WATCHERS

Dean Koontz was born into a very poor family and learned early on to escape into fiction — though books were scorned by his parents as a waste of time. Since then eleven of his books have appeared on the US bestseller lists, two made into films and six others in the process of development for filming. His work is read throughout the world and has been praised by many including Stephen King, Mary Higgins Clark and John D. MacDonald. *The Times* describes his work as being "emotionally and intellectually stimulating" and the *New York Times* says he is "more imaginative than most writers".

He now lives in California with his wife, Gerda. Between writing his novels he enjoys interior decorating, collecting art glass and, of course, reading.

Watchers

Dean R Koontz

HEADLINE FEATURE

Copyright © 1987 Nkui, Inc.

First published in Great Britain in 1987
by HEADLINE BOOK PUBLISHING PLC

First published in paperback in Great Britain in 1988
by HEADLINE BOOK PUBLISHING PLC

A HEADLINE FEATURE paperback

20 19 18 17 16 15 14 13

ISBN 0 7472 3061 7

Printed and bound in Great Britain by
Collins Manufacturing, Glasgow

HEADLINE BOOK PUBLISHING PLC
Headline House
79 Great Titchfield Street
London W1P 7FN

This book is dedicated to
Lennart Sane
who is not only the best at what he does
but who is also a nice guy.
And to
Elisabeth Sane
who is as charming as her husband.

PART ONE

Shattering the Past

The past is but the beginning of a beginning,
and all that is and has been
is but the twilight of the dawn.
— H. G. Wells

The meeting of two personalities is like the contact of two
chemical substances: if there is any reaction, both are
transformed.
— C. G. Jung

ONE

1

On his thirty-sixth birthday, May 18, Travis Cornell rose at five o'clock in the morning. He dressed in sturdy hiking boots, jeans, and a long-sleeved, blue-plaid cotton shirt. He drove his pickup south from his home in Santa Barbara all the way to rural Santiago Canyon on the eastern edge of Orange County, south of Los Angeles. He took only a package of Oreo cookies, and a large canteen full of orange-flavored Kool-Aid, and a fully loaded Smith & Wesson .38 Chief's Special.

During the two-and-a-half-hour trip, he never switched on the radio. He never hummed, whistled, or sang to himself as men alone frequently do. For part of the drive, the Pacific lay on his right. The morning sea was broodingly dark toward the horizon, as hard and cold as slate, but nearer shore it was brightly spangled with early light the colors of pennies and rose petals. Travis did not once glance appreciatively at the sun-sequined water.

He was a lean, sinewy man with deep-set eyes the same dark brown as his hair. His face was narrow, with a patrician nose, high cheekbones, and a slightly pointed chin. It was an ascetic face that would have suited a monk in some holy order that still believed in self-flagellation, in the purification of the soul through suffering. God knows, he'd had his share of suffering. But it could be a pleasant face, too, warm and open. His smile had once charmed women, though not recently. He had not smiled in a long time.

The Oreos, the canteen, and the revolver were in a small green nylon backpack with black nylon straps, which lay on the seat beside him. Occasionally, he glanced at the pack, and it seemed as if he could see straight through the fabric to the loaded Chief's Special.

From Santiago Canyon Road in Orange County, he turned onto a much narrower route, then onto a tire-eating dirt lane. At a few minutes past eight-thirty, he parked the red pickup in a lay-by, under the immense bristly boughs of a big-cone spruce.

He slipped the harness of the small backpack over his shoulders and set out into the foothills of the Santa Ana Mountains. From his boyhood, he knew every slope, vale, narrow defile, and ridge. His father had owned a stone cabin in upper Holy Jim Canyon, perhaps the most remote of all the inhabited canyons, and Travis had spent weeks exploring the wild land for miles around.

He loved these untamed canyons. When he was a boy, black bears had roamed the woods; they were gone now. Mule deer could still be found, though not in the great numbers he had seen two decades ago. At least the beautiful folds and thrusts of land, the profuse and varied brush, and the trees were still as they had been: for long stretches he walked beneath a canopy of California live oaks and sycamores.

Now and then he passed a lone cabin or a cluster of them. A few canyon dwellers were half-hearted survivalists who believed the end of civilization was approaching, but who did not have the heart to move to a place even more forbidding. Most were ordinary people who were fed up with the hurly-burly of modern life and thrived in spite of having no plumbing or electricity.

Though the canyons seemed remote, they would soon be overwhelmed by encroaching suburbs. Within a hundred-mile radius, nearly ten million people lived in the interconnecting communities of Orange and Los Angeles counties, and growth was not abating.

10

But now crystalline, revelatory light fell on the untamed land with almost as much substance as rain, and all was clean and wild.

On the treeless spine of a ridge, where the low grass that had grown during the short rainy season had already turned dry and brown, Travis sat upon a broad table of rock and took off his backpack.

A five-foot rattlesnake was sunning on another flat rock fifty feet away. It raised its mean wedge-shaped head and studied him.

As a boy, he had killed scores of rattlers in these hills. He withdrew the gun from the backpack and rose from the rock. He took a couple of steps toward the snake.

The rattler rose farther off the ground and stared intensely.

Travis took another step, another, and assumed a shooter's stance, with both hands on the gun.

The rattler began to coil. Soon it would realize that it could not strike at such a distance, and would attempt to retreat.

Although Travis was certain his shot was clear and easy, he was surprised to discover that he could not squeeze the trigger. He had come to these foothills not merely to attempt to recall a time when he had been glad to be alive, but also to kill snakes if he saw any. Lately, alternately depressed and angered by the loneliness and sheer pointlessness of his life, he had been wound as tight as a crossbow spring. He needed to release that tension through violent action, and the killing of a few snakes — no loss to anyone — seemed the perfect prescription for his distress. However, as he stared at this rattler, he realized that its existence was less pointless than his own: it filled an ecological niche, and it probably took more pleasure in life than he had in a long time. He began to shake, and the gun kept straying from the target, and he could not find the will to fire. He was not a worthy executioner, so he lowered the gun and returned to the rock where he had left his backpack.

The snake was evidently in a peaceable mood, for its head lowered sinuously to the stone once more, and it lay still.

After a while, Travis tore open the package of Oreos, which had been his favorite treat when he was young. He had not eaten one in fifteen years. They were almost as good as he remembered them. He drank Kool-Aid from the canteen, but it wasn't as satisfying as the cookies. To his adult palate, the stuff was far too sweet.

The innocence, enthusiasms, joys, and voracities of youth can be recalled but perhaps never fully regained, he thought.

Leaving the rattlesnake in communion with the sun, shouldering his backpack once more, he went down the southern slope of the ridge into the shadows of the trees at the head of the canyon, where the air was freshened by the fragrant spring growth of the evergreens. On the west-sloping floor of the canyon, in deep gloom, he turned west and followed a deer trail.

A few minutes later, passing between a pair of large California sycamores that bent together to form an archway, he came to a place where sunlight poured into a break in the forest. At the far side of the clearing, the deer trail led into another section of woods in which spruces, laurels and sycamores grew closer together than elsewhere. Ahead, the land dropped steeply as the canyon sought bottom. When he stood at the edge of the sunfall with the toes of his boots in shadow, looking down that sloped path, he could see only fifteen yards before a surprisingly seamless darkness fell across the trail.

As Travis was about to step out of the sun and continue, a dog burst from the dry brush on his right and ran straight to him, panting and chuffing. It was a golden retriever, pure of breed by the look of it. A male. He figured it was little more than a year old, for though it had attained the better part of its full growth, it retained some of the sprightliness of a puppy. Its thick coat was damp, dirty, tangled, snarled, full or burrs and broken bits of weeds and leaves. It stopped in front of him, sat, cocked its head, and looked up at him with an undeniably friendly expression.

Filthy as it was, the animal was nonetheless appealing. Travis stooped, patted its head, and scratched behind its ears.

He half-expected an owner, gasping and perhaps angry at this runaway, to follow the retriever out of the brush. Nobody came. When he thought to check for a collar and license, he found none.

"Surely you're not a wild dog — are you, boy?"

The retriever chuffed.

"No, too friendly for a wild one. Not lost, are you?"

It nuzzled his hand.

He noticed that, in addition to its dirty and tangled coat, it had dried blood on its right ear. Fresher blood was visible on its front paws, as if it had been running so long and so hard over rugged terrain that the pads of its feet had begun to crack.

"Looks like you've had a difficult journey, boy."

The dog whined softly, as if agreeing with what Travis had said.

He continued to stroke its back and scratch its ears, but after a minute or two he realized he was seeking something from the dog that it could not provide: meaning, purpose, relief from despair.

"On your way now." He gave the retriever a light slap on its side, rose, and stretched.

The dog remained in front of him.

He stepped past it, heading for the narrow path that descended into darkness.

The dog bolted around him and blocked the deer trail.

"Move along, boy."

The retriever bared its teeth and growled low in its throat.

Travis frowned. "Move along. That's a good dog."

When he tried to step past it, the retriever snarled. It snapped at his legs. Travis danced back two steps. "Hey, what's gotten into you?"

The dog stopped growling and just panted.

He advanced again, but the dog lunged at him more ferociously than before, still not barking but growling even deeper and snapping repeatedly at his legs, driving him backward across the clearing. He took eight or ten clumsy steps on a slippery carpet of dead spruce and pine needles, stumbled over his own feet, and fell on his butt.

The moment Travis was down, the dog turned away from him. It padded across the clearing to the brink of the sloping path and peered into the gloom below. Its floppy ears had pricked up as much as a retriever's ears can.

"Damn dog," Travis said.

It ignored him.

"What the hell's the matter with you, mutt?"

Standing in the forest's shadow, it continued to stare down the deer trail, into the blackness at the bottom of the wooded canyon slope. Its tail was down, almost tucked between its legs.

Travis gathered half a dozen small stones from the ground around him, got up, and threw one of the missiles at the retriever. Struck on the backside hard enough to be stung, the dog did not yelp but whipped around in surprise.

Now I've done it, Travis thought. He'll go for my throat.

But the dog only looked at him accusingly — and continued to block the entrance to the deer trail.

Something in the tattered beast's demeanor — in the wide-set dark eyes or in the tilt of its big squarish head — made Travis feel guilty for having stoned it. The sorry damn dog looked disappointed in him, and he was ashamed.

"Hey, listen," he said, "*you* started it, you know."

The dog just stared at him.

Travis dropped the other stones.

The dog glanced at the relinquished missiles, then raised its eyes once more, and Travis swore he saw approval in that canine face.

Travis could have turned back. Or he could have found another way down the canyon. But he was seized by an irrational determination to forge ahead, to go where he *wanted* to go, by God. This day of all days, he was not going to be deterred or even delayed by something as trivial as an obstructive dog.

He got up, shrugged his shoulders to resettle the back-pack, took a deep breath of the piny air, and walked boldly across the clearing.

The retriever began to growl again, softly but menacingly. Its lips skinned back from its teeth.

Step by step, Travis's courage faded, and when he was within a few feet of the dog, he opted for a different approach. He stopped and shook his head and gently berated the animal: "Bad dog. You're being a very bad dog. You know that? What's gotten into you? Hmmmm? You don't look as if you were born bad. You look like a good dog."

As he continued to sweet-talk the retriever, it ceased growling. Its bushy tail wagged once, twice, tentatively.

"That's a good boy," he said slyly, coaxingly. "That's better. You and I can be friends, huh?"

The dog issued a conciliatory whine, that familiar and appealing sound all dogs make to express their natural desire to be loved.

"Now, we're getting somewhere," Travis said, taking another step toward the retriever with the intention of stooping and petting it.

Immediately, the dog leaped at him, snarling, and drove him back across the clearing. It got its teeth in one leg of his jeans, shook its head furiously. He kicked at it, missed. As Travis staggered out of balance from the misplaced kick, the dog snatched the other leg of his pants and ran a circle around him, pulling him with it. He hopped desperately to keep up with his adversary but toppled and slammed to the ground again.

"Shit!" he said, feeling immeasurably foolish.

Whining again, having reverted to a friendly mood, the dog licked one of his hands.

"You're schizophrenic," Travis said.

The dog returned to the other end of the clearing. It stood with its back to him, staring down the deer trail that descended through the cool shadows of the trees. Abruptly, it lowered its head, hunched its shoulders. The muscles in its back and haunches visibly tensed as if it were preparing to move fast.

"What're you looking at?" Travis was suddenly aware that the dog was not fascinated by the trail itself but, perhaps, by something *on* the trail. "Mountain lion?" he wondered aloud as he got to his feet. In his youth, mountain

15

lions — specifically, cougars — had prowled these woods, and he supposed some still hung on.

The retriever grumbled, not at Travis this time but at whatever had drawn its attention. The sound was low, barely audible, and to Travis it seemed as if the dog was both angry and afraid.

Coyotes? Plenty of them roamed the foothills. A pack of hungry coyotes might alarm even a sturdy animal like this golden retriever.

With a startled yelp, the dog executed a leaping-scrambling turn away from the shadowed deer trail. It dashed toward him, past him, to the other arm of the woods, and he thought it was going to disappear into the forest. But at the archway formed by two sycamores, through which Travis had come only minutes ago, the dog stopped and looked back expectantly. With an air of frustration and anxiety, it hurried in his direction again, swiftly circled him, grabbed at his pants leg, and wriggled backward, trying to drag him with it.

"Wait, wait, okay," he said. "Okay."

The retriever let go. It issued one woof, more a forceful exhalation than a bark.

Obviously — and astonishingly — the dog had purposefully prevented him from proceeding along the gloomy stretch of the deer trail because something was down there. Something dangerous. Now the dog wanted him to flee because that dangerous creature was drawing nearer.

Something was coming. But what?

Travis was not worried, just curious. Whatever was approaching might frighten a dog, but nothing in these woods, not even a coyote or a cougar, would attack a grown man.

Whining impatiently, the retriever tried to grab one leg of Travis's jeans again.

Its behaviour was extraordinary. If it was frightened, why didn't it run off, forget him? He was not its master; it owed him nothing, neither affection nor protection. Stray dogs do not possess a sense of duty to strangers, do not have a moral perspective, a conscience. What did this animal think it was, anyway — a freelance Lassie?

16

"All right, all right," Travis said, shaking the retriever loose and accompanying it to the sycamore arch.

The dog dashed ahead, along the ascending trail, which led up toward the canyon rim, through thinning trees and brighter light.

Travis paused at the sycamores. Frowning, he looked across the sun-drenched clearing at the night-dark hole in the forest where the descending portion of the trail began. What was coming?

The shrill cries of the cicadas cut off simultaneously, as if a phonograph needle was lifted from a recording. The woods were preternaturally silent.

Then Travis heard something rushing up the lightless trail. A scrabbling noise. A clatter as of dislodged stones. A faint rustle of dry brush. The thing sounded closer than it probably was, for sound was amplified as it echoed up through the narrow tunnel of trees. Nevertheless, the creature was coming fast. Very fast.

For the first time, Travis sensed that he was in grave peril. He knew that nothing in the woods was big or bold enough to attack him, but his intellect was overruled by instinct. His heart hammered.

Above him, on the higher path, the retriever had become aware of his hesitation. It barked agitatedly.

Decades ago, he might have thought an enraged black bear was racing up the deer trail, driven mad by disease or pain. But the cabin dwellers and weekend hikers — outriders of civilization — had pushed the few remaining bears much farther back into the Santa Anas.

From the sound of it, the unknown beast was within seconds of reaching the clearing between the lower and higher trails.

The length of Travis's spine, shivers tracked like melting bits of sleet trickling down a windowpane.

He wanted to see what the thing was, but at the same time he had gone cold with dread, a purely instinctive fear.

Farther up the canyon, the golden retriever barked urgently.

Travis turned and ran.

He was in excellent shape, not a pound overweight. With the panting retriever leading, Travis tucked his arms close to his sides and sprinted up the deer trail, ducking under the few low-hanging branches. The studded soles of his hiking boots gave good traction; he slipped on loose stones and on slithery layers of dry pine needles, but he did not fall. As he ran through a false fire of flickering sunlight and shadow, another fire began to burn in his lungs.

Travis Cornell's life had been full of danger and tragedy, but he'd never flinched from anything. In the worst of times, he calmly confronted loss, pain, and fear. But now something peculiar happened. He lost control. For the first time in his life, he panicked. Fear pried into him, touching a deep and primitive level where nothing had ever reached him before. As he ran, he broke out in gooseflesh and cold sweat, and he did not know *why* the unknown pursuer should fill him with such absolute terror.

He did not look back. Initially, he did not want to turn his eyes away from the twisting trail because he was afraid he would crash into a low branch. But as he ran, his panic swelled, and by the time he had gone a couple of hundred yards, the reason he did not look back was because he was afraid of what he might see.

He knew that his response was irrational. The prickly sensation along the back of his neck and the iciness in his gut were symptoms of a purely superstitious terror. But the civilized and educated Travis Cornell had turned over the reins to the frightened child-savage that lives in every human being — the genetic ghost of what we once were — and he could not easily regain control even though he was aware of the absurdity of his behavior. Brute instinct ruled, and instinct told him that he must run, run, stop thinking and just run.

Near the head of the canyon, the trail turned left and carved a winding course up the steep north wall toward the ridge. Travis rounded a bend, saw a log lying across the path, jumped but caught one foot on the rotting wood. He fell forward, flat on his chest. Stunned, he could not get his breath, could not move.

18

He expected something to pounce on him and tear out his throat.

The retriever dashed back down the trail and leaped over Travis, landing surefootedly on the path behind him. It barked fiercely at whatever was chasing them, much more threateningly than when it had challenged Travis in the clearing.

Travis rolled over and sat up, gasping. He saw nothing on the trail below. Then he realized the retriever was not concerned about anything in that direction but was standing sideways on the trail, facing the underbrush in the forest to the east of them. Spraying saliva, it barked stridently, so hard and loud that each explosive sound hurt Travis's ears. The tone of savage fury in its voice was daunting. The dog was warning the unseen enemy to stay back.

"Easy, boy," Travis said softly. "Easy."

The retriever stopped barking but did not glance at Travis. It stared intently into the brush, peeling its pebbly black lips off its teeth and growling deep in its throat.

Still breathing hard, Travis got to his feet and look east into the woods. Evergreens, sycamores, a few larches. Shadows like swatches of dark cloth were fastened here and there by golden pins and needles of light. Brush. Briars. Climbing vines. A few well-worn toothlike formations of rock. He saw nothing out of the ordinary.

When he reached down and put a hand upon the retriever's head, the dog stopped growling, as if it understood his intentions. Travis drew a breath, held it, and listened for movement in the brush.

The cicadas remained silent. No birds sang in the trees. The woods were as still as if the vast, elaborate clockwork mechanism of the universe had ceased ticking.

He was sure that he was not the cause of the abrupt silence. His passage through the canyon had not previously disturbed either birds or cicadas.

Something *was* out there. An intruder of which the ordinary forest creatures clearly did not approve.

He took a deep breath and held it again, straining to hear the slightest movement in the woods. This time he detected the rustle of brush, a snapping twig, the soft crunch of dry leaves — and the unnervingly peculiar, heavy, ragged breathing of something big. It sounded about forty feet away, but he could not pinpoint its location.

At his side, the retriever had gone rigid. Its floppy ears were slightly pricked, straining forward.

The unknown adversary's raspy breathing was so creepy — whether because of the echo effect of the forest and canyon, or because it was just creepy to begin with — that Travis quickly took off his backpack, unsnapped the flap, and withdrew the loaded .38.

The dog stared at the gun. Travis had the weird feeling that the animal knew what the revolver was — and approved of the weapon.

Wondering if the thing in the woods was a man, Travis called out: "Who's there? Come on out where I can see you."

The hoarse breathing in the brush was now underlaid with a thick menacing gnarl. The eerie guttural resonance electrified Travis. His heart beat even harder, and he went as rigid as the retriever beside him. For interminable ticking seconds, he could not understand why the noise itself had sent such a powerful current of fear through him. Then he realized that what frightened him was the noise's ambiguity: the beast's growl was definitely that of an animal ... yet there was also an indescribable quality that bespoke intelligence, a tone and modulation almost like the sound that an enraged *man* might make. The more he listened, the more Travis decided it was neither strictly an animal nor human sound. But if neither ... then what the hell was it?

He saw the high brush stirring. Straight ahead. Something was coming toward him.

"Stop," he said sharply. "No closer."

It kept coming.

Now just thirty feet away.

Moving slower than it had been. A bit wary perhaps. But closing in nevertheless.

The golden retriever began to growl threateningly, again warning off the creature that stalked them. But tremors were

20

visible in its flanks, and its head shook. Though it was challenging the thing in the brush, it was profoundly frightened of a confrontation.

The dog's fear unnerved Travis. Retrievers were renowned for boldness and courage. They were bred to be the companions of hunters, and were frequently used in dangerous rescue operations. What peril or foe could provoke such dread in a strong, proud dog like this?

The thing in the brush continued toward them, hardly more than twenty feet away now.

Though he had as yet seen nothing extraordinary, he was filled with superstitious terror, a perception of indefinable but uncanny presences. He kept telling himself he had chanced upon a cougar, just a cougar, that was probably more frightened than he was. But the icy prickling that began at the base of his spine and extended up across his scalp now intensified. His hand was so slick with sweat that he was afraid the gun would slip out of his grasp.

Fifteen feet.

Travis pointed the .38 in the air and squeezed off a single warning shot. The blast crashed through the forest and echoed down the long canyon.

The retriever did not even flinch, but the thing in the brush immediately turned away from them and ran north, upslope, toward the canyon rim. Travis could not see it, but he could clearly mark its swift progress by the waist-high weeds and bushes that shook and parted under its assault.

For a second or two, he was relieved because he thought he had frightened if off. Then he saw it was not actually running away. It was heading north-northwest on a curve that would bring it to the deer trail above them. Travis sensed that the creature was trying to cut them off and force them to go out of the canyon by the lower route, where it would have more and better opportunities to attack. He did not understand how he knew such a thing, just that he *did* know it.

His primordial survival instinct drove him into action without the need to *think* about each move he made; he automatically did what was required. He had not felt that animal surety since he had seen military action almost a decade ago.

Trying to keep his eye on the telltale tremble of the brush to his right, abandoning his backpack and keeping only the gun, Travis raced up the steep trail, and the retriever ran behind him. Fast as he was, however, he was not fast enough to overtake the unknown enemy. When he realized that it was going to reach the path well above him, he fired another warning shot, which did not startle or deflect the adversary this time. He fired twice into the brush itself, toward the indications of movement, not caring if it *was* a man out there, and that worked. He did not believe he hit the stalker, but he scared it at last, and it turned away.

He kept running. He was eager to reach the canyon rim, where the trees were thin along the ridge top, where the brush was sparse, and where a brighter fall of sunlight did not permit concealing shadows.

When he arrived at the crest a couple of minutes later, he was badly winded. The muscles of his calves and thighs were hot with pain. His heart thumped so hard in his chest that he would not have been surprised to hear the echo of it bouncing off another ridge and coming back to him across the canyon.

This was where he had paused to eat some Oreos. The rattlesnake, which earlier had been sunning on a large flat rock, was gone.

The golden retriever had followed Travis. It stood beside him, panting, peering down the slope they had just ascended.

Slightly dizzy, wanting to sit and rest but aware that he was still in danger of an unknown variety, Travis looked down the deer trail, too, and scanned what underbrush he could see. If the stalker remained in pursuit of them, it was being more circumspect, climbing the slopes without disturbing the weeds and bushes.

The retriever whined and tugged once at Travis's pants leg. It scurried across the top of the narrow ridge to a declivity by which they could make their way down into the next canyon. Clearly, the dog believed they were not out of danger and ought to keep moving.

Travis shared that conviction. His atavistic fear — and the reliance on instinct that it invoked — sent him hurrying after the dog, over the far side of the ridge, into another tree-filled canyon.

2

Vincent Nasco had been waiting in the dark garage for hours. He did not look as if he would be good at waiting. He was big — over two hundred pounds, six-three, muscular — and he always seemed to be so full of energy that he might burst at any moment. His broad face was placid, usually as expressionless as the face of a cow. But his green eyes flashed with vitality, with an edgy nervous watchfulness — and with a strange hunger that was like something you expected to see in the eyes of a wild animal, some jungle cat, but never in the eyes of a man. Like a cat, in spite of his tremendous energy, he was patient. He could crouch for hours, motionless and silent, waiting for prey.

At nine-forty Tuesday morning, much later than Nasco expected, the deadbolt lock on the door between the garage and the house was disengaged with a single hard *clack*. The door opened, and Dr. Davis Weatherby flicked on the garage lights, then reached for the button that would raise the big sectional door.

"Stop right there," Nasco said, rising and stepping from in front of the doctor's pearl-gray Cadillac.

Weatherby blinked at him, surprised. "Who the hell —"

Nasco raised a silencer-equipped Walther P-38 and shot the doctor once in the face.

Ssssnap.

Cut off in midsentence, Weatherby fell backward into the cheery yellow and white laundry room. Going down, he struck his head on the clothes dryer and knocked a wheeled metal laundry cart into the wall.

Vince Nasco was not worried about the noise because Weatherby was unmarried and lived alone. He stooped over the corpse, which had wedged the door open, and tenderly put one hand on the doctor's face.

The bullet had hit Weatherby in the forehead, less than an inch above the bridge of his nose. There was little blood because death had been instantaneous, and the slug had not been quite powerful enough to smash through the back of the man's skull. Weatherby's brown eyes were open wide. He looked startled.

With his fingers, Vince stroked Weatherby's warm cheek, the side of his neck. He closed the sightless left eye, then the right, although he knew that postmortem muscle reactions would pop them open again in a couple of minutes. With a profound gratefulness evident in his tremulous voice, Vince said, "Thank you. Thank you, Doctor." He kissed both of the dead man's closed eyes. "Thank you."

Shivering pleasantly, Vince plucked the car keys off the floor where the dead man had dropped them, went into the garage, and opened the Cadillac's trunk, being careful not to touch any surface on which he might leave a clear fingerprint. The trunk was empty. Good. He carried Weatherby's corpse out of the laundry room, put it in the trunk, closed and locked the lid.

Vince had been told that the doctor's body must not be discovered until tomorrow. He did not know why the timing was important, but he prided himself on doing flawless work. Therefore, he returned to the laundry room, put the metal cart where it belonged, and looked around for signs of violence. Satisfied, he closed the door on the yellow and white room, and locked it with Weatherby's keys.

He turned out the garage lights, crossed the darkened space, and let himself out the side door, where he had entered during the night by quietly loiding the flimsy lock with a credit card. Using the doctor's keys, he relocked the door and walked away from the house.

Davis Weatherby lived in Corona Del Mar, within sight of the Pacific Ocean. Vince had left his two-year-old Ford van three blocks from the doctor's house. The walk back to the van was very pleasant, invigorating. This was a fine neighborhood boasting a variety of architectural styles; expensive

Spanish casas sat beside beautifully detailed Cape Cod homes with a harmony that had to be seen to be believed. The landscaping was lush and well tended. Palms and ficus and olive trees shaded the sidewalks. Red, coral, yellow, and orange bougainvillaeas blazed with thousands of flowers. The bottlebrush trees were in bloom. The branches of jacarandas dripped lacy purple blossoms. The air was scented with star jasmine.

Vincent Nasco felt wonderful. So strong, so powerful, so *alive*.

3

Sometimes the dog led, and sometimes Travis took the lead. They went a long way before Travis realized that he had been completely jolted out of the despair and desperate loneliness that had brought him to the foothills of the Santa Ana Mountains in the first place.

The big tattered dog stayed with him all the way to his pickup, which was parked along the dirt lane under the overhanging boughs of an enormous spruce. Stopping at the truck, the retriever looked back the way they had come.

Behind them, black birds swooped through the cloudless sky, as if engaged in reconnaissance for some mountain sorcerer. A dark wall of trees loomed like the ramparts of a sinister castle.

Though the woods were gloomy, the dirt road onto which Travis had stepped was fully exposed to the sun, baked to a pale brown, mantled in fine, soft dust that plumed around his boots with each step he took. He was surprised that such a bright day could have been abruptly filled with an overpowering palpable sense of evil.

Studying the forest out of which they had fled, the dog barked for the first time in half an hour.

"Still coming, isn't it?" Travis said.

The dog glanced at him and mewled unhappily.

"Yeah," he said, "I feel it too. Crazy . . . yet I feel it too.

25

But what the hell's out there, boy? Huh? What the hell is it?''

The dog shuddered violently.

Travis's own fear was amplified every time he saw the dog's terror manifested.

He put down the tailgate of the truck and said, "Come on. I'll give you a lift out of this place.''

The dog sprang into the cargo hold.

Travis slammed the gate shut and went around the side of the truck. As he pulled open the driver's door, he thought he glimpsed movement in nearby brush. Not back toward the forest but at the far side of the dirt road. Over there, a narrow field was choked with waist-high brown grass as crisp as hay, a few bristly clumps of mesquite, and some sprawling oleander bushes with roots deep enough to keep them green. When he stared directly at the field, he saw none of the movement he thought he had caught from the corner of his eye, but he suspected that he had not imagined it.

With a renewed sense of urgency, he climbed into the truck and put the revolver on the seat beside him. He drove away from there as fast as the washboard lane permitted, and with constant consideration for the four-legged passenger in the cargo bed.

Twenty minutes later, when he stopped along Santiago Canyon Road, back in the world of blacktop civilization, he still felt weak and shaky. But the fear that lingered was different from that he'd felt in the forest. His heart was no longer drumming. The cold sweat had dried on his hands and brow. The odd prickling of nape and scalp was gone — and the memory of it seemed unreal. Now he was afraid not of some unknown creature but of his own strange behavior. Safely out of the woods, he could not quite recall the degree of terror that had gripped him; therefore, his actions seemed irrational.

He pulled on the handbrake and switched off the engine. It was eleven o'clock, and the flurry of morning traffic had gone; only an occasional car passed on the rural two-lane blacktop. He sat for a minute, trying to convince himself that he had acted on instincts that were good, right, and reliable.

26

He had always taken pride in his unshakable equanimity and hardheaded pragmatism — in that if in nothing else. He could stay cool in the middle of a bonfire. He could make hard decisions under pressure and accept the consequences.

Except — he found it increasingly difficult to believe something strange had actually been stalking him out there. He wondered if he had misinterpreted the dog's behavior and had imagined the movement in the brush merely to give himself an excuse to turn his mind away from self-pity.

He got out of the truck and stepped back to the side of it, where he came face-to-face with the retriever, which stood in the cargo bed. It shoved its burly head toward him and licked his neck, his chin. Though it had snapped and barked earlier, it was an affectionate dog, and for the first time its bedraggled condition struck him as having a comical aspect. He tried to hold the dog back. But it strained forward, nearly clambering over the side of the cargo hold in its eagerness to lick his face. He laughed and ruffled its tangled coat.

The retriever's friskiness and the frenzied wagging of its tail had an unexpected effect on Travis. For a long time his mind had been a dark place, filled with thoughts of death, culminating in today's journey. But this animal's un-adulterated joy in being alive was like a spotlight that pierced Travis's inner gloom and reminded him that life had a brighter side from which he had long ago turned away.

"What *was* that all about back there?" he wondered aloud.

The dog stopped licking him, stopped wagging its matted tail. It regarded him solemnly, and he was suddenly trans-fixed by the animal's gentle, warm brown eyes. Something in them was unusual, compelling. Travis was half mes-merized, and the dog seemed equally captivated. As a mild spring breeze rose from the south, Travis searched the dog's eyes for a clue to their special power and appeal, but he saw nothing extraordinary about them. Except ... well, they seemed somehow more expressive than a dog's eyes usually were, more intelligent and aware. Given the short attention span of any dog, the retriever's unwavering stare *was* damned unusual. As the seconds ticked past and as neither

Travis nor the dog broke the encounter, he felt increasingly peculiar. A shiver rippled through him, occasioned not by fear but by a sense that something uncanny was happening, that he was teetering on the threshold of an awesome revelation.

Then the dog shook its head and licked Travis's hand, and the spell was broken.

"Where'd you come from, boy?"

The dog cocked its head to the left.

"Who's your owner?"

The dog cocked its head to the right.

"What should I do with you?"

As if in answer, the dog jumped over the truck's tailgate, ran past Travis to the driver's door, and climbed into the pickup's cab.

When Travis peered inside, the retriever was in the passenger's seat, looking straight ahead through the windshield. It turned to him and issued a soft woof, as if impatient with his dawdling.

He got in behind the wheel, tucked the revolver under his seat. "Don't believe I can take care of you. Too much responsibility, fella. Doesn't fit in with my plans. Sorry about that."

The dog regarded him beseechingly.

"You look hungry, boy."

It woofed once, softly.

"Okay, maybe I can help you that much. I think there's a Hershey's bar in the glove compartment . . . and there's a McDonald's not far from here, where they've probably got a couple of hamburgers with your name on them. But after that . . . well, I'll either have to let you loose again or take you to the pound."

Even as Travis was speaking, the dog raised one foreleg and hit the glove-compartment release button with a paw. The lid fell open.

"What the hell —"

The dog leaned forward, put its snout into the open box, and withdrew the candy in its teeth, holding the bar so lightly that the wrapping was not punctured.

Travis blinked in surprise.

The retriever held forth the Hershey's bar, as if requesting that Travis unwrap the treat.

Startled, he took the candy and peeled off the paper.

The retriever watched, licking his lips.

Breaking the bar into pieces, Travis paid out the chocolate in morsels. The dog took them gratefully and ate almost daintily.

Travis watched in confusion, not certain if what had happened was truly extraordinary or had a reasonable explanation. Had the dog actually understood him when he had said there was candy in the glove box? Or had it detected the scent of chocolate? Surely the latter.

To the dog, he said, "But how did you know to press the button to pop the lid open?"

It stared, licked its chops, and accepted another bit of candy.

He said, "Okay, okay, so maybe that's a trick you've been taught. Though it's not the sort of thing anyone would ordinarily train a dog to do, is it? Roll over, play dead, sing for your supper, even walk on your hind feet a little ways . . . yeah, those're things that dogs are trained to do . . . but they're not trained to open locks and latches."

The retriever gazed longingly at the last morsel of chocolate, but Travis withheld the goody for a moment.

The *timing*, for God's sake, had been uncanny. Two seconds after Travis had referred to the chocolate, the dog had gone for it.

"Did you understand what I said?" Travis asked, feeling foolish for suspecting a dog of possessing language skills. Nevertheless, he repeated the question: "Did you? Did you understand?"

Reluctantly, the retriever raised its gaze from the last of the candy. Their eyes met. Again Travis sensed that something uncanny was happening; he shivered not unpleasantly, as before.

He hesitated, cleared his throat. "Uh . . . would it be all right with you if I had the last piece of chocolate?"

The dog turned its eyes to the two small squares of the

Hershey's bar still in Travis's hand. It chuffed once, as if with regret, then looked through the windshield.

"I'll be damned," Travis said.

The dog yawned.

Being careful not to move his hand, not holding the chocolate out, not calling attention to the chocolate in any manner except with words, he addressed the big tattered dog again: "Well, maybe you need it more than I do, boy. If you want it, the last bit's yours."

The retriever looked at him.

Still not moving his hand, keeping it close to his own body in a way that implied he was withholding the chocolate, he said, "If you want it, take it. Otherwise, I'll just throw it away."

The retriever shifted on the seat, leaned close to him, and gently snatched the chocolate off his palm.

"I'll be double-damned," he said.

The dog rose onto all fours, standing on the seat, which brought its head almost to the roof. It looked through the back window of the cab and growled softly.

Travis glanced at the rearview mirror, then at the side-mounted mirror, but he saw nothing unusual behind them. Just the two-lane blacktop, the narrow berm, the weed-covered hillside sloping down on their right side.

"You think we should get moving? Is that it?"

The dog looked at him, peered out of the rear window, then turned and sat with its hind legs tucked to one side, facing forward again.

Travis started the engine, put the truck in gear, pulled onto Santiago Canyon Road, and headed north. Glancing at his companion, he said, "Are you really more than you appear to be ... or am I just cracking up? And if you are more than you appear to be ... what the devil *are* you?"

At the rural eastern end of Chapman Avenue, he turned west toward the McDonald's of which he'd spoken.

He said, "Can't turn you loose now or take you to a pound."

And a minute later, he said, "If I didn't keep you, I'd die of curiosity, wondering about you."

They drove about two miles and swung into the McDonald's parking lot.

Travis said, "So I guess you're my dog now."

The retriever said nothing.

TWO

1

Nora Devon was afraid of the television repairman. Although he appeared to be about thirty (her age), he had the offensive cockiness of a know-it-all teenager. When she answered the doorbell, he boldly looked her up and down as he identified himself—"Art Streck, Wadlow's TV"—and when he met her eyes again, he winked. He was tall and lean and well-scrubbed, dressed in white uniform slacks and shirt. He was clean-shaven. His darkish-blond hair was cut short and neatly combed. He looked like any mother's son, not a rapist or psycho, yet Nora was instantly afraid of him, maybe because his boldness and cockiness seemed at odds with his appearance.

"You need service?" he asked when she hesitated in the doorway.

Although his question appeared innocent, the inflection he put on the word 'service' seemed creepy and sexually suggestive to Nora. She did not think she was overreacting. But she had called Wadlow TV, after all, and she could not turn Streck away without explanation. An explanation would probably lead to an argument, and she was not a confrontational person, so she let him inside.

As she escorted him along the wide, cool hallway to the living-room arch, she had the uneasy feeling that his good grooming and big smile were elements of a carefully calculated disguise. He had a keen animal watchfulness, a coiled tension, that further disquieted her with every step they took away from the front door.

Following her much too closely, virtually looming over her from behind, Art Streck said, "You've got a nice house here, Mrs. Devon. Very nice. I really like it."

"Thank you," she said stiffly, not bothering to correct his misapprehension of her marital status.

"A man could be happy here. Yeah, a man could be very happy."

The house was of that style of architecture sometimes called Old Santa Barbara Spanish: two stories, cream-colored stucco with a red-tile roof, verandas, balconies, all softly rounded lines instead of squared-off corners. Lush red bougainvillaea climbed the north face of the structure, dripping bright blossoms. The place was beautiful.

Nora hated it.

She had lived there since she was only two years old, which now added up to twenty-eight years, and during all but one of them, she had been under the iron thumb of her Aunt Violet. Hers had not been a happy childhood or, to date, a happy life. Violet Devon had died a year ago. But, in truth, Nora was still oppressed by her aunt, for the memory of that hateful old woman was formidable, stifling.

In the living room, putting his repair kit beside the Magnavox, Streck paused to look around. He was clearly surprised by the decor.

The flowered wallpaper was dark, funereal. The Persian carpet was singularly unattractive. The color scheme—gray, maroon, royal blue—was unenlivened by a few touches of faded yellow. Heavy English furniture from the mid-nineteenth century, trimmed with deeply carved molding, stood on clawed feet: massive armchairs, footstools, cabinets suitable for Dr. Caligari, credenzas that looked as if they each weighed half a ton. Small tables were draped with weighty brocade. Some lamps were pewter with pale-gray shades, and others had maroon ceramic bases, but none threw much light. The drapes looked as heavy as lead;

age-yellowed sheers hung between the side panels, permitting only a mustard-colored drizzle of sunlight to enter the room. None of it complemented the Spanish architecture; Violet had willfully imposed her ponderous bad taste upon the graceful house.

"You decorate?" Art Streck asked.

"No. My aunt," Nora said. She stood by the marble fireplace, almost as far from him as she could get without leaving the room. "This was her place. I ... inherited it."

"If I was you," he said, "I'd heave all this stuff out of here. Could be a bright, cheery room. Pardon my saying so, but this isn't you. This might be all right for someone's maiden aunt ... She was a *maiden* aunt, huh? Yeah, thought so. Might be all right for a dried-up maiden aunt, but definitely not for a pretty lady like yourself."

Nora wanted to criticize his impertinence, wanted to tell him to shut up and fix the television, but she had no experience at standing up for herself. Aunt Violet had preferred her meek, obedient.

Streck was smiling at her. The right corner of his mouth curled in a most unpleasant way. It was almost a sneer.

She forced herself to say, "I like it well enough."

"Not really?"

"Yes."

He shrugged. "What's the matter with the set?"

"The picture won't stop rolling. And there's static, snow."

He pulled the television away from the wall, switched it on, and studied the tumbling, static-slashed images. He plugged in a small portable lamp and hooked it to the back of the set.

The grandfather clock in the hall marked the quarter-hour with a single chime that reverberated hollowly through the house.

"You watch a lot of TV?" he asked as he unscrewed the dust shield from the set.

"Not much," Nora said.

"I like those nighttime soaps. *Dallas, Dynasty*, that stuff."

35

"I never watch them."

"Yeah? Oh, now, come on, I bet you do." He laughed slyly. "Everybody watches 'em, even if they don't want to admit it. Just isn't anything more interesting than stories full of backstabbing, scheming, thieving, lying . . . and adultery. You know what I'm saying? People sit and watch it and cluck their tongues and say, 'Oh, how awful,' but they really get off on it. That's human nature."

"I . . . I've got things to do in the kitchen," she said nervously. "Call me when you've fixed the set." She left the room and went down the hall through the swinging door into the kitchen.

She was trembling. She despised herself for her weakness, for the ease with which she surrendered to fear, but she could not help being what she was. A mouse.

Aunt Violet had often said, "Girl, there are two kinds of people in the world—cats and mice. Cats go where they want, do what they want, take what they want. Cats are aggressive and self-sufficient by nature. Mice, on the other hand, don't have an ounce of aggression in them. They're naturally vulnerable, gentle, and timid, and they're happiest when they keep their heads down and accept what life gives them. You're a mouse, dear. It's not bad to be a mouse. You can be perfectly happy. A mouse might not have as colorful a life as a cat, but if it stays safely in its burrow and keeps to itself, it'll live longer than the cat, and it'll have a lot less turmoil in its life."

Right now, a cat lurked in the living room, fixing the TV set, and Nora was in the kitchen, gripped by mouselike fear. She was not actually in the middle of cooking anything, as she had told Streck. For a moment she stood by the sink, one cold hand clasped in the other—her hands *always* seemed to be cold—wondering what to do until he finished his work and left. She decided to bake a cake. A yellow cake with chocolate icing. That task would keep her occupied and help turn her mind away from the memory of Streck's suggestive winking.

She got bowls, utensils, an electric mixer, plus the cake mix and other ingredients out of the cupboards, and she set to work. Soon her frayed nerves were soothed by the mundane domestic activity.

Just as she finished pouring the batter into the two baking pans, Streck stepped into the kitchen and said, "You like to cook?"

Surprised, she nearly dropped the empty metal mixing bowl and the batter-smeared spatula. Somehow, she managed to hold on to them and—with only a little clatter to betray her tension—put them into the sink to be washed. "Yes. I like to cook."

"Isn't that nice? I admire a woman who enjoys doing woman's work. Do you sew, crochet, do embroidery, anything like that?"

"Needlepoint," she said.

"That's even nicer."

"Is the TV fixed?"

"Almost."

Nora was ready to put the cake in the oven, but she did not want to carry the pans while Streck was watching her because she was afraid she would shake too much. Then he'd realize that she was intimidated by him, and he would probably get bolder. So she left the full pans on the counter and tore open the box of icing mix instead.

Streck came farther into the big kitchen, moving casually, very relaxed, looking around with an amiable smile, but coming straight toward her. "Think I could have a glass of water?"

Nora almost sighed with relief, eager to believe that a drink of cold water was all that had brought him here. "Oh, yes, of course," she said. She took a glass from the cupboard, ran the cold water.

When she turned to hand it to him, he was standing close behind her, having crept up with catlike quiet. She gave an involuntary start. Water slopped out of the glass and splattered on the floor.

She said, "You—"

"Here," he said, taking the glass from her hand.

"—startled me."

"Me?" he said, smiling, fixing her with icy blue eyes.

37

"Oh, I certainly didn't mean to. I'm harmless, Mrs. Devon. Really, I am. All I want is a drink of water. You didn't think I wanted anything else—did you?"

He was so damned bold. She couldn't *believe* how bold he was, how smart-mouthed and cool and aggressive. She wanted to slap his face, but she was afraid of what would happen after that. Slapping him—in any way acknowledging his insulting double entendres or other offenses—seemed sure to encourage rather than deter him.

He stared at her with unsettling intensity, voraciously. His smile was that of a predator.

She sensed the best way to handle Streck was to pretend innocence and monumental thickheadedness, to ignore his nasty sexual innuendos as if she had not understood them. She must, in short, deal with him as a mouse might deal with any threat from which it was unable to flee. Pretend you do not see the cat, pretend that it is not there, and perhaps the cat will be confused and disappointed by the lack of reaction and will seek more responsive prey elsewhere.

To break away from his demanding gaze, Nora tore a couple of paper towels from the dispenser beside the sink and began to mop up the water she had spilled on the floor. But the moment she stooped before Streck, she realized she'd made a mistake, because he did not move out of her way but stood over her, loomed over her, while she squatted in front of him. The situation was full of erotic symbolism. When she realized the submissiveness implied by her position at his feet, she popped up again and saw that his smile had broadened.

Flushed and flustered, Nora threw the damp towels into the wastecan under the sink.

Art Streck said, "Cooking, needlepoint ... yeah, I think that's real nice, real nice. What other things do you like to do?"

"That's it, I'm afraid," she said. "I don't have any unusual hobbies. I'm not a very interesting person. Low-key. Dull, even."

Damning herself for being unable to order the bastard out of her house, she slipped past him and went to the oven, ostensibly to check that it was finished preheating, but she was really just trying to get out of Streck's reach.

He followed her, staying close. "When I pulled up out front, I saw lots of flowers. You tend the flowers?"

Staring at the oven dials, she said, "Yes ... I like gardening."

"I approve of that," he said, as if she ought to care whether he approved or not. "Flowers ... that's a good thing for a woman to have an interest in. Cooking, needlepoint, gardening—why you're just full of womanly interests and talents. I'll bet you do everything well, Mrs. Devon. I mean everything a woman should do. I'll bet you're a first-rate woman in every department."

If he touches me, I'll scream, she thought.

However, the walls of the old house were thick, and the neighbours were some distance away. No one would hear her or come to her rescue.

I'll kick him, she thought. I'll fight back.

But, in fact, she was not sure that she would fight, was not sure that she had the gumption to fight. Even if she did attempt to defend herself, he was bigger and stronger than she was.

"Yeah, I'll bet you're a first-rate woman in every department," he repeated, delivering the line more provocatively than before.

Turning from the oven, she forced a laugh. "My husband would be astonished to hear that. I'm not too bad at cakes, but I've still not learned to make a decent piecrust, and my pot roast always turns out bone-dry. My needlepoint's not half bad, but it takes me forever to get anything done." She slipped past him and returned to the counter. She was amazed to hear herself chattering on as she opened the box of icing mix. Desperation made her garrulous. "I've got a green thumb with flowers, but I'm not much of a housekeeper, and if my husband didn't help out—why, this place would be a disaster."

She thought she sounded phony. She detected a note of hysteria in her voice that had to be evident to him. But the mention of a husband had obviously given Art Streck

39

second thoughts about pushing her further. As Nora poured the mix into a bowl and measured out the required butter, Streck drank the water she had given him. He went to the sink and put the empty glass in the dishpan with the dirty bowls and utensils. This time he did not press unnecessarily close to her.

"Well, I better get back to work," he said.

She gave him a calculatedly distracted smile, and nodded. She began to hum softly as she returned to her own task, as if untroubled.

He crossed the kitchen and pushed open the swinging door, then stopped and said, "Your aunt really liked dark places, didn't she? This kitchen would be swell, too, if you brightened it up."

Before she could respond, he went out, letting the door swing shut behind him.

In spite of his unasked-for opinion of the kitchen decor, Streck seemed to have pulled in his horns, and Nora was pleased with herself. Using a few white lies about her non-existent husband, delivered with admirable equanimity, she had handled him after all. That was not exactly the way a cat would have dealt with an aggressor, but it was not the timid, frightened behavior of a mouse, either.

She looked around at the high-ceilinged kitchen and decided it *was* too dark. The walls were a muddy blue. The frosted globes of the overhead lights were opaque, shedding a drab, wintry glow. She considered having the kitchen repainted, the lights replaced.

Merely to contemplate making major changes in Violet Devon's house was dizzying, exhilarating. Nora had redone her own bedroom since Violet's death, but nothing else. Now, wondering if she could follow through with extensive redecoration, she felt wildly daring and rebellious. Maybe. Maybe she could. If she could fend off Streck, maybe she could dredge up the courage to defy her dead aunt.

Her upbeat self-congratulatory mood lasted just twenty minutes, which was long enough to put the cake pans in the oven and whip up the icing and wash some of the bowls and utensils. Then Streck returned to tell her the TV set was

repaired and to give her the bill. Though he had seemed subdued when he left the kitchen, he was as cocky as ever when
he entered the second time. He looked her up and down as
if undressing her in his imagination, and when he met her
eyes he gave her a challenging look.

She thought the bill was too high, but she did not question
it because she wanted him out of the house quickly. As she
sat at the kitchen table to write the check, he pulled the now-
familiar trick of standing too close to her, trying to cow her
with his masculinity and superior size. When she stood and
handed him the check, he contrived to take it in such a way
that his hand touched hers suggestively.

All the way along the hall, Nora was more than half-
convinced that he would suddenly put down his tool kit and
attack her from behind. But she got to the door, and he
stepped past her onto the veranda, and her racing heart
began to slow to a more normal pace.

He hesitated just outside the door. "What's your
husband do?"

The question disconcerted her. It was something he might
have asked earlier, in the kitchen, when she had spoken of
her husband, but now his curiosity seemed inappropriate.

She should have told him it was none of his business, but
she was still afraid of him. She sensed that he could be easily
angered, that the pent-up violence in him could be triggered
with minor effort. So she answered him with another lie,
one she hoped would make him reluctant to harass her any
further: "He's a ... policeman."

Streck raised his eyebrows. "Really? Here in Santa
Barbara?"

"That's right."

"Quite a house for a policeman."

"Excuse me?" she said.

"Didn't know policemen were paid so well."

"Oh, but I told you—I inherited the house from my
aunt."

"Of course, I remember now. You told me. That's
right."

Trying to reinforce the lie, she said, "We were living in an

41

apartment when my aunt died, and then we moved here. You're right—we wouldn't have been able to afford it otherwise.''

"Well," he said, "I'm happy for you. I sure am. A lady as pretty as you deserves a pretty house.''

He tipped an imaginary hat to her, winked, and went along the walk toward the street, where his white van was parked at the curb.

She closed the door and watched him through a clear segment of the leaded, stained-glass oval window in the center of the door. He glanced back, saw her, and waved. She stepped away from the window, into the gloomy hallway, and watched him from a point at which she could not be seen.

Clearly, he hadn't believed her. He knew the husband was a lie. She shouldn't have said she was married to a cop, for God's sake; that was too obvious an attempt to dissuade him. She should have said she was married to a plumber or doctor, anything but a cop. Anyway, Art Streck was leaving. Though he knew she was lying, he was leaving.

She did not feel safe until his van was out of sight.

Actually, even then, she did not feel safe.

2

After murdering Dr. Davis Weatherby, Vince Nasco had driven his gray Ford van to a service station on Pacific Coast Highway. In the public phone booth, he deposited coins and called a Los Angeles number that he had long ago committed to memory.

A man answered by repeating the number Vince had dialed. It was one of the usual three voices that responded to calls, the soft one with a deep timbre. Often, there was another man with a hard sharp voice that grated on Vince.

Infrequently, a woman answered; she had a sexy voice, throaty and yet girlish. Vince had never seen her, but he had often tried to imagine what she looked like.

Now, when the soft-spoken man finished reciting the number, Vince said, "It's done. I really appreciate your calling me, and I'm always available if you have another job." He was confident that the guy on the other end of the line would recognize his voice, too.

"I'm delighted to hear all went well. We've the highest regard for your workmanship. Now remember this," the contact said. He recited a seven-digit telephone number.

Surprised, Vince repeated it.

The contact said, "It's one of the public phones at Fashion Island. In the open-air promenade near Robinson's Department Store. Can you be there in fifteen minutes?"

"Sure," Vince said. "Ten."

"I'll call in fifteen with the details."

Vince hung up and walked back to the van, whistling. Being sent to another public telephone to receive 'the details' could mean only one thing: they had a job for him already, two in one day!

3

Later, after the cake was baked and iced, Nora retreated to her bedroom at the southwest corner of the second floor.

When Violet Devon had been alive, this had been Nora's sanctuary in spite of the lack of a lock on the door. Like all the rooms in the large house, it had been crammed with heavy furniture, as if the place served as a warehouse instead of a home. It had been dreary in all other details as well. Nevertheless, when finished with her chores, or when dismissed after one of her aunt's interminable lectures, Nora had fled to her bedroom, where she escaped into books or vivid daydreams.

Violet inevitably checked on her niece without warning, creeping soundlessly along the hall, suddenly throwing open the unlockable door, entering with the hope of catching Nora in a forbidden pastime or practice. These unannounced inspections had been frequent during Nora's childhood and adolescence, dwindling in number thereafter, though they had continued through the final weeks of Violet Devon's life, when Nora had been a grown woman of twenty-nine. Because Violet had favored dark dresses, had worn her hair in a tight bun, and had gone without a trace of makeup on her pale, sharp-featured face, she had often looked less like a woman than like a man, a stern monk in coarse penitential robes, prowling the corridors of a bleak medieval retreat to police the behavior of fellow monastics.

If caught daydreaming or napping, Nora was severely reprimanded and punished with onerous chores. Her aunt did not condone laziness.

Books were permitted—if Violet had first approved of them—because, for one thing, books were educational. Besides, as Violet often said, "Plain, homely women like you and me will never lead a glamorous life, never go to exotic places. So books have a special value to us. We can experience most everything vicariously, through books. This isn't bad. Living through books is even *better* than having friends and knowing . . . men."

With the assistance of a pliable family doctor, Violet had kept Nora out of public school on the pretense of poor health. She had been educated at home, so books were her only school as well.

In addition to having read thousands of books by the age of thirty, Nora had become a self-taught artist in oils, acrylics, watercolors, pencil. Drawing and painting were activities of which Aunt Violet approved. Art was a solitary pursuit that took Nora's mind off the world beyond the house and helped her avoid contact with people who would inevitably reject, hurt, and disappoint her.

One corner of Nora's room had been furnished with a drawing board, an easel, and a cabinet for supplies. Space for her miniature studio was created by pushing other pieces of furniture together, not by removing anything, and the effect was claustrophobic.

Many times over the years, especially at night but even in the middle of the day, Nora had been overcome by a feeling that the floor of the bedroom was going to collapse under all the furniture, that she was going to crash down into the chamber below, where she would be crushed to death beneath her own massive four-poster bed. When that fear overwhelmed her, she had fled onto the rear lawn, where she sat in the open air, hugging herself and shuddering. She'd been twenty-five before she realized that her anxiety attacks arose not only from the overfurnished rooms and dark decor of the house but from the domineering presence of her aunt.

On a Saturday morning four months ago, eight months after Violet Devon's death, Nora had abruptly been seized by an acute need for change and had frantically reordered her bedroom-studio. She carried and dragged out all the smaller pieces of furniture, distributing them evenly through the other five crowded chambers on the second floor. Some of the heavier things had to be dismantled and taken away in sections, but finally she succeeded in eliminating everything but the four-poster bed, one nightstand, a single armchair, her drawing board and stool, the supply cabinet, and the easel, which was all she needed. Then she stripped off the wallpaper.

Throughout that dizzying weekend, she'd felt as if the revolution had come, as if her life would never be the same. But by the time she had redone her bedroom, the spirit of rebellion had evaporated, and she had left the rest of the house untouched.

Now this one place, at least, was bright, even cheerful. The walls were painted the palest yellow. The drapes were gone, and in their place were Levolor blinds that matched the paint. She had rolled up the dreary carpet and had polished the beautiful oak floor.

More than ever, this was her sanctuary. Without fail, upon passing through the door and seeing what she had wrought, her spirits lifted and she found some surcease from her troubles.

After her frightening encounter with Streck, Nora was soothed, as always, by the bright room. She sat at the drawing board and began a pencil sketch, a preliminary study for an oil painting that she had been contemplating for some time. Initially, her hands shook, and she had to pause repeatedly to regain sufficient control to continue drawing, but in time her fear abated.

She was even able to think about Streck as she worked and to try to imagine just how far he might have gone if she had not managed to maneuver him out of the house. Recently, Nora had wondered if Violet Devon's pessimistic view of the outside world and of all other people was accurate; though it was the primary view that Nora, herself, had been taught, she had the nagging suspicion that it might be twisted, even sick. But now she had encountered Art Streck, and he seemed to be ample proof of Violet's contentions, proof that interacting too much with the outside world was dangerous.

But after a while, when her sketch was half finished, Nora began to think that she had misinterpreted everything Streck had said and done. Surely he could not have been making sexual advances toward her. Not toward *her*.

She was, after all, quite undesirable. Plain. Homely. Perhaps even ugly. Nora knew this was true because, regardless of Violet's faults, the old woman had some virtues, one of which was a refusal to mince words. Nora was unattractive, drab, not a woman who could expect to be held, kissed, cherished. This was a fact of life that Aunt Violet made her understand at an early age.

Although his personality was repellent, Streck was a physically attractive man, one who could have his choice of pretty women. It was ridiculous to assume he would be interested in a drudge like her.

Nora still wore the clothes that her aunt had bought for her—dark, shapeless dresses and skirts and blouses similar to those that Violet had worn. Brighter and more feminine dresses would only call attention to her bony, graceless body and to the characterless and uncomely lines of her face.

But why had Streck said that she was pretty?

Oh, well, that was easily explained. He was making fun of her, perhaps. Or, more likely, he was being polite, kind.

The more she thought about it, the more Nora believed

that she had misjudged the poor man. At thirty, she was already a nervous old maid, as fear-ridden as she was lonely.

That thought depressed her for a while. But she redoubled her efforts on the sketch, finished it, and began another from a different perspective. As the afternoon waned she escaped into her art.

From downstairs the chimes of the ancient grandfather clock rose punctually on the hour, half-hour, and quarter-hour.

The west-falling sun turned more golden as time passed, and as the day wore on the room grew brighter. The air seemed to shimmer. Beyond the south window a king palm stirred gently in the May breeze.

By four o'clock, she was at peace, humming as she worked.

When the telephone rang, it startled her.

She put down her pencil and reached for the receiver. "Hello?"

"Funny," a man said.

"Excuse me?"

"They never heard of him."

"I'm sorry," she said, "but I think you've got the wrong number."

"This *is* you, Mrs. Devon?"

She recognized the voice now. It was him. Streck.

For a moment, she could not speak.

He said, "They never heard of him. I called the Santa Barbara police and asked to speak to Officer Devon, but they said they don't have an Officer Devon on the force. Isn't that odd, Mrs. Devon?"

"What do you want?" she asked shakily.

"I figure it's a computer error," Streck said, laughing quietly. "Yeah, sure, some sort of computer error dropped your husband from their records. I think you'd better tell him as soon as he gets home, Mrs. Devon. If he doesn't get this straightened out ... why, hell, he might not get his paycheck at the end of the week."

He hung up, and the sound of the dial tone made her realize that she should have hung up first, should have slammed down the handset as soon as he said that he'd called the police station. She dared not encourage him even to the extent of listening to him on the phone.

She went through the house, checking all the windows and doors. They were securely locked.

4

At McDonald's on East Chapman Avenue in Orange, Travis Cornell had ordered five hamburgers for the golden retriever. Sitting on the front seat of the pickup, the dog had eaten all of the meat and two buns, and it had wanted to express its gratitude by licking his face.

"You've got the breath of a dyspeptic alligator," he protested, holding the animal back.

The return trip to Santa Barbara took three and a half hours because the highways were much busier than they had been that morning. Throughout the journey, Travis glanced at his companion and spoke to it, anticipating a display of the unnerving intelligence it had shown earlier. His expectations were unfulfilled. The retriever behaved like any dog on a long trip. Once in a while, it *did* sit very erect, looking through the windshield or side window at the scenery with what seemed an unusual degree of interest and attention. But most of the time it curled up and slept on the seat, snuffling in its dreams—or it panted and yawned and looked bored.

When the odor of the dog's filthy coat became intolerable, Travis rolled down the windows for ventilation, and the retriever stuck its head out in the wind. With its ears blown back, hair streaming, it grinned the foolish and charmingly witless grin of all dogs who had ever ridden shotgun in such a fashion.

In Santa Barbara, Travis stopped at a shopping center, where he bought several cans of Alpo, a box of Milk-Bone dog biscuits, heavy plastic dishes for pet food and water, a galvanized tin washtub, a bottle of pet shampoo with flea-

and tick-killing compound, a brush to comb out the animal's tangled coat, a collar, and a leash.

As Travis loaded those items into the back of the pickup, the dog watched him through the rear window of the cab, its damp nose pressed to the glass.

Getting behind the wheel, he said, "You're filthy, and you stink. You're not going to be a lot of trouble about taking a bath, are you?"

The dog yawned.

By the time Travis pulled into the driveway of his four-room rented bungalow on the northern edge of Santa Barbara and switched off the pickup's engine, he was beginning to wonder if the pooch's actions that morning had really been as amazing as he remembered.

"If you don't show me the right stuff again soon," he told the dog as he slipped his key into the front door of the house, "I'm going to have to assume that I stripped a gear out there in the woods, that I'm just nuts and that I imagined everything."

Standing beside him on the stoop, the dog looked up quizzically.

"Do you want to be responsible for giving me doubts about my own sanity? Hmmmmm?"

An orange and black butterfly swooped past the retriever's face, startling it. The dog barked once and raced after the fluttering prey, off the stoop, down the walkway. Dashing back and forth across the lawn, leaping high, snapping at the air, repeatedly missing its bright quarry, it nearly collided with the diamond-patterned trunk of a big Canary island date palm, then narrowly avoided knocking itself unconscious in a head-on encounter with a concrete bird-bath, and at last crashed clumsily into a bed of New Guinea impatiens over which the butterful soared to safety. The retriever rolled once, scrambled to its feet, and lunged out of the flowers.

When it realized that it had been foiled, the dog returned to Travis. It gave him a sheepish look.

"Some wonder dog," he said. "Good grief."

He opened the door, and the retriever slipped in ahead of

him. It padded off immediately to explore these new rooms.

"You better be housebroken!" Travis shouted after it.

He carried the galvanized washtub and the plastic bag full of other purchases into the kitchen. He left the food and pet dishes there, and took everything else outside through the back door. He put the bag on the concrete patio and set the tub beside it, near a coiled hose that was attached to an outdoor faucet.

Inside again, he removed a bucket from beneath the kitchen sink, filled it with the hottest water he could draw, carried it outside, and emptied it into the tub. When Travis had made four trips with the hot water, the retriever appeared and began to explore the backyard. By the time Travis filled the tub more than half full, the dog had begun to urinate every few feet along the whitewashed concrete-block wall that defined the property line, marking its territory.

"When you finish killing the grass," Travis said, "you'd better be in the mood for a bath. You reek."

The retriever turned toward him and cocked its head and appeared to listen when he spoke. But it did not look like one of those smart dogs in the movies. It did not look as if it understood him. It just looked dumb. As soon as he stopped talking, it hurried a few steps farther along the wall and peed again.

Watching the dog relieve itself, Travis felt an urge of his own. He went inside to the bathroom, then changed into an older pair of jeans and a T-shirt for the sloppy job ahead.

When Travis came outside again, the retriever was standing beside the steaming washtub, the hose in its teeth. Somehow, it had managed to turn the faucet. Water gushed out of the hose, into the tub.

For a dog, successfully manipulating a water faucet would be very difficult if not impossible. Travis figured that an equivalent test of his own ingenuity and dexterity would be trying to open a child-proof safety cap on an aspirin bottle with one hand behind his back.

Astonished, he said, "Water's too hot for you?"

The retriever dropped the hose, letting water pour across

the patio, and stepped almost daintily into the tub. It sat and looked at him, as if to say, *Let's get on with it, you dink.*

He went to the tub and squatted beside it. "Show me how you can turn off the water."

The dog looked at him stupidly.

"Show me," Travis said.

The dog snorted and shifted its position in the warm water.

"If you could turn it on, you can turn it off. How did you do it? With your teeth? Had to be with your teeth. Couldn't do it with a paw, for God's sake. But that twisting motion would be tricky. You could've broken a tooth on the cast-iron handle."

The dog leaned slightly out of the tub, just far enough to bite at the neck of the bag that held the shampoo.

"You won't turn off the faucet?" Travis asked.

The dog just blinked at him, inscrutable.

He sighed and turned off the water. "All right. Okay. Be a wiseass." He took the brush and shampoo out of the bag and held them toward the retriever. "Here. You probably don't even need me. You can scrub yourself, I'm sure."

The dog issued a long, drawn-out *woooooof* that started deep in its throat, and Travis had the feeling it was calling *him* a wiseass.

Careful now, he told himself. You're in danger of leaping off the deep end, Travis. This is a damn smart dog you've got here, but he can't really understand what you're saying, and he can't talk back.

The retriever submitted to its bath without protest, enjoying itself. After ordering the dog out of the tub and rinsing off the shampoo, Travis spent an hour brushing its damp coat. He pulled out burrs, bits of weeds that hadn't flushed away, unsnarled the tangles. The dog never grew impatient, and by six o'clock it was transformed.

Groomed, it was a handsome animal. Its coat was predominantly medium gold with feathering of a lighter shade on the backs of its legs, on its belly and buttocks, and on the underside of the tail. The undercoat was thick and soft to provide warmth and repel water. The outer coat was also

51

soft but not as thick, and in some places these longer hairs were wavy. The tail had a slight upward curve, giving the retriever a happy, jaunty look, which was emphasized by its tendency to wag continuously.

The dried blood on the ear was from a small tear already healing. The blood on the paws resulted not from serious injury but from a lot of running over difficult ground. Travis did nothing except pour boric-acid solution, a mild antiseptic, on these minor wounds. He was confident that the dog would experience only slight discomfort—or maybe none at all, for it was not limping—and that it would be completely well in a few days.

The retriever looked splendid now, but Travis was damp, sweaty, and stank of dog shampoo. He was eager to shower and change. He had also worked up an appetite.

The only task remaining was to collar the dog. But when he attempted to buckle the new collar in place, the retriever growled softly and backstepped out of his reach.

"Whoa now. It's only a collar, boy."

The dog snarled at the loop of red leather in Travis's hand and continued to growl.

"You had a bad experience with a collar, huh?"

The dog stopped growling, but it did not take a step toward him.

"Mistreated?" Travis asked. "That must be it. Maybe they choked you with a collar, twisted it and choked you, or maybe they put you on a short chain. Something like that?"

The retriever barked once, padded across the patio, and stood in the farthest corner, looking at the collar from a distance.

"Do you trust me?" Travis asked, remaining on his knees in an unthreatening posture.

The dog shifted its attention from the loop of leather to Travis, meeting his eyes.

"I will never mistreat you," he said solemnly, feeling not at all foolish for speaking so directly and sincerely to a mere dog. "You must know that I won't. I mean, you have good instincts about things like that, don't you? Rely on your instincts, boy, and trust me."

The dog returned from the far end of the patio and stopped just beyond Travis's reach. It glanced once at the collar, then fixed him with that uncannily intense gaze. As before, he felt a degree of communion with the animal that was as profound as it was eerie—and as eerie as it was indescribable.

He said, "Listen, there'll be times I'll want to take you places where you'll need a leash. Which has to be attached to a collar, doesn't it? That's the only reason I want you to wear a collar—so I can take you everywhere with me. That and to ward off fleas. But if you really don't want to submit to it, I won't force you."

For a long time they faced each other as the retriever mulled over the situation. Travis continued to hold the collar out as if it represented a gift rather than a demand, and the dog continued to stare into his new master's eyes. At last, the retriever shook itself, sneezed once, and slowly came forward.

"That's a good boy," Travis said encouragingly.

When it reached him, the dog settled on its belly, then rolled onto its back with all four legs in the air, making itself vulnerable. It gave him a look that was full of love, trust, and a little fear.

Crazily, Travis felt a lump form in his throat and was aware of hot tears scalding the corners of his eyes. He swallowed hard and blinked back the tears and told himself he was being a sentimental dope. But he knew why the dog's considered submission affected him so strongly. For the first time in three years, Travis Cornell felt needed, felt a deep connection with another living creature. For the first time in three years, he had a reason to live.

He slipped the collar in place, buckled it, gently scratched and rubbed the retriever's exposed belly.

"Got to have a name for you," he said.

The dog scrambled to its feet, faced him, and pricked its ears as if waiting to hear what it would be called.

God in heaven, Travis thought, I'm attributing human intentions to him. He's a mutt, special maybe but still only a mutt. He may look as if he's waiting to hear what he'll be called, but he sure as hell doesn't understand English.

"Can't think of a single name that's fitting," Travis said at last. "We don't want to rush this. It's got to be just the right name. You're no ordinary dog, fur face. I've got to think on it a while until I hit the right moniker."

Travis emptied the washtub, rinsed it out, and left it to dry. Together, he and the retriever went into the home they now shared.

5

Dr. Elisabeth Yarbeck and her husband Jonathan, an attorney, lived in Newport Beach in a sprawling, single-storey, ranch-style home with a shake-shingle roof, cream-colored stucco walls, and a walkway of Bouquet Canyon stone. The waning sun radiated copper and ruby light that glinted and flashed in the beveled glass of the narrow leaded windows flanking the front door, giving those panes the look of enormous gemstones.

Elisabeth answered the door when Vince Nasco rang the bell. She was about fifty, trim and attractive, with shaggy silver-blond hair and blue eyes. Vince told her his name was John Parker, that he was with the FBI, and that he needed to speak with her and her husband in regards to a case currently under investigation.

"Case?" she said. "What case?"

"It involves a government-financed research project on which you were once involved," Vince told her, for that was the opening line that he had been told to use.

She examined his photo ID and Bureau credentials carefully.

He was not concerned. The phony papers had been prepared by the same people who had hired him for this job. The forged documents had been provided ten months ago to assist him on a hit in San Francisco, and had served him well on three other occasions.

Though he knew the ID would meet with her approval, he

was not sure that he, himself, would pass inspection. He was wearing a dark blue suit, white shirt, blue tie, and highly polished black shoes—correct attire for an agent. His size and his expressionless face also served him well in the role he was playing. But the murder of Dr. Davis Weatherby and the prospect of two more murders within the next few minutes had wildly excited him, had filled him with a manic glee that was almost uncontainable. Laughter kept building within him, and the struggle to repress it grew more difficult by the minute. In the drab green Ford sedan, which he had stolen forty minutes ago expressly for this one job, he had been seized by a fit of shakes induced not by nervousness but by intense pleasure of an almost sexual nature. He'd been forced to pull the car to the side of the road and sit for ten minutes, breathing deeply, until he had calmed down a bit.

Now, Elisabeth Yarbeck looked up from the forged ID, met Vince's eyes, and frowned.

He risked a smile, though there was a danger of slipping into uncontrollable laughter that would blow his cover. He had a boyish smile that, by its marked contrast with his size, could be disarming.

After a moment, Dr. Yarbeck also smiled. Satisfied, she returned his credentials and welcomed him into her house.

"I'll need to speak with your husband, too," Vince reminded her as she closed the front door behind them.

"He's in the living room, Mr. Parker. This way, please."

The living room was large and airy. Cream-colored walls and carpet. Pale-green sofas. Big plate-glass windows, partly shielded by green awnings, provided views of the meticulously landscaped property and of houses on the hills below.

Jonathan Yarbeck was stuffing handfuls of wood chips in among the logs that he'd piled in the brick fireplace, getting ready to light a fire. He stood up, dusting his hands together, as his wife introduced Vince. " ... John Parker of the FBI."

"FBI?" Yarbeck said, raising his eyebrows inquiringly.

"Mr. Yarbeck," Vince said, "if there are other members

of the family at home, I'd also like to speak with them now, so I don't have to repeat myself.''

Shaking his head, Yarbeck said, ''There's just Liz and me. Kids are away at college. What's this all about?''

Vince drew the silencer-equipped pistol from inside his suit jacket and shot Jonathan Yarbeck in the chest. The attorney was flung backward against the mantel, where he hung for a moment as if nailed in place, then fell atop the brass fireplace tools.

Sssssnap.

Elisabeth Yarbeck was briefly frozen by astonishment and horror. Vince quickly moved on her. He grabbed her left arm and twisted it up behind her back, hard. When she cried out in pain, he put the pistol against the side of her head and said, ''Be quiet, or I'll blow your fuckin' brains out.''

He forced her to accompany him across the room to her husband's body. Jonathan Yarbeck was face-down on top of a small brass coal shovel and a brass-handled poker. He was dead. But Vince did not want to take chances. He shot Yarbeck twice in the back of the head at close range.

A strange, thin, catlike sound escaped Liz Yarbeck—then she began to sob.

Because of the distance and the smoky tint on the glass, Vince did not believe even the neighbors could see through the big windows, but he wanted to deal with the woman in a more private place. He forced her into the hall and headed deeper into the house, looking in doors as they went until he found the master bedroom. There, he gave her a hard shove, and she sprawled on the floor.

''Stay put,'' he said.

He switched on the bedside lamps. He went to the big sliding-glass doors that opened onto the patio and began to close the drapes.

The moment his back was turned, the woman scrambled to her feet and ran toward the hall door.

He caught her, slammed her up against the wall, drove a fist into her stomach, knocking the wind out of her, then threw her to the floor again. Lifting her head by a handful of hair, he forced her to look him in the eyes. "Listen, lady, I'm not going to shoot you. I came here to get your husband. Just your husband. But if you try to slip away from me before I'm ready to let you go, I'll have to waste you, too. Understand?"

He was lying, of course. She was the one he was being paid to hit, and the husband had to be removed simply because he was there. However, it was true that Vince was not going to shoot her. He wanted her to be cooperative until he could tie her up and deal with her at a more leisurely pace. The two shootings had been satisfying, but he wanted to draw this one out, kill her more slowly. Sometimes, death could be savored like good food, fine wine, and glorious sunsets.

Gasping for breath, sobbing, she said, "Who *are* you?"

"None of your business."

"What do you want?"

"Just shut up, cooperate, and you'll get out of this alive."

She was reduced to urgent prayer, running the words together and sometimes punctuating them with small desperate wordless sounds.

Vince finished with the drapes.

He tore the phone out of the wall and pitched it across the room.

Taking the woman by the arm again, he pulled her to her feet and dragged her into the bathroom. He searched through drawers until he found first-aid supplies; the adhesive tape was just what he needed.

In the bedroom once more, he made her lie on her back on the bed. He used the tape to bind her ankles together and to secure her wrists in front of her. From a bureau drawer, he got a pair of her flimsy panties, which he wadded up and stuffed into her mouth. He sealed her mouth shut with a final strip of tape.

She was shaking violently, blinking through tears and sweat.

He left the bedroom, went to the living room, and knelt beside Jonathan Yarbeck's corpse, with which he had unfinished business. He turned it over. One of the bullets that had entered the back of Yarbeck's head had punched out through his throat, just under his chin. His open mouth was full of blood. One eye was rolled back in his skull, so only the white showed.

Vince looked into the other eye. "Thank you," he said sincerely, reverently. "Thank you, Mr Yarbeck."

He closed both eyelids. He kissed them.

'Thank you.'

He kissed the dead man's forehead.

"Thank you for what you've given me."

Then he went into the garage, where he searched through cabinets until he found some tools. He selected a hammer with a comfortable rubberized handle and a polished steel head.

When he returned to the quiet bedroom and put the hammer on the mattress beside the bound woman, her eyes widened almost comically.

She began to twist and squirm, tried to wrench her hands loose of the looped adhesive tape, to no avail.

Vince stripped out of his clothes.

Seeing the woman's eyes fix on him with the same terror with which she had regarded the hammer, he said, "No, please, don't worry, Dr. Yarbeck. I'm not going to molest you." He hung his suit jacket and shirt on the back of a chair. "I have no sexual interest in you." He slipped out of his shoes, socks, and trousers. "You won't have to suffer that humiliation. I'm not that sort of man. I'm just removing my clothes to avoid getting blood all over them."

Naked, he picked up the hammer and swung it at her left leg, shattering her knee. Perhaps fifty or sixty hammer strikes after he began, The Moment arrived.

Sssssnap.

Sudden energy blasted through him. He felt inhumanly alert, acutely sensitive of the color and texture of everything around him. And he felt far stronger than ever before in his life, like a god in a man's body.

He dropped the hammer and fell to his bare knees beside the bed. He put his forehead on the bloodied bedspread and took deep breaths, shuddering with pleasure so intense it could almost not be borne.

A couple of minutes later, when he had recovered, when he had adjusted to his new and more powerful condition, he got up, turned to the dead woman, and bestowed kisses on her battered face, plus one in the palm of each of her hands.

"Thank you."

He was so deeply moved by the sacrifice she had made for him that he thought he might weep. But his joy at his own good fortune was greater than his pity for her, and the tears would not flow.

In the bathroom he took a quick shower. As the hot water sluiced the soap from him, he thought about how lucky he was to have found a way to make murder his business, to be paid for what he would have done anyway, without remuneration.

When he had dressed again, he used a towel to wipe off the few things he had touched since entering the house. He always remembered *every* move he'd made, and he never worried about missing an object in the wipe-down and leaving a stray fingerprint. His perfect memory was just another part of his Gift.

When he let himself out of the house, he discovered that night had fallen.

THREE

1

Throughout the early part of the evening, the retriever exhibited none of the remarkable behavior that had stirred Travis's imagination. He kept a watch on the dog, sometimes directly, sometimes out of the corner of his eye, but he saw nothing that engaged his curiosity.

He made a dinner of bacon, lettuce, and tomato sandwiches for himself, and he opened a can of Alpo for the retriever. It liked the Alpo well enough, consuming the stuff in great gulps, but it clearly preferred his food. It sat on the kitchen floor beside his chair, looking at him forlornly as he ate two sandwiches at the red Formica-topped table. At last he gave it two strips of bacon.

Nothing about its doggy begging was extraordinary. It performed no startling tricks. It merely licked its chops, whined now and then, and repeatedly employed a limited repertoire of sorrowful expressions designed to elicit pity and compassion. Any mutt would have tried to cadge a treat in the same fashion.

Later, in the living room, Travis switched on the television, and the dog curled up on the couch beside him. After a while it put its head on his thigh, wanting to be petted and scratched behind the ears, and he obliged. The dog glanced occasionally at the television but had no great interest in the programs.

Travis was not interested in TV, either. He was intrigued only by the dog. He wanted to study it and encourage it to perform more tricks. Although he tried to think of ways to elicit displays of its astonishing intelligence, he could come up with no tests that would reliably gauge the animal's mental capacity.

Besides, Travis had a hunch that the dog would not cooperate in a test. Most of the time it seemed instinctively to conceal its cleverness. He recalled its witlessness and comical clumsiness in pursuit of the butterfly, then contrasted that behavior with the wit and agility required to turn on the patio water faucet: those actions appeared to be the work of two different animals. Though it was a crazy idea, Travis suspected that the retriever did not wish to draw attention to itself and that it revealed its uncanny intelligence only in times of crisis (as in the woods), or if it was very hungry (as when it had opened the glove compartment in the truck to obtain the candy bar), or if no one was watching (as when it had turned on the water faucet).

This was a preposterous idea because it suggested that the dog was not only highly intelligent for one of its species *but was aware of the extraordinary nature of its own abilities*. Dogs—all animals, in fact—simply did not possess the high degree of self awareness required to analyze themselves in comparison to others of their kind. Comparative analysis was strictly a human quality. If a dog was especially bright and capable of many tricks, it would still not be aware it was different from most of its kind. To assume this dog was, in fact, aware of such things was to credit it not only with remarkable intelligence but with a capacity for reason and logic, and with a facility for rational judgement superior to the instinct that ruled the decisions of all other animals.

"You," Travis told the retriever, gently stroking its head, "are an enigma wrapped in a mystery. Either that, or I'm a candidate for a rubber room."

The dog looked at him in response to his voice, gazed into his eyes for a moment, yawned—and suddenly jerked its head up and stared beyond him at the bookshelves that flanked the archway between the living and dining rooms.

The satisfied, dopey, doggy expression on its face had vanished, replaced by the keen interest Travis had seen before, which transcended ordinary canine alertness.

Scrambling off the sofa, the retriever dashed to the bookshelves. It ran back and forth beneath them, looking up at the colorful spines of the neatly arranged volumes.

The rental house came fully—if unimaginatively and cheaply—furnished, with upholstery chosen for durability (vinyl) or for the ability to conceal ineradicable stains (eye-searing plaids). Instead of wood, there was lots of wood-finish Formica that was resistant to chipping, scratching, abrasion, and cigarette burns. Virtually the only things in the place reflecting Travis Cornell's own tastes and interests were the books—both paperbacks and hardcovers—that filled the shelves in the living room.

The dog appeared to be intensely curious about at least some of those few hundred volumes.

Getting to his feet, Travis said, "What is it, boy? What's got your tail in an uproar?"

The retriever jumped onto its hind feet, put its forepaws on one of the shelves, and sniffed the spines of the books. It glanced at Travis, then returned to its eager examination of his library.

He went to the shelf in question, withdrew one of the volumes to which the dog had pressed its nose—*Treasure Island* by Robert Louis Stevenson—and held it out. "This? You're interested in this?"

The dog studied the painting of Long John Silver and a pirate ship that adorned the dust jacket. It looked up at Travis, then down at Long John Silver again. After a moment, it dropped back from the shelf, onto the floor, dashed to the shelves on the other side of the archway, leaped up again, and began sniffing other books.

Travis replaced *Treasure Island* and followed the retriever. It was now applying its damp nose to his collection of Charles Dickens's novels. Travis picked up a paperback of *A Tale of Two Cities*.

Again, the retriever carefully studied the cover illustration as if actually trying to determine what the book was about, then looked up expectantly at Travis.

Utterly baffled, he said, "The French Revolution. Guillotines. Beheadings. Tragedy and heroism. It's ... uh ... well, it's all about the importance of valuing individuals over groups, about the need to place a far greater value on one man's or woman's life than on the advancement of the masses."

The dog returned its attention to the tomes shelved in front of it, sniffing, sniffing.

"This is nuts," Travis said, putting *A Tale of Two Cities* back where he'd gotten it. "I'm giving plot synopses to a dog, for God's sake!"

Dropping its big forepaws down to the next shelf, the retriever panted and snuffled over the literature on that row. When Travis did not pull any of those books out for inspection, the dog tilted its head to get into the shelf, gently gripped a volume in its teeth, and tried to withdraw it for further examination.

"Whoa," Travis said, reaching for the book. "Keep your slobber off the fine bindings, fur face. This one's *Oliver Twist*. Another Dickens. The story of an orphan in Victorian England. He gets involved with shady characters, the criminal underworld, and they—"

The retriever dropped to the floor and padded back to the shelves on the other side of the archway, where it continued to sniff at those volumes within its reach. Travis could have sworn it even gazed up wistfully at the books that were above its head.

For perhaps five minutes, in the grip of an eerie premonition that something of tremendous importance was about to happen, Travis followed the dog, showing it the covers of a dozen novels, providing a line or two of plot description of each story. He had no idea if that was what the precocious pooch wanted him to do. Surely, it could not understand the synopses he provided. Yet it seemed to listen raptly as he spoke. He knew he must be misinterpreting essentially meaningless animal behavior, attributing complex intentions to the dog when it had none. Still, a premonitory tingle coursed along the back of his neck. As their peculiar search continued, Travis half-expected some startling revelation at any moment—and at the same time felt increasingly gullible and foolish.

His taste in fiction was eclectic. Among the volumes he took off the shelves were Bradbury's *Something Wicked This Way Comes* and Chandler's *The Long Goodbye*. Cain's *The Postman Always Rings Twice* and Hemingway's *The Sun Also Rises*. Two books by Richard Condon and one by Anne Tyler. Dorothy Sayer's *Murder Must Advertise* and Elmore Leonard's *52 Pick-Up*.

At last the dog turned away from the books and went to the middle of the room, where it padded back and forth, back and forth, clearly agitated. It stopped, confronted Travis, and barked three times.

"What's wrong, boy?"

The dog whined, looked at the laden shelves, walked in a circle, and peered up at the books again. It seemed frustrated. Thoroughly, maddeningly frustrated.

"I don't know what more to do, boy," he said, "I don't know what you're after, what you're trying to tell me."

The dog snorted and shook itself. Lowering its head in defeat, it returned resignedly to the sofa and curled up on the cushions.

"That's all?" Travis asked. "We're just giving up?"

Putting its head down on the sofa, it regarded him with moist soulful eyes.

Travis turned from the dog and let his gaze travel slowly over the books, as if they not only offered the information printed on their pages but also contained an important message that could not be as easily read, as if their colorful spines were the strange runes of a long-lost language and, once deciphered, would reveal wondrous secrets. But he could not decipher them.

Having believed that he was on the trembling edge of some great revelation, Travis felt enormously let down. His own frustration was considerably worse than what the dog had exhibited, and he could not merely curl up on the sofa, put his head down, and forget the whole thing as the retriever had done.

"What the hell was that all about?" he demanded.

The dog looked up at him, inscrutable.

"Was there any point to all of that stuff with the books?"

The dog stared.

"Is there something special about you—or have I popped the pull-tab on my brain and emptied it?"

The dog was perfectly limp and still, as if it might close its eyes at any moment and doze off.

"If you yawn at me, damn you, I'll kick your butt."

The dog yawned.

"Bastard," Travis said.

It yawned again.

"Now *there*. What does that mean? Are you yawning on purpose because of what I said, because you're playing with me? Or are you just yawning? How am I to interpret anything you do? How am I to know whether any of it has meaning?"

The dog sighed.

With a sigh of his own, Travis went to one of the front windows and stared out at the night, where the feathery fronds of the large Canary Island date palm were backlit by the vaguely yellow glow of the sodium-vapor streetlamps. He heard the dog get off the sofa and hurry out of the room, but he refused to inquire into its activities. For the moment, he could not handle more frustration.

The retriever was making noise in the kitchen. A clink. A soft clatter. Travis figured it was drinking from its bowl.

Seconds later, he heard it returning. It came to his side and rubbed against his leg.

He glanced down and, to his surprise, saw the retriever was holding a can of beer in its teeth. Coors. He took the proffered can and discovered it was cold.

"You got this from the refrigerator!"

The dog appeared to be grinning.

2

When Nora Devon was in the kitchen making dinner, the phone rang again. She prayed it would not be *him*.

But it was. "I know what you need," Streck said. "I know what you need."

I'm not even pretty, she wanted to say. *I'm a plain, dumpy old maid, so what do you want with me? I'm safe from the likes of you because I'm not pretty. Are you blind?* But she could say nothing.

"Do *you* know what you need?" he asked.

Finding her voice at last, she said, "Go away."

"I know what you need. You might not know, but I do."

This time she hung up first, slamming the handset down so hard that it must have hurt his ear.

Later, at eight-thirty, the phone rang again. She was sitting in bed, reading *Great Expectations* and eating ice cream. She was so startled by the first ring that the spoon popped out of her hand into the dish, and she nearly spilled the dessert.

Putting the dish and the book aside, she stared anxiously at the telephone, which stood on the nightstand. She let it ring ten times. Fifteen. Twenty. The strident sound of the bell filled the room, echoing off the walls, until each ring seemed to drill into her skull.

Eventually she realized she would be making a big mistake if she did not answer. He'd know she was here and was too frightened to pick up the receiver, which would please him. More than anything, he desired domination. Perversely, her timid withdrawal would encourage him. Nora had no experience at confrontation, but she saw that she was going to have to learn to stand up for herself—and fast.

She lifted the receiver on the thirty-first ring.

Streck said, "I can't get you out of my mind."

Nora did not reply.

Streck said, "You have beautiful hair. So dark. Almost black. Thick and glossy. I want to run my hands through your hair."

She had to say something to put him in his place—or hang up. But she could not bring herself to do either.

"I've never seen eyes like yours," Streck said, breathing hard. "Gray but not like other gray eyes. Deep, warm, *sexy* eyes."

Nora was speechless, paralyzed.

'You're very pretty, Nora Devon. Very pretty. And I know what you need. I do. I really do, Nora. I know what you need, and I'm going to give it to you."

Her paralysis was shattered by a fit of the shakes. She dropped the phone into its cradle. Bending forward in bed, she felt as if she were shaking herself to pieces before the tremors slowly subsided.

She did not own a gun.

She felt small, fragile, and terribly alone.

She wondered if she should call the police. But what would she tell them? That she was the object of sexual harassment? They'd get a big laugh out of that. Her? A sex object? She was an old maid, as plain as mud, not remotely the type to turn a man's head and give him erotic dreams. The police would suppose that she either was making it up or was hysterical. Or they would assume she had misinterpreted Streck's politeness as sexual interest, which is what even *she* thought at first.

She pulled a blue robe on over the roomy men's pajamas that she wore, belted it. Barefoot, she hurried downstairs to the kitchen, where she hesitantly withdrew a butcher's knife from the rack near the stove. Light trickled like a thin stream of quicksilver along the well-honed cutting edge.

As she turned the gleaming knife in her hand, she saw her eyes reflected in the broad, flat blade. She stared at herself in the polished steel, wondering if she could possibly use such a horrible weapon against another human being even in self-defense.

She hoped she would never have to find out.

Upstairs again, she put the butcher's knife on the night-stand, within easy reach.

She took off her robe and sat on the edge of the bed, hugging herself and trying to stop shaking.

"Why me?" she said aloud. "Why does he want to pick on *me*?"

Streck said that she was pretty, but Nora knew it was not true. Her own mother had abandoned her to Aunt Violet and had returned only twice in twenty-eight years, the last time when Nora was six. Her father remained unknown to her, and no other Devon relatives were willing to take her in, a situation which Violet frankly attributed to Nora's uncomely appearance. So although Streck said she was pretty, it could not possibly be her that he wanted. No, what he wanted was the thrill of scaring and dominating and hurting her. There were such people. She read about them in books, newspapers. And Aunt Violet had warned her a thousand times that if a man ever came onto her with sweet talk and smiles, he would only want to lift her up so he could later cast her down from a greater height and hurt her all the worse.

After a while, the worst of the tremors passed. Nora got into bed again. Her remaining ice cream had melted, so she put the dish aside, on the nightstand. She picked up the novel by Dickens and tried to involve herself once more with Pip's tale. But her attention repeatedly strayed to the phone, to the butcher's knife—and to the open door and the second-floor hall beyond where she kept imagining she saw movement.

3

Travis went into the kitchen, and the dog followed him.

He pointed to the refrigerator and said, "Show me. Do it again. Get me a beer. Show me how you did it."

The dog did not move.

Travis squatted. "Listen, fur face, who got you out of those woods, away from whatever was chasing you? I did. And who bought hamburgers for you? I did. I bathed you, fed you, gave you a home. Now you owe me. Stop being coy. If you can open that thing, *do it!*"

The dog went to the aging Frigidaire, lowered its head to the bottom corner of the enamel-coated door, gripped the edge in its jaws, and pulled backward, straining with its entire body. The rubber seal let loose with a barely audible sucking sound. The door swung open. The dog quickly insinuated itself into the gap, then jumped up and braced itself with a forepaw on each side of the storage compartment.

"I'll be damned," Travis said, moving closer.

The retriever peered into the second shelf, where Travis had stored cans of beer, Diet Pepsi, and V-8 vegetable juice. It plucked another Coors from the supply, dropped to the floor, and let the refrigerator door slip shut again as it came to Travis.

He took the beer from it. Standing with a Coors in each hand, studying the dog, he said, more to himself than to the animal, "Okay, so somebody could have taught you to open a refrigerator door. And he could even have taught you how to recognize a certain brand of beer, how to distinguish it from other cans, and how to carry it to him. But we still have some mysteries here. Is it likely that the brand you were taught to recognize would be the same one I'd have in my refrigerator? Possible, yes, but not likely. Besides, I didn't give you any command. I didn't ask you to get me a beer. You did it on your own hook, as if you figured a beer was exactly what I needed at the moment. And it *was*."

Travis put one can down on the table. He wiped the other on his shirt, popped it open, and took a few swallows. He was not concerned that the can had been in the dog's mouth. He was too excited by the animal's amazing performance to worry about germs. Besides, it had held each can by the bottom, as if concerned about hygiene.

The retriever watched him drink.

When he had finished a third of the beer, Travis said, "It was almost as if you understood that I was tense, upset— and that a beer would help relax me. Now, is that crazy or what? We're talking analytical reasoning. Okay, so pets can *sense* their masters' moods a lot of the time. But how many

70

pets know what beer is, and how many realize what it can do to make the master more mellow? Anyway, how'd you know there was beer in the fridge? I guess you could've seen it sometime during the evening when I was fixing dinner, but still . . .''

His hands were shaking. He drank more of the beer, and the can rattled lightly against his teeth.

The dog went around the red Formica table to the twin cabinet doors below the sink. It opened one of these, stuck its head into the dark space, and pulled out the bag of Milk-Bone biscuits, which it brought straight to Travis.

He laughed and said, "Well, if I can have a beer, I guess you deserve a treat of your own, huh?" He took the bag from the dog and tore it open. "Do a few Milk-Bones mellow you out, fur face?" He put the open bag on the floor. "Serve yourself. I trust you not to overindulge like an ordinary dog." He laughed again. "Hell, I think I might trust you to drive the car!"

The retriever finessed a biscuit out of the package, sat down with its hind legs splayed, and happily crunched up the treat.

Pulling out a chair and sitting at the table, Travis said, "You give me reason to believe in miracles. Do you know what I was doing in those woods this morning?"

Working its jaws, industriously grinding up the biscuit, the dog seemed to have lost interest in Travis for the moment.

"I went out there on a sentimental journey, hoping to recall the pleasure I got from the Santa Anas when I was a boy, in the days before . . . everything turned so dark. I wanted to kill a few snakes like I did when I was a kid, hike and explore and feel in tune with life like in the old days. Because for a long time now, I haven't cared whether I live or die."

The dog stopped chewing, swallowed hard, and focused on Travis with undivided attention.

"Lately, my depressions have been blacker than midnight on the moon. Do you understand about depression, pooch?"

Leaving the Milk-Bone biscuits behind, the retriever got

71

up and came to him. It gazed into his eyes with that unnerving directness and intensity that it had shown before.

Meeting its stare, he said, "Wouldn't consider suicide, though. For one thing, I was raised a Catholic, and though I haven't gone to Mass in ages, I still sort of believe. And for a Catholic, suicide is a mortal sin. Murder. Besides, I'm too mean and too stubborn to give up, no matter how dark things get."

The retriever blinked but did not break eye contact.

"I was in those woods searching for the happiness I once knew. And then I ran into you."

"Woof," it said, as if it were saying, *Good*.

He took its head in both his hands, lowered his face to it, and said, "Depression. A feeling that existence is pointless. How would a dog know about those things, hmmm? A dog has no worries, does it? To a dog, every day is a joy. So do you really understand what I'm talking about, boy? Honest to God, I think maybe you do. But am I crediting you with too much intelligence, too much wisdom even for a magical dog! Huh! Sure, you can do some amazing tricks, but that's not the same as *understanding* me."

The retriever pulled away from him and returned to the Milk-Bone package. It took the bag in its teeth and shook out twenty or thirty biscuits onto the linoleum.

"There you go again," Travis said. "One minute, you seem half human—and the next minute you're just a dog with a dog's interests."

However, the retriever was not seeking a snack. It began to push the biscuits around with the black tip of its snout, maneuvering them into the open center of the kitchen floor one at a time, ordering them neatly end to end.

"What the hell is this?"

The dog had five biscuits arranged in a row that gradually curved to the right. It pushed a sixth into place, emphasizing the curve.

As he watched, Travis hastily finished his first beer and opened the second. He had a feeling he was going to need it.

The dog studied the row of biscuits for a moment, as if not quite sure what it had begun to do. It padded back and forth a few times, clearly uncertain, but eventually nudged two more biscuits into line. It looked at Travis, then at the shape it was creating on the floor, then nosed a ninth biscuit into place.

Travis sipped some beer and waited tensely to see what would happen next.

With a shake of its head and a snort of frustration, the dog went to the far end of the room and stood facing into the corner, its head hung low. Travis wondered what it was doing, and then somehow he got the idea that it had gone into the corner to concentrate. After a while, it returned and pushed the tenth and eleventh Milk-Bones into place, enlarging the pattern.

He was stricken again by the premonition that something of great importance was about to happen. Gooseflesh dimpled his arms.

This time he was not disappointed. The golden retriever used nineteen biscuits to form a crude but recognizable question mark on the kitchen floor, then raised its expressive eyes to Travis.

A question mark.

Meaning: *Why?* Why have you been so depressed? Why do you feel life is pointless, empty?

The dog aparently understood what he had told it. All right, okay, so maybe it didn't understand language exactly, didn't follow every word that he spoke, but it somehow perceived the meaning of what he was saying, or at least enough of the meaning to arouse its interest and curiosity.

And, by God, if it also understood the purpose of a question mark, then it was capable of abstract thinking! The very concept of simple symbols—like alphabets, numbers, question marks, and exclamation points—serving as shorthand for communicating complex ideas ... well, that required abstract thinking. And abstract thinking was reserved for only one species on earth: humankind. This golden retriever was demonstrably *not* human, but somehow it had come into possession of intellectual skills that no other animal could claim.

Travis was stunned. But there was nothing accidental

73

about the question mark. Crude but not accidental. Somewhere, the dog must have seen the symbol and been taught its meaning. Statistical theorists said an infinite number of monkeys, equipped with an infinite number of typewriters, would eventually be able to recreate every line of great English prose merely by random chance. He figured that this dog forming a Milk-Bone question mark in about two minutes flat, merely by purest chance, was about ten times as unlikely as all those damn monkeys recreating Shakespeare's plays.

The dog was watching him expectantly.

Getting up, he found he was a bit shaky in the legs. He went to the carefully arranged biscuits, scattered them across the floor, and returned to his chair.

The retriever studied the disarranged Milk-Bones, regarded Travis inquiringly, sniffed at the biscuits again, and seemed baffled.

Travis waited.

The house was unnaturally quiet, as if the flow of time had been suspended for every living creature, machine, and object on earth—though not for him, the retriever, or the contents of the kitchen.

At last, the dog began to push the biscuits around with its nose as it had done before. In a minute or two, it formed a question mark.

Travis chugged some Coors. His heart was hammering. His palms were sweaty. He was filled with both wonder and trepidation, with both wild joy and fear of the unknown, simultaneously awestricken and bewildered. He wanted to laugh because he had never seen anything half as delightful as this dog. He also wanted to cry because only hours ago he'd thought life was bleak, dark, and pointless. But no matter how painful it was sometimes, life was (he now realized) nonetheless precious. He actually felt as if God had sent the retriever to intrigue him, to remind him that the world was full of surprises and that despair made no sense when one had no understanding of the purpose—and strange possibilities—of existence. Travis wanted to laugh, but his laughter teetered on the brink of a sòb. Yet when he surrendered to the sob, it became a laugh. When he attempted to stand, he knew that he was even shakier than before, too shaky, so he did the only thing he could do: he stayed in his chair and took another long swallow of Coors.

Cocking its head one way and then the other, looking slightly wary, the dog watched him as if it thought he had gone mad. He had. Months ago. But he was all better now.

He put down the Coors and wiped tears out of his eyes with the backs of his hands. He said, "Come here, fur face."

The retriever hesitated, then came to him.

He ruffled and stroked its coat, scratched behind its ears. "You amaze me and scare me. I can't figure where you came from or how you got to be what you are, but you couldn't have come where you're more needed. A question mark, huh? Jesus. All right. You want to know why I felt life had no purpose or joy for me? I'll tell you. I will, by God, I'll sit right here and have another beer and tell it to a dog. But first ... I'm going to name you."

The retriever blew air out of its nostrils, as if to say, *Well, it's about time.*

Holding the dog's head, looking straight into its eyes, Travis said, "Einstein. From now on, fur face, your name is Einstein."

4

Streck called again at ten minutes past nine.

Nora snatched up the phone on the first ring, fiercely determined to tell him off and make him leave her alone. But for some reason she clenched up again and was unable to speak.

In a repulsively intimate tone of voice, he said, "You miss me, prettiness? Hmmmm? Do you wish I'd come to you, be a man for you?"

She hung up.

What's wrong with me? she wondered. Why can't I tell him to go away and stop bothering me?

Maybe her speechlessness grew from a secret desire to hear a man—any man, even a disgusting specimen like Streck—call her pretty. Although he was not the kind who would be capable of tenderness or affection, she could listen to him and imagine what it would be like to have a *good* man say sweet things to her.

"Well, you're not pretty," she told herself, "and you never ever will be, so stop mooning around. Next time he calls, tell him off."

She got out of bed and went down the hall to the bathroom, where there was a mirror. Following Violet Devon's example, Nora did not have mirrors anywhere in the house except the bathrooms. She did not like to look at herself because what she saw was saddening.

This one night, however, she wanted to take a look at herself because Streck's flattery, though cold and calculated, had stirred her curiosity. Not that she hoped to see some fine quality that she had never seen before. No. From duckling to swan overnight . . . that was a frivolous, hopeless dream. Rather, she wanted to confirm that she was undesirable. Streck's unwanted interest rattled Nora because she was *comfortable* in her homeliness and solitude and she wanted to reassure herself that he was mocking her, that he could not act upon his threats, that her peaceful solitude would endure. Or so she told herself as she stepped into the bathroom and switched on the light.

The narrow chamber had pale-blue tile from floor to ceiling with a white-tile border. A huge claw-foot tub. White porcelain and brass fixtures. The large mirror was somewhat streaked with age.

She looked at her hair, which Streck said was beautiful, dark, glossy. But it was of one shade, without natural highlights; to her it wasn't glossy but oily, although she had washed it that morning.

She looked quickly at her brow, cheekbones, nose, jaw line, lips, and chin. She tentatively traced her features with one hand, but she saw nothing to intrigue a man.

At last, reluctantly, she stared into her eyes, which Streck had called lovely. They were a dreary, lusterless shade of gray. She could not bear to meet her own gaze for more than a few seconds. Her eyes confirmed her low opinion of her appearance. But also ... well, in her own eyes she saw a smoldering anger that disturbed her, that was not like her, an anger at what she had let herself become. Of course, that made no sense whatsoever because she was what nature had made her—a mouse—and she could do nothing about that.

Turning from the mottled mirror, she felt a pang of disappointment that her self-inspection had not resulted in a single surprise or reevaluation. Immediately, however, she was shocked and appalled by that disappointment. She stood in the bathroom doorway, shaking her head, amazed by her own befuddled thought processes.

Did she *want* to be appealing to Streck? Of course not. He was weird, sick, dangerous. The very last thing she wanted was to appeal to him. Maybe she wouldn't mind if another man looked on her with favor, but not Streck. She should get on her knees and thank God for creating her as she was, because if she were at all attractive, Streck would make good on his threats. He'd come here, and he'd rape here ... maybe murder her. Who knew about a man like that? Who knew what his limits were? She wasn't being a nervous old maid when she worried about murder, not these days: the newspapers were full of it.

She realized that she was defenseless, and she hurried back to the bedrom where she had left the butcher's knife.

5

Most people believe psychoanalysis is a cure for unhappiness. They are sure they could overcome all their problems and achieve peace of mind if only they could understand their own psychology, understand the reasons for their negative moods and self-destructive behavior. But Travis had learned this was not the case. For years, he engaged in unsparing self-analysis, and long ago he figured out why he had become a loner who was unable to make friends.

However, in spite of that understanding, he had not been able to change.

Now, as midnight approached, he sat in the kitchen, drank another Coors, told Einstein about his self-imposed emotional isolation. Einstein sat before him, unmoving, never yawning, as if intently interested in his tale.

"I was a loner as a kid, right from the start, though I wasn't entirely without friends. It was just that I always preferred my own company. I guess it's my nature. I mean, when I was a kid, I hadn't yet decided that my being friends with someone was a danger to him."

Travis's mother had died giving birth to him, and he knew all about that from an early age. In time her death would seem like an omen of what was to come, and it would take on a terrible importance, but that was later. As a kid, he wasn't yet burdened with guilt.

Not until he was ten. That was when his brother Harry died. Harry was twelve, two years older than Travis. One Monday morning in June, Harry talked Travis into walking three blocks to the beach, although their father had expressly forbidden them to go swimming without him. It was a private cove without a public lifeguard, and they were the only two swimmers in sight.

"Harry got caught in an undertow," Travis told Einstein. "We were in the water together no more than ten feet apart, and the damn undertow got him, sucked him away, but it didn't get me. I even went after him, tried to save him, so I should've swum straight into the same current, but I guess it changed course just after it snatched Harry away, 'cause I came out of the water alive." He stared at the top of the kitchen table for a long moment, seeing not the red Formica but the rolling, treacherous, blue-green sea. "I loved my big brother more than anyone in the world."

Einstein whined softly, as in commiseration.

"Nobody blamed me for what happened to Harry. He was the older one. He was supposed to be the most responsible. But I felt ... well, if the undertow took Harry, it should've taken me, too."

A night wind blew in from the west, rattled a loose windowpane.

After taking a swallow of beer, Travis said, "The summer I was fourteen, I wanted very badly to go to tennis camp. Tennis was my big enthusiasm then. So my dad enrolled me in a place down near San Diego, a full month of intense instruction. He drove me there on a Sunday, but we never made it. Just north of Oceanside, a trucker fell asleep at the wheel, his rig jumped the median, and we were wiped. Dad was killed instantly. Broken neck, broken back, skull crushed, chest caved in. I was in the front seat beside him, and I came out of it with a few cuts, bruises, and two broken fingers."

The dog was studying him intently.

"It was just like with Harry. Both of us should have died, my father and me, but I escaped. And we wouldn't have been making the damn drive if I hadn't agitated like hell about tennis camp. So this time, there was no getting around it. Maybe I couldn't be blamed for my mother dying in childbirth, and maybe I couldn't be pinned with Harry's death, but *this* one . . . Anyway, although I wasn't always at fault, it began to be clear that I was jinxed, that it wasn't safe for people to get too close to me. When I loved somebody, really loved them, they were sure as shit going to die."

Only a child could have been convinced that those tragic events meant he was a walking curse, but Travis was a child then, only fourteen, and no other explanation was so neat. He was too young to understand that the mindless violence of nature and fate often had no meaning that could be ascertained. At fourteen, he *needed* meaning in order to cope, so he told himself that he was cursed, that if he made any close friends he would be sentencing them to early death. Being somewhat of an introvert to begin with, he found it almost too easy to turn inward and make do with his own company.

By the time he graduated from college at the age of twenty-one, he was a confirmed loner, though maturity had given him a healthier perspective on the deaths of his mother, brother, and father. He no longer consciously thought of himself as jinxed, no longer blamed himself for what had happened to his family. He remained an introvert, without close friends, partly because he had lost the ability to form and nurture intimate relationships and partly because he figured he could not be shattered by grief if he had no friends to lose.

"Habit and self-defense kept me emotionally isolated," he told Einstein.

The dog rose and crossed the few feet of kitchen floor that separated them. It insinuated itself between his legs and put its head in his lap.

Petting Einstein, Travis said, "Had no idea what I wanted to do after college, and there was a military draft then, so I joined up before they could call me. Chose the army. Special Forces. Liked it. Maybe because ... well, there was a sense of camaraderie, and I was *forced* to make friends. See, I pretended not to want close ties with anyone, but I must have because I put myself in a situation where it was inevitable. Decided to make a career out of the service. When Delta Force—the antiterrorist group—was formed, that's where I finally landed. The guys in Delta were tight, real buddies. They called me 'The Mute' and 'Harpo' because I wasn't a talker, but in spite of myself I made friends. Then, on our eleventh operation, my squad was flown into Athens to take the U.S. embassy back from a group of Palestinian extremists who'd seized it. They'd killed eight staff members and were still killing one an hour, wouldn't negotiate. We hit them quick and sneaky—and it was a fiasco. They'd booby-trapped the place. Nine men in my squad died. I was the only survivor. A bullet in my thigh. Shrapnel in my ass. But a survivor."

Einstein raised his head from Travis's lap.

Travis thought he saw sympathy in the dog's eyes. Maybe because that was what he wanted to see.

"That's eight years ago, when I was twenty-eight. Left the army. Came home to California. Got a real-estate license because my dad had sold real estate, and I didn't know what else to do. Did real well, maybe 'cause I didn't care if they bought the houses I showed them, didn't push, didn't act like a salesman. Fact is, I did so well that I became a broker, opened my own office, hired salespeople.''

Which was how he had met Paula. She was a tall blond beauty, bright and amusing, and she could sell real estate so well that she joked about having lived an earlier life in which she had represented the Dutch colonists when they had bought Manhattan from the Indians for beads and trinkets. She was smitten with Travis. That's what she told him: "Mr. Cornell, sir, I am smitten. I think it's your strong, silent act. Best Clint Eastwood imitation I've ever seen.'' Travis resisted her at first. He did not believe he would jinx Paula; at least, he didn't consciously believe it; he had not openly reverted to childhood superstition. But he did not want to risk the pain of loss again. Undeterred by his hesitancy, she pursued him, and in time he had to admit he was in love with her. So in love that he told her about his lifelong tag game with Death, something of which he spoke to no one else. "Listen,'' Paula said, "you won't have to mourn me. I'm going to outlive you because I'm not the type to bottle up my feelings. I take out my frustrations on those around me, so I'm bound to shave a decade off *your* life.''

They had been married in a simple courthouse ceremony four years ago, the summer after Travis's thirty-second birthday. He had loved her. Oh God, how he had loved her.

To Einstein, he said, "We didn't know it then, but she had cancer on our wedding day. Ten months later, she was dead.''

The dog put its head down in his lap again.

For a while, Travis could not continue.

He drank some beer.

He stroked the dog's head.

In time he said, "After that, I tried to go on as usual. Always prided myself in going on, facing up to anything, keeping my chin up, all that bullshit. Kept the real-estate office running another year. But none of it mattered any more. Sold it two years ago. Cashed in all my investments, too. Turned everything into cash and socked it in the bank. Rented this house. Spent the last two years ... well, brooding. And I got squirrelly. Hardly a surprise, huh?

Squirrelly as hell. Came full circle, you see, right back to what I believed when I was a kid. That I was a danger to anyone who gets close to me. But you changed me, Einstein. You turned me around in one day. I swear, it's like you were *sent* to show me that life's mysterious, strange, and full of wonders—and that only a fool withdraws from it willingly and lets it pass him by.''

The dog was peering at him again.

He lifted his beer can, but it was empty.

Einstein went to the fridge and got another Coors.

Taking the can from the dog, Travis said, ''Now, after hearing the whole sorry thing, what do you think? You think it's wise for you to hang around with me? You think it's safe?''

Einstein woofed.

''Was that a yes?''

Einstein rolled onto his back and put all four legs in the air, baring his belly as he had done earlier when he had permitted Travis to collar him.

Putting his beer aside, Travis got off his chair, settled on the floor, and stroked the dog's belly. ''All right,'' he said. ''All right. But don't die on me, damn you. Don't you dare die on me.''

6

Nora Devon's telephone rang again at eleven o'clock.

It was Streck. ''Are you in bed now, prettiness?''

She did not reply.

''Do you wish I was there with you?''

Since the previous call, she had thought about how to handle him and had come up with several threats she hoped might work. She said, ''If you don't leave me alone, I'll go to the police.''

''Nora, do you sleep in the nude?''

She was sitting in bed. She sat up straighter, tense, rigid. ''I'll go to the police and say you tried to . . . to force yourself on me. I will, I swear I will.''

"I'd like to see you in the nude,'' he said, ignoring her threat.

"I'll lie. I'll say you r-raped me.''

"Wouldn't you like me to put my hands on your breasts, Nora?''

Dull cramps in her stomach forced her to bend forward in bed. 'I'll have the telephone company put a tap on my line, record all the calls I get, so I'll have proof.''

"Kiss you all over, Nora. Wouldn't that be nice?''

The cramps were getting worse. She was shaking uncontrollably, too. Her voice cracked repeatedly as she employed her final threat: "I have a gun. I have a gun.''

"Tonight you'll dream about me, Nora. I'm sure you will. You'll dream about me kissing you everywhere, all over your pretty body—''

She slammed the phone down.

Rolling on to her side on the bed, she hunched her shoulders and drew up her knees and hugged herself. The cramps had no physical cause. They were strictly an emotional reaction, generated by fear and shame and rage and enormous frustration.

Gradually, the pain passed. Fear subsided, leaving only rage.

She was so wrenchingly innocent of the world and its ways, so unaccustomed to dealing with people, that she couldn't function unless she restricted herself to the house, to a private world without human contact. She knew nothing about social interaction. She had not even been capable of holding a polite conversation with Garrison Dilworth, Aunt Violet's attorney—Nora's attorney now—during their meetings to settle the estate. She had answered his questions as succinctly as possible and had sat in his presence with her eyes downcast and her cold hands fidgeting in her lap, crushingly shy. Afraid of her own lawyer! If she couldn't deal with a kind man like Garrison Dilworth, how could she ever handle a beast like Art Streck? In the future, she wouldn't dare have a repairman in her home, no matter what broke down; she would just have to live in ever-worsening decay and ruin because the next man might be another Streck—or worse. In the tradition established by her aunt, Nora already had groceries delivered from a neighborhood market, so she did not have to go out to shop, but now she would be afraid to let the delivery boy into the house; he had never been the least aggressive, suggestive, or in any way insulting, but one day he might see the vulnerability that Streck had seen . . .

She *hated* Aunt Violet.

On the other hand, Violet had been right: Nora was a mouse. Like all mice, her destiny was to run, to hide, and to cower in the dark.

Her fury abated just as her cramps had done.

Loneliness took the place of anger, and she wept quietly.

Later, sitting with her back against the headboard, blotting her reddened eyes with Kleenex and blowing her nose, she bravely vowed not to become a recluse. Somehow she would find the strength and courage to venture out into the world more than she'd done before. She would meet people. She would get to know the neighbors that Violet had more or less shunned. She would make friends. By God, she *would*. And she wouldn't let Streck intimidate her. She would learn how to handle other problems that came along as well, and in time she would be a different woman from the one she was now. A promise to herself. A sacred vow.

She considered unplugging the telephone, thus foiling Streck, but she was afraid she might need it. What if she woke, heard someone in the house, and was unable to plug in the phone fast enough?

Before turning out the lights and pulling up the covers, she closed the lockless bedroom door and braced it shut with the armchair, which she tilted under the knob. In bed, in the dark, she felt for the butcher's knife, which she'd placed on the nightstand, and she was reassured when she put her hand directly upon it without fumbling.

Nora lay on her back, eyes open, wide awake. Pale amber light from the streetlamps found its way through the shuttered windows. The ceiling was banded with alternating strips of black and faded gold, as if a tiger of infinite length were leaping over the bed in a jump that would never end. She wondered if she would ever sleep easily again.

She also wondered if she would find anyone who could care about her—and for her—out there in the bigger world that she had vowed to enter. Was there no one who could love a mouse and treat it gently?

Far away, a train whistle played a one-note dirge in the night. It was a hollow, cold, and mournful sound.

7

Vince Nasco had never been so busy. Or so happy.

When he called the usual Los Angeles number to report success at the Yarbeck house, he was referred to another public phone. This one was between a frozen yogurt shop and a fish restaurant on Balboa Island in Newport Harbor.

There, he was called by the contact with the sexy, throaty, yet little-girl voice. She spoke circumspectly of murder, never using incriminating words but employing exotic euphemisms that would mean nothing in a court of law. She was calling from another pay phone, one she had chosen at random, so there was virtually no chance that either of them was tapped. But it was a Big Brother world where you didn't dare take risks.

The woman had a third job for him. Three in one day.

As Vince watched the evening traffic inching past on the narrow island street, the woman—whom he had never seen and whose name he didn't know—gave him the address of Dr. Albert Hudston in Laguna Beach. Hudston lived with his wife and sixteen-year-old son. Both Dr. and Mrs. Hudston had to be hit; however, the boy's fate was in Vince's hands. If the kid could be kept out of it, fine. But if he saw Vince and could serve as a witness, he had to be eliminated, too.

"Your discretion," the woman said.

Vince already knew that he would erase the kid, because killing was more useful to him, more energizing, if the victim was young. It had been a long time since he'd blown away a really young one, and the prospect excited him.

"I can only emphasize," the contact said, driving Vince a little nuts with her breathy pauses, "that this option must be exercised with all due speed. We want the deal concluded tonight. By tomorrow, the competition will be aware of what we're trying to swing, and they'll get in our way."

Vince knew the "competition" must be the police. He was being paid to kill three doctors in a single day—*doctors*, when he had never killed a doctor before—so he knew there was something that linked them, something the cops would pick up on when they found Weatherby in the trunk of his car and Elisabeth Yarbeck beaten to death in her bedroom. Vince didn't know what the link was because he never knew anything about the people he was hired to kill and he didn't really want to know anything. It was safer that way. But the cops would link Weatherby with Yarbeck and both of them with Hudston, so if Vince did not get to Hudston tonight, the police would be providing the man with protection by tomorrow.

Vince said, "I wonder ... do you want the option exercised in the same way as the other two deals today? You want a pattern?"

He was thinking maybe he should burn the Hudston house to the ground with them in it to cover the murders.

"No, we absolutely do want a pattern," the woman said. "Same as the others. We want them to *know* we've been busy."

"I see."

"We want to tweak their noses," she said, and laughed softly. "We want to rub in the salt."

Vince hung up and walked to the Jolly Roger for dinner. He had vegetable soup, a hamburger, fries, onion rings, coleslaw, chocolate cake with ice cream, and (as an afterthought) apple pie, all of which he washed down with five cups of coffee. He was ordinarily a big eater, but his appetite increased dramatically after a job. In fact, when he finished the pie, he wasn't full. Understandable. In one busy day, he had absorbed the life energies of Davis

86

Weatherby and the Yarbecks; he was overcharged, a racing engine. His metabolism was in high gear; he would need more fuel for a while, until his body stored the excess life energies in biological batteries for future use.

The ability to absorb the very life force of his victim was the Gift that made him different from all other men. Because of the Gift, he would always be strong, vital, alert. He would live forever.

He had never divulged the secret of his splendid Gift to the throaty-voiced woman or to any of the people for whom he worked. Few people were imaginative and open-minded enough to consider seriously such an amazing talent. Vince kept it to himself because he was afraid they'd think he was crazy.

Outside the restaurant, he stood on the sidewalk for a while, just breathing deeply, savoring the crisp sea air. A chilly night wind blew off the harbor, sweeping scrap paper and purple jacaranda blossoms along the pavement.

Vince felt terrific. He believed he was as much of an elemental force as were the sea and wind.

From Balboa Island, he drove south to Laguna Beach. At eleven-twenty, he parked his van across the street from the Hudston house. It was in the hills, a single-storey home slung on a steep slope to take advantage of ocean views. He saw lights in a couple of windows.

He climbed between the seats and sat down in the back of the van, out of sight, to wait until all of the Hudstons had gone to bed. Soon after leaving the Yarbeck house, he had changed out of his blue suit into gray slacks, a white shirt, a maroon sweater, and a dark-blue nylon jacket. Now, in the darkness, he had nothing to do except take his weapons out of a cardboard box, where they were hidden beneath two loaves of bread, a four-roll package of toilet tissue, and other items that gave the impression he had just been to the market.

The Walther P-38 was fully loaded. After finishing the job at the Yarbeck house, he had screwed a fresh silencer onto the barrel, one of the new short ones that, thanks to the high-tech revolution, was half the length of older models. He set the gun aside.

He had a six-inch switchblade knife. He put it in the right front pocket of his trousers.

When he had wound the wire garrote into a tight coil, he tucked it into the left inside pocket of his jacket.

He had a sap weighted with lead pellets. That went into his right exterior jacket pocket.

He did not expect to use anything but the gun. However, he liked to be prepared for any eventuality.

On some jobs he had used an Uzi submachine gun that had been illegally converted for automatic fire. But the current assignment did not require heavy armament.

He also had a small leather packet, half the size of a shaving kit, which contained a few simple burglary tools. He did not bother to inspect those instruments. He might not even need them because a lot of people were amazingly lax about home security, leaving doors and windows unlocked during the night, as if they believed they were living in a nineteenth-century Quaker village.

At eleven-forty he leaned between the front seats and looked through the side window at the Hudston house. All the lights were out. Good. They were in bed.

To give them time to fall asleep, he sat down in the back of the van again, ate a Mr. Goodbar, and thought about how he'd spend some of the substantial fees that he had earned just since this morning.

He'd been wanting a power ski, one of those clever machines that made it possible to water-ski without a boat. He was an ocean lover. Something about the sea drew him; he felt at home in the tides and was most fully alive when he was moving in harmony with great, surging, dark masses of water. He enjoyed scuba diving, windsailing, and surfing. His teenage years had been spent more on the beach than in school. He still rode the board now and then, when the surf was high. But he was twenty-eight, and surfing now seemed tame to him. He wasn't as easily thrilled as he had once been. He liked *speed* these days. He pictured himself skimming over a slate-dark sea on power skis, hammered by the wind, jolted by an endless series of impacts with eternally incoming breakers, riding the Pacific as a rodeo cowboy would ride a bronc . . .

At twelve-fifteen he got out of the van. He tucked the pistol under the waistband of his trousers and crossed the silent, deserted street to the Hudston house. He let himself through an unlocked wooden gate onto a side patio brightened only by moonlight filtered through the leafy branches of an enormous sheltering coral tree.

He paused to pull on a pair of supple leather gloves.

Mirrored by moonbeams, a sliding glass door connected the patio with the living room. It was locked. A penlight, extracted from the packet of burglary tools, also revealed a wooden pole laid in the interior track of the door to prevent it from being forced.

The Hudstons were more security-conscious than most people, but Vince was unconcerned. He fixed a small suction cup to the glass, used a diamond cutter to carve a circle in the pane near the door handle, and quietly removed the cutout with the cup. He reached through the hole and disengaged the lock. He cut another circle near the sill, reached inside, and removed the wooden pole from the track, pushing it under the drawn drapes, into the room beyond.

He did not have to worry about dogs. The woman with the sexy voice had told him that the Hudstons had no house pets. That was one reason why he liked working for these particular employers: their information was always extensive and accurate.

Easing the door open, he slipped through the closed drapes into the dark living room. He stood for a moment, letting his eyes adjust to the gloom, listening. The house was tomb-silent.

He found the boy's room first. It was illuminated by the green glow of the numerals on a digital clock-radio. The teenager was lying on his side, snoring softly. Sixteen. Very young. Vince like them very young.

He moved around the bed and crouched along the side of it, face-to-face with the sleeper. With his teeth, he pulled the glove off his left hand. Holding the pistol in his right hand, he touched the muzzle to the underside of the boy's chin.

The kid woke at once.

Vince slapped his bare hand firmly against the boy's forehead and simultaneously fired the gun. The bullet smashed up through the soft underside of the kid's chin, through the roof of his mouth, into his brain, killing him instantly.

Ssssnap.

An intense charge of life energy burst out of the dying body and into Vince. It was such pure, vital energy that he whimpered with pleasure as he felt it surge into him.

For a while he crouched beside the bed, not trusting himself to move. Transported. Breathless. At last, in the dark he kissed the dead boy on the lips and said, "I accept. Thank you. I accept."

He crept cat-swift, cat-silent through the house and quickly found the master bedroom. Sufficient light was provided by another digital clock with green numerals and the soft glow of a night-light coming through the open bathroom door. Dr. and Mrs. Hudston were both asleep. Vince killed her first—

Ssssnap.

—without waking her husband. She slept in the nude, so after he received her sacrifice, he put his head to her bare breasts and listened to the stillness of her heart. He kissed her nipples and murmured, "Thank you."

When he circled the bed, turned on a nightstand lamp, and woke Dr. Hudston, the man was at first confused. Until he saw his wife's staring, sightless eyes. Then he shouted and grabbed for Vince's arm, and Vince clubbed him over the head twice with the butt of the gun.

Vince dragged the unconscious Hudston, who also slept in the nude, into the bathroom. Again, he found adhesive tape, with which he was able to bind the doctor's wrists and ankles.

He filled the tub with cold water and wrestled Hudston into it. That frigid bath revived the doctor.

In spite of being naked and bound, Hudston tried to push up out of the cold water, tried to launch himself at Vince.

Vince hit him in the face with the pistol and shoved him down into the tub again.

"Who are you? What do you want?" Hudston spluttered

as his face came up out of the water.

"I've killed your wife *and* your son, and I'm going to kill you."

Hudston's eyes seemed to sink back into his damp, pasty face. "Jimmy? Oh, not Jimmy, really no."

"Your boy is dead," Vince insisted. "I blew his brains out."

At the mention of his son, Hudston broke. He did not burst into tears, did not begin to keen, nothing as dramatic as that. But his eyes went dead—*blink*—just that abruptly. Like a light going out. He stared at Vince, but there was no fear or anger in him any more.

Vince said, "What you've got here is two choices: die easy or die hard. You tell me what I want to know, and I let you die easy, quick and painless. You get stubborn on me, and I can draw it out for five or six hours."

Dr. Hudston stared. Except for bright ribbons of fresh blood that banded his face, he was very white, wet and sickly pale like some creature that swam eternally in the deepest reaches of the sea.

Vince hoped the guy wasn't catatonic. "What I want to know is what you have in common with Davis Weatherby and Elisabeth Yarbeck."

Hudston blinked, focused on Vince. His voice was hoarse and tremulous. "Davis and Liz? What are you talking about?"

"You know them?"

Hudston nodded.

"How do you know them? Go to school together? Live next door at one time?"

Shaking his head, Hudston said, "We ... we used to work together at Banodyne."

"What's Banodyne?"

"Banodyne Laboratories."

"Where's that?"

"Here in Orange County," Hudston said. He gave an address in the city of Irvine.

"What'd you do there?"

"Research. But I left months ago. Weatherby and

Yarbeck still work there, but I don't.''

"What sort of research?" Vince asked.

Hudston hesitated.

Vince said, "Quick and painless—or hard and nasty?"

The doctor told him about the research he had been involved with at Banodyne. The Francis Project. The experiments. The dogs.

The story was incredible. Vince made Hudston run through some of the details three or four times before he was finally convinced the story was true.

When he was sure he had squeezed everything out of the man, Vince shot Hudston in the face, point-blank, the quick death he'd promised.

Ssssnap.

Back in the van, driving down the night-draped Laguna Hills, away from the Hudston house, Vince thought about the dangerous step he had taken. Usually, he knew nothing about his targets. That was safest for him and for his employers. Ordinarily he didn't *want* to know what the poor saps had done to bring so much grief on themselves, because knowing would bring *him* grief. But this was no ordinary situation. He had been paid to kill three doctors—not medical doctors, as it turned out now, but scientists—all of them upstanding citizens, plus any members of their families who happened to get in the way. Extraordinary. Tomorrow's papers weren't going to have enough room for all the news. Something very big was going on, something so important that it might provide him with a once-in-a-lifetime edge, with a shot at money so big he would need help to count it. The money might come from selling the forbidden knowledge he had pried out of Hudston . . . if he could figure out who would like to buy it. But knowledge was not only saleable; it was also dangerous. Ask Adam. Ask Eve. If his current employers, the sexy-voiced lady and the other people in L.A., learned that he had broken the most basic rule of his trade, if they knew that he had interrogated one of his victims before wasting him, they would put out a contract on Vince. The hunter would become the hunted.

Of course, he didn't worry a lot about dying. He had too much life stored up in him. Other people's life. More lives than ten cats. He was going to live forever. He was pretty sure of that. But ... well, he didn't know for certain how *many* lives he had to absorb in order to insure immortality. Sometimes he felt that he'd already achieved a state of invincibility, eternal life. But at other times, he felt that he was still vulnerable and that he would have to take more life energy into himself before he would reach the desired state of godhood. Until he knew, beyond doubt, that he had arrived at Olympus, it was best to exercise a little caution.

Banodyne.

The Francis Project.

If what Hudston said was true, the risk Vince was taking would be well-rewarded when he found the right buyer for the information. He was going to be a rich man.

8

Wes Dalberg had lived alone in a stone cabin in upper Holy Jim Canyon on the eastern edge of Orange County for ten years. His only light came from Coleman lanterns, and the only running water in the place was from a hand pump in the kitchen sink. His toilet was in an outhouse with a quarter-moon carved on the door (as a joke), about a hundred feet from the back of the cabin.

Wes was forty-two, but he looked older. His face was wind-scoured and sun-leathered. He wore a neatly trimmed beard with a lot of white whiskers. Although he appeared aged beyond his true years, his physical condition was that of a twenty-five-year-old. He believed his good health resulted from living close to nature.

Tuesday night, May 18, by the silvery light of a hissing Coleman lantern, he sat at the kitchen table until one in the morning, sipping homemade plum wine and reading a McGee novel by John D. MacDonald. Wes was, as he put it, "an antisocial curmudgeon born in the wrong century," who had little use for modern society. But he liked to read about McGee because McGee swam in that messy, nasty world out there and never let the murderous currents sweep him away.

When he finished the book at one o'clock, Wes went outside to get more wood for the fireplace. Wind-swayed branches of sycamores cast vague moon-shadows on the ground, and the glossy surfaces of rustling leaves shone dully with pale reflections of the lunar light. Coyotes howled in the distance as they chased down a rabbit or other small creature. Nearby, insects sang in the brush, and a chill wind soughed through the higher reaches of the forest.

His supply of cordwood was stored in a lean-to that extended along the entire north side of the cabin. He pulled the latch-peg out of the hasp on the double doors. He was so familiar with the arrangement of the wood on the storage space that he worked blindly in its lightless confines, filling a sturdy tin hod with half a dozen logs. He carried the hod out in both hands, put it down, and turned to close the doors.

He realized the coyotes and the insects had all fallen silent. Only the wind still had a voice.

Frowning, he turned to look at the dark forest that encircled the small clearing in which his cabin stood.

Something growled.

Wes squinted at the night-swaddled woods, which suddenly seemed less well illuminated by the moon than they had been a moment ago.

The growling was deep and angry. Not like anything he had heard out there before in ten years of nights alone.

Wes was curious, even concerned, but not afraid. He stood very still, listening. A minute ticked by, and he heard nothing further.

He finished closing the lean-to doors, pegged the latch, and picked up the hod full of cordwood.

Growling again. Then silence. Then the sound of dry brush and leaves crackling, crunching, snapping underfoot.

Judging by the sound, it was about thirty yards away. Just a bit west of the outhouse. Back in the forest.

The thing grumbled again, louder this time. Closer, too. Not more than twenty yards away now.

He could still not see the source of the sound. The deserter moon continued to hide behind a narrow filigree band of clouds.

Listening to the thick, guttural, yet ululant growling, Wes was suddenly uneasy. For the first time in ten years as a resident of Holy Jim, he felt he was in danger. Carrying the hod, he headed quickly toward the back of the cabin and the kitchen door.

The rustling of displaced brush grew louder. The creature in the woods was moving faster than before. Hell, it was running.

Wes ran, too.

The growling escalated into hard, vicious snarls: an eerie mix of sounds that seemed one part dog, part pig, part cougar, part human, and one part something else altogether. It was almost at his heels.

As he sprinted around the corner of the cabin. Wes swung the hod and threw it toward where he judged the animal to be. He heard the cordwood flying loose and slamming to the ground, heard the metal hod clanging end over end, but the snarling only grew closer and louder, so he knew he had missed.

He hurried up the three back steps, threw open the kitchen door, stepped inside, and slammed the door behind him. He slipped the latch bolt in place, a security measure he had not used in nine years, not since he had grown accustomed to the peacefulness of the canyon.

He went through the cabin to the front door and latched it, too. He was surprised by the intensity of the fear that had overcome him. Even if a hostile animal was out there—perhaps a crazed bear that had come down from the mountains—it could not open doors and follow him into the cabin. There was no need to engage the locks, yet he felt better for having done so. He was operating on instinct, and he was a good enough outdoorsman to know that instincts ought to be trusted even when they resulted in seemingly irrational behavior.

Okay, so he was safe. No animal could open a door. Certainly, a bear couldn't, and it was most likely a bear.

But it hadn't sounded like a bear. That's what had Wes Dalberg so spooked: it had not sounded like anything that could possibly be roaming those woods. He was familiar with his animal neighbors, knew all the howls, cries, and other noises they made.

The only light in the front room was from the fireplace, and it did not dispel the shadows in the corners. Phantoms of reflected firelight cavorted across the walls. For the first time, Wes would have welcomed electricity.

He owned a Remington 12-gauge shotgun with which he hunted small game to supplement his diet of store-bought foods. It was on a rack in the kitchen. He considered getting it down and loading it, but now that he was safely behind locked doors, he was beginning to be embarrassed about having panicked. Like a greenhorn, for God's sake. Like some lardass suburbanite shrieking at the sight of a field-mouse. If he had just shouted and clapped his hands, he would most likely have frightened off the thing in the brush. Even if his reaction could be blamed on instinct, he had not behaved in accordance with his self-image as a hard-bitten canyon squatter. If he armed himself with the rifle now, when there was no compelling need for it, he'd lose a large measure of self-respect, which was important because the only opinion of Wes Dalberg that Wes cared about was his own. No gun.

Wes risked going to the living room's big window. This was an alteration made by someone who held the Forest Service lease on the cabin about twenty years ago; the old, narrow, multipane window had been taken out, a larger hole cut in the wall, and a big single-pane window installed to take advantage of the spectacular forest view.

A few moon-silvered clouds appeared phosphorescent against the velvety blackness of the night sky. Moonlight dappled the front yard, glistered on the grill and hood and windshield of Wes's Jeep Cherokee, and outlined the shadowy shapes of the encroaching trees. At first nothing moved except a few branches swaying gently in the mild wind.

He studied the woodland scene for a couple of minutes. Neither seeing nor hearing anything out of the ordinary, he decided the animal had wandered off. With considerable relief and with a resurgence of embarrassment, he started to turn away from the window—then glimpsed movement near the Jeep. He squinted, saw nothing, remained watchful for another minute or two. Just when he decided he had imagined the movement, he saw it again: something coming out from behind the Jeep.

He leaned closer to the window.

Something was rushing across the yard toward the cabin, coming fast and low to the ground. Instead of revealing the nature of the enemy, the moonlight made it more mysterious, shapeless. The thing was *hurtling* at the cabin. Abruptly— Jesus, God!—the creature was airborne, a strangeness flying straight at him through the darkness, and Wes cried out, and an instant later the beast exploded through the big window, and Wes screamed, but the scream was cut short.

9

Because Travis was not much of a drinker, three beers were enough to insure against insomnia. He was asleep within seconds of putting his head on the pillow. He dreamed that he was the ringmaster in a circus where all the performing animals could speak, and after each show he visited them in their cages, where each animal told him a secret that amazed him even though he forgot it as soon as he moved along to the next cage and the next secret.

At four o'clock in the morning, he woke and saw Einstein at the bedroom window. The dog was standing with its fore-paws on the sill, its face limned by moonlight, staring out at the night, very alert.

"What's wrong, boy?" Travis asked.

Einstein glanced at him, then returned his attention to the moon-washed night. He whined softly, and his ears perked up slightly.

"Somebody out there?" Travis asked, getting out of the bed, pulling on his jeans.

The dog dropped onto all fours and hurried out of the bedroom.

Travis found him at another window in the darkened living room, studying the night on that side of the house. Crouching beside the dog, putting a hand on the broad furry back, he said, "What's the matter? Huh?"

Einstein pressed his snout to the glass and mewled nervously.

Travis could see nothing threatening on the front lawn or on the street. Then a thought struck him, and he said, "Are you worried about whatever was chasing you in the woods this morning?"

The dog regarded him solemnly.

"What *was* it out there in the forest?" Travis wondered.

Einstein whined again and shuddered.

Remembering the retriever's—and his own—stark fear in the Santa Ana foothills, recalling the uncanny feeling that something unnatural had been stalking them, Travis shivered. He looked out at the night-draped world. The spiky black patterns of the date palm's fronds were edged in wan yellow light from the nearest streetlamp. A fitful wind harried small funnels of dust and leaves and bits of litter along the pavement, dropped them for a few seconds and left them for dead, then enlivened them again. A lone moth bumped softly against the window in front of Travis's and Einstein's faces, evidently mistaking the reflection of the moon or streetlamp for a flame.

"Are you worried that it's still after you?" he asked.

The dog woofed once, quietly.

"Well I don't think it is," Travis said. "I don't think you understand how far north we've come. We had wheels, but it would have had to follow on foot, which it couldn't have done. Whatever it was, it's far behind us, Einstein, far down there in Orange County, with no way of knowing where we've gone. You don't have to worry about it any more. You understand?"

Einstein nuzzled and licked Travis's hand as if reassured

and grateful. But he looked out the window again and issued a barely audible whimper.

Travis had to coax him back into the bedroom. There, the dog wanted to lie on the bed beside his master, and in the interest of calming the animal, Travis did not object.

Wind murmured and moaned in the bungalow's eaves.

Now and then the house creaked with ordinary middle-of-the-night settling noises.

Engine purring, tires whispering, a car went by on the street.

Exhausted from the emotional as well as the physical exertions of the day, Travis was soon asleep.

Near dawn he came half awake and realized that Einstein was at the bedroom window again, keeping watch. He murmured the retriever's name and wearily patted the mattress. But Einstein remained on guard, and Travis drifted off once more.

FOUR

1

The day following her encounter with Art Streck, Nora Devon went for a long walk, intending to explore parts of the city that she had never seen before. She had taken short walks with Violet once a week. Since the old woman's death, Nora still went out, though less often, and she never ventured farther than six or eight blocks from home. Today, she would go much farther. This was to be the first small step in a long journey toward liberation and self-respect.

Before setting out, she considered having a light lunch later at a restaurant chosen at random along the way. But she had never been in a restaurant. The prospect of dealing with a waiter and dining in the company of strangers was daunting. Instead, she packed one apple, one orange, and two oatmeal cookies in a small paper bag. She would eat lunch alone, in a park somewhere. Even that would be revolutionary. One small step at a time.

The sky was clear. The air was warm. With vivid green spring growth, the trees looked fresh; they stirred in a breeze just strong enough to take the searing edge off the hot sunlight.

As Nora strolled past the well-kept houses, the vast majority of which were in one style of Spanish architecture

101

or another, she looked at doors and windows with a new curiosity, wondering about the people who lived within. Were they happy? Sad? In love? What music and books did they enjoy? What food? Were they planning vacations to exotic places, evenings at the theater, visits to nightclubs?

She had never wondered about them before because she had known their lives and hers would never cross. Wondering about them would have been a waste of time and effort. But *now* ...

When she encountered other walkers, she kept her head down and averted her face, as she had always done before, but after a while she found the courage to look at some of them. She was surprised when many smiled at her and said hello. In time, she was even more surprised when she heard herself respond.

At the county courthouse she paused to admire the yellow blossoms of the yucca plants and the rich red bougainvillaea that climbed the stucco wall and twined through the ornate wrought-iron grille over one of the tall windows.

At the Santa Barbara Mission, built in 1815, she stood at the foot of the front steps and studied the handsome facade of the old church. She explored the courtyard with its Sacred Garden and climbed the west bell tower.

Gradually, she began to understand why, in some of the many books she had read, Santa Barbara had been called one of the most beautiful places on earth. She had lived there nearly all her life, but because she had cowered in the Devon house with Violet and, on venturing out, had looked at little more than her own shoes, she was seeing the town for the first time. It both charmed and thrilled her.

At one o'clock, in Alameda Park within sight of the pond, she sat on a bench near three ancient and massive date palms. Her feet were getting sore, but she did not intend to go home early. She opened the paper bag and began lunch with the yellow apple. Never had anything tasted half as delicious. Famished, she quickly ate the orange, too, dropping the pieces of peel into the bag, and she was starting on the first of the oatmeal cookies when Art Streck sat down beside her.

"Hello, prettiness."

He was wearing only blue running shorts, running shoes, and thick white athletic socks. However, he clearly hadn't been running, for he wasn't sweating. He was muscular with a broad chest, deeply tanned, exceedingly masculine. The whole purpose of his attire was to display his physique, so Nora at once averted her eyes.

"Shy?" he asked.

She could not speak because the bite she had taken from the oatmeal cookie was stuck in her mouth. She couldn't work up any saliva. She was afraid she would choke if she tried to swallow the piece of cookie, but she couldn't very well just spit it out.

"My sweet, shy Nora," Streck said.

Looking down, she saw how badly her right hand was trembling. The cookie was being shaken to pieces in her fingers; bits of it dropped onto the paving between her feet.

She had told herself that she would go for a daylong walk as a first step toward liberation, but now she had to admit there had been another reason for getting out of the house. She had been trying to avoid Streck's attentions. She was afraid to stay home, afraid that he'd call and call and call. But now he had found her in the open, beyond the protection of her locked windows and bolted doors, which was worse than the telephone, infinitely worse.

"Look at me, Nora."

No.

"Look at me."

The last of the disintegrating cookie fell from her right hand.

Streck took her left hand, and she tried to resist him, but he squeezed. grinding the bones of her fingers, so she surrendered. He put her hand palm-down on his bare thigh. His flesh was firm and hot.

Her stomach twisted, and her heart thumped, and she did not know which she would do first—puke or pass out.

Moving her hand slowly up and down his bare thigh, he said, "I'm what you need, prettiness. I can take care of you."

103

As if it were a wad of paste, the oatmeal cookie glued her mouth shut. She kept her head down, but she raised her eyes to look out from under her brow. She hoped to see someone nearby to whom she could call for help, but there were only two young mothers with their small children, and even they were too far away to be of assistance.

Lifting her hand from his thigh, putting it on his bare chest, Streck said, "Having a nice stroll today? Did you like the mission? Hmmm? And weren't the yucca blossoms pretty at the courthouse?"

He rambled on in that cool, smug voice, asking her how she had liked other things she'd seen, and she realized he had been *following* her all morning, either in his car or on foot. She hadn't seen him, but there was no doubt he had been there because he knew every move she had made since leaving the house, which frightened and infuriated her more than anything else he had done.

She was breathing hard and fast, yet she felt as if she could not get her breath. Her ears were ringing, yet she could hear every word he said too clearly. Though she thought she might strike him and claw at his eyes, she was also paralyzed, on the verge of striking but unable to strike, simultaneously strong with rage and weak with fear. She wanted to scream, not for help but in frustration.

"Now," he said, "you've had a real nice stroll, a nice lunch in the park and you're in a relaxed mood. So you know what would be nice now? You know what would make this a terrific day, prettiness? A really special day? What we'll do is get in my car, go back to your place, up to your yellow room, get in that four-poster bed—"

He'd been in her bedroom! He must have done it yesterday. When he was supposed to have been in the living room fixing the TV, he must have sneaked upstairs, the bastard, prowling through her most private place, invading her sanctuary, poking through her belongings.

"—that big old bed, and I'm going to strip you down, honey, strip you down and fuck you—"

Nora would never be able to decide whether her sudden courage arose from the horrible realization that he'd

104

violated her sanctuary, whether it was that he had spoken an obscenity in her presence for the first time, or whether both, but she snapped her head up and glared at him and spat the wad of uneaten cookie in his face. Flecks of spittle and damp spatters of food stuck on his right cheek, right eye, and on the side of his nose. Bits of oatmeal clung in his hair and speckled his forehead. When she saw anger flash into Streck's eyes and contort his face, Nora felt a surge of terror at what she'd done. But she was also elated that she had been able to break the bonds of emotional paralysis that had immobilized her, even if her actions brought her grief, even if Streck retaliated.

And he did retaliate swiftly, brutally. He still held her left hand, and she was unable to wrench free. He squeezed hard, as he had done before, grinding her bones. It hurt, Jesus, it hurt. But she did not want to give him the satisfaction of seeing her cry, and she was determined not to whimper or beg, so she clenched her teeth and endured. Sweat prickled her scalp, and she thought she might pass out. But the pain was not the worst of it; the worst was looking into Streck's disturbing ice-blue eyes. As he crushed her fingers, he held her not merely with his hand but with his gaze, which was cold and infinitely strange. He was trying to intimidate and cow her, and it was working—by God, it was—because she saw in him a madness with which she would never be able to cope.

When he saw her despair, which evidently pleased him more than a cry of pain could have done, he stopped grinding her hand, but he did not let go. He said, "You'll pay for that, for spitting in my face. And you'll *enjoy* paying for it."

Without conviction, she said, "I'll complain to your boss, and you'll lose your job."

Streck only smiled. Nora wondered why he did not bother to wipe the bits of oatmeal cookie from his face, but even as she wondered about it she knew the reason: he was going to make her do it for him. First, he said, "Lose my job? Oh, I already quit working for Wadlow TV. Walked out yesterday afternoon. So I'd have time for you, Nora."

She lowered her eyes. She could not conceal her fear, was shaken by it until she thought her teeth would chatter.

"I never do stay too long in a job. Man like me, full of so much energy, gets bored easy. I need to move around. Besides, life's too short to waste all of it working, don't you think? So I keep a job for a while, till I've got some money saved, then I coast as long as I can. And once in a while I run into a lady like you, someone who has a powerful need for me, someone who's just crying out for a man like me, and so I help her along."

Kick him, bite him, go for his eyes, she told herself.

She did nothing.

Her hand ached dully. She remembered how hot and intense the pain had been.

His voice changed, became softer, soothing, reassuring, but that frightened her even more. "And I'm going to help you, Nora. I'll be moving in for a while, It's going to be fun. You're a little nervous about me, sure, I understand that, I really do. But believe me, this is what you need, girl, this is going to turn your life upside down, nothing's ever going to be the same again, and that's the best thing could happen to you."

2

Einstein loved the park.

When Travis slipped off the leash, the retriever trotted to the nearest bed of flowers—big yellow marigolds surrounded by a border of purple polyanthuses—and walked slowly around it, obviously fascinated. He went to a blazing bed of late-blooming ranunculuses, to another of impatiens, and his tail wagged faster with each discovery. They said dogs could see in only black and white, but Travis would not have bet against the proposition that Einstein possessed full-color vision. Einstein sniffed everything—flowers, shrubbery, trees, rocks, trash cans, crumpled litter, the base of the drinking fountain, and every foot of ground he covered—no doubt turning up olfactory "pictures" of people and dogs that had passed this way before, images as clear to him as photographs would have been to Travis.

Throughout the morning and early afternoon, the retriever had done nothing amazing. In fact, his I'm-just-an-ordinary-dumb-dog behavior was so convincing that Travis wondered if the animal's nearly human intelligence came only in brief flashes, sort of the beneficial equivalent of epileptic seizures. But after all that had happened yesterday, Einstein's extraordinary nature, though seldom revealed, was no longer open to debate.

As they were strolling around the pond, Einstein suddenly went rigid, lifted his head, raised his floppy ears a bit, and stared at a couple sitting on a park bench about sixty feet away. The man was in running shorts, and the woman wore a rather baggy gray dress; he was holding her hand, and they appeared to be in deep conversation.

Travis started to turn away from them, heading out toward the open green of the park to give them privacy.

But Einstein barked once and raced straight toward the couple.

"Einstein! Here! Come back here!"

The dog ignored him and, nearing the pair on the bench, began to bark furiously.

By the time Travis reached the bench, the guy in running shorts was standing. His arms were raised defensively, and his hands were fisted as he warily moved back a step from the retriever.

"*Einstein!*"

The retriever stopped barking, turned away from Travis before the leash could be clipped to the collar again, went to the woman on the bench, and put his head in her lap. The change from snarling dog to affectionate pet was so sudden that everyone was startled.

Travis said, "I'm sorry. He never—"

"For Christ's sake," said the guy in running shorts, "you can't let a vicious dog run loose in a park!"

"He's not vicious," Travis said. "He—"

"Bullshit," the runner said, spraying spittle. "The damn

107

thing tried to bite me. You *enjoy* lawsuits or something?''

"I don't know what got into—"

"Get it out of here," the runner demanded.

Nodding, embarrassed, Travis turned to Einstein and saw that the woman had coaxed the retriever onto the bench. Einstein was sitting with her, facing her, his forepaws in her lap, and she was not merely petting him but hugging him. In fact, there was something a little desperate about the way she was holding on to him.

"Get it *out* of here!" the runner said furiously.

The guy was taller, broader in the shoulders, and thicker in the chest than Travis, and he took a couple of steps forward, looming over Travis, using his superior size to intimidate. By being aggressive, by looking and acting a little dangerous, he was accustomed to getting his way. Travis despised such men.

Einstein turned his head to look at the runner, bared his teeth, and growled low in his throat.

"Listen, buddy," the runner said angrily, "are you deaf, or what? I said that dog's got to be put on a leash, and I see the leash there in your hand, so what the hell are you waiting for?"

Travis began to realize something was wrong. The runner's self-righteous anger was overdone—as if he had been caught in a shameful act and was trying to conceal his guilt by going immediately and aggressively on the offensive. And the woman was behaving peculiarly. She had not spoken a word. She was pale. Her thin hands trembled. But judging by the way she petted and clung to the dog, it wasn't Einstein that frightened her. And Travis wondered why a couple would go to the park dressed so differently from each other, one in running shorts and the other in a drab housedress. He saw the woman glance surreptitiously and fearfully at the runner, and suddenly he knew that these two were not together—at least not by the woman's choice—and that the man had, indeed, been up to something about which he felt guilty.

"Miss," Travis said, "are you all right?"

"Of course she's not all right," the runner said. "Your

damn dog came barking and snapping at us—''

"He doesn't seem to be terrorizing her right now," Travis said, meeting and holding the other man's gaze.

Bits of what appeared to be oatmeal batter were stuck on the guy's cheek. Travis had noticed an oatmeal cookie spilling from a bag on the bench beside the woman, and another one crumbled on the ground between her feet. What the hell had been going on here?

The runner glared at Travis and started to speak. But then he looked at the woman and Einstein, and he evidently realized that his calculated outrage would no longer be appropriate. He said sullenly, "Well . . . you should still get the damn hound under control."

"Oh, I don't think he'll bother anyone now," Travis said, coiling the leash. "It was just an aberration."

Still furious but uncertain, the runner looked at the huddled woman and said, "Nora?"

She did not respond. She just kept petting Einstein.

"I'll see you later," the runner told her. Getting no response, he refocused on Travis, narrowed his eyes, and said, "If that hound comes nipping at my heels—"

"He won't," Travis interrupted. "You can get on with your run. He won't bother you."

Several times as he jogged slowly across the park to the nearest exit, the man glanced back at them. Then he was gone.

On the bench, Einstein had settled down on his belly with his head on the woman's lap.

Travis said, "He's sure taken a liking to you."

Without looking up, smoothing Einstein's coat with one hand, she said, "He's a lovely dog."

"I just got him yesterday."

She said nothing.

He sat down on the other end of the bench, with Einstein between them. "My name's Travis."

Unresponsive, she scratched behind Einstein's ears. The dog made a contented sound.

"Travis Cornell," he said.

At last she raised her head and looked at him. "Nora Devon."

"Glad to meet you."

She smiled, but nervously.

Though she wore her hair straight and lank, though she used no makeup, she was quite attractive. Her hair was dark and glossy, her skin flawless, and her gray eyes were accented with green striations that seemed luminous in the bright May sunshine.

As if sensing his approval and frightened of it, she immediately broke eye contact, lowered her head once more.

He said, "Miss Devon . . . is something wrong?"

She said nothing.

"Was that man . . . bothering you?"

"It's all right," she said.

With her head bowed and shoulders hunched, sitting there under a ton-weight of shyness, she looked so vulnerable that Travis could not just get up, walk away, and leave her with her problems. He said, "If that man was bothering you, I think we ought to find a cop—"

"No," she said softly but urgently. She slipped out from under Einstein and got up.

The dog scrambled off the bench to stand beside her, gazing at her with affection.

Rising, Travis said, "I don't mean to pry, of course—"

She hurried away, heading out of the park on a different path from the one the runner had taken.

Einstein started after her but halted and reluctantly returned when Travis called to him.

Puzzled, Travis watched her until she disappeared, an enigmatic and troubled woman in a gray dress as drab and shapeless as the garb of an Amish lady or a member of some other sect that took great pains to cloak the female figure in garments that would not lead a man into temptation.

He and Einstein continued their walk through the park. Later, they went to the beach, where the retriever seemed astounded by the endless vistas of rolling sea and by the breakers foaming on the sand. He repeatedly stopped to stare out at the ocean for a minute or two at a time, and he frolicked happily in the surf. Later still, back at the house, Travis tried to interest Einstein in the books that had caused such excitement last evening, hoping this time to be able to figure out what the dog expected to find in them. Einstein sniffed without interest at the volumes Travis brought to him—and yawned.

Throughout the afternoon, the memory of Nora Devon returned to Travis with surprising frequency and vividness. She did not require alluring clothes to capture a man's interest. That face and those green-flecked gray eyes were enough.

3

After only a few hours of deep sleep, Vincent Nasco took an early-morning flight to Acapulco, Mexico. He checked into a huge bayfront hotel, a gleaming but soulless highrise where everything was glass, concrete, and terrazzo. After he had changed into ventilated white Top-Siders, white cotton pants, and a pale-blue Ban-Lon shirt, he went looking for Dr. Lawton Haines.

Haines was vacationing in Acapulco. He was thirty-nine years old, five-eleven, one hundred and sixty pounds, with unruly dark brown hair, and he was purported to look like Al Pacino, except that he had a red birthmark the size of a half-dollar on his forehead. He came to Acapulco at least twice a year, always stayed at the elegant Hotel Las Brisas on the headland at the eastern end of the bay, and frequently enjoyed long lunches at a restaurant adjacent to the Hotel Caleta, which he favored for its margaritas and its view of Playa de Caleta.

By twelve-twenty in the afternoon, Vince was seated in a rattan chair with comfortable yellow and green cushions at a table by the windows in that same restaurant. He'd spotted Haines on entering. The doctor was at another window table, three away from Vince, half-screened by a potted palm. Haines was eating shrimp and drinking margaritas with a stunning blonde. She was wearing white slacks and a gaily striped tube-top, and half

111

the men in the place were staring at her.

As far as Vince was concerned, Haines looked more like Dustin Hoffman than like Pacino. He had those bold features of Hoffman's, including the nose. Otherwise, he was exactly as he'd been described. The guy was wearing pink cotton trousers and a pale-yellow shirt and white sandals, which seemed, to Vince, to be taking tropical resort attire to an extreme.

Vince finished a lunch of albondiga soup, seafood enchiladas in salsa verde, and a nonalcholic margarita, and paid the check by the time Haines and the blonde were ready to leave.

The blonde drove a red Porsche. Vince followed in a rental Ford, which had too many miles on it, rattled with the exuberance of percussion instruments in a mariachi band, and had fragrant moldy carpet.

At Las Brisas, the blonde dropped Haines in the parking lot, though not until they stood beside her car for at least five minutes, holding each other's asses and soul-kissing in broad daylight.

Vince was dismayed. He expected Haines to have a stronger sense of propriety. After all, the man had a *doctorate*. If educated people did not uphold traditional standards of conduct, who would? Weren't they teaching manners and deportment in the universities these days? No wonder the world got ruder and cruder every year.

The blonde departed in her Porsche, and Haines left the lot in a white Mercedes 560 SL sports coupe. It sure wasn't a rental, and Vince wondered where the doctor had gotten it.

Haines checked his car with the valet at another hotel, as did Vince. He tailed the doctor through the lobby, out to the beach, where at first they seemed embarked on an uneventful stroll along the shore. But Haines settled down beside a gorgeous Mexican girl in a string bikini. She was dark, superbly proportioned, and fifteen years younger than the doctor. She was sunbathing on a lounge, her eyes closed. Haines kissed her throat, startling her. Evidently, she knew him, for she threw her arms around him, laughing.

Vince walked down the beach and back, then sat on the

sand behind Haines and the girl, with a pair of sunbathers interposed between them. He was not concerned that Haines would notice him. The doctor seemed to have eyes only for choice female anatomy. Besides, in spite of his size, Vince Nasco had a knack for fading into the background.

Out on the bay, a tourist was taking a parachute ride, hanging high in the air behind the towboat. Sun fell like an endless rain of gold doubloons on the sand and the sea.

After twenty minutes, Haines kissed the girl on the lips, and on the slopes of her breasts, then set off back the way he had come. The girl called out, "Tonight at six!" And Haines said, "I'll be there."

Then Haines and Vince went for a pleasure drive. At first Vince thought Haines had a destination in mind, but after a while it seemed they were just heading aimlessly down the coast road, taking in the scenery. They passed Revolcadero Beach and kept going, Haines in his white Mercedes, Vince following as far back as he dared in his Ford.

Eventually they came to a scenic overlook, where Haines pulled off the road and parked beside a car from which four garishly dressed tourists were emerging. Vince parked, too, and walked to the iron railing at the outer edge of the escarpment, where there was a truly magnificent view of the coastline and of waves breaking thunderously on the rocky shore more than a hundred feet below.

The tourists, in their parrot shirts and striped pants, finished exclaiming over the sights, took their last pictures, discarded their last bits of litter, and departed, leaving Vince and Haines alone on the cliff. The only traffic on the highway was an approaching black Trans Am. Vince was waiting for the car to pass. Then he was going to take Haines by surprise.

Instead of going by, the Trans Am pulled off the road and parked beside Haines's Mercedes, and a gorgeous girl, about twenty-five, got out. She hurried to Haines. She looked Mexican but with a measure of Chinese blood, very exotic. She was wearing a white halter top and white shorts, and she had the best legs Vince had ever seen. She and Haines moved farther along the railing, until they were about forty feet from Vince, where they went into a clinch that made Vince blush.

For the next few minutes, Vince edged along the railing toward them, leaning out dangerously now and then, craning his neck to gawk down at the crashing waves that threw water twenty feet into the air—saying "Whooo boy!" when a particularly big breaker hit the craggy outcroppings of stone—trying to make it look as if his movement in their direction was entirely innocent.

Though they had turned their backs to him, the breeze carried bits of their conversation. The woman seemed worried that her husband might find out that Haines was in town, and Haines was pushing her to make up her mind about tomorrow night. The guy was shameless.

The highway cleared of traffic again, and Vince decided he might not get another opportunity to nail Haines. He closed the last few feet between him and the girl, grabbed her by the nape of the neck and the belt of her shorts, plucked her off the ground, and threw her over the railing. Screaming, she plummeted toward the rocks below.

It happened so fast that Haines didn't even have time to react. The instant the woman was airborne, Vince turned on the startled doctor and punched him in the face twice, splitting both his lips, breaking his nose, and knocking him unconscious.

As Haines crumpled to the ground, the woman hit the rocks below, and Vince received her gift even at that distance: *Ssssnap*.

He would have liked to lean over the railing to take a long look at her shattered body on the rocks down there, but unfortunately he had no time to spare. The highway would not long be free of traffic.

He carried Haines back to the Ford and put him in the front seat, letting him slump against the door as if sleeping peacefully. He made sure the man's head tipped back to let the blood from his nose trickle down this throat.

From the coast highway, which was twisty and frequently in poor repair for such a major route, Vince followed a series of lesser unpaved roads, each narrower and more

114

rugged than the one before, traveling from gravel to dirt surfaces, heading deeper into the rain forest, until he came to a lonely dead end at a green wall of immense trees and lush vegetation. Twice during the drive, Haines had begun to regain consciousness, but Vince had quieted the doctor by thumping his head against the dashboard.

Now, he dragged the unconscious man out of the Ford, through a gap in the brush, and deep under the trees, until he found a shady clearing floored with hairy moss. Cawing and trilling birds fell silent, and unknown animals with peculiar voices moved off through the underbrush. Large insects, including a beetle as big as Vince's hand, scuttled out of his way, and lizards scampered up tree trunks.

Vince returned to the Ford, where he had left some interrogation equipment in the trunk. A packet of syringes and two vials of sodium pentothal. A leather sap weighted with lead pellets. A hand-applied Taser that resembled a remote-control device for a television set. And a corkscrew with a wooden handle.

Lawton Haines was still unconscious when Vince returned to the clearing. His breath rattled in his broken nose.

Haines should have been dead twenty-four hours ago. The people who had employed Vince for three jobs yesterday had expected to use another free-lancer who lived in Acapulco and operated throughout Mexico. But that guy had died yesterday morning when a long-awaited air-mail package from Fortnum & Mason in London surprisingly contained two pounds of plastic explosives instead of assorted jellies and marmalades. Out of desperate necessity, the outfit in Los Angeles had given the job to Vince, though he was getting to be dangerously overworked. It was a big break for him, for he was sure *this* must also be connected with Banodyne Laboratories and could provide more details about the Francis Project.

Now, exploring the rain forest around the clearing where Haines lay, Vince found a fallen tree from which he was able to pull off a loose, curved section of thick bark that would serve as a ladle. He located an algae-mottled stream and scooped up nearly a quart of water in the bark vessel. The stuff looked foul. No telling what exotic bacteria thrived in it. But, of course, at this point the possibility of disease would not matter to Haines.

Vince threw the first ladle of water in Haines's face. A minute later he returned with a second scoopful from which he forced the doctor to drink. After a lot of spluttering, choking, gagging, and a little vomiting, Haines was at last clearheaded enough to understand what was being said to him, and to respond intelligibly.

Holding up the leather sap, the Taser, and the corkscrew, Vince explained how he'd use each of them if Haines was uncooperative. The doctor—who revealed himself to be a specialist in brain physiology and function—proved more intelligent than patriotic, and he eagerly divulged every detail of the top-secret defense work in which he was engaged at Banodyne.

When Haines swore there was no more to be told, Vince prepared the sodium pentothal. As he drew the drug into the syringe, he said, conversationally, "Doctor, what *is* it with you and women?"

Haines, lying on his back in the hairy moss with his arms at his sides, exactly as Vince had told him to lie, was not able to adjust quickly to the change of subject. He blinked in confusion.

"I been following you since lunch, and I know you got three of them on a string in Acapulco—"

"Four," Haines said, and in spite of his terror a visible pride surfaced. "That Mercedes I'm driving belongs to Giselle, the sweetest little—"

"You're using one woman's car to cheat on her with three others?"

Haines nodded and tried to smile, but he winced as the smile sent new waves of pain through his ruined nose. "I've always . . . had this way with the ladies."

"For God's sake!" Vince was appalled. "Don't you realize these aren't the sixties or seventies any more? Free love's dead. It's got a price now. Steep price. Haven't you heard about herpes, AIDS, all that stuff?" Administering

116

the pentothal, he said, "You must be a carrier for every veneral disease known to man."

Blinking stupidly at him, Haines at first looked baffled and then was deep in a pentothal sleep. Under the drug, he confirmed all that he had already told Vince about Banodyne and the Francis Project.

When the drug wore off, Vince used the Taser on Haines, just for the fun of it, until the batteries wore out. The scientist twitched and kicked like a half-crushed water bug, back bowed, digging at the moss with his heels and head and hands.

When the Taser was of no further use, Vince beat him unconscious with the leather sap and killed him by applying the corkscrew to the space between two ribs, angling it up into the beating heart.

Ssssnap.

Throughout, a sepulchral silence hung over the rain forest, but Vince sensed a thousand eyes watching, the eyes of wild things. He believed that the hidden watchers approved of what he had done to Haines because the scientist's lifestyle made him an affront to the natural order of things, the natural order that all the creatures of the jungle obeyed.

He said, "Thank you," to Haines, but he did not kiss the man. Not on the mouth. Not even on the forehead. Haines's life energy was as invigorating and welcome as anyone's but his body and spirit were unclean.

4

Nora went straight home from the park. The mood of adventure and the spirit of freedom that had colored the morning and the early afternoon could not be recaptured. Streck had sullied the day.

Closing the front door behind her, she engaged the regular lock, the deadbolt lock, and the brass safety chain. She went through the downstairs rooms, drawing the drapes tightly shut at all the windows to prevent Arthur Streck from seeing inside if he should come prowling around. But she could not tolerate the resultant darkness, so she turned on every lamp in every room. In the kitchen, she closed the shutters and checked the lock on the back door.

Her contact with Streck had not only terrified her but had left her feeling dirty. More than anything, she wanted a long, hot shower.

But her legs were suddenly shaky and weak, and she was seized by a spell of dizziness. She had to grab hold of the kitchen table to steady herself. She knew she would fall if she tried to climb the stairs just then, so she sat down, folded her arms on the table, put her head in her arms, and waited until she felt better.

When the worst of the dizziness passed, she remembered the bottle of brandy in the cupboard by the refrigerator, and she decided a drink might help steady her. She had bought the brandy—Remy Martin—after Violet had died because Violet had not approved of any stronger drink than partially fermented apple cider. As an act of rebellion, Nora had poured a glass of brandy for herself when she had come home from her aunt's funeral. She had not enjoyed it and had emptied most of the contents of the glass down the drain. But now it seemed that a shot of brandy would stop her shivering.

First she went to the sink and washed her hands repeatedly under the hottest water she could tolerate, using both soap and then a lot of Ivory dishwashing liquid, scrubbing away every trace of Streck. When she was done, her hands were red and looked raw.

She brought the brandy bottle and a glass to the table. She had read books in which characters had sat down with a fifth of booze and a heavy load of despair, determined to use the former to wash away the latter. Sometimes it worked for them, so maybe it would work for her. If the brandy could improve her state of mind even marginally, she was prepared to drink the whole damn bottle.

But she did not have it in her to be a lush. She spent the next two hours sipping at a single glass of Remy Martin.

When she tried to turn her mind away from thoughts of Streck, she was relentlessly tormented by memories of Aunt Violet, and when she tried not to think of Violet, she was right back to Streck again, and when she forced herself to put *both* of them out of her mind, she thought of Travis Cornell, the man in the park, and dwelling on him gave her no comfort either. He had seemed nice—gentle, polite, concerned—and he had gotten rid of Streck. But he was probably just as bad as Streck. If she gave him half a chance, Cornell would probably take advantage of her the same way Streck was trying to do. Aunt Violet had been a tyrant, twisted and sick, but increasingly it seemed that she had been right about the dangers of interacting with other people.

Ah, but the *dog*. That was a different story. She had not been afraid of the dog, not even when he had dashed toward the park bench, barking ferociously. Somehow, she knew that the retriever—Einstein, his master had called him—was not barking at her, that his anger was focused on Streck. Clinging to Einstein, she'd felt safe, protected, even with Streck still looming over her.

Maybe she should get a dog of her own. Violet had abhorred the very idea of house pets. But Violet was dead, forever dead, and there was nothing to prevent Nora from having a dog of her own.

Except . . .

Well, she had the peculiar notion that no other dog would give her the profound feeling of security she had gotten from Einstein. She and the retriever had enjoyed instant rapport.

Of course, because the dog rescued her from Streck, she might be attributing qualities to him that he did not possess. Naturally, she would view him as a savior, her valiant guardian. But no matter how vigorously she tried to disabuse herself of the notion that Einstein was only a dog like any other, she still felt he was special, and she was convinced no other dog would give her the degree of protection and companionship that Einstein could provide.

A single glass of Remy Martin, consumed over two hours,

plus thoughts of Einstein, did in fact lift her spirits. More important, the brandy and memories of the dog also gave her the courage to go to the kitchen telephone with the determination to call Travis Cornell and offer to buy his retriever. After all, he had told her he'd owned the dog only one day, so he couldn't be deeply attached to it. For the right price, he might sell. She paged through the directory, found Cornell's number, and dialed it.

He answered on the second ring, "Hello?"

On hearing his voice, she realized that any attempt to buy the dog from him would give him a lever with which he could attempt to pry his way into her life. She had forgotten that he might be just as dangerous as Streck.

"Hello?" he repeated.

Nora hesitated.

"Hello? Is anyone there?"

She hung up without saying a word.

Before she spoke with Cornell about the dog, she needed to devise an approach that would somehow discourage him from thinking he could make a move on her if, in fact, he was like Streck.

5

When the telephone rang at a few minutes before five o'clock, Travis was emptying a can of Alpo into Einstein's bowl. The retriever was watching with interest, licking his chops but waiting until the last scraps had been scraped from the can, exhibiting restraint.

Travis went for the phone, and Einstein went for the food. When no one answered Travis's first greeting, he said hello again, and the dog glanced away from his bowl. When Travis still got no answer, he asked if anyone was on the line, which seemed to intrigue Einstein because the dog padded across the kitchen to look up at the receiver in Travis's hand.

Travis hung up and turned away, but Einstein stood

there, gazing at the wall phone.

"Probably a wrong number."

Einstein glanced at him, then at the phone again.

"Or kids thinking they're being clever."

Einstein whined unhappily.

"What's eating you?"

Einstein just stood there, riveted by the phone.

With a sigh, Travis said, "Well, I've had all the bewilderment I can handle for one day. If you're going to wax mysterious, you'll have to do it without me."

He wanted to watch the early news before preparing dinner for himself, so he got a Diet Pepsi from the fridge and went into the living room, leaving the dog in peculiar communion with the telephone. He switched on the TV, sat in the big armchair, popped the tab on his Pepsi—and heard Einstein getting into some kind of trouble in the kitchen.

"What're you doing out there?"

A clank. A clatter. The sound of claws scrabbling against a hard surface. A thump, and another.

"Whatever damage you do," Travis warned, "you're going to have to pay for. And how're you going to earn the bucks? Might have to go up to Alaska and work as a sled dog."

The kitchen got quiet. But only for a moment. Then there were a couple of clunks, a rattle, a rustle, more scrabbling of claws.

Travis was intrigued in spite of himself. He used the remote-control unit to mute the TV.

Something hit the kitchen floor with a bang.

Travis was about to go and see what had happened, but before he rose from the chair, Einstein appeared. The industrious dog was carrying the telephone directory in his jaws. He must have leaped repeatedly at the kitchen counter where the book lay, pawing it, until he pulled it onto the floor. He crossed the living room and deposited the book in front of the armchair.

"What do you want?" Travis asked.

The dog nudged the directory with his nose, then gazed at Travis expectantly.

"You want me to call someone?"

"Woof."

"Who?"

Einstein nosed the phone book again.

Travis said, "Now who would you want me to call? Lassie, Rin Tin Tin, Old Yeller?"

The retriever stared at him with those dark, undoglike eyes, which were more expressive than ever but insufficient to communicate what the animal wanted.

"Listen, maybe you can read my mind," Travis said, "but I can't read yours."

Whining in frustration, the retriever padded out of the room, disappearing around the corner into the short hallway that served the bath and two bedrooms.

Travis considered following, but he decided to wait and see what happened next.

In less than a minute, Einstein returned, carrying a gold-framed eight-by-ten photograph in his mouth. He dropped it beside the phone directory. It was the picture of Paula that Travis kept on the bedroom dresser. It had been taken on their wedding day, ten months before she died. She looked beautiful—and deceptively healthy.

"No good, boy. I can't call the dead."

Einstein huffed as if to say Travis was thickheaded. He went to a magazine rack in the corner, knocked it over, spilling its contents, and came back with an issue of *Time*, which he dropped beside the gold-framed photograph. With his forepaws, he scraped at the magazine, pulling it open and leafing through its pages, tearing a few in the process.

Moving to the edge of the armchair, leaning forward, Travis watched with interest.

Einstein paused a couple of times to study the open pages of the magazine, then continued to paw through it. Finally, he came to an automobile advertisement that prominently featured a striking brunette model. He looked up at Travis, down at the ad, up at Travis again, and woofed.

"I don't get you."

Pawing the pages again, Einstein found an ad in which a smiling blonde was holding a cigarette. He snorted at Travis.

"Cars and cigarette? You want me to buy you a car and a pack of Virginia Slims?"

After another trip to the overturned magazine rack, Einstein returned with a copy of a real estate magazine that still showed up in the mail every month even though Travis had been out of the racket for two years. The dog pawed through that one as well until he found an ad that featured a pretty brunette real-estate saleswoman in a Century 21 jacket.

Travis looked at Paula's photograph, at the blonde smoking the cigarette, at the perky Century 21 agent, and he remembered the other ad with the brunette and the automobile, and he said, "A woman? You want me to call . . . some woman?"

Einstein barked.

"Who?"

With his jaws, Einstein gently took hold of Travis's wrist and tried to pull him out of the chair.

"Okay, okay, let go. I'll follow you."

But Einstein was taking no chances. He would not let go of Travis's wrist, forcing his master to walk in a half-stoop all the way across the living room and dining room, into the kitchen, to the wall phone. There, he finally released Travis.

"Who?" Travis asked again, but suddenly he understood. There was only one woman whose acquaintance both he and the dog had made. "Not the lady we met in the park today?"

Einstein began to wag his tail.

"And you think that's who just called us?"

The tail wagged faster.

"How could you know who was on the line? She didn't say a word. And what are you up to here, anyway? Matchmaking?"

The dog woofed twice.

"Well, she was certainly pretty, but she wasn't my type, fella. A little strange, didn't you think?"

Einstein barked at him, ran to the kitchen door and jumped at it twice, turned to Travis and barked again, ran around the table, barking all the way, dashed to the door and jumped at it once more, and gradually it became apparent that he was deeply disturbed about something.

About the woman.

She had been in some kind of trouble this afternoon in the park. Travis remembered the bastard in the running shorts. He had offered to help the woman, and she had refused. But had she reconsidered and phoned him a few minutes ago, only to discover that she did not have the courage to explain her plight?

"You really think that's who called?"

The tail started wagging again.

"Well . . . even if it was her, it's not wise to get involved."

The retriever rushed at him, seized the right leg of his jeans, and shook the denim furiously, nearly tugging Travis off balance.

"All right, already! I'll do it. Get me the damn directory."

Einstein let go of him and raced out of the room, slipping on the slick linoleum. He returned with the directory in his jaws.

Only as Travis took the phone book did he realize that he had expected the dog to understand his request. The animal's extraordinary intelligence and abilities were now things that Travis took for granted.

With a jolt, he also realized that the dog would not have brought the directory to him in the living room if it had not understood the purpose of such a book.

"By God, fur face, you *have* been well named, haven't you?"

6

Although Nora usually ate dinner no earlier than seven, she was hungry. The morning walk and the glass of brandy had given her an appetite that even thoughts of Streck could not spoil. She didn't feel like cooking, so she prepared a platter of fresh fruit and some cheese, plus a croissant heated in the oven.

Nora usually ate dinner in her room, in bed with a magazine or book, because she was happiest there. Now, as she prepared a platter to take upstairs, the telephone rang.

Streck.

It must be him. Who else? She received few calls.

She froze, listening to the phone. Even after it stopped, she leaned against the kitchen counter, feeling weak, waiting for the ringing to start again.

7

When Nora Devon did not answer her telephone, Travis was ready to go back to the evening news on TV, but Einstein was still agitated. The retriever leaped up against the counter, pawed at the directory, pulled it to the floor again, took it in his jaws, and hurried out of the kitchen.

Curious about the dog's next move, Travis followed and found him waiting at the front door with the phone book still in his mouth.

"What now?"

Einstein put one paw on the door.

"You want to go out?"

The dog whined, but the sound was muffled by the directory in his mouth.

"What're you going to do with the phone book out there? Bury it like a bone? What's up?"

Although he received answers to none of his questions, Travis opened the door and let the retriever out into the golden, late-afternoon sunshine. Einstein dashed straight to the pickup parked in the driveway. He stood at the passenger door, looking back with what might have been impatience.

Travis walked to the truck and looked down at the retriever. He sighed. "I suspect you want to go somewhere, and I suspect you don't have in mind the offices of the telephone company."

Dropping the directory, Einstein jumped up, put his

forepaws against the door of the truck and stood there, looking over his shoulder at Travis. He barked.

"You want me to look up Miss Devon's address in the phone book and go there. Is that it?"

One woof.

"Sorry," Travis said. "I know you liked her, but I'm not in the market for a woman. Besides, she's not my type. I already told you that. And I'm not her type, either. Fact is, I have a hunch that *nobody's* her type."

The dog barked.

"No."

The dog dropped to the ground, rushed at Travis, and took hold of one leg of his jeans again.

"No," he said, reaching down and grabbing Einstein by the collar. "There's no point chewing my wardrobe, because I'm not going."

Einstein let go, twisted out of his grasp, and sprinted to the long bed of brightly blooming impatiens, where he started to dig furiously, tossing mangled flowers onto the lawn behind him.

"What're you doing, now, for God's sake?"

The dog kept digging industriously, working his way through the bed, back and forth, apparently bent on totally destroying it.

"Hey, stop that!" Travis hurried toward the retriever.

Einstein fled to the other end of the front yard and commenced digging a hole in the grass.

Travis went after him.

Einstein escaped once more to another corner of the lawn, where he began ripping out more grass, then to the birdbath, which he tried to undermine, then back to what was left of the impatiens.

Unable to catch the retriever, Travis finally halted, gasped for breath, and shouted, "Enough!"

Einstein stopped digging in the flowers and raised his head, snaky trailers of coral-red impatiens dangling from his mouth.

"We'll go," Travis said.

Einstein dropped the flowers and came out of the ruins, onto the lawn—warily.

"No tricks," Travis promised. "If it means that much to you, then we'll go see the woman. But God knows what I'm going to say to her."

8

With her dinner platter in one hand and a bottle of Evian in the other, Nora went along the downstairs hallway, comforted by the sight of lights blazing in every room. On the upstairs landing, she used her elbow to flick the switch for the second-floor hall lights. She would need to include a lot of light bulbs in her next grocery order because she intended to leave all the lights burning day and night for the foreseeable future. It was an expense she did not in the least begrudge.

Still buoyed by the brandy, she began to sing softly to herself as she headed for her room: "Moon River, wider than a mile . . ."

She stepped through the door. Streck was lying on the bed.

He grinned and said, "Hi, babe."

For an instant she thought he was an hallucination, but when he spoke she knew he was real, and she cried out, and the platter fell from her hand, scattering fruit and cheese across the floor.

"Oh my, what an awful mess you've made," he said, sitting up and swinging his legs over the edge of the bed. He was still wearing his running shorts, athletic socks, and running shoes; nothing else. "But there's no need to clean it up now. There's other business to take care of first. I been waiting a long time for you to come upstairs. Waiting and thinking about you . . . getting primed for you . . ." He stood. "And now it's time to teach you what you've never learned."

Nora could not move. Could not breathe.

He must have come to the house directly from the park, arriving before she did. He had forced entry, leaving no trace of a break-in, and he'd been waiting here on the bed all the time she'd been sipping brandy in the kitchen. There was something about his *waiting* up here that was creepier than anything else he had done, waiting and teasing himself with the promise of her, getting a kick out of listening to her putter around downstairs in ignorance of his presence.

When he was finished with her, would he kill her?

She turned and ran into the second-floor hallway.

As she put her hand on the newel post at the head of the stairs and started down, she heard Streck behind her.

She plunged down the steps, taking them two and three at a time, terrified that she was going to twist an ankle and fall, and at the landing her knee nearly buckled, and she stumbled but kept going, *leaped* down the last flight, into the first-floor hall.

Seizing her from behind, catching the baggy shoulders of her dress, Streck spun her around to face him.

9

As Travis swung to the curb in front of the Devon house, Einstein stood on the front seat, placed both forepaws on the door handle, bore down with all of his weight, and opened the door. Another neat trick. He was out of the truck and galloping up the front walkway before Travis had engaged the hand brake and switched off the engine.

Seconds later, Travis reached the foot of the veranda steps in time to see the retriever on the porch as he stood on his hind paws and hit the doorbell with one forepaw. The bell was audible from inside.

Climbing the steps, Travis said, "Now, what the devil's gotten into you?"

The dog rang the bell again.

"Give her a chance—"

As Einstein hit the button a third time, Travis heard a man shout in anger and pain. Then a woman's cry for help.

Barking as ferociously as he had done in the woods

yesterday, Einstein clawed at the door as if he actually believed he could tear his way through it.

Pressing forward, Travis peered through a clear segment in the stained-glass window. The hallway was brightly lit, so he was able to see two people struggling only a few feet away.

Einstein was barking, snarling, going crazy.

Travis tried the door, found it locked. He used his elbow to smash in a couple of the stained-glass segments, reached inside, fumbled for the lock, located it and and the security chain, and went inside just as the guy in running shorts pushed the woman aside and turned to face him.

Einstein didn't give Travis a chance to act. The retriever bolted along the hallway, straight toward the runner.

The guy reacted as anyone would upon seeing a charging dog the size of this one: he ran. The woman tried to trip him, and he stumbled but did not fall. At the end of the corridor, he slammed through a swinging door, out of sight.

Einstein raced past Nora Devon and reached the still-swinging door at full tilt, timing his approach perfectly, streaking through the opening as the door rocked inward. He vanished after the runner. In the room beyond the swinging door—the kitchen, Travis figured—there was much barking, snarling, and shouting. Something fell with a crash, then something else made an even louder crash, and the runner cursed, and Einstein made a vicious sound that gave Travis a chill, and the din grew worse.

He went to Nora Devon. She was leaning against the newel post at the bottom of the stairs. He said, "You okay?"

"He almost . . . almost . . . "

"But he didn't," Travis guessed.

"No."

He touched the blood on her chin. "You're hurt."

"His blood," she said, seeing it on Travis's fingertips. "I bit the bastard." She looked toward the swinging door, which had stopped moving now. "Don't let him hurt the dog."

"Not likely," Travis said.

The noise in the kitchen subsided as Travis pushed through the swinging door. Two ladder-back chairs had been knocked over. A large blue-flowered ceramic cookie jar lay in pieces on the tile floor, and oatmeal cookies were scattered across the room, some whole and some broken and some squashed. The runner was sitting in a corner, his bare legs pulled up, hands crossed defensively on his chest. One of the man's shoes was missing, and Travis suspected the dog had gotten hold of it. The runner's right hand was bleeding, which was evidently Nora Devon's work. He was also bleeding from his left calf, but that wound appeared to be a dog bite. Einstein was guarding him, staying back out of range of a kick, but ready to tear at the runner if the guy was foolish enough to attempt to leave the corner.

"Nice job," Travis told the dog. "Very nice indeed."

Einstein made a whining sound that indicated acceptance of the praise. But when the runner started to move, the happy whine turned instantly to a snarl. Einstein snapped at the man, who jerked back into the corner again.

"You're finished," Travis told the runner.

"He bit me! They *both* bit me." Petulant rage. Astonishment. Disbelief. "*Bit* me."

Like a lot of bullies who'd had their way all of their lives, this man was shocked to discover he could be hurt, beaten. Experience had taught him that people would always back down if he pressed them hard enough and if he kept a crazy-man look in his eyes. He thought he could never lose. Now, his face was pale, and he looked as if he was in a state of shock.

Travis went to the phone and called the police.

FIVE

1

Late Thursday morning, May 20, when Vincent Nasco returned from his one-day vacation in Acapulco, he picked up the *Times* at the Los Angeles International Airport before taking the commuter van—they called it a limousine, but it was a van—back to Orange County. He read the newspaper during the trip to his townhouse in Huntington Beach, and on page three he saw the story about the fire at Banodyne Laboratories in Irvine.

The blaze had broken out shortly after six o'clock yesterday morning, when Vince had been on his way to the airport to catch the plane to Acapulco. One of the two Banodyne buildings had been gutted before the firemen had brought the flames under control.

The people who had hired Vince to kill Davis Weatherby, Lawton Haines, the Yarbecks, and the Hudstons had almost certainly employed an arsonist to torch Banodyne. They seemed to be trying to eradicate all records of the Francis Project, both those stored in Banodyne files and those in the minds of the scientists who had participated in the research.

The newspaper said nothing about Banodyne's defense contracts, which were apparently not public knowledge. The company was referred to as ''a leader in the genetic-engineering industry, with a special focus on the development of revolutionary new drugs derived from recombinant-DNA research.''

A night watchman had died in the blaze. The *Times* offered no explanation as to why he had been unable to flee the fire. Vince figured the guy had been killed by intruders, then incinerated to cover the murder.

The commuter van ferried Vince to the front door of his townhouse. The rooms were cool and shadowy. On the uncarpeted floors, each footstep was heard and clearly defined, echoing hollowly through the nearly empty house.

He had owned the place for two years, but he had not fully furnished it. In fact, the dining room, den, and two of the three bedrooms contained nothing except cheap drapes for privacy.

Vince believed that the townhouse was a way station, a temporary residence from which he would one day move to a house on the beach at Rincon, where the surf and the surfers were legendary, where the vast rolling sea was the overwhelming fact of life. But his failure to furnish his current residence had nothing to do with its temporary status in his plans. He simply liked bare white walls, clean concrete floors, and empty rooms.

When he eventually purchased his dream house, Vince intended to have polished white ceramic tile installed on the floors and walls in every one of its big rooms. There would be no wood, no stone or brick, no textured surfaces to provide the visual ''warmth'' that other people seemed to prize. The furniture would be built to his specifications, with several coats of glossy white enamel, upholstered in white vinyl. The only deviations that he would permit from all those shiny white surfaces would be the necessary use of glass and highly polished steel. Then, there, thus encapsulated, he would at least feel at peace and at home for the first time in his life.

Now, after unpacking his suitcase, he went down to the kitchen to prepare lunch. Tunafish. Three hard-boiled eggs. Half a dozen rye crackers. Two apples and an orange. A bottle of Gatorade.

The kitchen had a small table and one chair in the corner,

but he ate upstairs in the sparsely furnished master bed-room. He sat in a chair at the window that faced west. The ocean was only a block away, on the other side of the Coast Highway and beyond a wide public beach, and from the second floor he could see the rolling water.

The sky was partially overcast, so the sea was dappled with sunshine and shadows. In some places it looked like molten chrome, but in other places it might have been a surging mass of dark blood.

The day was warm, though it looked strangely cold, wintry.

Staring at the ocean, he always felt that the ebb and flow of blood through his veins and arteries was in perfect sympathy with the rhythm of the tides.

When he finished eating, he sat for a while in communion with the sea, crooning to himself, looking through his faint reflection on the glass as if peering through the wall of an aquarium, although he felt himself to be within the ocean even now, far beneath the waves in a clean, cool, endless world of silence.

Later in the afternoon, he drove his van to Irvine and located Banodyne Laboratories. Banodyne was set against the backdrop of the Santa Ana Mountains. The company had two buildings on a multiple-acre lot that was surprisingly large in an area of such expensive real estate: one L-shaped two-story structure and a larger V-shaped single story with only a few narrow windows that made it look fortresslike. Both were very modern in design, a striking mix of flat planes and sensuous curves faced in dark green and gray marble, quite attractive. Surrounded by an employee parking lot and by immense expanses of well-maintained grass, shaded by a few palms and coral trees, the buildings were actually larger than they appeared to be, for their true scale was distorted and diminished by that enormous piece of flat land.

The fire had been confined to the V-shaped building that housed the labs. The only indications of destruction were a few broken windows and soot stains on the marble above those narrow openings.

The property was not walled or fenced, so Vince could have walked onto it from the street if he had wished, although there was a simple gate and guard booth at the three-lane entrance road. Judging by the guard's sidearm and by the subtly forbidding look of the building that housed the research labs, Vince suspected the lawns were monitored electronically and that, at night, sophisticated alarm systems would alert watchmen to an intruder's presence before he had taken more than a few steps across the grass. The arsonist must have been skilled at more than setting fires; he must also have had a wide knowledge of security systems.

Vince cruised past the place, then turned and drove by from the other direction. Like spectral presences, cloud shadows moved slowly across the lawn and slid up the walls of the buildings. Something about Banodyne gave it a portentous—perhaps even slightly ominous—look. And Vince did not think that he was letting his view of the place be unduly colored by the research that he knew to have been conducted there.

He drove home to Huntington Beach.

Having gone to Banodyne in the hope that seeing the place would help him decide how to proceed, he was disappointed. He still did not know what to do next. He could not figure out to whom he could sell his information for a price worth the risk he was taking. Not to the U.S. government: it was their information to begin with. And not to the Soviets, the natural adversary, for it was the Soviets who had paid him to kill Weatherby, the Yarbecks, the Hudstons, and Haines.

Of course, he couldn't *prove* he had been working for the Soviets. They were clever when they hired a freelancer like him. But he had worked for these people as often as he had taken contracts from the mob, and based on dozens of clues over the years, he had decided they were Soviets. Once in a while he dealt with people other than the usual three contacts in L.A., and invariably they spoke with what sounded like Russian accents. Furthermore, their targets were usually political to at least some degree—or, as in the

134

case of the Banodyne kills, military targets. And their information always proved more thorough, accurate, and sophisticated than the information he was given by the mob when he contracted for a simple gangland hit.

So who would pay for such sensitive defense information if not the U.S. or the Soviets? Some third-world dictator looking for a way to circumvent the nuclear capabilities of the most powerful countries? The Francis Project might give some pocket Hitler that edge, elevate him to a world power, and he might pay well for it. But who wanted to risk dealing with Qaddafi types? Not Vince.

Besides, he possessed information about the *existence* of the revolutionary research at Banodyne, but he did not have detailed files on how the Francis Project's miracles had been accomplished. He had less to sell than he'd first thought.

However, in the back of his mind, an idea had been growing since yesterday. Now, as he continued to puzzle over a potential buyer for his information, that idea flowered.

The dog.

At home again, he sat in his bedroom, staring out at the sea. He sat there even after nightfall, after he could no longer see the water, and he thought about the dog.

Hudston and Haines had told him so much about the retriever that he'd begun to realize his knowledge of the Francis Project, although potentially explosive and valuable, was not one-thousandth as valuable as the dog itself. The retriever could be exploited in many ways; it was a money machine with a tail. For one thing, he could probably sell it back to the government or to the Russians for a bargeload of cash. If he could find the dog, he would be able to achieve financial independence.

But how could he locate it?

All over southern California, a quiet search—almost secret yet gigantic—must be under way. The Defense Department would be putting tremendous manpower into the hunt, and if Vince crossed paths with those searchers, they would want to know who he was. He could not afford to draw attention to himself.

Furthermore, if he conducted his own search of the nearest Santa Ana foothills, into which the lab escapees had almost surely fled, he might encounter the wrong one. He might miss the golden retriever and stumble upon The Outsider, and that could be dangerous. Deadly.

Beyond the bedroom window, the cloud-armored night sky and the sea flowed together in blackness as dark as the far side of the moon.

2

On Thursday, one day after Einstein cornered Arthur Streck in Nora Devon's kitchen, Streck was arraigned on charges of breaking and entering, assault and battery, and attempted rape. Because he had previously been convicted of rape and had served two years of a three-year sentence, his bail was high; he could not meet it. And since he could not locate a bondsman who would trust him, he seemed destined to remain in jail until his case came to trial, which was a great relief to Nora.

On Friday, she went to lunch with Travis Cornell.

She was startled to hear herself accept his invitation. It was true that Travis had seemed genuinely shocked to learn of the terror and harassment she had endured at Streck's hands, and it was also true that to some extent she owed her dignity and perhaps her life to his arrival at the penultimate moment. Yet years of indoctrination in Aunt Violet's paranoia could not be washed away in a few days, and a residue of unreasonable suspicion and wariness clung to Nora. She would have been dismayed, maybe even shattered, if Travis had suddenly tried to force himself upon her, but she would not have been surprised. Having been encouraged since early childhood to expect the worst from people, she could be surprised only by kindness and compassion.

Nevertheless, she went to lunch with him.

At first, she did not know why.

136

However, she did not have to think long to find the answer: the dog. She wanted to be near the dog because he made her feel secure and because she'd never before been the recipient of such unrestrained affection as Einstein lavished on her. She had never previously been the object of any affection from anyone, and she liked it even if it came from an animal. Besides, in her heart Nora knew that Travis must be completely trustworthy because Einstein trusted him, and Einstein did not seem easily fooled.

They ate lunch at a café that had a few linen-draped tables outside on a brick patio, under white- and blue-striped umbrellas, where they were permitted to clip the dog's leash to the wrought-iron table leg and keep him with them. Einstein was well-behaved, lying quietly most of the time. Occasionally he raised his head to gaze at them with his soulful eyes until they relinquished scraps of food, though he was not a pest about it.

Nora did not have much experience with dogs, but she thought that Einstein was unusually alert and inquisitive. He frequently shifted his position in order to watch the other diners, with whom he seemed intrigued.

Nora was intrigued with *everything*. This was her first meal in a restaurant, and although she had read about people having lunch and dinner in thousands of restaurants in countless novels, she was still amazed and delighted by every detail. The single rose in the milk-white vase. The matchbooks with the establishment's name embossed on them. The way the butter had been molded into round pats with a flower pattern on each, then served on a bowl of crushed ice. The slice of lemon in the ice water. The chilled salad fork was an especially amazing touch.

"Look at this," she said to Travis after their entrées had been served and the waiter had departed.

He frowned at her plate and said, "Something wrong?"

"No, no. I mean ... these vegetables."

"Baby carrots, baby squash."

"Where do they get them so tiny? And look how they've scalloped the edge of this tomato. Everything's so pretty.

137

How do they ever find the time to make everything so pretty?"

She knew these things that astonished her were things he took for granted, knew that her amazement revealed her lack of experience and sophistication, making her seem like a child. She frequently blushed, sometimes stammered in embarrassment, but she could not restrain herself from commenting on these marvels. Travis smiled at her almost continuously, but it was not a patronizing smile, thank God; he seemed genuinely delighted by the pleasure she took in new discoveries and small luxuries.

By the time they finished coffee and dessert—a kiwi tart for her, strawberries and cream for Travis, and a chocolate éclair that Einstein did not have to share with anyone—Nora had been engaged in the longest conversation of her life. They passed two and a half hours without an awkward silence, mainly discussing books because—given Nora's reclusive life—a love of books was virtually the only thing they had in common. That and loneliness. He seemed genuinely interested in her opinions of novelists, and he had some fascinating insights into books, insights which had eluded her. She laughed more in one afternoon than she had laughed in an entire year. But the experience was so exhilarating that she occasionally felt dizzy, and by the time they left the restaurant she could not precisely remember anything they had actually said; it was all a colorful blur. She was experiencing sensory overload analogous to what a primitive tribesman might feel if suddenly deposited in the middle of New York City, and she needed time to absorb and process all that had happened to her.

Having walked to the café from her house, where Travis had left his pickup truck, they now made the return trip on foot, and Nora held the dog's leash all the way. Einstein never tried to pull away from her, never tangled the leash around her legs, but padded along at her side or in front of her, docile, now and then looking up at her with a sweet expression that made her smile.

"He's a good dog," she said.

"Very good," Travis agreed.

"So well behaved."

"Usually."

"And so cute."

"Don't flatter him too much."

"Are you afraid he'll become vain?"

"He's already vain," Travis said. "If he were any more vain, he'd be impossible to live with."

The dog looked back and up at Travis, and sneezed loudly as if ridiculing his master's comment.

Nora laughed. "Sometimes it almost seems he can understand every word you're saying."

"Sometimes," Travis agreed.

When they arrived at the house, Nora wanted to invite him in. But she wasn't sure if the invitation would seem too bold, and she was afraid Travis would misinterpret it. She knew she was being a nervous old maid, knew she could—and ought to—trust him, but Aunt Violet suddenly loomed in her memory, full of dire warnings about men, and Nora could not bring herself to do what she knew was right. The day had been perfect, and she dreaded extending it further for fear something would happen to sully the entire memory, leaving her with nothing good, so she merely thanked him for lunch and did not even dare to shake his hand.

She did, however, stoop down and hug the dog. Einstein nuzzled her neck and licked her throat once, making her giggle. She had *never* heard herself giggle before. She would have clung to him and petted him for hours if her enthusiasm for the dog had not, by comparison, made her wariness of Travis even more evident.

Standing in the open door, she watched them as they got into the pickup and drove away.

Travis waved at her.

She waved, too.

Then the truck reached the corner and began to turn right, out of sight, and Nora regretted her cowardice, wished she'd asked Travis in for a while. She almost ran after them, almost shouted his name and almost rushed down the sidewalk in pursuit. But then the truck was gone, and she was alone again. Reluctantly, she went into the house and closed the door on the brighter world outside.

3

The Bell JetRanger executive helicopter flashed over the tree-filled ravines and balding ridges of the Santa Ana foothills, its shadow running ahead of it because the sun was in the west as Friday afternoon waned. Approaching the head of Holy Jim Canyon, Lemuel Johnson looked out the window in the passenger compartment and saw four of the county sheriff's squad cars lined up along the narrow dirt lane down there. A couple of other vehicles, including the coroner's wagon and a Jeep Cherokee that probably belonged to the victim, were parked at the stone cabin. The pilot had barely enough room to put the chopper down in the clearing. Even before the engine died and the sun-bronzed rotors began to slow, Lem was out of the craft, hurrying toward the cabin, with his right-hand man, Cliff Soames, close behind him.

Walt Gaines, the county sheriff, stepped out of the cabin as Lem approached. Gaines was a big man, six-four and at least two hundred pounds, with enormous shoulders and a barrel chest. His corn-yellow hair and cornflower-blue eyes would have lent him a movie-idol look if his face had not been so broad and his features blunt. He was fifty-five. looked forty, and wore his hair only slightly longer than he had during his twenty years in the Marine Corps.

Although Lem Johnson was a black man, every bit as dark as Walt was white, though he was seven inches shorter and sixty pounds lighter than Walt, though he had come from an upper-middle-class black family while Walt's folks had been poor white trash from Kentucky, though Lem was ten years younger than the sheriff, the two were friends. More than friends. Buddies. They played bridge together, went deep-sea fishing together, and found unadulterated pleasure in sitting in lawn chairs on one or the other's patio, drinking Corona beer and solving all of the world's problems. Their wives even became best friends, a serendipitous development that was, according to Walt, "a miracle, 'cause the woman's never liked anyone else I've introduced her to in thirty-two years."

To Lem, his friendship with Walt Gaines was also a miracle, for he was not a man who made friends easily. He was a workaholic and did not have the leisure to nurture an acquaintance carefully into a more enduring relationship. Of course, careful nurturing hadn't been necessary with Walt; they had clicked the first time they'd met, had recognized similar attitudes and points of view in each other. By the time they had known each other six months, it seemed they had been close since boyhood. Lem valued their friendship nearly as much as he valued his marriage to Karen. The pressure of his job would be harder to endure if he couldn't let off some steam with Walt once in a while.

Now, as the chopper's blades fell silent, Walt Gaines said, "Can't figure why the murder of a grizzled old canyon squatter would interest you feds."

"Good," Lem said. "You're not supposed to figure it, and you really don't want to know."

"Anyway, I sure didn't expect you'd come yourself. Thought you'd send some of your flunkies."

"NSA agents don't like to be called flunkies," Lem said.

Looking at Cliff Soames, Walt said, "But that's how he treats you fellas, isn't it? Like flunkies?"

"He's a tyrant," Cliff confirmed. He was thirty-one, with red hair and freckles. He looked more like an earnest young preacher than like an agent of the National Security Agency.

"Well, Cliff," Walt Gaines said, "you've got to understand where Lem comes from. His father was a downtrodden black businessman who never made more than two hundred thousand a year. Deprived, you see. So Lem, he figures he's got to make you white boys jump through hoops whenever he can, to make up for all those years of brutal oppression."

"He makes me call him 'Massah,' " Cliff said.

"I don't doubt it," Walt said.

Lem sighed and said, "You two are about as amusing as a groin injury. Where's the body?"

"This way, Massah," Walt said.

As a gust of warm afternoon wind shook the surrounding trees, as the canyon hush gave way to the whispering of leaves, the sheriff led Lem and Cliff into the first of the cabin's two rooms.

Lem understood, at once, why Walt had been so jokey. The forced humor was a reaction to the horror inside the cabin. It was somewhat like laughing aloud in a graveyard at night to chase away the willies.

Two armchairs were overturned, upholstery slashed. Cushions from the sofa had been ripped to expose the white foam padding. Paperbacks had been pulled off a corner bookcase, torn apart, and scattered all over the room. Glass shards from the big window sparkled gemlike in the ruins. The debris and the walls were spattered with blood, and a lot of dried blood darkened the light-pine floor.

Like a pair of crows searching for brightly colored threads with which to dress up their nest, two lab technicians in black suits were carefully probing through the ruins. Occasionally one of them made a soft wordless cawing sound and plucked at something with tweezers, depositing it in a plastic envelope.

Evidently, the body had been examined and photographed, for it had been transferred into an opaque plastic mortuary bag and was lying near the door, waiting to be carried out to the meat wagon.

Looking down at the half-visible corpse in the sack, which was only a vaguely human shape beneath the milky plastic, Lem said, "What was his name?"

"Wes Dalberg," Walt said. "Lived here ten years or more."

"Who found him?"

"A neighbor."

"When was he killed?"

"Near as we can tell, about three days ago. Maybe Tuesday night. Have to wait for lab tests to pinpoint it.

Weather's been pretty warm lately, which makes a difference in the rate of decomposition."

Tuesday night ... In the predawn hours of Tuesday morning, the breakout had occurred at Banodyne. By Tuesday night, The Outsider could have traveled this far.

Lem thought about that—and shivered.

"Cold?" Walt asked sarcastically.

Lem didn't respond. They were friends, yes, and they were both officers of the law, one local and one federal, but in this case they served opposing interests. Walt's job was to find the truth and bring it to the public, but Lem's job was to put a lid on the case and keep it clamped down tight.

"Sure stinks in here," Cliff Soames said.

"You should've smelled it before we got the stiff in the bag," Walt said. "Ripe."

"Not just ... decomposition," Cliff said.

"No," Walt said, pointing here and there to stains that were not caused by blood. "Urine and feces, too."

"The victim's?"

"Don't think so," Walt said.

"Done any preliminary tests of it?" Lem asked, trying not to sound worried. "On-site microscopic exam?"

"Nope. We'll take samples back to the lab. We think it belongs to whatever came crashing through that window."

Looking up from the body bag, Lem said, "You mean the man who killed Dalberg."

"Wasn't a man," Walt said, "and I figure you know that."

"Not a man?" Lem said.

"At least not a man like you or me."

"Then what do you think it was?"

"Damned if I know," Walt said, rubbing the back of his bristly head with one big hand. "But judging from the body, the killer had sharp teeth, maybe claws, and a nasty disposition. Does that sound like what you're looking for?"

Lem could not be baited.

For a moment, no one spoke.

A fresh piny breeze came through the shattered window,

blowing away some of the noxious stench.

One of the lab men said, "Ah," and plucked something from the rubble with his tweezers.

Lem sighed wearily. This situation was no good. They would not find enough to tell them what killed Dalberg, though they would gather sufficient evidence to make them curious as hell. However, this was a matter of national defense, in which no civilian would be wise to indulge his curiosity. Lem was going to have to put a stop to their investigation. He hoped he could intervene without angering Walt. It would be a real test of their friendship.

Suddenly, staring at the body bag, Lem realized something was wrong with the shape of the corpse. He said, "The head isn't here."

"You feds don't miss a trick, do you?" Walt said.

"He was decapitated?" Cliff Soames asked uneasily.

"This way," Walt said, leading them into the second room.

It was a large—if primitive—kitchen with a hand pump in the sink and an old-fashioned wood-burning stove.

Except for the head, there were no signs of violence in the kitchen. Of course, the head was bad enough. It was in the center of the table. On a plate.

"Jesus," Cliff said softly.

When they had entered the room, a police photographer had been taking shots of the head from various angles. He was not finished, but he stepped back to given them a better view.

The dead man's eyes were missing, torn out. The empty sockets seemed as deep as wells.

Cliff Soames had turned so white that, by contrast, his freckles burned on his skin as if they were flecks of fire.

Lem felt sick, not merely because of what had happened to Wes Dalberg but because of all the deaths yet to come. He was proud of both his management and investigatory skills, and he knew he could handle this case better than anyone else. But he was also a hardheaded pragmatist, incapable of underestimating the enemy or of pretending there would be a quick ending to this nightmare. He would need time and patience and luck to track down the killer, and meanwhile more bodies would pile up.

The head had not been cut off the dead man. It was not as neat as that. It appeared to have been clawed and chewed and wrenched off.

Lem's palms were suddenly damp.

Strange . . . how the empty sockets of the head transfixed him as surely as if they had contained wide, staring eyes.

In the hollow of his back, a single droplet of sweat traced the course of his spine. He was more scared than he had ever been—or had ever thought he could be—but he did not want to be taken off the job for any reason. It was vitally important to the very security of the nation and the safety of the public that this emergency be handled right, and he knew no one was likely to perform as well as he could. That was not just ego talking. Everyone said he was the best, and he knew they were right; he had a justifiable pride and no false modesty. This was his case, and he would stay with it to the end.

His folks had raised him with an almost too-keen sense of duty and responsibility. "A black man," his father used to say, "has to do a job twice as well as a white man in order to get any credit at all. That's nothing to be bitter about. Nothing worth protesting. It's just a fact of life. Might as well protest the weather turning cold in winter. Instead of protesting, the thing to do is just face facts, work twice as hard, and you'll get where you want to go. And you must succeed because you carry the flag for all your brothers." As a result of that upbringing, Lem was incapable of less than total, unhesitating commitment to every assignment. He dreaded failure, rarely encountered it, but could be thrown into a deep funk for weeks when the successful conclusion of a case eluded him.

"Talk to you outside a minute?" Walt asked, moving to the open rear door of the cabin.

Lem nodded. To Cliff, he said, "Stay here. Make sure nobody—pathologists, photographer, uniformed cops, *nobody*—leaves before I've had a chance to talk to them."

"Yes, sir," Cliff said. He headed quickly toward the

front of the cabin to inform everyone that they were temporarily quarantined—and to get away from the eyeless head.

Lem followed Walt Gaines into the clearing behind the cabin. He noticed a metal hod and firewood scattered over the ground, and paused to study those objects.

"We think it started out here," Walt said. "Maybe Dalberg was getting wood for the fireplace. Maybe something came out of those trees, so he threw the hod at it and ran into the house."

They stood in the bloody-orange late-afternoon sunlight, at the perimeter of the trees, peering into the purple shadows and mysterious green depths of the forest.

Lem was uneasy. He wondered if the escapee from Weatherby's lab was nearby, watching them.

"So what's up?" Walt asked.

"Can't say."

"National security?"

"That's right."

The spruces and pines and sycamores rustled in the breeze, and he thought he heard something moving furtively through the brush.

Imagination, of course. Nevertheless, Lem was glad that both he and Walt Gaines were armed with reliable pistols in accessible shoulder holsters.

Walt said, "You can keep your lip zipped if you insist, but you can't keep me totally in the dark. I can figure out a few things for myself. I'm not stupid."

"Never thought you were."

"Tuesday morning, every damn police department in Orange and San Bernardino counties gets an urgent request from your NSA asking us to be prepared to cooperate in a manhunt, details to follow. Which puts us all on edge. We know what you guys are responsible for—guarding defense research, keeping the vodka-pissing Russians from stealing our secrets. And since Southern California's the home of half of the defense contractors in the country, there's plenty to be stolen here."

Lem kept his eyes on the woods, kept his mouth shut.

"So," Walt continued, "we figure we're going to be looking for a Russian agent with something hot in his pockets, and we're happy to have a chance to help kick some ass for Uncle Sam. But by noon, instead of getting details we get a cancellation of the request. No manhunt after all. Everything's under control, your office tells us. Original alert was issued in error, you say."

"That's right." The agency had realized that local police could not be sufficiently controlled and, therefore, could not be fully trusted. It was a job for the military. "Issued in error."

"Like hell. By late afternoon of the same day, we learn Marine choppers from El Toro are quartering the Santa Ana foothills. And by Wednesday morning, a hundred Marines with high-tech tracking gear are flown in from Camp Pendleton to carry on the search at ground level."

"I heard about that, but it had nothing to do with my agency," Lem said.

Walt studiously avoided looking at Lem. He stared off into the trees. Clearly, he knew Lem was lying to him, knew that Lem *had* to lie to him, and he felt it would be a breach of good manners to make Lem do it while they maintained eye contact. Though he looked crude and ill-mannered, Walt Gaines was an unusually considerate man with a rare talent for friendship.

But he was also the county sheriff, and it was his duty to keep probing even though he knew Lem would reveal nothing. He said, "Marines tell us it's just a training exercise."

"That's what I heard."

"We're always notified of training exercises ten days ahead."

Lem did not reply. He thought he saw something in the forest, a flicker of shadows, a darkish presence moving through piny gloom.

"So the Marines spend all day Wednesday and half of Thursday out there in the hills. But when reporters hear about this 'exercise' and come snooping around, the leathernecks suddenly call it off, pack up, go home. It was

147

almost as if ... whatever they were looking for was so worrisome, so damn top-secret that they'd rather not find it at all if finding it meant letting the press know about it.''

Squinting into the forest, Lem strained to see through steadily deepening shadows, trying to catch another glimpse of the movement that had drawn his attention a moment ago.

Walt said, "Then yesterday afternoon the NSA asks to be kept informed about any 'peculiar reports, unusual assaults, or exceedingly violent murders'. We ask for clarification, don't get any.''

There. A ripple in the murkiness beneath the evergreen boughs. About eighty feet in from the perimeter of the woods. Something moving quickly and stealthily from one sheltering shadow to another. Lem put his right hand under his coat, on the butt of the pistol in his shoulder holster.

"But then just one day later," Walt said, "we find this poor son of a bitch Dalberg torn to pieces—and the case is peculiar as hell and about as 'exceedingly violent' as I ever hope to see. Now here *you* are, Mr. Lemuel Asa Johnson, director of the Southern California Office of the NSA, and I know you didn't come choppering in here just to ask me whether I want onion or guacamole dip at tomorrow night's bridge game.''

The movement was closer than eighty feet, much closer. Lem had been confused by the layers of shadows and by the queerly distorting late-afternoon sunlight that penetrated the trees. The thing was no more than forty feet away, maybe closer, and suddenly it came straight at them, *bounded* at them through the brush, and Lem cried out, drew the pistol from his holster, and involuntarily stumbled backward a few steps before taking a shooter's stance with his legs spread wide, both hands on the gun.

"It's just a mule deer!" Walt Gaines said.

Indeed it was. Just a mule deer.

The deer stopped a dozen feet away, under the drooping boughs of a spruce, peering at them with huge brown eyes that were bright with curiosity. Its head was held high, ears pricked up.

"They're so used to people in these canyons that they're almost tame," Walt said.

Lem let out a stale breath as he holstered his pistol.

The mule deer, sensing their tension, turned from them and loped away along the trail, vanishing into the woods.

Walt was staring hard at Lem. "What's out there, buddy?"

Lem said nothing. He blotted his hands on his suit jacket.

The breeze was stiffening, getting cooler. Evening was on its way, and night was close behind it.

"Never saw you spooked before," Walt said.

"A caffeine jag. I've had too much coffee today."

"Bullshit."

Lem shrugged.

"It seems to've been an *animal* that killed Dalberg, something with lots of teeth, claws, something savage," Walt said. "Yet no damn animal would carefully place the guy's head on a plate in the center of the kitchen table. That's a sick joke. Animals don't make jokes, not sick or otherwise. Whatever killed Dalberg . . . it left the head like that to taunt us. So what in Christ's name are we dealing with?"

"You don't want to know. And you don't *need* to know 'cause I'm assuming jurisdiction in this case."

"Like hell."

"I've got the authority," Lem said. "It's now a federal matter, Walt. I'm impounding all the evidence your people have gathered, all reports they've written thus far. You and your men are to talk to no one about what you've seen here. No one. You'll have a file on the case, but the only thing in it will be a memo from me, asserting the federal prerogative under the correct statute. You're out from under. No matter what happens, no one can blame you, Walt."

"Shit."

"Let it go."

Walt scowled. "I've got to know—"

"Let it go."

"—are people in my county in danger? At least tell me that much, damn it."

"Yes."

"In danger?"

"Yes."

"And if I fought you, if I tried to hang on to jurisdiction in this case, would there be anything I could do to lessen that danger, to insure the public safety?"

"No. Nothing," Lem said truthfully.

"Then there's no point in fighting you."

"None," Lem said.

He started back toward the cabin because the daylight was fading fast, and he did not want to be near the woods as darkness crept in. Sure, it had only been a mule deer. But next time?

"Wait a minute," Walt said. "Let me tell you what I think, and you just listen. You don't have to confirm or deny what I say. All you've got to do is hear me out."

"Go on," Lem said impatiently.

The shadows of the trees crept steadily across the bristly dry grass of the clearing. The sun was balanced on the western horizon.

Walt paced out of the shadows into the waning sunlight, hands in his back pockets, looking down at the dusty ground, taking a moment to collect his thoughts. Then: "Tuesday afternoon, somebody walked into a house in Newport Beach, shot a man named Yarbeck, and beat his wife to death. That night, somebody killed the Hudston family in Laguna Beach—husband, wife, and teenage son. Police in both communities use the same forensics lab, so it didn't take long to discover one gun was used both places. But that's about all the police in either case are going to learn because your NSA has quietly assumed jurisdiction in those crimes, too. In the interest of national security."

Lem did not respond. He was sorry he had even agreed to listen. Anyway, he was not taking direct charge of the investigation into the murders of the scientists, which were almost surely Soviet-inspired. He'd delegated that task to other men, so he'd be free to concentrate on finding the dog and The Outsider.

The sunlight was burnt orange. The cabin windows smoldered with reflections of that fading fire.

Walt said, "Okay. Then there's Dr. Davis Weatherby of

Corona Del Mar. Missing since Tuesday. This morning, Weatherby's brother finds the doctor's body in the trunk of his car. Local pathologists hardly arrive at the scene before NSA agents show up.''

Lem was slightly unnerved by the swiftness with which the sheriff evidently gathered, coordinated, and absorbed information from various communities that were not in the unincorporated part of the county and were not, therefore, under his authority.

Walt grinned but with little or no humor. "Didn't expect me to have made all these connections, huh? Each of these things happened in a different police jurisdiction, but as far as I'm concerned this county is one sprawling city of two million people, so I make it my business to work hand in glove with all the local departments.

"What's your point?"

"My point is that it's astonishing to have six murders of upstanding citizens in one day. This is Orange Country, after all, not L.A. And it's even more astonishing that all six deaths are related to urgent matters of national security. So it arouses my curiosity. I start checking into the backgrounds of these people, looking for something that links them—"

"Walt, for Christ's sake!"

"—and I discover they all work—or did work—for something called Banodyne Laboratories."

Lem was not angry. He couldn't get angry with Walt— they were tighter than brothers—but the big man's canniness was maddening right now. Lem said, "Listen, you've no right to conduct an investigation."

"I'm sheriff, remember?"

"But none of these murders—except Dalberg here—falls into your jurisdiction to begin with," Lem said. "And even if it did . . . once the NSA steps in, you've got no right to continue. In fact, you're expressly *forbidden* by law to continue."

Ignoring him, Walt said, "So I look up Banodyne, see what kind of work they do, and I discover they're into genetic engineering, recombinant DNA—"

"You're incorrigible."

"There's no indication Banodyne's at work on defense projects, but that doesn't mean anything. Could be blind contracts, projects so secret that the funding doesn't even appear on public record."

"Jesus," Lem said irritably. "Don't you understand how damn mean we can get when we've got national security laws on our side?"

"Just speculating now," Walt said.

"You'll speculate your honky ass right into a prison cell."

"Now, Lemuel, let's not have an ugly racial confrontation here."

"You're incorrigible."

"Yeah, and you're repeating yourself. Anyway, I did some heavy thinking, and I figure the murders of these people who work at Banodyne must be connected somehow to the manhunt the Marines conducted on Wednesday and Thursday. And to the murder of Wesley Dalberg."

"There's no similarity between Dalberg's murder and the others."

"Of course there's not. Wasn't the same killer. I can see that. The Yarbecks, the Hudstons, and Weatherby were hit by a pro, while poor Wes Dalberg was torn to pieces. Still, there's a connection, by God, or you wouldn't be interested, and the connection must be Banodyne."

The sun was sinking. Shadows pooled and thickened.

Walt said, "Here's what I figure: they were working on some new bug at Banodyne, a genetically altered germ, and it got loose, contaminated someone, but it didn't just make him sick. What it did was severely damage his brain, turn him into a savage or something—"

"An updated Dr. Jekyll for the high-tech age?" Lem interrupted sarcastically.

"—so he slipped out of the lab before anyone knew what happened to him, fled into the foothills, came here, attacked Dalberg."

"You watch a lot of bad horror movies or what?"

"As for Yarbeck and the others, maybe they were eliminated 'cause they knew what happened and were so

152

scared about the consequences that they intended to go public."

Off the dusty canyon, a soft, ululant howl arose. Probably just a coyote.

Lem wanted to get out of there, away from the forest. But he felt that he had to deal with Walt Gaines, deflect the sheriff from these lines of inquiry and consideration.

"Let me get this straight, Walt. Are you saying the United States government had its own scientists *killed* to shut them up?"

Walt frowned, knowing how unlikely—if not downright impossible—his scenario was.

Lem said, "Is life really just a Ludlum novel? Killed our own people? Is it National Paranoia Month or something? Do you really believe that crap?"

"No," Walt admitted.

"And how could Dalberg's killer be a contaminated scientist with brain damage? I mean, Christ, you yourself said it was some animal that killed Dalberg, something with claws, sharp teeth."

"Okay, okay, so I don't have it figured. Not all of it, anyway. But I'm sure it's all tied in with Banodyne somehow. I'm not entirely on the wrong track—am I?"

"Yes, you are," Lem said. "Entirely."

"Really?"

"Really." Lem felt bad about lying to Walt and manipulating him, but he did it anyway. "I shouldn't even tell you that you're chasing after false spoor, but as a friend I guess I owe you something."

Additional wild voices had joined the eerie howling in the woods, confirming that the cries were only those of coyotes, yet the sound chilled Lem Johnson and made him eager to depart.

Rubbing the nape of his bull neck with one hand, Walt said, "It doesn't have anything at all to do with Banodyne?"

"Nothing. It's just a coincidence that Weatherby and Yarbeck both worked there—and that Hudston used to work there. If you insist on making the connection, you'll just be spinning your wheels—which is fine by me."

The sun set and, in passing, seemed to unlock a door through which a much cooler, brisker breeze swept into the darkening world.

Still rubbing his neck, Walt said, "Not Banodyne, huh?" He sighed. "I know you too well, buddy. You've got such a strong sense of duty that you'd lie to your own mother if that was in the best interests of the country."

Lem said nothing.

"All right," Walt said. "I'll drop it. Your case from here on. Unless more people in my jurisdiction get killed. If that happens ... well, I might try to take control of things again. Can't promise you that I won't. I've got a sense of duty, too, you know."

"I know," Lem said, feeling guilty, feeling like a total shit.

At last, they both headed back to the cabin.

The sky—which was dark in the east, still streaked with deep orange and red and purple light in the west—seemed to be descending like the lid of a box.

Coyotes howled.

Something out in the night woods howled back at them.

Cougar, Lem thought, but he knew that now he was even lying to himself.

4

On Sunday, two days after their successful Friday lunch date, Travis and Nora drove to Solvang, a Danish-style village in the Santa Ynez Valley. It was a touristy place with hundreds of shops selling everything from exquisite Scandinavian crystal to plastic imitations of Danish beer steins. The quaint architecture (though calculated) and the tree-lined streets enhanced the simple pleasures of window shopping.

Several times Travis felt the urge to take Nora's hand and hold it while they strolled. It seemed natural, right. Yet he sensed that she might not be ready for even such harmless contact as hand-holding.

She was wearing another drab dress, dull blue this time, nearly as shapeless as a sack. Sensible shoes. Her thick dark hair still hung limp and unstyled, as it had been when he'd first seen her.

Being with her was pure pleasure. She had a sweet temperament and was unfailingly sensitive and kind. Her innocence was refreshing. Her shyness and modesty, though excessive, endeared her to him. She viewed everything with a wide-eyed wonder that was charming, and he delighted in surprising her with simple things: a shop that sold only cuckoo clocks; another that sold only stuffed animals; a music box with a mother-of-pearl door that opened to reveal a pirouetting ballerina.

He bought her a T-shirt with a personalized message that he would not let her see until it was ready: *NORA LOVES EINSTEIN*. Though she professed she could never wear a T-shirt, that it wasn't her style, Travis knew she would wear it because she did, indeed, love the dog.

Perhaps Einstein could not read the words on the shirt, but he seemed to understand what was meant. When they came out of the shop and unhooked his leash from the parking meter where they'd tethered him, Einstein regarded the message on the shirt solemnly while Nora held it up for his inspection, then happily licked and nuzzled her.

The day held only one bad moment for them. As they turned a corner and approached another shop window, Nora stopped suddenly and looked around at the crowds on the sidewalks—people eating ice cream in big homemade waffle-cookie cones, people eating apple tarts wrapped in wax paper, guys in feather-decorated cowboy hats they'd bought in one of the stores, pretty young girls in short-shorts and halters, a very fat woman in a yellow muumuu, people speaking English and Spanish and Japanese and Vietnamese and all the other languages you could hear at any Southern California tourist spot—and then she looked along the busy street at a gift shop built in the form of a three-story stone-and-timber windmill, and she stiffened, looked stricken.

Travis had to guide her to a bench in a small park, where she sat trembling for a few minutes before she could even tell him what was wrong.

"Overload," she said at last, her voice shaky. "So many . . . new sights . . . new sounds . . . so many different things all at once. I'm so sorry."

"It's all right," he said, touched.

"I'm used to a few rooms, familiar things. Are people staring?"

"No one's noticed anything. There's nothing to stare at."

She sat with her shoulders hunched, her head hung forward, her hands fisted in her lap—until Einstein put his head on her knees. As she petted the dog, she began gradually to relax.

"I was enjoying myself," she said to Travis, though she did not raise her head, "really enjoying myself, and I thought how far from home I was, how wonderfully far from home—"

"Not really. Less than an hour's drive," he assured her.

"A long, long way," she said.

Travis supposed that for her it was, in fact, a great distance.

She said, "And when I realized how far from home I was and how . . . *different* everything was . . . I clenched up, afraid, like a child."

"Would you like to go back to Santa Barbara now?"

"No!" she said, meeting his eyes at last. She shook her head. She dared to look around at the people moving through the small park and at the gift shop shaped like a windmill. "No. I want to stay a while. All day. I want to have dinner in a restaurant here, not a sidewalk café but inside, like other people do, inside, and then I want to go home after dark." She blinked and repeated those two words wonderingly, "After dark."

"All right."

"Unless, of course, you hoped to get back sooner."

"No, no," he said. "I planned on making a day of it."

"This is very kind of you."

156

Travis raised one eyebrow. "What do you mean?"

"You know."

"I'm afraid I don't."

"Helping me step out into the world," she said. "Giving up your time to help someone ... like me. It's very generous of you."

He was astonished. "Nora, let me assure you, it's not charity work I'm involved in here!"

"I'm sure a man like you has better things to do with a Sunday afternoon in May."

"Oh, yes," he said self-mockingly, "I could have stayed at home and given all my shoes a meticulous shining with a toothbrush. Could have counted the number of pieces in a box of elbow macaroni."

She stared at him in disbelief.

"By God, you're serious," Travis said. "You think I'm just here because I've taken pity on you."

She bit her lip and said, "It's all right." She looked down at the dog again. "I don't mind."

"But I'm not here out of pity, for God's sake! I'm here because I like being with you, I really do, I like you very much."

Even with her head lowered, the blush that crept into her cheeks was visible.

For a while neither of them spoke.

Einstein looked up at her adoringly as she petted him, though once in a while he rolled his eyes at Travis as if to say, *All right, you've opened the door of a relationship, so don't just sit there like a fool, say something, move forward, win her over.*

She scratched the retriever's ears and stroked him for a couple of minutes, and then she said, "I'm okay now."

They left the little park and strolled past the shops again, and in a while it was as if her moment of panic and his clumsy proclamation of affection had not happened.

He felt as if he were courting a nun. Eventually, he realized that the situation was even worse than that. Since the death of his wife three years ago, he had been celibate. The whole subject of sexual relations seemed strange and

157

new to him again. So it was almost as if he were a *priest* wooing a nun.

Nearly every block had a bakery, and the wares in the display windows of each shop looked more delicious than what had been for sale in the previous place. The scents of cinnamon, powdered sugar, nutmeg, almonds, apples, and chocolate eddied in the warm spring air.

Einstein stood on his hind feet at each bakery, paws on the windowsill, and stared longingly through the glass at the artfully arranged pastries. But he didn't go into any of the shops, and he never barked. When he begged for a treat, his soulful whining was discreetly low, so as not to bother the swarming tourists. Rewarded with a bit of pecan fudge and a small apple tart, he was satisfied and did not persist in begging.

Ten minutes later, Einstein revealed his exceptional intelligence to Nora. He had been a good dog around her, affectionate and bright and well-behaved, and he had shown considerable initiative in chasing and cornering Arthur Streck, but he had not previously allowed her a glimpse of his uncanny intelligence. And when she witnessed it, she did not at first realize what she was seeing.

They were passing the town pharmacy, which also sold newspapers and magazines, some of which were displayed outside in a rack near the entrance. Einstein surprised Nora with a sudden lurch toward the pharmacy, tearing his leash out of her hand. Before either Nora or Travis could regain control of him, Einstein used his teeth to pull a magazine from the rack and brought it to them, dropping it at Nora's feet. It was *Modern Bride*. As Travis grabbed for him, Einstein eluded capture and snatched up another copy of *Modern Bride*, which he deposited at Travis's feet just as Nora was picking up her copy to return it to the rack.

"You silly pooch," she said. "What's gotten into you?"

Taking up the leash, Travis stepped through the passersby and put the second copy of the magazine back where the dog had gotten it. He thought he knew exactly what Einstein had in mind, but he said nothing, afraid of embarrassing Nora, and they resumed their walk.

Einstein looked at everything, sniffing with interest at the people who passed, and he seemed immediately to have forgotten his enthusiasm for matrimonial publications.

However, they had taken fewer than twenty steps when the dog abruptly turned and ran between Travis's legs, jerking the leash out of his hand and nearly knocking him down. Einstein went directly to the pharmacy, snatched a magazine out of the rack, and returned.

Modern Bride.

Nora still did not get it. She thought it was funny, and she stooped to ruffle the retriever's coat. "Is this your favorite reading material, you silly pooch? Read it every month, do you? You know, I'll bet you do. You strike me as a complete romantic."

A couple of tourists had noticed the playful dog and were smiling, but they were even less likely than Nora to realize there was a complex intention behind the animal's game with the magazine.

When Travis bent down to pick up *Modern Bride*, intending to return it to the pharmacy, Einstein got to it first, took it in his jaws, and shook his head violently for a moment.

"Bad dog," Nora said with evident surprise that Einstein had such a devilish streak in him.

Einstein dropped the magazine. It was badly rumpled, and some of the pages were torn, and here and there the paper was damp with saliva.

"I guess we'll have to buy it now," Travis said.

Panting, the retriever sat on the sidewalk, cocked his head, and grinned up at Travis.

Nora remained innocently unaware that the dog was trying to tell them something. Of course, she had no reason to make a sophisticated interpretation of Einstein's behavior. She was unfamiliar with the degree of his genius and did not expect him to perform miracles of communication.

Glaring at the dog, Travis said, "You stop it, fur face. No more of this. Understand me?"

Einstein yawned.

With the magazine paid for and tucked into a pharmacy

bag, they resumed their tour of Solvang, but before they reached the end of the block, the dog began to elaborate on his message. He suddenly gripped Nora's hand gently but firmly in his teeth and, to her startlement, pulled her along the sidewalk to an art gallery, where a young man and woman were admiring the landscape paintings in the window. The couple had a baby in a stroller, and it was the child to whom Einstein was directing Nora's attention. He wouldn't let go of her hand until he had forced her to touch the pink-outfitted infant's chubby arm.

Embarrassed, Nora said, "He thinks your baby's exceptionally cute, I guess—which she certainly is."

The mother and father were wary of the dog at first but quickly realized he was harmless.

"How old's your little girl?" Nora asked.

"Ten months," the mother said.

"What's her name?"

"Lana."

"That's pretty."

Finally, Einstein was willing to release Nora's hand.

A few steps away from the young couple, in front of an antique shop that looked as if it had been transported brick by brick and timber by timber from seventeeth-century Denmark, Travis stopped, crouched beside the dog, lifted one of its ears, and said, "Enough. If you ever want your Alpo again, cut it out."

Nora looked baffled. "What's gotten into him?"

Einstein yawned, and Travis knew they were in trouble.

In the next ten minutes, the dog took hold of Nora's hand twice again and led her, both times, to babies.

Modern Bride and babies.

The message was painfully clear now, even to Nora: *You and Travis belong together. Get married. Have babies. Raise a family. What're you waiting for?*

She was blushing furiously and seemed unable to look directly at Travis. He was somewhat embarrassed, too.

At last Einstein seemed satisfied that he had gotten his point across, and he stopped misbehaving. Until now, if asked, Travis would have said that a dog could not look smug.

160

Later, at dinnertime, the day was still pleasantly warm, and Nora changed her mind about eating inside, in an ordinary restaurant. She chose a place with sidewalk tables under red umbrellas that were, in turn, sheltered by the boughs of a giant oak. Travis sensed that she was not now intimidated by the prospect of a real restaurant experience but wanted to eat in the open air so they could keep Einstein with them. Repeatedly throughout dinner, she looked at Einstein, sometimes glancing surreptitiously at him, sometimes studying him openly and intently.

Travis made no reference to what had happened and pretended to have forgotten the whole affair. But when he had the dog's attention, and when Nora was not looking, he mouthed threats at the mutt: *No more apple tarts. Choke chain. Muzzle. Straight to the dog pound.*

Einstein took every threat with great equanimity, either grinning or yawning or blowing air out his nostrils.

5

Early Sunday evening, Vince Nasco paid a visit to Johnny "The Wire" Santini. Johnny was called "The Wire" for several reasons, not least of which was that he was tall and lean and taut, and he looked as if he was constructed of knotted wires in various gauges. He also had frizzy hair the shade of copper. He had made his bones at the tender age of fifteen, when to please his uncle, Religio Fustino, don of one of New York's Five Families, Johnny had taken it upon himself to strangle a freelance shit-and-coke dealer who was operating in the Bronx without the permission of the Family. Johnny used a length of piano wire for the job. This display of initiative and dedication to the principles of the Family had filled Don Religio with pride and love, and he had wept for only the second time in his life, promising his nephew the eternal respect of the Family and a well-paid position in the business.

Now Johnny The Wire was thirty-five and lived in a

million-dollar beach house in San Clemente. The ten rooms and four baths had been remade by an interior designer commissioned to create an authentic—and expensive— private Art Deco retreat from the modern world. Everything was in shades of black, silver and deep blue, with accents of turquoise and peach. Johnny had told Vince that he liked Art Deco because it reminded him of the Roaring Twenties, and he liked the twenties because that was the romantic era of legendary gangsters.

To Johnny The Wire, crime was not just a means to make money, not simply a way to rebel against the constraints of civilized society, and not only a genetic compulsion, but it was also—and primarily—a magnificent romantic tradition. He saw himself as a brother of every eye-patched hook-handed pirate who ever sailed in search of plunder, of every highwayman who had robbed a mail coach, of every safecracker and kidnapper and embezzler and thug in all the ages of criminal endeavor. He was, he insisted, mystical kin to Jesse James, Dillinger, Al Capone, the Dalton boys, Lucky Luciano, and legions of others, and Johnny loved them all, these legendary brothers in blood and theft.

Greeting Vince at the front door, Johnny said, "Come in, come in, big guy. Good to see you again."

They hugged. Vince didn't like being hugged, but he had worked for Johnny's Uncle Religio when he'd lived back in New York, and he still did a West Coast job for the Fustino Family now and then, so he and Johnny went back a long way, long enough that a hug was required.

"You're looking good," Johnny said. "Taking care of yourself, I see. Still mean as a snake?"

"A rattlesnake," Vince said, a little embarrassed to be saying such a stupid thing, but he knew it was the kind of outlaw crap that Johnny liked to hear.

"Hadn't seen you in so long I thought maybe the cops busted your ass."

"I'll never do time," Vince said, meaning that he knew prison was not part of his destiny.

Johnny took it to mean that Vince would go down

shooting rather than submit to the law, and he scowled and nodded approval. "They ever get you in a corner, blow away as many of 'em as you can before they take you out. That's the only *clean* way to go down."

Johnny The Wire was an astonishingly ugly man, which probably explained his need to feel that he was a part of a great romantic tradition. Over the years Vince had noticed that the better-looking hoods never glamorized what they did. They killed in cold blood because they liked killing or found it necessary, and they stole and embezzled and extorted because they wanted easy money, and that was the end of it: no justifications, no self-glorification, which was the way it ought to be. But those with faces that appeared to have been crudely molded from concrete, those who resembled Quasimodo on a bad day—well, many of them tried to compensate for their unfortunate looks by casting themselves as Jimmy Cagney in *Public Enemy*.

Johnny was wearing a black jumpsuit, black sneakers. He always wore black, probably because he thought it made him look sinister instead of just ugly.

From the foyer, Vince followed Johnny into the living room, where the furniture was upholstered in black fabric and the end tables were finished in glossy black lacquer. There were ormolu table lamps by Ranc, large silver-dusted Deco vases by Daum, a pair of antique chairs by Jacques Ruhlmann. Vince knew the history of these things only because, on previous visits, Johnny The Wire had stepped out of his tough-guy persona long enough to babble about his period treasures.

A good-looking blonde was reclining on a silver-and-black chaise longue, reading a magazine. No older than twenty, she was almost embarrassingly ripe. Her silver-blond hair was cut short, in a pageboy. She was wearing Chinese-red silk lounging pajamas that clung to the contours of her full breasts, and when she glanced up and pouted at Vince, she seemed to by trying to look like Jean Harlow.

"This is Samantha," Johnny The Wire said. To Samantha, he said, "Toots, this here is a mad man that nobody messes with, a legend in his own time.''

Vince felt like a jackass.

"What's a 'made man'?" the blonde asked in a high-pitched voice she'd no doubt copied from the old movie star Judy Holliday.

Standing beside the longue, cupping one of the blonde's breasts and fondling it through the silk pajamas, Johnny said, "She doesn't know the lingo, Vince. She's not of the *fratellanza*. She's a valley girl, new to the life, unaware of our customs."

"He means I'm no greaseball guinea," Samantha said sourly.

Johnny slapped her so hard that he nearly knocked her off the chaise longue. "You watch your mouth, bitch."

She put a hand to her face, and tears shimmered in her eyes, and in a little-girl voice, she said, "I'm sorry, Johnny."

"Stupid bitch," he muttered.

"I don't know what gets into me," she said. "You're good to me, Johnny, and I hate myself when I act like that."

To Vince, it appeared to be a rehearsed scene, but he supposed that was just because they'd been through it so many times before, both privately and publicly. From the shine in Samantha's eyes, Vince could tell she enjoyed being slapped around; she smart-mouthed Johnny just so he'd hit her. Johnny clearly liked slapping her, too.

Vince was disgusted.

Johnny The Wire called her a "bitch" again, then led Vince out of the living room and into the big study, closing the door behind them. He winked and said, "She's a little uppity, that one, but she can just about suck your brains out through your cock."

Half-sickened by Johnny Santini's sleaziness, Vince refused to be drawn into such a conversation. Instead, he withdrew an envelope from his jacket pocket. "I need information."

Johnny took the envelope, looked inside, thumbed casually through the wad of hundred-dollar bills, and said,

"What you want, you got."

The study was the only room in the house untouched by Art Deco. It was strictly high-tech. Sturdy metal tables were lined up along three walls, and eight computers stood on them, different makes and models. Every computer had its own phone line and modem, and every display screen was aglow. On some screens, programs were running; data flicked across them or scrolled from top to bottom. Drapes were drawn over the windows, and the two flexible-neck work lamps were hooded to prevent glare on the monitors, so the predominant light was electronic-green, which gave Vince a peculiar feeling of being under the surface of the sea. Three laser printers were producing hard copies with only vague whispering sounds that for some reason brought to mind images of fish swimming through ocean-floor vegetation.

Johnny The Wire had killed half a dozen men, had managed bookie and numbers operations, had planned and executed bank robberies and jewelry heists. He had been involved in the Fustino Family's drug operations, extortion rackets, kidnapping, labor-union corruption, record and videotape counterfeiting, interstate truck hijacking, political bribery, and child pornography. He had done it all, seen it all, and although he had never exactly been bored by any criminal undertaking, no matter how long or often he had been involved in it, he *had* grown somewhat jaded. During the past decade, as the computer opened exciting new areas of criminal activity, Johnny had seized the opportunity to move where no mafia wiseguy had gone before, into challenging frontiers of electronic thievery and mayhem. He had a gift for it, and he soon became the mob's premier hacker.

Given time and motivation, he could break any computer security system and pry through a corporation's or a government agency's most sensitive information. If you wanted to run a major credit-card scam, charging a million bucks' worth of purchases to other people's American Express accounts, Johnny The Wire could suck some suitable names and credit histories out of TRW's files and matching card numbers from American Express's data banks, and you were in business. If you were a don under indictment and about to go to trial on heavy charges, and if you were afraid of the testimony to be given by one of your cronies who had turned state's evidence, Johnny could invade the Department of Justice's most well-guarded data banks, discover the new identity that had been given the stool pigeon through the Federal Witness Relocation Program, and tell you where to send the hit men. Johnny rather grandly called himself the "Silicon Sorcerer," though everyone else still called him The Wire.

As the mob's hacker, he was more valuable than ever to all the Families nationwide, so valuable that they didn't even mind if he moved to a comparative backwater like San Clemente, where he could live the good beach life while he worked for them. In the age of the microchip, Johnny said, the world was one small town, and you could sit in San Clemente—or Oshkosh—and pick someone's pocket in New York City.

Johnny dropped into a high-backed black leather chair equipped with rubber wheels, in which he could roll swiftly from one computer to the next. He said, "So! What can the Silicon Sorcerer do for you, Vince?"

"Can you tap into police computers?"

"It's a snap."

"I need to know if, since last Tuesday, any police agency in the county has opened a file on any particularly strange murders."

"Who're the victims?"

"I don't know. I'm just looking for strange murders."

"Strange in what way?"

"I'm not exactly sure. Maybe ... somebody with his throat torn out. Somebody ripped to pieces. Somebody all chewed up and gouged by an animal."

Johnny gave him a peculiar look. "That's strange, all right. Something like that would be in the newspapers."

"Maybe not," Vince said, thinking of the army of government security agents that would be working diligently to keep the press in the dark about the Francis

166

Project and to conceal the dangerous developments on Tuesday at the Banodyne labs. "The murders might be in the news, but the police will probably be suppressing the gory details, making them look like ordinary homicides. So from what the papers print, I won't be able to tell which victims are the ones I'm interested in."

"All right. Can do."

"You'd also better prowl around at the County Animal Control authority to see if they're getting any reports of unusual attacks by coyotes or cougars or other predators. And not just attacks on people, but on livestock—cows, sheep. There might even be some neighborhood, probably on the eastern edge of the county, where a lot of family pets are disappearing or being chewed up real bad by something wild. If you run across that, I want to know."

Johnny grinned and said, "You tracking down a werewolf?"

It was a joke; he did not expect or want an answer. He had not asked why this information was needed, and he would never ask, because people in their line of work did not poke into each other's business. Johnny might be curious, but Vince knew that The Wire would never indulge his curiosity.

Vince was unnerved not by the question but by the grin. The green light from the computer screens was reflected by Johnny's eyes and by the saliva on his teeth and, to a lesser extent, by his wiry copper-colored hair. As ugly as he was to begin with, the eerie luminescence made him look like a revived corpse in a Romero film.

Vince said, "Another thing. I need to know if any police agency in the county is running a quiet search for a golden retriever."

"A dog?"

"Yeah."

"Cops don't usually look for lost dogs."

"I know," Vince said.

"This dog got a name?"

"No name."

"I'll check it out. Anything else?"

"That's it. When can you put it together?"

"I'll call you in the morning. Early."

Vince nodded. "And depending on what you turn up, I might need you to keep tracking these things on a daily basis."

"Child's play," Johnny said, spinning around once in his black leather chair, then jumping to his feet with a grin. "Now, I'm gonna fuck Samantha. Hey! You want to join in! Two studs like us, going at her at the same time, we could reduce that bitch to a little pile of jelly, have her begging for mercy. How about it?"

Vince was glad for the weird green lighting because it covered the fact that he had gone ghost-pale. The idea of messing around with that infected slut, that diseased whore, that rotting and festering round-heeled pump, was enough to make him sick. He said, "Got an appointment I can't break."

"Too bad," Johnny said.

Vince forced himself to say, "Would have been fun."

"Maybe next time."

The very idea of the three of them going at it . . . well, it made Vince feel unclean. He was overcome by a desire for a steaming-hot shower.

6

Sunday night, pleasantly tired from a long day in Solvang, Travis thought he would fall asleep the moment he put his head on his pillow, but he did not. He couldn't stop thinking about Nora Devon. Her gray eyes flecked with green. Glossy black hair. The graceful, slender line of her throat. The musical sound of her laughter, the curve of her smile.

Einstein was lying on the floor in the pale-silver light that came through the window and vaguely illuminated one small section of the dark room. But after Travis tossed and turned for an hour, the dog finally joined him on the bed and put his burly head and forepaws on Travis's chest.

"She's so sweet, Einstein. One of the gentlest, sweetest people I've ever known."

The dog was silent.

"And she's very bright. She's got a sharp mind, sharper than she realizes. She sees things I don't see. She has a way of describing things that make them fresh and new. The whole *world* seems fresh and new when I see it with her."

Though still and quiet, Einstein had not fallen asleep. He was very attentive.

"When I think about all that vitality, intelligence, and love of life being suppressed for thirty years, I want to cry. Thirty years in that old dark house. Jesus. And when I think of how she endured those years without letting it make her bitter, I want to hug her and tell her what an incredible woman she is, what a strong and courageous and incredible woman."

Einstein was silent, unmoving.

A vivid memory flashed back to Travis: the clean shampoo smell of Nora's hair when he had leaned close to her in front of a gallery window in Solvang. He breathed deep and could actually smell it again, and the scent accelerated his heartbeat.

"Damn," he said. "I've only known her a few days, but damn if I don't think I'm falling in love."

Einstein lifted his head and woofed once, as if to say it was about time that Travis realized what was happening, and as if to say that he had brought them together and was pleased to take credit for their future happiness, and as if to say that it was all part of some grand design and that Travis was to stop fretting about it and just go with the flow.

For another hour, Travis talked about Nora, about the way she looked and moved, about the melodic quality of her soft voice, about her unique perspective on life and her way of thinking, and Einstein listened with the attentiveness and genuine interest that was the mark of a true, concerned friend. It was an exhilarating hour. Travis had never thought he would love anyone again. Not anyone, not at all, and certainly not this intensely. Less than a week ago, his abiding loneliness had seemed unconquerable.

Later, thoroughly exhausted both physically and emotionally, Travis slept.

Later still, in the hollow heart of night, he came half awake and was dimly aware that Einstein was at the window. The retriever's forepaws were on the windowsill, his snout against the glass. He was staring out at the darkness, alert.

Travis sensed that the dog was troubled.

But in his dream, he had been holding Nora's hand under a harvest moon, and he did not want to come fully awake for fear he would not be able to regain that pleasant fantasy.

7

On Monday morning, May 24, Lemuel Johnson and Cliff Soames were at the small zoo—mostly a petting zoo for children—in sprawling Irvine Park, on the eastern edge of Orange County. The sky was cloudless, the sun bright and hot. The immense oaks did not stir a leaf in the motionless air, but birds swooped from branch to branch, peeping and trilling.

Twelve animals were dead. They lay in bloody heaps.

During the night, someone or something had climbed the fences into the pens and had slaughtered three young goats, a white-tailed deer and her recently born fawn, two peacocks, a lop-eared rabbit, a ewe and two lambs.

A pony was dead, though it had not been savaged. Apparently, it had died of fright while throwing itself repeatedly against the fence in an attempt to escape whatever had attacked the other animals. It lay on its side, neck twisted in an improbable angle.

The wild boars had been left unharmed. They snorted and sniffed continuously at the dusty earth around the feeding trough in their separate enclosure, looking for bits of food that might have spilled yesterday and been missed until now.

Other surviving animals, unlike the boars, were skittish.

Park employees—also skittish—were gathered near an orange truck that belonged to the county, talking with two Animal Control officers and with a young, bearded biologist from the California Department of Wildlife.

Crouching beside the delicate and pathetic fawn, Lem studied the wounds in its neck until he could no longer tolerate the stench. Not all of the foul odors were caused by the dead animals. There was evidence that the killer had deposited feces and sprayed urine on its victims, just as it had done at Dalberg's place.

Pressing a handkerchief against his nose to filter the reeking air, he moved to a dead peacock. Its head had been torn off, as had one leg. Both of its clipped wings were broken, and its iridescent feathers were dulled and pasted together with blood.

"Sir," Cliff Soames called from the adjoining pen.

Lem left the peacock, found a service gate that opened into the next enclosure, and joined Cliff at the carcass of the ewe.

Flies swarmed around them, buzzing hungrily, settling upon the ewe, then darting off as the men fanned them away.

Cliff's face was bloodless, but he did not look as shocked or as nauseated as he had been last Friday, at Dalberg's cabin. Perhaps this slaughter didn't affect him as strongly because the victims were animals instead of human beings. Or perhaps he was consciously hardening himself against the extreme violence of their adversary.

"You'll have to come to this side," Cliff said from where he crouched beside the ewe.

Lem stepped around the sheep and squatted beside Cliff. Though the ewe's head was in the shadow of an oak bough overhanging the pen, Lem saw that her right eye had been torn out.

Without comment, Cliff used a stick to lever the left side of the ewe's head off the ground, revealing that the other socket was also vacant.

The cloud of flies thickened around them.

"Looks like it was our runaway, all right," Lem said.

Lowering his own handkerchief from his face, Cliff said, "There's more." He led Lem to three additional carcasses —both lambs and one of the goats—that were eyeless. "I'd say it's beyond argument. The damn thing that killed Dalberg last Tuesday night, then roamed the foothills and canyons for five days, doing ..."

"What?"

"God knows what. But it wound up here last night."

Lem used his handkerchief to mop the sweat off his dark face. "We're only a few miles north-northwest of Dalberg's cabin."

Cliff nodded.

"Which way you think it's headed?"

Cliff shrugged.

"Yeah," Lem said. "No way of knowing where it's going. Can't begin to outthink it because we haven't the slightest idea *how* it thinks. Let's just pray to God it stays out here in the unpopulated end of the county. I don't want to even consider what could happen if it decides to head into the easternmost suburbs like Orange Park Acres and Villa Park."

On the way out of the compound, Lem saw that the flies were gathered on the dead rabbit in such numbers that they looked like a piece of dark cloth draped over the carcass and rippling in a light breeze.

Eight hours later, at seven o'clock Monday evening, Lem stepped up to the lectern in a large meeting room on the grounds of the Marine Air Station at El Toro. He leaned toward the microphone, tapped it with a finger to be sure it was active, heard a loud hollow *thump*, and said, "May I have your attention, please?"

A hundred men were seated on metal folding chairs. They were all young, well-built, and healthy-looking, for they were members of elite Marine Intelligence units. Five two-squad platoons had been drawn from Pendleton and other bases in California. Most of them had been involved in the search of the Santa Ana foothills last Wednesday and Thursday, following the breakout at the Banodyne labs.

They were *still* searching, having just returned from a full day in the hills and canyons, but they were no longer conducting the operation in uniform. To deceive reporters and local authorities, they had driven in cars and pickups and Jeep wagons to various points along the current search perimeter. They had gone into the wilds in groups of three or four, dressed as ordinary hikers: jeans or khaki pants in the rugged Banana Republic style; T-shirts or cotton safari shirts; Dodger or Budweiser or John Deere caps, or cowboy hats. They went armed with powerful handguns that could be quickly concealed in nylon backpacks or under their loose T-shirts if they encountered real hikers or state authorities. And in Styrofoam coolers, they carried compact Uzi submachine guns that could be brought into service in seconds if they found the adversary.

Every man in the room had signed a secrecy oath, which put him in jeopardy of a long prison term if he ever divulged the nature of this operation to anyone. They knew what they were hunting, though Lem was aware that some of them had trouble believing the creature really existed. Some were afraid. But others, especially those who had previously served in Lebanon or Central America, were familiar enough with death and horror to be unshaken by the nature of their current quarry. A few oldtimers went as far back as the final year of the Vietnam War, and they professed to believe that the mission was a piece of cake. In any event, they were all good men, and they had a wary respect for the strange enemy they were stalking, and if The Outsider could be found, they would find it.

Now, when Lem asked for their attention, they immediately fell silent.

"General Hotchkiss tells me that you've had another fruitless day out there," Lem said, "and I know you're as unhappy about that as I am. You've been working long

173

hours in rugged terrain for six days now, and you're tired, and you're wondering how long this is going to drag on. Well, we're going to keep looking until we find what we're after, until we corner The Outsider and kill it. There is no way we can stop if it's still loose. No way."

None of the hundred even grumbled in disagreement.

"And always remember—we're also looking for the dog."

Every man in the room probably hoped that he would be the one to find the dog and that someone else would encounter The Outsider.

Lem said, "On Wednesday, we're bringing in another four Marine Intelligence squads from more distant bases, and they'll spell you on a rotating basis, giving you a couple of days off. But you'll all be out there tomorrow morning, and the search area has been redefined."

A county map was on the wall behind the lectern, and Lem Johnson pointed to it with a yardstick. "We'll be shifting north-northwest, into the hills and canyons around Irvine Park."

He told them about the slaughter at the petting zoo. He gave a graphic description of the condition of the carcasses, for he did not want any of these men to get careless.

"What happened to those zoo animals," Lem said, "could happen to any of you if you let your guard down at the wrong place and time."

A hundred men regarded him with utmost seriousness, and in their eyes he saw a hundred versions of his own tightly controlled fear.

8

Tuesday night, May 25, Tracy Leigh Keeshan could not sleep. She was so excited she felt as if she might burst. She pictured herself as a dandelion gone to seed, a puffball of fragile white fuzz, and then a gust of wind would come along and all the bits of fluff would be sent spinning in every direction—*poof*—to the far corners of the world, and Tracy Keeshan would exist no more, destroyed by her own excitement.

She was an unusually imaginative thirteen-year-old.

Lying in bed in her dark room, she did not even have to close her eyes to see herself on horseback—on her own chestnut stallion, Goodheart, to be precise—thundering along the racetrack, the rails flashing past, the other horses in the field left far behind, the finish line less than a hundred yards ahead, and the adoring crowds cheering wildly in the grandstand . . .

In school, she routinely got good grades, not because she was a diligent student but because learning came easily to her, and she could do well without much effort. She didn't really care about school. She was slender, blond, with eyes the precise shade of a clear summer sky, very pretty, and boys were drawn to her, but she didn't spend any more time thinking about boys than she did worrying about her school work, not yet anyway, although her girlfriends were so fixated on boys, so *consumed* by the subject that they sometimes bored Tracy half to death.

What Tracy cared about—deeply, profoundly, passionately—was horses, racing thoroughbreds. She had been collecting pictures of horses since she was five and had been taking riding lessons since she was seven, though for the longest time her parents had not been able to afford to buy her a horse of her own. During the past two years, however, her father's business had prospered, and two months ago they had moved into a big new house on two acres in Orange Park Acres, which was a horsey community with plenty of riding trails. At the back end of their lot was a private stable for six horses, though only one stall was occupied. Just today—Tuesday, May 25, a day of glory, a day that would live forever in Tracy Keeshan's heart, a day that just *proved* there was a God—she had been given a horse of her own, the splendid and beautiful and incomparable Goodheart.

So she could not sleep. She went to bed at ten, and by midnight she was more awake than ever. By one o'clock Wednesday morning, she could not stand it any longer. She had to go out to the stables and look at Goodheart. Make sure he was all right. Make sure he was comfortable in his new home. Make sure he was *real*.

She threw off the sheet and thin blanket and got quietly out of bed. She was wearing panties and a Santa Anita Racetrack T-shirt, so she just pulled on a pair of jeans and slipped her bare feet into blue Nike running shoes.

She turned the knob on her door slowly, quietly, and went out into the hall, letting the door stand open.

The house was dark and quiet. Her parents and her nine-year-old brother Bobby were asleep.

Tracy went down the hall, through the living room and the dining room, not turning on lights, relying on the moonlight that penetrated the large windows.

In the kitchen, she silently pulled open the utility drawer on the corner secretary and withdrew a flashlight. She unlocked the back door and let herself out onto the rear patio, stealthily easing the door shut behind her, not yet switching on the flashlight.

The spring night was cool but not chilly. Silvered by moonlight above but with dark undersides, a few big clouds glided like white-sailed galleons across the sea of night, and Tracy stared up at them for a while, enjoying the moment. She wanted to absorb every detail of this special time, letting her anticipation build. After all, this would be her first moment *alone* with the proud and noble Goodheart, just the two of them sharing their dreams of the future.

She crossed the patio, went around the swimming pool, where the reflection of the moon rippled gently in the chlorinated water, and stepped out onto the sloping lawns. The dew-damp grass seemed to shimmer in the lambent lunar beams.

Off to the left and right, the property line was defined by white ranch fencing that appeared vaguely phosphorescent in the moonglow. Beyond the fences were other properties of at least an acre and some as large as the Keeshan place, and all across Orange Park Acres the night was still but for a few crickets and nocturnal frogs.

Tracy walked slowly toward the stables at the end of the

yard, thinking about the triumphs that lay ahead for her and Goodheart. He would not race again. He had placed in the money at Santa Anita, Del Mar, Hollywood Park, and other tracks throughout California, but he had been injured and could no longer race safely. However, he could still be put to stud, and Tracy had no doubt that he'd sire winners. Within a week they hoped to add two good mares to the stable, and then they'd take the horses immediately to a breeding farm, where Goodheart would impregnate the mares. All three would be brought back here, where Tracy would care for them. Next year two healthy colts would be born, and then the young ones would be boarded with a trainer near enough so Tracy could visit constantly, and she'd help out with their training, learn all there was to learn about rearing a champion, and then—and *then*—she and the offspring of Goodheart would make racing history, oh yes, she was quite confident of making racing history—

Her fantasizing was interrupted when, about forty yards from the stables, she stepped in something mushy and slippery, and nearly fell. She didn't smell manure, but she figured it must be a pile left by Goodheart when they'd had him out in the yard last evening. Feeling stupid and clumsy, she switched on the flashlight and directed it at the ground, and instead of manure she found the remains of a brutally mutilated cat.

Tracy made a hissing sound of disgust and instantly switched off the flashlight.

The neighborhood was crawling with cats, partly because they were useful for controlling the mouse population around everyone's stables. Coyotes regularly ventured in from the hills and canyons to the east, in search of prey. Although cats were quick, coyotes were sometimes quicker, and at first Tracy thought a coyote had dug under the fence or leaped over it and had gotten hold of this unfortunate feline, which had probably been prowling for rodents.

But a coyote would have eaten the cat right on the spot, leaving little more than a bit of tail and a scrap or two of fur, for a coyote was a gourmand rather than gourmet and had a ravenous appetite. Or it would have carried the cat away for leisurely consumption elsewhere. Yet this cat had not looked even half-eaten, merely torn to pieces, as if something or someone had killed it merely for the sick pleasure of rending it apart . . .

Tracy shuddered.

And remembered the rumors about the zoo.

In Irvine Park, which was only a couple of miles away, someone apparently had killed several caged animals in the small petting zoo two nights ago. Drug-crazed vandals. Thrill killers. The story was just a hot rumor, and no one was able to confirm it, but there were indications that it was true. Some kids had bicycled out to the park yesterday after school, and they'd not seen any mangled carcasses, but they'd reported that there seemed to be fewer animals in the pens than usual. And the Shetland pony was definitely missing. Park employees had been uncommunicative when approached.

Tracy wondered if the same psychos were prowling Orange Park Acres, killing cats and other family pets, a possibility that was spooky and sickening. Suddenly, she realized that people deranged enough to slaughter cats for the sheer fun of it would also be sufficiently twisted to get a kick out of killing horses.

An almost crippling pang of fear flashed through her as she thought of Goodheart out there in the stable all by himself. For a moment, she could not move.

Around her, the night seemed even quieter than it had been.

It *was* quieter. The crickets were no longer chirruping. The frogs had stopped croaking, too.

The galleon clouds seemed to have dropped anchor in the sky, and the night appeared to have frozen in the ice-pale glow of the moon.

Something moved in the shrubbery.

Most of the enormous lot was devoted to open expanses of lawn, but a score of trees stood in artfully placed groups—mostly Indian laurels and jacarandas, plus a couple of corals—and there were beds of azaleas, California lilac bushes, Cape honeysuckles.

Tracy distinctly heard shrubbery rustling as something pushed roughly and hurriedly through it. But when she switched on the flashlight and swept the beam around the nearest plantings, she could not see anything moving.

The night was silent again.

Hushed.

Expectant.

She considered returning to the house, where either she could wake her father to ask him to investigate, or she could go to bed and wait until morning to investigate the situation herself. But what if it *was* only a coyote in the shrubbery? In that case, she was in no danger. Though a hungry coyote would attack a very young child, it would run from anyone Tracy's size. Besides, she was too worried about her noble Goodheart to waste any more time; she had to be sure that the horse was all right.

Using the flashlight to avoid any more dead cats that might be strewn about, she headed toward the stable. She had taken only a few steps when she heard the rustling again and, worse, an eerie growling that was unlike the sound of any animal she'd ever heard before.

She began to turn, might have run for the house then, but in the stable Goodheart whinnied shrilly, as if in fear, and kicked at the board walls of his stall. She pictured a leering psycho going after Goodheart with hideous instruments of torture. Her concern for her own welfare was not half as strong as her fear that something terrible would happen to her beloved breeder of champions, so she sprinted to his rescue.

Poor Goodheart began kicking even more frantically. His hooves slammed repeatedly against the walls, drummed furiously, and the night seemed to echo with the thunder of an oncoming storm.

She was still about fifteen yards from the stable when she heard the strange guttural growling again and realized that something was coming after her, bearing down on her from behind. She skidded on the damp grass, whirled, and brought up her flashlight.

Rushing toward her was a creature that had surely

escaped from Hell. It let out a shriek of madness and rage.

In spite of the flashlight, Tracy did not get a clear look at the attacker. The beam wavered, and the night grew darker as the moon slipped behind a cloud, and the hateful beast was moving fast, and she was too scared to understand what she was seeing. Nevertheless, she saw enough to know it was nothing she had ever seen before. She had an impression of a dark, misshapen head with asymmetrical depressions and bulges, enormous jaws full of sharp curved teeth, and amber eyes that blazed in the flashlight beam the way a dog's or a cat's will glow in a car's headlights.

Tracy screamed.

The attacker shrieked again and leaped at her.

It hit Tracy hard enough to knock the breath clear out of her. The flashlight flew from her hand, tumbled across the lawn. She fell, and the creature came down on top of her, and they rolled over and over toward the stable. As they rolled, she flailed desperately at the thing with her small fists, and she felt its claws sinking into the flesh along her right side. Its gaping mouth was at her face, she felt its hot rank breath washing over her, smelled blood and decay and worse, and she sensed it was going for her throat—she thought, *I'm dead, oh God, it's going to kill me, I'm dead, like the cat*—and she would have been dead in seconds, for sure, if Goodheart, less than fifteen feet away now, had not kicked out the latched half-door of his stall and bolted straight at them in panic.

The stallion screamed and reared up on its hind feet when it saw them, as if it would trample them underfoot.

Tracy's monstrous attacker shrieked again, though not in rage this time but in surprise and fear. It released her and flung itself to one side, out from under the horse.

Goodheart's hooves slammed into the earth inches from Tracy's head, and he reared up again, pawing at the air, screaming, and she knew that in his terror he might unwittingly trample her skull to mush. She threw herself out from under him, and also away from the amber-eyed beast, which had disappeared in the darkness on the other side of the stallion.

Still, Goodheart reared and screamed, and Tracy was screaming as well, and dogs were howling all over the neighborhood, and now lights appeared in the house, which gave her hope of survival. However, she sensed that the attacker wasn't ready to give up, that it was already circling the frantic stallion to make another try for her. She heard it snarling, spitting. She knew she would never reach the distant house before the thing dragged her down again, so she scrambled toward the nearby stable, to one of the empty stalls. As she went, she heard herself chanting, "Jesus, oh Jesus, Jesus, Jesus, Jesus ..."

The two halves of the Dutch-style stall door were bolted firmly together. Another bolt fastened the entire door to the frame. She unlatched that second bolt, pulled open the door, rushed into the straw-scented darkness, shut the door behind her, and held it with all the strength she possessed, for it could not be latched from inside.

An instant later, her assailant slammed into the other side of the door, trying to knock it open, but the frame prevented that. The door would only move outward, and Tracy hoped the amber-eyed creature was not smart enough to figure out how the door worked.

But it *was* smart enough—

(Dear Lord in Heaven, why wasn't it as dumb as it was ugly!)

—and after hitting the barrier only twice, it began to pull instead of push. The door was almost yanked out of Tracy's grasp.

She wanted to scream for help, but she needed every ounce of energy to dig in her heels and hold the stall door shut. It rattled and thumped against the frame as her demonic assailant wrestled with it. Fortunately, Goodheart was still letting loose shrill squeals and whinnies of terror, and the assailant was also shrieking—a sound that was strangely animal and human at the same time—so her father could have no doubt where the trouble was.

The door jerked open a few inches.

181

She yelped and pulled it shut.

Instantly the attacker yanked it partway open again and held it ajar, striving to pull the door wider even as she struggled to reclose it. She was losing. The door inched open. She saw the shadowy outline of the malformed face. The sharply pointed teeth gleamed dully. The amber eyes were faint now, barely visible. It hissed and snarled at her, and its pungent breath was stronger than the scent of straw.

Whimpering in terror and frustration, Tracy drew back on the door with all of her strength.

But it opened another inch.

And another.

Her heart was hammering loud enough to muffle the first shotgun blast. She didn't know what she'd heard until a second shot boomed through the night, and then she knew her father had grabbed his 12-gauge on the way out of the house.

The stall door slammed shut in front of her as the attacker, frightened by the gunfire, let go of it. Tracy held fast.

Then she thought that maybe, in all the confusion, Daddy might believe that Goodheart was to blame, that the poor horse had gone loco or something. From within the stall she cried out, "Don't shoot Goodheart! Don't shoot the horse!"

No more shots rang out, and Tracy immediately felt stupid for thinking her father would blow away Goodheart. Daddy was a cautious man, especially with loaded guns, and unless he knew exactly what was happening, he wouldn't fire anything but warning shots. More likely than not, he'd just blasted some shrubbery to bits.

Goodheart was probably all right, and the amber-eyed assailant was surely hightailing it for the foothills or the canyons or back to wherever it had come from—

(What *was* that crazy damn thing?)

—and the ordeal was over, thank God.

She heard running footsteps, and her father called her name.

She pushed open the stall door and saw Daddy rushing toward her in a pair of blue pajama bottoms, barefoot, with the shotgun cradled in his arm. Mom was there too, in a short yellow nightie, hurrying behind Daddy with a flashlight.

Up near the top of the sloped yard stood Goodheart, the sire of future champions, his panic gone, unhurt.

Tears of relief sprang from Tracy at the sight of the unharmed stallion, and she stumbled out of the stall, wanting to go have a closer look at him. With her second or third step, a fiercely hot pain flamed along her entire right side and she was suddenly dizzy. She staggered, fell, put one hand to her side, felt something wet, and realized that she was bleeding. She remembered the claws sinking into her just before Goodheart had burst from his stall, frightening off the assailant, and as if from a great distance she heard herself saying, "Good horse ... what a good horse ..."

Daddy dropped to his knees beside her. "Baby, what the hell happened, what's wrong?"

Her mother arrived too.

Daddy saw the blood. "Call an ambulance!"

Her mother, not given to hesitation or hysterics in time of trouble, turned immediately and ran back toward the house.

Tracy was getting dizzier. Creeping in at the edges of her vision was a darkness that was not part of the night. She wasn't afraid of it. It seemed like a welcoming, healing darkness.

"Baby," her father said, putting a hand on her wounds.

Weakly, realizing she was slightly delirious and wondering what she was going to say, she said, "Remember when I was very little ... just a little girl ... and I thought some horrible thing ... lived in my closet ... at night?"

He frowned worriedly. "Honey, maybe you'd better be still, be quiet and still."

As she lost consciousness, Tracy heard herself say, with a seriousness that both amused and frightened her, "Well ... I think maybe it was the boogeyman who used to live in the closet at the other house. I think maybe ... he was real ... and he's come back."

At four-twenty Wednesday morning, only hours after the attack at the Keeshan house, Lemuel Johnson reached Tracy Keeshan's hospital room at St. Joseph's in Santa Ana. Quick as he was, however, Lem found Sheriff Walt Gaines had arrived ahead of him. Walt stood in the corridor, towering over a young doctor in surgical greens and a white lab coat; they seemed to be arguing quietly.

The NSA's Banodyne crisis team was monitoring all police agencies in the county, including the police department in the city of Orange, in whose jurisdiction the Keeshan house fell. The team's night-shift leader had called Lem at home with news of this case, which fitted the profile of expected Banodyne-related incidents.

"You relinquished jurisdiction," Lem pointedly reminded Walt when he joined the sheriff and doctor at the girl's closed door.

"Maybe this isn't part of the same case."

"You know it is."

"Well, that determination hasn't been made."

"It *was* made—back at the Keeshans' house when I talked with your men."

"Okay, so let's say I'm just here as an observer."

"My ass," Lem said.

"What about your ass?" Walt asked, smiling.

"It's got a pain in it, and the name of the pain is Walter."

"How interesting," Walt said. "You *name* your pains. Do you give names to toothaches and headaches as well?"

"I've got a headache right now, and its name is Walter, too."

"That's too confusing, my friend. Better call the headache Bert or Harry or something."

Lem almost laughed—he loved this guy—but he knew that, in spite of their friendship, Walt would use the laughter as a lever to pry himself back into the case. So Lem remained stone-faced, though Walt obviously knew that Lem *wanted* to laugh. The game was ridiculous, but it had to be played.

The doctor, Roger Selbok, resembled a young Rod Steiger. He frowned when they raised their voices, and he possessed some of the powerful presence of Steiger, too, because his frown was enough to chasten and quiet them.

Selbok said the girl had been put through tests, had been treated for her wounds, and had been given a painkiller. She was tired. He was just about to administer a sedative to guarantee her a restful sleep, and he did not think it was a good idea for policemen of any stripe to be asking her questions just now.

The whispering, the early-morning hush of the hospital, the scent of disinfectants that filled the hall, and the sight of a white-robed nun gliding past was enough to make Lem uneasy. Suddenly, he was afraid that the girl was in far worse condition than he had been told, and he voiced his concern to Selbok.

"No, no. She's in pretty good shape," the doctor said. "I've sent her parents home, which I wouldn't have done if there was anything to worry about. The left side of her face is bruised, and the eye is blackened, but there's nothing serious in that. The wounds along her right side required thirty-two stitches, so we'll need to take precautions to keep the scarring to a minimum, but she's in no danger. She's had a bad scare. However, she's a bright kid, and self-reliant, so I don't think she'll suffer lasting psychological trauma. Still, I don't think it's a good idea to subject her to an interrogation tonight."

"Not an interrogation," Lem said. "Just a few questions."

"Five minutes," Walt said.

"Less," Lem said.

They kept at Selbok, and at last they wore him down. "Well . . . I guess you've got your job to do, and if you promise not to be too insistent with her—"

"I'll handle her as if she's made of soap bubbles," Lem said.

"*We'll* handle her as if she's made of soap bubbles," Walt said.

Selbok said, "Just tell me . . . what the devil happened to her?"

185

"She hasn't told you herself?" Lem asked.

"Well, she talks about being attacked by a coyote ..."

Lem was surprised, and he saw Walt was startled, too. Maybe the case had nothing to do with Wes Dalberg's death and the dead animals at the Irvine Park petting zoo, after all.

"But," the physician said, "no coyote would attack a girl as big as Tracy. They're only a danger to very small children. And I don't believe her wounds are like those a coyote would inflict."

Walt said, "I understand her father drove the assailant off with a shotgun. Doesn't he know what attacked her?"

"No," Selbok said. "He couldn't see what was happening in the dark, so he only fired two warning shots. He says something dashed across the yard, leaped the fence, but he couldn't see any details. He says that Tracy first told him it was the boogeyman who used to live in her closet, but she was delirious then. She told *me* it was a coyote. So ... do you know what's going on here? Can you tell me anything I need to know to treat the girl?"

"I can't," Walt said. "But Mr. Johnson here knows the whole situation."

"Thanks a lot," Lem said.

Walt just smiled.

To Selbok, Lem said, "I'm sorry, Doctor, but I'm not at liberty to discuss the case. Anyway, nothing I could tell you would alter the treatment you'd give Tracy Keeshan."

When Lem and Walt finally got into Tracy's hospital room, leaving Dr. Selbok in the corridor to time their visit, they found a pretty thirteen-year-old who was badly bruised and as pale as snow. She was in bed, the sheets pulled up to her shoulders. Though she had been given painkillers, she was alert, even edgy, and it was obvious why Selbok wanted to give her a sedative. She was trying not to show it, but she was scared.

"I wish you'd leave," Lem told Walt Gaines.

"If wishes were filet mignon, we'd always eat well at dinner," Walt said. "Hi, Tracy, I'm Sheriff Walt Gaines, and this is Lemuel Johnson. I'm about as nice as they come, though Lem here is a real stinker—everybody says so — but you don't have to worry because I'll keep him in line and make him be nice to you. Okay?"

Together, they coaxed Tracy into a conversation. They quickly discovered that she'd told Selbok she'd been attacked by a coyote because, though she knew it wasn't true, she didn't believe she could convince the physician— or anyone else—of the truth of what she'd seen. "I was afraid they'd think I'd been hit real hard on the head, had my brains scrambled," she said, "and then they'd keep me here a lot longer."

Sitting on the edge of the girl's bed, Lem said, "Tracy, you don't have to worry that I'll think you're scrambled. I believe I know what you saw, and all I want from you is confirmation."

She stared at him disbelievingly.

Walt stood at the foot of her bed, smiling down at her as if he were a big, affectionate teddy bear come to life. He said, "Before you passed out, you told your dad you'd been attacked by the boogeyman who used to live in your closet."

"It was sure ugly enough," the girl said quietly. "But that's not what it was, I guess."

"Tell me," Lem said.

She stared at Walt, at Lem, then sighed. "You tell me what you think I should've seen, and if you're close, I'll tell you what I can remember. But I'm not going to start it 'cause I know you'll think I'm looney tunes."

Lem regarded Walt with unconcealed frustration, realizing there was no way to avoid divulging some of the facts of the case.

Walt grinned.

To the girl, Lem said, "Yellow eyes."

She gasped and went rigid. "Yes! You do know, don't you! You know what was out there." She started to sit up, winced in pain as she pulled the stitches in her wound, and slumped back against the bed. "What was it, what *was* it?"

"Tracy," Lem said, "I can't tell you what it was. I've signed a secrecy oath. If I violated it, I could be put in jail, but more important ... I wouldn't have much respect for myself."

She frowned, finally nodded. "I guess I can understand that."

"Good. Now tell me everything you can about your assailant."

As it turned out, she had not seen much because the night was dark and her flashlight had illuminated The Outsider for only an instant. "Pretty big for an animal ... maybe as big as me. The yellow eyes." She shuddered. "And its face was ... strange."

"In what way?"

"Lumpy ... deformed," the girl said. Though she had been very pale at the start, she grew paler now, and fine beads of sweat appeared along her hairline, dampening her brow.

Walt was leaning on the footrail of the bed, straining forward, intensely interested, not wanting to miss a word.

A sudden Santa Ana wind buffeted the building, startling the girl. She looked fearfully at the rattling window, where the wind moaned, as if she was afraid something would come smashing through the glass.

Which was, Lem reminded himself, exactly how The Outsider had gotten to Wes Dalberg.

The girl swallowed hard. "Its mouth was huge ... and the teeth ..."

She could not stop shaking, and Lem put a reassuring hand on her shoulder. "It's okay, honey. It's over now. It's all behind you."

After a pause to regain control of herself, but still shivering, Tracy said, "I think it was kind of hairy ... or furry ... I'm not sure, but it was very strong."

"What kind of animal did it resemble?" Lem asked.

She shook her head. "It wasn't like anything else."

"But if you had to say it was like some other animal, would you say it was more like a cougar than anything else?"

"No. Not a cougar."

"Like a dog?"

She hesitated. "Maybe . . . a little bit like a dog."

"Maybe a little bit like a bear, too?"

"No."

"Like a panther?"

"No. Not like any cat."

"Like a monkey?"

She hesitated again, frowned, thinking. "I don't know why . . . but, yeah, maybe a little like a monkey. Except, no dog and no monkey has *teeth* like that."

The door opened from the hall, and Dr. Selbok appeared. "You're already past five minutes."

Walt started to wave the doctor out.

Lem said, "No, it's okay. We're finished. Half a minute yet."

"I'm counting the seconds," Selbok said, retreating.

To the girl Lem said, "Can I rely on you?"

She matched his gaze and said, "To keep quiet?"

Lem nodded.

She said, "Yeah. I sure don't *want* to tell anybody. My folks think I'm mature for my age. Mentally and emotionally mature, I mean. But if I start telling wild stories about . . . about monsters, they're going to think I'm not so mature after all, and maybe they'll figure I'm not responsible enough to take care of the horses, and so maybe they'll slow down the breeding plans. I won't risk that, Mr. Johnson. No, sir. So as far as I'm concerned, it was a loco coyote. But . . ."

"Yes?"

"Can you tell me . . . is there any chance it'll come back?"

"I don't think so. But it would be wise, for a while, not to go out to the stable at night. All right?"

"All right," she said. Judging by her haunted expression, she would remain indoors after dusk for weeks to come.

They left the room, thanked Dr. Selbok for his cooperation, and went down to the hospital's parking garage. Dawn had not yet arrived, and the cavernous concrete structure was empty, desolate. Their footsteps echoed hollowly off the walls.

Their cars were on the same floor, and Walt accompanied Lem to the green, unmarked NSA sedan. As Lem put the key in the door to unlock it, Walt looked around to be sure they were alone, then said, "Tell me."

"Can't."

"I'll find out."

"You're off the case."

"So take me to court. Get a bench warrant."

"I might."

"For endangering the national security."

"It would be a fair charge."

"Throw my ass in jail."

"I might," Lem said, though he knew he would not.

Curiously, though Walt's doggedness was frustrating and more than a little irritating, it was also pleasing to Lem. He had few friends, of which Walt was the most important, and he liked to think the reason he had few friends was because he was selective, with high standards. If Walt had backed off entirely, if he had been completely cowed by federal authority, if he'd been able to turn off his curiosity as easily as turning off a light switch, he would have been slightly tarnished and diminished in Lem's eyes.

"What reminds you of a dog *and* an ape and has yellow eyes?" Walt asked. "Aside from your mama, that is."

"You leave my mama out of this, honky," Lem said. Smiling in spite of himself, he got into the car.

Walt held the door open and leaned down to look in at him. "What in the name of God escaped from Banodyne?"

"I told you this has nothing to do with Banodyne."

"And the fire they had at the labs the next day . . . did they set it themselves to destroy the evidence of what they'd been up to?"

"Don't be ridiculous," Lem said wearily, thrusting the key into the ignition. "Evidence could be destroyed in a more efficient and less drastic manner. *If* there was evidence to destroy. Which there isn't. Because Banodyne has nothing to do with this."

Lem started the car, but Walt would not give up. He held the door open and leaned in even closer to be heard above

190

the rumble of the engine: "Genetic engineering. That's what they're involved with at Banodyne. Tinkering with bacteria and virus to make new bugs that do good deeds like manufacture insulin or eat oil slicks. And they tinker with the genes of plants as well, I guess, to produce corn that grows in acidic soil or wheat that thrives with half the usual water. We always think of gene tinkering as being done on a small scale—plants and germs. But could they screw around with an animal's genes so it produced bizarre offspring, a whole new species! Is that what they've done, and is that what's escaped from Banodyne?"

Lem shook his head exasperatedly. "Walt, I'm not an expert on recombinant DNA, but I don't think the science is nearly sophisticated enough to work with any degree of confidence on that sort of thing. And what would be the point anyway! Okay, just supposing they could make a weird new animal by fiddling with the genetic structure of an existing species— what *use* would there be for it! I mean, aside from exhibition in a carnival freak show?"

Walt's eyes narrowed. "I don't know. You tell me."

"Listen, research money is always damn tight, and there's fierce competition for every major and minor grant, so no one's going to be able to afford to experiment with something that has no *use*. Get me? Now, because I'm involved here, you know this has to be a matter of national defense, which would mean Banodyne was squandering Pentagon money to make a carnival freak."

"The words 'squander' and 'Pentagon' have sometimes been used in the same sentence," Walt said drily.

"Be real, Walt. It's one thing for the Pentagon to let some of its contractors waste money in the production of a needed weapons system. But it's altogether another thing for them to knowingly hand out funds for experiments with no defense potential. The system is sometimes inefficient, sometimes even corrupt, but it's never outright stupid. Anyway, I'll say it one more time: This entire conversation is pointless because *this has nothing to do with Banodyne.*"

Walt stared in at him for a long moment, then sighed. "Jesus, Lem, you're good. I know you've got to be lying to me, but I half-think you're telling the truth."

"I am telling the truth."

"You're good. So tell me ... what about Weatherby, Yarbeck, and the others? Got their killer yet?"

"No." In fact, the man Lem had put in charge of the case had reported that it appeared as if the Soviets had used a killer outside of their own agencies and perhaps outside of the political world entirely. The investigation seemed stymied. But all he said to Walt was, "No."

Walt started to straighten up and close the car door, then leaned down and in again. "One more thing. You notice it seems to have a meaningful destination?"

"What're you talking about?"

"It's been moving steadily north or north-north-west ever since it broke out of Banodyne," Walt said.

"It didn't break out of Banodyne, damn it."

"From Banodyne to Holy Jim Canyon, from there to Irvine Park, and from there to the Keeshan house tonight. Steadily north or north-north-west. I suppose you know what that might mean, where it might be headed, but of course I daren't ask you about it or you'll heave me straight into prison and let me rot there."

"I'm telling you the truth about Banodyne."

"So you say."

"You're impossible, Walt."

"So *everyone* says. Now will you let me go home? I'm beat."

Smiling, Walt closed the door at last.

Lem drove out of the hospital garage to Main Street, then to the freeway, heading home toward Placentia. He hoped to make it back into bed no later than dawn.

As he piloted the NSA sedan through streets as empty as midocean sealanes, he thought about The Outsider heading northward. He'd noticed the same thing himself. And he was convinced that he knew what it was seeking even if he did not know where, precisely, it was going. From the first, the dog and The Outsider had possessed a special awareness of each other, an uncanny instinctual awareness of each other's moods and activities even when they were not in the same room. Davis Weatherby had suggested, more than half seriously, that there was something telepathic about the relationship of those two creatures. Now, The Outsider was very likely still in tune with the dog and, by some sixth sense, was following it.

For the dog's sake, Lem hoped to God that was not the case.

It had been evident in the lab that the dog had always feared The Outsider, and with good reason. The two were the yin and yang of the Francis Project, the success and the failure, the good and the bad. As wonderful, right, and good as the dog was—well, The Outsider was every bit as hideous, wrong, and evil. And the researchers had seen that The Outsider did not fear the dog but *hated* it with a passion that no one had been able to understand. Now that both were free, The Outsider might single-mindedly pursue the dog, for it had never wanted anything more than to tear the retriever limb from limb.

Lem realized that, in his anxiety, he had put his foot down too hard on the accelerator. The car was rocketing along the freeway. He eased back on the pedal.

Wherever the dog was, with whomever it had found shelter, it was in jeopardy. And those who had given it shelter were also in grave danger.

SIX

1

Through the last week of May and the first week of June, Nora and Travis—and Einstein—were together nearly every day.

Initially, she had worried that Travis was somehow dangerous, not as dangerous as Art Streck but still to be feared; however, she'd soon gotten through that spell of paranoia. Now she laughed at herself when she remembered how wary of him she had been. He was sweet and kind, precisely the sort of man who, according to her Aunt Violet, did not exist anywhere in the world.

Once Nora's paranoia had been overcome, she'd then been convinced that the only reason Travis continued to see her was because he pitied her. Being the compassionate man he was, he would not be able to turn his back on anyone in desperate need or trouble. Most people, meeting Nora, would not think of her as desperate—perhaps strange and shy and pathetic, but not desperate. Yet she was—or had been—desperately unable to cope with the world beyond her own four walls, desperately afraid of the future, and desperately lonely. Travis, being every bit as perceptive as he was kind, saw her desperation and responded to it. Gradually, as May faded into June and the days grew hotter under the summer sun, she dared to consider the possibility that he was helping her not because he pitied her but because he really liked her.

But she couldn't understand what a man like him would see in a woman like her. She seemed to have nothing whatsoever to offer.

All right, yes, she had a self-image problem. Maybe she was not really as hopelessly drab and dull as she felt. Still, Travis clearly deserved—and could surely have—better female companionship than she could provide.

She decided not to question his interest. The thing to do was just relax and enjoy it.

Because Travis had sold his real-estate business after the death of his wife and was essentially retired, and because Nora had no job either, they were free to be together most of the day if they wanted—and they were. They went to galleries, haunted bookstores, took long walks, went on longer drives into the picturesque Santa Ynez Valley or up along the gorgeous Pacific coast.

Twice they set out early in the morning for Los Angeles and spent a long day there, and Nora was as overwhelmed by the sheer size of the city as she was by the activities they pursued: a movie-studio tour, a visit to the zoo, and a matinée performance of a hit musical.

One day Travis talked her into having her hair cut and styled. He took her to a beauty parlor that his late wife had frequented, and Nora was so nervous that she stuttered when she spoke to the beautician, a perky blonde named Melanie. Violet always cut Nora's hair at home, and after Violet's death, Nora cut it herself. Being tended by a beautician was a new experience, as unnerving as eating in a restaurant for the first time. Melanie did something she called "feathering", and cut off a lot of Nora's hair while somehow still leaving it full. They did not allow Nora to watch in the mirror, did not let her get a glimpse of herself until she was blown dry and combed out. Then they spun her around in the chair and confronted her with herself, and when she saw her reflection, she was stunned.

"You look terrific," Travis said.

"It's a total transformation," Melanie said.

"Terrific," Travis said.

"You've got such a pretty face, great bone structure," Melanie said, "but all that straight, long hair made your face look elongated and pointy. *This* frames your face to its best advantage."

Even Einstein seemed to like the change in her. When they left the beauty shop, the dog was waiting for them where they had left him tethered to a parking meter. He did a canine double-take when he saw Nora, jumped up with his front paws on her, and sniffed her face and hair, whining happily and wagging his tail.

She hated the new look. When they had turned her to the mirror, she'd seen a pathetic old maid trying to pass for a pretty, vivacious young thing. The styled hair was simply not *her.* It only emphasized that she was basically a plain, drab woman. She would never be sexy, charming, with-it, or any of the other things that the new hairstyle tried to say she was. It was rather like fastening a brightly colored feather duster to the back end of a turkey and attempting to pass it off as a peacock.

Because she did not want to hurt Travis's feelings, she pretended to like what had been done to her. But that night she washed her hair and brushed it dry, pulling on it until all the so-called style had been tugged from it. Because of the feathering, it did not hang as straight and lank as it had previously, but she did the best with it that she could.

The next day, when Travis picked her up for lunch, he was clearly startled to find that she had reverted to her previous look. However, he said nothing about it, asked no questions. She was so embarrassed and afraid of having hurt his feelings that, for the first couple of hours, she was not able to meet his eyes for more than a second or two at a time.

In spite of her repeated and increasingly vigorous demurrals, Travis insisted on taking her shopping for a new dress, a bright and summery frock that she could wear to dinner at Talk of the Town, a dressy restaurant on West Gutierrez, where he said you could sometimes see some of the movie stars who lived in the area, members of a film colony second only to that in Beverly Hills—Bel Air. They went to an expensive store, where she tried on a score of dresses, modeling each for Travis's reaction, blushing and *mortified*. The saleswoman seemed genuinely approving of the way everything looked on Nora, and she kept telling Nora that her figure was perfect, but Nora couldn't shake the feeling that the woman was laughing at her.

The dress Travis liked best was from the Diane Freis collection. Nora couldn't deny that it was lovely: predominantly red and gold, though with an almost riotous background of other colors somehow more right in combination than they should have been (which apparently was a trait of Freis's designs). It was exceedingly feminine. On a beautiful woman it would have been a knockout. But it just was not *her*. Dark colors, shapeless cuts, simple fabrics, no ornamentation whatsoever—that was her style. She tried to tell him what was best for her, explained that she could never wear such a dress as this, but he said, "You look gorgeous in it, really, you look gorgeous."

She let him buy it. Dear God, she really did. She knew it was a big mistake, was wrong, and that she would never wear it. As the dress was being wrapped, Nora wondered why she had acquiesced, and she realized that, in spite of being mortified, she was flattered to have a man buying clothes for her, to have a man take an interest in her appearance. She never dreamed such a thing would happen to her, and she was overwhelmed.

She couldn't stop blushing. Her heart pounded. She felt dizzy, but it was a good dizziness.

Then, as they were leaving the store, she learned that he had paid five hundred dollars for the dress. Five hundred dollars! She had intended to hang it in the closet and look at it a lot, use it as a starting point for pleasant daydreams, which was all fine and dandy if it had cost fifty dollars, but for five hundred she would have to wear it even if it made her feel ridiculous, even if she did look like a poseur, a scrubwoman pretending to be a princess.

The following evening, during the two hours before Travis was to pick her up and escort her to Talk of the Town, she put the dress on and took it off a half dozen times. She repeatedly sorted through the contents of her closet, searching frantically for something else to wear, something more sensible, but she didn't have anything because she had never before needed clothes for a dressy restaurant.

Scowling at herself in the bathroom mirror, she said, "You look like Dustin Hoffman in *Tootsie*."

She suddenly laughed because she knew she was being too hard on herself. But she couldn't go easier on herself because that was how she felt: like a guy in drag. In this case, feelings were more important than facts, so her laughter quickly soured.

She broke down and cried twice, and considered calling him to cancel their date. But she wanted more than anything to see him, no matter how horribly humiliating the evening was going to be. She used Murine to get the red out of her eyes, and she tried the dress on again—and took it off.

When he arrived at a few minutes past seven, he looked handsome in a dark suit.

Nora was wearing a shapeless blue shift with dark-blue shoes.

He said, "I'll wait."

She said, "Huh? For what?"

"You know," he said, meaning, *Go change*.

The words came out in a nervous rush, and her excuse was limp: "Travis, I'm sorry, this is terrible, I'm so sorry, but I spilled coffee all over the dress."

"I'll wait in here," he said, walking to the living room archway.

She said, "A whole pot of coffee."

"Better hurry. Our reservation is for seven-thirty."

Steeling herself for the amused whispers if not outright laughter of everyone who saw her, telling herself that Travis's opinion was the only one that mattered, she changed into the Diane Freis dress.

She wished she had not undone the hairstyle that Melanie had given her a couple of days ago. Maybe that would help.

No, it would probably just make her look more ludicrous.

When she came downstairs again, Travis smiled at her and said, "You're lovely."

She didn't know whether the food at Talk of the Town was as good as its reputation or not. She tasted nothing. Later, she could not clearly remember the decor of the place, either, though the faces of the other customers—including the actor Gene Hackman—were burned into her memory because she was certain that, all evening, they were staring at her with amazement and disdain.

In the middle of dinner, evidently well aware of her discomfort, Travis put down his wineglass and leaned toward her and said quietly, "You really *do* look lovely, Nora, no matter what you think. And if you had the experience to be aware of such things, you'd realize that most of the men in the room are attracted to you."

But she knew the truth, and she could face it. If men really were staring at her, it was not because she was pretty. People could be expected to stare at a turkey with a feather duster trying to pass itself off as a peacock.

"Without a trace of makeup," he said, "you look better than any woman in the room."

No makeup. That was another reason they were staring at her. When a woman put on a five-hundred-dollar dress to be taken to an expensive restaurant, she made herself look as good as possible with lipstick, eyeliner, makeup, skin blush, and God knew what else. But Nora had never even *thought* about makeup.

The chocolate mousse dessert, though surely delicious, tasted like library paste to her and repeatedly stuck in her throat.

She and Travis had talked for long hours during the past couple of weeks, and they had found it surprisingly easy to reveal intimate feelings and thoughts to each other. She had learned why he was alone in spite of his good looks and relative wealth, and he had learned why she harbored a low opinion of herself. So when she could not choke down any more of the mousse, when she implored Travis to take her home right away, he said softly, "If there's any justice, Violet Devon is sweating in Hell tonight."

Shocked, Nora said, "Oh, no. She wasn't *that* bad."

All the way home, he was silent, brooding.

When he left her at her door, he insisted she set up a meeting with Garrison Dilworth, who had been her aunt's attorney and now took care of Nora's minor legal business. "From what you've told me," Travis said, "Dilworth knew your aunt better than anyone, so I'd bet dollars to doughnuts he can tell you things about her that will break this goddamn stranglehold she had on you even from the grave."

Nora said, "But there're no great dark secrets about Aunt Violet. She was what she appeared to be. She was a very simple woman, really. A sort of sad woman."

"Sad my ass," Travis said.

He persisted until she agreed to make the appointment with Garrison Dilworth.

Later, upstairs in her bedroom, when she tried to take off the Diane Freis, she discovered she didn't want to undress. All evening, she had been impatient to get out of that costume, for it *had* seemed like a costume on her. But now, in retrospect, the evening possessed a warm glow, and she wanted to prolong that glow. Like a sentimental high school girl, she slept in the five-hundred-dollar dress.

Garrison Dilworth's office had been carefully decorated to convey respectability, stability, and reliability. Beautifully detailed oak paneling. Heavy royal-blue drapes hung from brass rods. Shelves full of leather-bound law books. A massive oak desk.

The attorney himself was an intriguing cross between a personification of Dignity and Probity—and Santa Claus. Tall, rather portly, with thick silver hair, past seventy but still working a full week, Garrison favored three-piece suits and subdued ties. In spite of his many years as a Californian, his deep and smooth and cultured voice clearly marked him as a product of the upper-class Eastern circles in which he had been born, raised, and educated. But there was also a decidedly merry twinkle in his eyes, and his smile was quick, warm, altogether Santalike.

He did not distance himself by staying behind his desk, but sat with Nora and Travis in comfortable armchairs around a coffee table on which stood a large Waterford bowl. "I don't know what you came here expecting to learn. There are no secrets about your aunt. No great dark revelations that will change your life—"

"I knew as much," Nora said. "I'm sorry we've bothered you."

"Wait," Travis said. "Let Mr. Dilworth finish."

The attorney said, "Violet Devon was my client, and an attorney has a responsibility to protect clients' confidences even after their death. At least that's my view, though some in the profession might not feel such a lasting obligation. Of course, as I'm speaking to Violet's closest living relative and heir, I suppose there's little I would choose not to divulge—if in fact there *were* any secrets to reveal. And I certainly see no moral constraint against my expressing an honest opinion of your aunt. Even attorneys, priests, and doctors are allowed to have opinions of people." He took a deep breath and frowned. "I never liked her. I thought she was a narrow-minded, totally self-involved woman who was at least slightly . . . well, mentally unstable. And the way she raised you was criminal, Nora. Not abusive in any legal sense that would interest the authorities, but criminal nonetheless. And cruel."

For as long as Nora could recall, a large knot had seemed to be tied tight inside of her, pinching vital organs and vessels, leaving her tense, restricting the flow of blood and making it necessary for her to live with all her senses damped down, forcing her to struggle along as if she were a machine getting insufficient power. Suddenly, Garrison Dilworth's words untied that knot, and a full, unrestricted current of life rushed through her for the first time.

She had known what Violet Devon had done to her, but knowing was not enough to help her overcome that grim upbringing. She needed to hear her aunt condemned by someone else. Travis had already denounced Violet, and Nora had felt some small release at hearing what he said. But that had not been enough to free her because Travis hadn't known Violet and, therefore, spoke without complete authority. Garrison knew Violet well, however, and his words released Nora from bondage.

She was trembling violently, and tears were trickling down her face, but she was unaware of both conditions until Travis reached out from his chair to put one hand consolingly upon her shoulder. She fumbled in her purse for a handkerchief. "I'm sorry."

"Dear lady," Garrison said, "don't apologize for breaking through that iron shell you've been in all your life. This is the first time I've seen you show a strong emotion, the first time I've seen you in any condition other than extreme shyness, and it's lovely to behold." Turning to Travis, giving Nora time to blot her eyes, he said, "What more *did* you hope to hear me say?"

"There are some things Nora doesn't know, things she ought to know and that I don't believe would violate even your strict code of client privilege if you were to divulge them."

"Such as?"

Travis said, "Violet Devon never worked yet lived reasonably well, never in want, and she left enough funds to keep Nora pretty much for the rest of her life, at least as long as Nora stays in that house and lives like a recluse. Where did her money come from?"

"Come from?" Garrison sounded surprised. "Nora knows that, surely."

"But she doesn't," Travis said.

Nora looked up and saw Garrison Dilworth staring at her in astonishment. He blinked and said, "Violet's husband was moderately well-to-do. He died quite young, and she inherited everything."

Nora gaped at him and could barely find sufficient

breath to speak. "*Husband?*"

"George Olmstead," the attorney said.

"I've never heard that name."

Garrison blinked rapidly again, as if sand had blown in his face. "She never mentioned a husband?"

"Never."

"But didn't a neighbor ever mention—"

"We had nothing to do with our neighbors," Nora said. "Violet didn't approve of them."

"And in fact," Garrison said, "now that I think about it, there might have been new neighbors on both sides by the time you came to live with Violet."

Nora blew her nose and put away her handkerchief. She was still trembling. Her sudden sense of release from bondage had generated powerful emotions, but now they subsided somewhat to make room for curiosity.

"All right?" Travis asked.

She nodded, then stared hard at him and said, "You knew, didn't you? About the husband, I mean. That's why you brought me here."

"I suspected," Travis said. "If she'd inherited everything from her parents, she would have mentioned it. The fact that she didn't talk about where the money came from ... well, it seemed to me to leave only one possibility—a husband, and very likely a husband with whom she'd had troubles. Which made even more sense when you think about how down she was on people in general and on men in particular."

The attorney was so dismayed and agitated that he could not sit still. He got up and paced past an enormous antique globe that was lighted from within and seemed made of parchment. "I'm flabbergasted. So you never really understood *why* she was bitterly misanthropic, why she suspected everyone of having her worst interests at heart?"

"No," Nora said. "I didn't need to know why, I guess. It was just the way she was."

Still pacing, Garrison said, "Yes. That's true. I'm convinced she was a borderline paranoid even in her youth. And then, when she discovered that George had betrayed her with other women, the switch clicked all the way over in her. She got much worse after that."

Travis said, "Why did Violet still use her maiden name, Devon, if she'd been married to Olmstead?"

"She didn't want his name any more. Loathed the name. She sent him packing, very nearly drove him out of the house with a stick! She was about to divorce him when he died," Garrison said. "She had learned about his affairs with other women, as I've said. She was furious. Ashamed and enraged. I must say ... I can't entirely blame poor George because I don't think he found much love and affection at home. He knew the marriage was a mistake within a month of the wedding."

Garrison paused beside the globe, one hand resting lightly on top of the world, staring far into the past. Ordinarily, he did not look his age. Now, as he gazed back across the years, the lines in his face seemed to deepen, and his blue eyes appeared faded. After a moment he shook his head and continued:

"Anyway, those were different times, when a woman betrayed by a husband was an object of pity, ridicule. But even for those days, I thought Violet's reaction was overblown. She burned all his clothes and changed the locks on the house ... she even killed a dog, a spaniel, of which he was fond. Poisoned it. And mailed it to him in a box."

"Dear God," Travis said.

Garrison said, "Violet took back her maiden name because she didn't want his any more. The thought of carrying George Olmstead's name through life repelled her, she said, even though he was dead. She was an unforgiving woman."

"Yes," Nora agreed.

His face pinched with distaste at the memory, Garrison said, "When George was killed, she didn't bother to conceal her pleasure."

"Killed?" Nora half expected to hear that Violet had murdered George Olmstead yet had somehow escaped prosecution.

"It was in an auto accident, forty years ago," Garrison

said. "He lost control on the Coast Highway driving home from Los Angeles, went over the edge where, in those days, there wasn't a guardrail. The embankment was sixty or eighty feet high, very steep, and George's car—a large black Packard—rolled over several times on the way down to the rocks below. Violet inherited everything because, though she had initiated divorce proceedings against him, George had not gotten around to changing his will."

Travis said, "So George Olmstead not only betrayed Violet but, in dying, left her with no target for her anger. So she directed that anger at the world in general."

"And at me in particular," Nora said.

That same afternoon, Nora told Travis about her painting. She had not mentioned her artistic pursuits before, and he had not been in her bedroom to see her easel, supply cabinet, and drawing board. She was not sure why she had kept this aspect of her life a secret from him. She had mentioned an interest in art, which was why they had gone to galleries and museums, but perhaps she had never spoken of her own work because she was afraid that, on seeing her canvases, he would be unimpressed.

What if he felt that she had no real talent?

Aside from the escape provided by books, the thing that kept Nora going through many grim, lonely years was her painting. She believed that she was good, perhaps very good, though she was too shy and too vulnerable to voice that conviction to anyone. What if she was wrong? What if she had no talent and had been merely filling time? Her art was the primary medium by which she defined herself. She had little else with which to sustain even her thin and shaky self-image, so she desperately needed to believe in her talent. Travis's opinion meant more to her than she could say, and if his reaction to her painting was negative, she would be devastated.

But after leaving Garrison Dilworth's office, Nora knew that the time had come to take the risk. The truth about

Violet Devon had been a key that had unlocked Nora's emotional prison. She would need a long time to move from her cell, down the long hall to the outside world but the journey would inevitably continue. Therefore, she would have to open herself to all the experiences that her new life provided, including the awful possibility of rejection and severe disappointment. Without risk, there was no hope of gain.

Back at the house, she considered taking Travis upstairs to have a look at a half dozen of her most recent paintings. But the idea of having a man in her bedroom, even with the most innocent intentions, was too unsettling. Garrison Dilworth's revelations freed her, yes, and her world was rapidly broadening, but she was not yet *that* free. Instead, she insisted that Travis and Einstein sit on one of the big sofas in the furniture-stuffed living room, where she would bring some of her canvases for viewing. She turned on all the lights, drew the drapes away from the windows, and said, "I'll be right back."

But upstairs she dithered over the ten paintings in her bedroom, unable to decide which two she should take to him first. Finally she settled on four pieces, though it was a bit awkward carrying that many at once. Halfway down the stairs, she halted, trembling, and decided to take the paintings back and select others. But she retreated only four steps before she realized that she could spend the entire day in vacillation. Reminding herself that nothing could be gained without risk, she took a deep breath and went quickly downstairs with the four paintings that she had originally chosen.

Travis liked them. More than liked them. He raved about them. "My God, Nora, this is no hobby painting. This is the real thing. This is *art*."

She propped the paintings on four chairs, and he was not content to study them from the sofa. He got up for a closer look, moved from one canvas to another and back again.

"You're a superb photorealist," he said. "Okay, so I'm no art critic, but by God you're as skilled as Wyeth. But this other thing ... this eerie quality in two of these ... "

His compliments had left her blushing furiously, and she had to swallow hard to find her voice. "A touch of surrealism."

She had brought two landscapes and two still lifes. One of each was, indeed, strictly a photorealist work. But the other two were photorealism with a strong element of surrealism. In the still life, for example, several water glasses, a pitcher, spoons, and a sliced lemon were on a table, portrayed in excruciating detail, and at first glance the scene looked very realistic; but at second glance you noticed that one of the glasses was melting into the surface on which it stood, and that one slice of lemon was penetrating the side of a glass as if the glass had been formed around it.

"They're brilliant, they really are," he said. "Do you have others?"

Did she have *others*!

She made two additional trips to her bedroom, returning with six more paintings.

With each new canvas, Travis's excitement grew. His delight and enthusiasm were genuine, too. Initially she thought that he might be humoring her, but soon she was certain he was not disguising his true reaction.

Moving from canvas to canvas and back again, he said, "Your sense of color is excellent."

Einstein accompanied Travis around the room, adding a soft woof after each of his master's statements and vigorously wagging his tail, as if expressing agreement with the assessment.

"There's such mood in these pieces," Travis said.

"Woof."

"Your control of the medium is astonishing. I've no sense that I'm looking at thousands of brush strokes. Instead, it seems as if the picture just *appeared* on the canvas magically."

"Woof."

"It's hard to believe you've had no formal schooling."

"Woof."

"Nora, these are easily good enough to sell. Any gallery

would take these in a minute."

"Woof."

"You could not only make a living at this . . . I think you could build one hell of a reputation."

Because she had not dared to admit how seriously she had always taken her work, Nora had often painted one picture over another, using a canvas again and again. As a consequence, many of her pieces were gone forever. But in the attic she had stored more than eighty of her best paintings. Now, because Travis insisted, they brought down more than a score of those wrapped canvases, tore off the brown paper, and propped them on the living-room furniture. For the first time in Nora's memory, that dark chamber looked bright and welcoming.

"Any gallery would be delighted to do a show of these," Travis said. "In fact, tomorrow, let's load some of them into the truck and take them around to a few galleries, hear what they say."

"Oh no, no."

"I promise you, Nora, you won't be disappointed."

She was suddenly in the clutches of anxiety. Although thrilled by the prospect of a career in art, she was also frightened by the big step she would be taking. Like walking off the edge of a cliff.

She said, "Not yet. In a week . . . or a month . . . we'll load them in the truck and take them to a gallery. But not yet, Travis. I just can't . . . I can't handle it yet."

He grinned at her. "Sensory overload again?"

Einstein came to her and rubbed against her leg, looking up with a sweet expression that made Nora smile.

Scratching behind the dog's ears, she said, "So much has happened so fast. I can't absorb it all. I keep having to fight off attacks of dizziness. I feel a little bit as if I'm on a carousel that's whirling around faster and faster, out of control."

What she said was true, to an extent, but that was not the only reason, she wished to delay going public with her art. She also wanted to move slowly in order to have time to savor every glorious development. If she rushed into things,

209

the transformation from reclusive spinster to a full-fledged participant in life would go too fast, and later it would be just a blur. She wanted to enjoy every moment of her metamorphosis.

As if she were an invalid who had been confined since birth to a single dark room full of life-support equipment, and as if she had just been miraculously cured, Nora Devon was coming cautiously out into a new world.

Travis was not solely responsible for Nora's emergence from reclusion. Einstein had an equally large role in her transformation.

The retriever had obviously decided that Nora could be trusted with the secret of his extraordinary intelligence. After the *Modern Bride* and baby business in Solvang, the dog gave her glimpse after glimpse of his undoglike mind at work.

Taking his lead from Einstein, Travis told Nora how he had found the retriever in the woods and how something strange—and never seen—had been pursuing it. He recounted all the amazing things the dog had done since then. He also told her of Einstein's occasional bouts with anxiety in the heart of the night, when he sometimes stood at a window and stared out at the darkness as if he believed the unknown creature in the woods would find him.

They sat for hours one evening in Nora's kitchen, drinking pots of coffee and eating homemade pineapple cake and discussing explanations for the dog's uncanny intelligence. When not cadging bits of cake, Einstein listened to them with interest, as if he understood what they were saying about him, and sometimes he whined and paced impatiently, as if frustrated that his canine vocal apparatus did not permit him to speak. But they were mostly spinning their wheels because they had no explanations *worth* discussing.

"I believe he could tell us where he comes from, why he's so damn different from other dogs," Nora said.

Einstein busily swept the air with his tail.

"Oh, I'm sure of it," Travis said. "He's got a humanlike self-awareness. He *knows* he's different, and I suspect he knows why, and I think he'd like to tell us about it if he could only find a way."

The retriever barked once, ran to the far end of the kitchen, ran back, looked up at them, did a frantic little dance of purely human frustration, and finally slumped on the floor with his head on his paws, alternately chuffing and whining softly.

Nora was most intrigued by the story of the night that the dog had gotten excited over Travis's book collection. "He recognizes that books are a means of communication," she said. "And maybe he senses there's a way to use books to bridge the communications gap between him and us."

"How?" Travis asked as he lifted another forkful of pineapple cake.

Nora shrugged. "I don't know. But maybe the problem was that your books weren't the right kind. Novels, you said?"

"Yeah. Fiction."

She said, "Maybe what we need is books with pictures, images he can react to. Maybe if we gathered up a lot of picture books of all kinds, and magazines with pictures, and maybe if we spread them out on the floor and *worked* with Einstein, maybe we'd find some way to communicate with him."

The retriever leaped to his feet and padded directly to Nora. From the expression on his face and from the intent look in his eyes, Nora knew that her proposal was a good one. Tomorrow, she would collect dozens of books and magazines, and put the scheme into operation.

"It's going to take a lot of patience," Travis warned her.

"I've got oceans of patience."

"You may think you have, but sometimes dealing with Eintsein gives a whole new meaning to the word."

Turning to Travis, the dog blew air out of his nostrils.

The prospects for more direct communication looked bleak during the first few sessions with the dog on

Wednesday and Thursday, but the big breakthrough was not long in coming. Friday evening, June 4, they found the way, and after that their lives could never be the same.

2

"*. . . reports of screaming in an unfinished housing tract, Bordeaux Ridge—*"

Friday evening, June 4, less than an hour before nightfall, the sun cast gold and copper light on Orange County. It was the second day of blistering temperatures in the mid-nineties, and the stored heat of the long summer day radiated off the pavement and buildings. Trees seemed to droop wearily. The air was motionless. On the freeways and surface streets, the sound of traffic was muffled, as if the thick air filtered the roar of engines and blaring of horns.

"*—repeat, Bordeaux Ridge, under construction at the east end—*"

In the gently rolling foothills to the northeast, in an unincorporated area of the county adjacent to Yorba Linda, where the suburban sprawl had only recently begun to reach, there was little traffic. The occasional blast of a horn or squeal of brakes was not merely muffled but curiously mournful, melancholy in the humid stillness.

Sheriff's Deputies Teel Porter and Ken Dimes were in a patrol car—Teel driving, Ken riding shotgun—with a broken ventilation system: no air-conditioning, not even forced air coming out of the vents. The windows were open, but the sedan was an oven.

"You stink like a dead hog," Teel Porter told his partner.

"Yeah?" Ken Dimes said. "Well, you not only stink like a dead hog, you *look* like a dead hog."

"Yeah? Well, you *date* dead hogs."

Ken smiled in spite of the heat. "That so? Well, I hear from your women that you make *love* like a dead hog."

Their tired humor could not mask the fact that they were weary and uncomfortable. And they were answering a call that didn't promise much excitement, probably kids playing games; kids loved to play on construction sites. Both deputies were thirty-two, husky former high school football players. They weren't brothers—but, as partners for six years, they were *brothers*.

Teel turned off the county road onto a lightly oiled dirt lane that led into the Bordeaux Ridge development. About forty houses were in various stages of construction. Most were still being framed, but a few had already been stuccoed.

"Now there," Ken said, "is the kind of shit I just can't believe people fall for. I mean, hell, what kind of name is 'Bordeaux' for a housing tract in Southern California? Are they trying to make you believe there's going to be vineyards here one day? And they call it 'Ridge', but the whole tract's in this stretch of flatland between the hills. Their sign promises serenity. Maybe now. But what about when they pitch up another three thousand houses out here in the next five years?"

Teel said, "Yeah, but the part gets me is 'miniestates.' What the fuck is a *miniestate*? Nobody in his right mind would think these are estates—except maybe Russians who've spent their lives twelve to an apartment. These are tract homes."

The concrete curb gutters had been poured along the streets of Bordeaux Ridge, but the pavement had not yet been put down. Teel drove slowly, trying not to raise a lot of dust, raising it anyway. He and Ken looked left and right at the skeletal forms of unfinished houses, searching for kids who were up to no good.

To the west, at the edge of the city of Yorba Linda and adjacent to Bordeaux Ridge, were finished tracts where people already lived. From those residents the Yorba Linda Police had received calls about screaming somewhere in this embryonic development. Because the area had not yet been annexed into the city, the complaint fell into the jurisdiction of the Sheriff's Department.

213

At the end of the street, the deputies saw a white pickup that belonged to the company that owned Bordeaux: Tulemann Brothers. It was parked in front of three almost-completed display models.

"Looks like there's a foreman still here," Ken said.

"Or maybe it's the night watchman on duty a little early," Teel said.

They parked behind the truck, got out of the stiflingly hot patrol car, and stood for a moment, listening. Silence.

Ken shouted, "Hello! Anybody here?"

His voice echoed back and forth through the deserted tract.

Ken said, "You want to look around?"

"Shit, no," Teel said. "But let's do it."

Ken still did not believe anything was wrong at Bordeaux Ridge. The pickup could have been left behind at the end of the day. After all, other equipment remained on the tract overnight: a couple of Bob-cats on a long-bed truck, a backhoe. And it was still likely that the reported screaming had been kids playing.

They grabbed flashlights from the car because, even if electric service to the tract had been connected, there were no lamps or ceiling lights in the unfinished structures.

Resettling their gunbelts on their hips more out of habit than out of any belief that they would need weapons, Ken and Teel walked through the nearest of the partially framed houses. They were not looking for anything in particular, just going through the motions, which was half of all police work.

A mild and inconstant breeze sprang up, the first of the day, and blew sawdust ghosts through the open sides of the house. The sun was falling rapidly westward, and the wall studs cast prison-bar shadows across the floor. The last light of the day, which was changing from gold to muddy red, imparted a soft glow to the air like that around the open door of a furnace. The concrete pad was littered with nails that winked in the fiery light and clinked underfoot.

"For a hundred and eighty thousand bucks," Teel said, probing into black corners with the beams of his flashlight,

214

"I'd expect rooms a little bigger than these."

Taking a deep breath of sawdust-scented air, Ken said, "Hell, I'd expect rooms as big as airport lounges."

They stepped out of the back of the house, into a shallow rear yard, where they switched off their flashes. The bare, dry earth was not landscaped. It was littered with the detritus of construction: scraps of lumber, chunks of broken concrete, rumpled pieces of tarpaper, tangled loops of wire, more nails, useless lengths of PVC pipe, cedar shingles discarded by roofers. Styrofoam soft-drink cups and Big Mac containers, empty Coke cans, and less identifiable debris.

No fences had yet been constructed, so they had a view of all twelve backyards along this street. Purple shadows seeped across the sandy soil, but they could see that all the yards were deserted.

"No signs of mayhem," Teel said.

"No damsels in distress," Ken said.

"Well, let's at least walk along here, look between buildings," Teel said. "We ought to give the public something for their money."

Two houses later, in the thirty-foot-wide pass-through between structures, they found the dead man.

"Damn," Teel said.

The guy was lying on his back, mostly in shadow, with only the lower half of his body revealed in the dirty-red light, and at first Ken and Teel didn't realize what a horror they'd stumbled across. But when he knelt beside the corpse, Ken was shocked to see that the man's gut had been torn open.

"Jesus Christ, his eyes," Teel said.

Ken looked up from the ravaged torso and saw empty sockets where the victim's eyes should have been.

Retreating into the littered yard, Teel drew his revolver.

Ken also backed away from the mutilated corpse and slipped his own gun out of his holster. Though he had been perspiring all day, he felt suddenly damper, slick with a different kind of sweat, the cool, sour sweat of fear.

PCP, Ken thought. Only some asshole stoned on PCP

would be violent enough to do something like this.

Bordeaux Ridge was silent.

Nothing moved except the shadows, which seemed to grow longer by the second.

"Some angel-dust junkie did this," Ken said, putting his fears about PCP into words.

"I was thinking the same thing," Teel said. "You want to look any farther?"

"Not just the two of us. Let's radio for assistance."

They began to retrace their steps, warily keeping a watch on all sides as they moved, and they did not go far before they heard the noises. A crash. A clatter of metal. Glass breaking.

Ken had no doubt whatsoever where the sounds were coming from. The racket originated inside the closest of the three houses that were nearing completion and that would serve as sales models.

With no suspect in sight and no clue as to where to begin looking for one, they would have been justified in returning to the patrol car and calling for assistance. But now that they'd heard the disturbance in the model home, their training and instinct required them to act more boldly. They moved toward the back of the house.

A plyboard skin had been nailed over the studs, so the walls were not open to the elements, and chicken wire had been fixed to the tar-papered boards, and half the place was stuccoed. In fact, the stucco looked damp, as if the job had been started only today. Most of the windows were installed; only a few cutouts were still covered with tattered sheets of opaque plastic.

Another crash, louder than the first, was followed by the sound of more glass shattering inside.

Ken Dimes tried the sliding glass door that connected the rear yard and the family room. It was not locked.

From outside, Teel studied the family room through the glass. Although some light still entered the house by way of undraped doors and windows, shadows ruled the interior. They could see that the family room was deserted, so Teel eased through the half-open door with his flashlight in one hand and his Smith & Wesson clutched firmly in the other.

"You go around front," Teel whispered, "so the bastard doesn't get out that way."

Bending down to stay below window level, Ken hurried around the corner, along the side of the house, around to the front, and every step of the way he half-expected someone to jump on him from the roof or leap out through one of the unfinished windows.

The interior had been Sheetrocked, the ceilings textured. The family room opened into a breakfast area adjoining the kitchen, all of it one large flowing space without partitions. Oak cabinets had been installed in the kitchen, but the tile floor had not yet been put down.

The air had the lime odor of drywaller's mud, with an underlying scent of wood stain.

Standing in the breakfast area, Teel listened for more sounds of destruction, movement.

Nothing.

If this was like most California tract homes, he would find the dining room to the left, beyond the kitchen, then the living room, the entrance foyer, and a den. If he went into the hallway that led out of the breakfast area, he would probably find a laundry room, the downstairs bath, a coat closet, then the foyer. He could see no advantage of one route over another, so he went into the hall and checked the laundry first.

The dark room had no windows. The door was standing half-open, and the flashlight showed only yellow cabinets and the spaces where the washer and dryer would be placed. However, Teel wanted to look at the section behind the door, where he figured there was a sink and work area. He pushed the door all the way open and went in fast, swinging the flashlight and the gun in that direction. He found the stainless-steel sink and built-in table that he expected, but no killer.

He was more on edge than he had been in years. He could

not keep the image of the dead man from flickering repeatedly through his mind: those empty eye sockets.

Not just on edge, he thought. Face it, you're scared shitless.

Out front, Ken jumped across a narrow ditch and headed for the house's double entrance doors, which were still closed. He surveyed the surrounding area and saw no one trying to escape. As twilight descended, Bordeaux Ridge looked less like a tract under development than like a bombed-out neighborhood. Shadows and dust created the illusion of rubble.

In the laundry room, Teel Porter turned, intending to step into the hall, and on his right, in the group of yellow cabinets, the two-foot-wide, six-foot-high door of a broom closet flew open, and this *thing* came at him as if it were a jack-in-the-box. Jesus, for a split second he was sure it must be a kid in a rubber fright mask. He could not see clearly in the backsplash of the flashlight, which was pointed away from the attacker, but then he knew it was real because those eyes, like circles of smoky lamplight, were not just plastic or glass, no way. He fired the revolver, but it was aimed ahead, into the hall, and the slug plowed harmlessly into the wall out there, so he tried to turn, but the thing was all over him, hissing like a snake. He fired again, into the floor this time—the sound was deafening in that enclosed space—then he was driven backward against the sink, and the gun was torn out of his hand. He also lost the flashlight, which spun off into the corner. He threw a punch, but before his fist was halfway through its arc, he felt a terrible pain in his belly, as if several stilettos had been thrust into him all at once, and he knew instantly what was happening to him. He screamed, screamed, and in the gloom the misshapen face of the jack-in-the-box loomed over him, its eyes radiantly yellow, and Teel screamed again, flailed, and more stilettos sank through the soft tissue of his throat—

Ken Dimes was four steps from the front doors when he heard Teel scream. A cry of surprise, fear, pain.

"Shit."

They were double doors, stained oak. The one on the right was secured to the sill and header by sliding bolts, while the one on the left was the active door—and unlocked. Ken rushed inside, caution briefly forgotten, then halted in the gloomy foyer.

Already, the screaming had stopped.

He switched on his flashlight. Empty living room to the right. Empty den to the left. A staircase leading up to the second floor. No one anywhere in sight.

Silence. Perfect silence. As in a vacuum.

For a moment Ken hesitated to call out to Teel, for fear he would be revealing his position to the killer. Then he realized that the flashlight, without which he could not proceed, was enough to give him away; it did not matter if he made noise.

"Teel!"

The name echoed through the vacant rooms.

"Teel, where are you?"

No reply.

Teel must be dead. Jesus. He would respond if he was alive.

Or he might just be injured and unconscious, wounded and dying. In that case, perhaps it would be best to go back to the patrol car and call for an ambulance.

No. No, if his partner *was* in desperate shape, Ken had to find him fast and administer first aid. Teel might die in the time it took to call an ambulance. Delaying that long was too great a risk.

Besides, the killer had to be dealt with.

Only the vaguest smoky-red light penetrated the windows

now, for the day was being swallowed by the night. Ken had to rely entirely on the flashlight, which was not ideal because, each time the beam moved, shadows leaped and swooped, creating illusory assailants. Those false attackers might distract him from real danger.

Leaving the front door wide open, he crept along the narrow hall that led to the back of the house. He stayed close to the wall. The sole of one of his shoes squeaked with nearly every step he took. He held the gun out in front of him, not aimed at the floor or ceiling, because for the moment, at least, he didn't give a damn about safe weapons procedure.

On the right, a door stood open. A closet. Empty.

The stink of his own perspiration grew greater than the lime and woodstain odors of the house.

He came to a powder room on his left. A quick sweep of the light revealed nothing out of the ordinary, though his own frightened face, reflected in the mirror, startled him.

The rear of the house—family room, breakfast area, kitchen—was directly ahead, and on his left was another door, standing open. In the beam of the flashlight, which suddenly began to quiver violently in his hand, Ken saw Teel's body on the floor of a laundry room, and so much blood that there could be no doubt he was dead.

Beneath the waves of fear that washed across the surface of his mind, there were undercurrents of grief, rage, hatred, and a fierce desire for vengeance.

Behind Ken, something thumped.

He cried out and turned to face the threat.

But the hall to the right and the breakfast area to the left were both deserted.

The sound had come from the front of the house. Even as the echo of it died away, he knew what he'd heard: the front door being closed.

Another sound broke the stillness, not as loud as the first but more unnerving: the *clack* of the door's dead bolt being engaged.

Had the killer departed and locked the door from the out-side, with a key? But where would he get a key? Off the foreman that he had murdered? And why would he pause to lock up?

More likely, he had locked the door from inside, not merely to delay Ken's escape but to let him know the hunt was still under way.

Ken considered dousing the flashlight because it pinpointed him for the enemy, but by now the twilight glow at the windows was purple-gray and did not reach into the house at all. Without the flashlight, he would be blind.

How the hell was the *killer* finding his way in this steadily deepening darkness? Was it possible that a PCP junkie's night vision improved when he was high, just as his strength increased to that of ten men as a side effect of the angel dust?

The house was quiet.

He stood with his back to the hallway wall.

He could smell Teel's blood. A vaguely metallic odor.

Click, click, click.

Ken stiffened and listened intently, but he heard nothing more after those three quick noises. They had sounded like swift footsteps crossing the concrete floor, taken by someone wearing boots with hard leather heels—or shoes with cleats.

The noises had begun and ended so abruptly that he had not been able to tell where they were coming from. Then he heard them again—*click, click, click, click*—four steps this time, and they were in the foyer, moving in this direction, toward the hall in which he stood.

He immediately pushed away from the wall, turning to face the adversary, dropping into a crouch and thrusting both the flashlight and the revolver toward where he had heard the steps. But the hallway was deserted.

Breathing through his open mouth to reduce the noise of his own rapid respiration, which he feared would mask the movements of the enemy, Ken eased along the hall, into the foyer. Nothing. The front door was closed all right, but the den and the living room and the staircase and the gallery above were deserted.

Click, click, click, click.

The noises arose from an entirely different direction now, from the back of the house, in the breakfast area. The killer had fled silently out of the foyer, across the living room and dining room, into the kitchen, into the breakfast area, circling through the house, coming around behind Ken. Now the bastard was entering the hall that Ken had just left. And though the guy had been silent while flitting through the other rooms, he was making those noises again, obviously not because he had to make them, not because his shoes clicked with every step the way Ken's shoes squeaked, but because he wanted to make the noises again, wanted to taunt Ken, wanted to say: *Hey, I'm behind you now, and here I come, ready or not, here I come.*

Click, click, click.

Ken Dimes was no coward. He was a good cop who had never walked away from trouble. He had received two citations for bravery in only seven years on the force. But this faceless, insanely violent son of a bitch, scurrying through the house in total darkness, silent when he wanted to be and making taunting sounds when it suited him—he baffled and scared Ken. And although Ken was as courageous as any cop, he was no fool, and only a fool would walk boldly into a situation that he did not understand.

Instead of returning to the hall and confronting the killer, he went to the front door and reached for the lever-action brass handle, intending to get the hell out. Then he noticed the door hadn't merely been closed and dead-bolted. A length of scrap wire had been wound around the handle on the fixed door and around that on the active door, linking them, fastening them together. He would have to unwind the wire before he could get out, which might take half a minute.

Click, click, click.

He fired once toward the hallway without even looking and ran in the opposite direction, crossing the empty living room. He heard the killer behind him. Clicking. Coming fast in the darkness. Yet when Ken reached the dining room and was almost to the doorway that led into the kitchen, intending to make a break for the family room and the patio

222

door by which Teel had entered, he heard the clicking coming from in *front* of him. He was sure the killer had pursued him into the living room, but now the guy had gone back into the lightless hallway and was coming at him from the other direction, making a crazy game of this. From the sounds the bastard was making, he seemed just about to enter the breakfast area, which would put only the width of the kitchen between him and Ken, so Ken decided to make a stand right there, decided to blow away this psycho the moment the guy appeared in the beam of the light—

Then the killer shrieked.

Clicking along the hallway, still out of sight but coming toward Ken, the attacker let out a shrill inhuman cry that was the essence of primal rage and hatred, the strangest sound that Ken had ever heard, not the sound a man would make, not even a lunatic. He gave up all thought of confrontation, pitched his flashlight into the kitchen to create a diversion, turned away from the approaching enemy and fled again, though not back into the living room, not toward any part of the house in which this game of cat and mouse could be extended, but straight across the dining room toward a window that glimmered vaguely with the last dim glow of twilight. He tucked his head down, brought his arms up against his chest, and turned sideways as he slammed into the glass. The window exploded, and he fell out into the rear yard, rolling through construction debris. Splintery scraps of two-by-fours and chunks of concrete poked painfully into his legs and ribs. He scrambled to his feet, spun toward the house, and emptied his revolver at the broken window in case the killer was in pursuit of him.

In the settling night, he saw no sign of the enemy.

Figuring he had not scored a hit, he wasted no time cursing his luck. He sprinted around the house, along the side of it, and out to the street. He had to get to the patrol car, where there was a radio—and a pump-action riot gun.

On Wednesday and Thursday, the second and third of June, Travis and Nora and Einstein searched diligently for a way to improve human-canine communications, and in the process man and dog had almost begun to chew up furniture in frustration. However, Nora proved to have enough patience and confidence for all of them. When the breakthrough came near sunset on Friday evening, the fourth of June, she was less surprised than either Travis or Einstein.

They had purchased forty magazines—everything from *Time* and *Life* to *McCall's* and *Redbook*—and fifty books of art and photography, and had brought them to the living room of Travis's rental house, where there was space to spread everything out on the floor. They had put pillows on the floor as well, so they could work at the dog's level and be comfortable.

Einstein had watched their preparations with interest.

Sitting on the floor with her back against the vinyl sofa, Nora took the retriever's head in both hands and, with her face close to his, their noses almost touching, she said, "Okay, now you listen to me, Einstein. We want to know all sorts of things about you: where you came from, why you're smarter than an ordinary dog, what you were afraid of in the woods that day Travis found you, why you sometimes stare out of the window at night as if you're frightened of something. Lots more. But you can't talk, can you? No. And so far as we know, you can't read. And even if you can read, you can't write. So we've got to do this with pictures, I think."

From where he sat near Nora, Travis could see that the dog's eyes never wavered from hers as she spoke. Einstein was rigid. His tail hung down, motionless. He not only seemed to understand what she was telling him, but he appeared to be electrified by the experiment.

How much does the mutt really perceive, Travis wondered, and how many of his reactions am I imagining because of pure wishful thinking?

People have a natural tendency to anthropomorphize their pets, to ascribe human perceptions and intentions to the animals where none exist. In Einstein's case, where there really was an exceptional intelligence at work, the temptation to see profound meaning in every meaningless doggy twitch was even greater than usual.

"We're going to study all these pictures, looking for things that interest you, for things that'll help us understand where you came from and how you got to be what you are. Every time you see something that'll help us put the puzzle together, you've got to somehow bring it to our attention. Bark at it or put a paw on it or wag your tail."

"This is nuts," Travis said.

"Do you understand me, Einstein?" Nora asked.

The retriever issued a soft woof.

"This will never work," Travis said.

"Yes, it will," Nora insisted. "He can't talk, can't write, but he can *show* us things. If he points out a dozen pictures, we might not immediately understand what meaning they have for him, how they refer to his origins, but in time we'll find a way to relate them to one another and to him, and we'll know what he's trying to tell us."

The dog, his head still trapped firmly in Nora's hands, rolled his eyes toward Travis and woofed again.

"We ready?" Nora asked Einstein.

His gaze flicked back to her, and he wagged his tail.

"All right," she said, letting go of his head, "Let's start."

Wednesday, Thursday, and Friday, for hours at a time, they leafed through scores of publications, showing Einstein pictures of all kinds of things—people, trees, flowers, dogs, other animals, machines, city streets, country lanes, cars, ships, planes, food, advertisements for a thousand products —hoping he would see something that would excite him. The problem was that he saw many things that excited him, too many. He barked at, pawed at, woofed at, put his nose to, or wagged his tail at perhaps a hundred out of the thousands of pictures, and his choices

225

were of such variety that Travis could see no pattern to them, no way to link them and divine meaning from their association to one another.

Einstein was fascinated by an automobile ad in which the car, being compared to a powerful tiger, was shown locked in an iron cage. Whether it was the car or the tiger that seized his interest was not clear. He also responded to several computer advertisements, Alpo and Purina Dog Chow ads, an ad for a portable stereo cassette player, and pictures of books, butterflies, a parrot, a forlorn man in a prison cell, four young people playing with a striped beach ball, Mickey Mouse, a violin, a man on an exercise treadmill, and many other things. He was tantalized by a photograph of a golden retriever like himself, and was downright excited by a picture of a cocker spaniel, but curiously he showed little or no interest in other breeds of dogs.

His strongest—and most puzzling—response was to a photo in a magazine article about an upcoming movie from 20th Century-Fox. The film's story involved the super-natural—ghosts, poltergeists, demons risen from Hell—and the photo that agitated him was of a slab-jawed, wickedly fanged, lantern-eyed demonic apparition. The creature was no more hideous than others in the film, less hideous than several of them, yet Einstein was affected by only that one demon.

The retriever barked at the photograph. He scurried behind the sofa and peeked around the end of it as if he thought the creature in the picture might rise off the page and come after him. He barked again, whined, and had to be coaxed back to the magazine. Upon seeing the demon a second time, Einstein growled menacingly. Frantically, he pawed at the magazine, turning its pages until, somewhat tattered, it was completely closed.

"What's so special about *that* picture?" Nora asked the dog.

Einstein just stared at her—and shivered slightly.

Patiently, Nora reopened the magazine to the same page. Einstein closed it again.

Nora opened it.

Einstein closed it a third time, snatched it up in his jaws, and carried it out of the room.

Travis and Nora followed the retriever into the kitchen, where they watched him go straight to the trash can. The can was one of those with a footpedal that opened a hinged lid. Einstein put a paw on the pedal, watched the lid open, dropped the magazine into the can, and released the pedal.

"What's that all about?" Nora wondered.

"I guess that's one movie he definitely doesn't want to see."

"Our own four-footed, furry critic."

That incident occurred Thursday afternoon. By early Friday evening, Travis's frustration—and that of the dog—were nearing critical mass.

Sometimes Einstein exhibited uncanny intelligence, but sometimes he behaved like an ordinary dog, and these oscillations between canine genius and dopey mutt were enervating for anyone trying to understand how he could be so bright. Travis began to think that the best way to deal with the retriever was to just accept him for what he was: be prepared for his amazing feats now and then, but don't expect him to deliver all the time. Most likely the mystery of Einstein's unusual intelligence would never be solved.

However, Nora remained patient. She frequently reminded them that Rome wasn't built in a day and that any worthwhile achievement required determination, persistence, tenacity, and time.

When she launched into these lectures about steadfastness and endurance, Travis sighed wearily—and Einstein yawned.

Nora was unperturbed. After they had examined the pictures in all of the books and magazines, she collected those to which Einstein had responded, spread them out across the floor, and encouraged him to make connections between one image and another.

"All of these are pictures of things that played important roles in his past," Nora said.

"I don't think we can be certain of that," Travis said.

227

"Well, that's what we've asked him to do," she said. "We've asked him to indicate pictures that might tell us something about where he's come from."

"But does he understand the game?"

"Yes," she said with conviction.

The dog woofed.

Nora lifted Einstein's paw and put it on the photograph of the violin. "Okay, pooch. You remember a violin from somewhere, and it was important to you somehow."

"Maybe he performed at Carnegie Hall," Travis said.

"Shut up." To the dog Nora said, "All right. Now is the violin related to any of these other pictures? Is there a link to another image that would help us understand what the violin means to you?"

Einstein stared at her intently for a moment, as if pondering her question. Then he crossed the room, walking carefully in the narrow aisles between the rows of photographs, sniffing, his gaze flicking left and right, until he found the ad for the Sony portable stereo cassette player. He put one paw on it and looked back at Nora.

"There's an obvious connection," Travis said. "The violin makes music, and the cassette deck reproduces music. That's an impressive feat of mental association for a dog, but does it really mean anything else, anything about his past?"

"Oh, I'm sure it does," Nora said. To Einstein she said, "Did someone in your past play the violin?"

The dog stared at her.

She said, "Did your previous master have a cassette player like that one?"

The dog stared at her.

She said, "Maybe the violinist in your past used to record his own music on a cassette system?"

The dog blinked and whined.

"All right," she said, "is there another picture here that you can associate with the violin and the tape deck?"

Einstein stared down at the Sony ad for a moment, as if thinking, then walked into another aisle between two more rows of pictures, this time stopping at a magazine open to a Blue Cross advertisement that showed a doctor in a white coat standing at the bedside of a new mother who was holding her baby. Doctor and mother were all smiles, and the baby looked as serene and innocent as the Christ child.

Crawling nearer to the dog on her hands and knees, Nora said, "Does that picture remind you of the family that owned you?"

The dog stared at her.

"Was there a mother, father, and new baby in the family you used to live with?"

The dog stared at her.

Still sitting on the floor with his back against the sofa, Travis said, "Gee, maybe we've got a real case of reincarnation on our hands. Maybe old Einstein remembers being a doctor, a mother, or a baby in a previous life."

Nora would not dignify that suggestion with a response.

"A violin-playing baby," Travis said.

Einstein mewled unhappily.

On her hands and knees in a doglike position, Nora was only two or three feet from the retriever, virtually face-to-face with him. "All right. This is getting us nowhere. We've got to do more than just have you associate one picture with another. We've got to be able to ask questions about these pictures and somehow get answers."

"Give him paper and pen," Travis said.

"This is serious," Nora said, impatient with Travis as she had never been with the dog.

"I know it's serious," he said, "but it's also ridiculous."

She hung her head for a moment, like a dog suffering in summer heat, then suddenly looked up at Einstein and said, "How smart are you really, pooch? You want to prove you're a genius? You want to have our everlasting admiration and respect? Then here's what you have to do: learn to answer my questions with a simple yes or no."

The dog watched her closely, expectantly.

"If the answer to my question is yes—wag your tail," Nora said. "But *only* if the answer is yes. While this test in under way, you've got to avoid wagging it out of habit or just because you get excited. Wagging is *only* for when you want to say yes. And when you want to say no, you bark once. Just once.''

Travis said, "Two barks mean 'I'd rather be chasing cats,' and three barks mean 'Get me a Budweiser'."

"Don't confuse him," Nora said sharply.

"Why not? He confuses me."

The dog did not even glance at Travis. His large brown eyes remained focused intently on Nora as she explained the wag-for-yes and bark-for-no system again.

"All right," she said, "let's try it. Einstein, do you understand the yes-no signs?"

The retriever wagged his tail five or six times, then stopped.

"Coincidence," Travis said. "Means nothing."

Nora hesitated a moment, framing her next question, then said, "Do you know my name?"

The tail wagged, stopped.

"Is my name . . . Ellen?"

The dog barked. *No.*

"Is my name . . . Mary?"

One bark. *No.*

"Is my name . . . Nona?"

The dog rolled his eyes, as if chastising her for trying to trick him. No wagging. One bark.

"Is my name . . . Nora?"

Einstein wagged his tail furiously.

Laughing with delight, Nora crawled forward, sat up, and hugged the retriever.

"I'll be damned," Travis said, crawling over to join them.

Nora pointed to the photo on which the retriever still had one paw. "Did you react to this picture because it reminds you of the family you used to live with?"

One bark. *No.*

Travis said, "Did you ever live with any family?"

One bark.

"But you're not a wild dog," Nora said. "You must've lived somewhere before Travis found you."

Studying the Blue Cross advertisement, Travis suddenly

thought he knew all the right questions. "Did you react to this picture because of the baby?"

One bark. *No*.

"Because of the woman?"

No.

"Because of the man in the white lab coat?"

Much wagging: *Yes, yes, yes*.

"So he lived with a doctor," Nora said. "Maybe a vet."

"Or maybe a scientist," Travis said as he followed the intuitive line of thought that had stricken him.

Einstein wagged a "yes" at the mention of "scientist".

"Research scientist," Travis said.

Yes.

"In a lab," Travis said.

Yes, yes, yes.

"You're a lab dog?" Nora asked.

Yes.

"A research animal," Travis said.

Yes.

"And that's why you're so bright."

Yes.

"Because of something they've done to you."

Yes.

Travis's heart raced. They actually were communicating, by God, not just in broad strokes, and not just in the comparatively crude way he and Einstein had communicated the night that the dog had formed a question mark out of Milk-Bones. This was communication with extreme specificity. Here they were, talking as if they were three people—well, almost talking—and suddenly nothing would ever be the same again. Nothing could *possibly* be the same in a world where men and animals possessed equal (if different) intellects, where they faced life on equal terms, with equal rights, with similar hopes and dreams. All right, okay, so maybe he was blowing this out of proportion. Not *all* animals had suddenly been given human-level consciousness and intelligence; this was only one dog, an experimental animal, perhaps the only one of his kind. But Jesus. *Jesus*. Travis stared in awe at the retriever, and a chill swept through him, not a chill of fear but of wonder.

Nora spoke to the dog, and in her voice was a trace of the same awe that had briefly rendered Travis speechless: "They didn't just let you go, did they?"

One bark. *No*.

"You escaped?"

Yes.

"That Tuesday morning I found you in the woods?" Travis asked. "Had you just escaped then?"

Einstein neither barked nor wagged his tail.

"Days before that?" Travis asked.

The dog whined.

"He probably has a sense of time," Nora said, "because virtually all animals follow natural day-night rhythms, don't they? They have instinctive clocks, biological clocks. But he probably doesn't have any concept of *calendar* days. He doesn't really understand how we divide time up into days and weeks and months, so he has no way of answering your question."

"Then that's something we'll have to teach him," Travis said.

Einstein vigorously wagged his tail.

Thoughtfully, Nora said, "Escaped ..."

Travis knew what she must be thinking. To Einstein, he said, "They'll be looking for you, won't they?"

The dog whined and wagged his tail—which Travis interpreted as a "yes" with a special edge of anxiety.

4

An hour after sunset, Lemuel Johnson and Cliff Soames, trailed by two additional unmarked cars carrying eight NSA agents, arrived at Bordeaux Ridge. The unpaved street through the center of the unfinished housing tract was lined with vehicles, mostly black-and-whites bearing the Sheriff's Department shield, plus cars and a van from the coroner's office.

Lem was dismayed to see that the press had already arrived. Both print journalists and television crews with minicams were being kept behind a police line, half a block from the apparent scene of the murder. By quietly suppressing details of the death of Wesley Dalberg in Holy Jim Canyon and of the associated murders of the scientists working at Banodyne, and by instituting an aggressive campaign of disinformation, the NSA had managed to keep the press ignorant of the connections among all these events. Lem hoped that the deputies manning these barriers were among Walt Gaine's most trusted men and that they would meet reporters' questions with stony silence until a convincing cover story could be developed.

Sawhorses were lifted out of the way to let the unmarked NSA cars through the police line, then were put into place again.

Lem parked at the end of the street, past the crime scene. He left Cliff Soames to brief the other agents, and he headed toward the unfinished house that appeared to be the focus of attention.

The patrol cars' radios filled the hot night air with codes and jargon—and with a hiss-pop-crackle of static, as if the whole world were being fried on a cosmic griddle.

Portable kliegs stood on tripods, flooding the front of the house with light to facilitate the investigation. Lem felt as if he were on a giant stage set. Moths swooped and fluttered around the kliegs. Their amplified shadows darted across the dusty ground.

Casting his own exaggerated shadow, he crossed the dirt yard to the house. Inside, he found more kliegs. Dazzlingly bright light bounced off white walls. Looking pale and sweaty in that harsh glare were a couple of young deputies, men from the coroner's office, and the usual intense types from the Scientific Investigation Division.

A photographer's strobe flashed once, twice, from farther back in the house. The hallway looked crowded, so Lem went around to the back by way of the living room, dining room, and kitchen.

Walt Gaines was standing in the breakfast area, in the

233

dimness behind the last of the hooded kliegs. But even in those shadows, his anger and grief were visible. He had evidently been at home when he had gotten word about the murder of a deputy, for he was wearing tattered running shoes, wrinkled tan chinos, a brown- and red-checkered short-sleeved shirt. In spite of his great size, bull neck, muscular arms, and big hands, Walt's clothes and slump-shouldered posture gave him the look of a forlorn little boy.

From the breakfast area, Lem could not see past the lab men and into the laundry room, where the body still lay. He said, "I'm sorry, Walt. I'm so sorry."

"Name was Teel Porter. His dad Red Porter and I been friends twenty-five years. Red just retired from the department last year. How am I going to tell him? Jesus. I've got to do it myself, us being so close. Can't pass the buck this time."

Lem knew that Walt never passed the buck when one of his men was killed in the line of duty. He always personally visited the family, broke the bad news, and sat with them through the initial shock.

"Almost lost *two* men," Walt said. "Other one's badly shaken."

"How was Teel . . . ?"

"Gutted like Dalberg. Decapitated."

The Outsider, Lem thought. No doubt about it now.

Moths had gotten inside and were bashing against the lens of the klieg light behind which Lem and Walt stood.

His voice thickening with anger, Walt said, "Haven't found . . . his head. How do I tell his dad that Teel's *head* is missing?"

Lem had no answer.

Walt looked hard at him. "You can't push me all the way out of it now. Not now that one of my men is dead."

"Walt, my agency works in purposeful obscurity. Hell, even the number of agents on the payroll is classified information. But your department is subject to full press attention. And in order to know how to proceed in this case, your people would have to be told exactly what they're looking for. That would mean revealing national defense secrets to a large group of deputies—''

"*Your* men all know what's up," Walt countered.

"Yes, but my men have signed secrecy oaths, undergone extensive security checks, and are trained to keep their mouths shut."

"My men can keep a secret, too."

"I'm sure they can," Lem said carefully. "I'm sure they don't talk outside the shop about ordinary cases. But this isn't ordinary. No, this has to remain in our hands."

Walt said, "My men can sign secrecy oaths."

"We'd have to background-check everyone in your department, not just deputies but file clerks. It'd take weeks, months."

Looking across the kitchen at the open door to the dining room, Walt noticed Cliff Soames and another NSA agent talking with two deputies in the next room. "You started taking over the minute you got here, didn't you? Before you even talked to me about it?"

"Yeah. We're making sure your people understand that they must not talk of anything they've seen here tonight, not even to their own wives. We're citing the appropriate federal laws to every man, 'cause we want to be sure they understand the fines and prison terms."

"Threatening me with jail again?" Walt asked, but there was no humor in his voice, as there had been when they'd spoken days ago in the garage of St. Joseph's Hospital after seeing Tracy Keeshan.

Lem was depressed not only by the deputy's death but by the wedge that this case was driving between him and Walt. "I don't want anyone in jail. That's why I want to be sure they grasp the consequences—''

Scowling, Walt said, "Come with me."

Lem followed him outside, to a patrol car in front of the house.

They sat in the front seat, Walt behind the steering wheel, with the doors closed. "Roll up the windows, so we'll have total privacy."

Lem protested that they'd suffocate in this heat without ventilation. But even in the dim light, he saw the purity and volatility of Walt's anger, and he realized his position was that of a man standing in gasoline while holding a burning candle. He rolled up his window.

"Okay," Walt said. "We're alone. Not NSA District Director and Sheriff. Just old friends. Buddies. So tell me all about it."

"Walt, damn it, I can't."

"Tell me now, and I'll stay off the case, I won't interfere."

"You'll stay off the case anyway. You have to."

"Damned if I do," Walt said angrily. "I can walk right down the road to those jackals." The car faced out of Bordeaux Ridge, toward the sawhorses where reporters waited, and Walt pointed at them through the dusty windshield. "I can tell them that Banodyne Laboratories was working on some defense project that got out of hand, tell them that someone or something strange escaped from those labs in spite of the security, and now it's loose, killing people."

"You do that," Lem said, "you wouldn't just wind up in jail. You'd lose your job, ruin your whole career."

"I don't think so. In court I'd claim I had to choose between breaching the national security and betraying the trust of the people who elected me to office in this county. I'd claim that, in a time of crisis like this, I had to put local public safety above the concerns of the Defense bureaucrats in Washington. I'm confident just about any jury would vindicate me. I'd stay out of jail, and in the next election I'd win by even more votes than I got the last time."

"Shit," Lem said because he knew Walt was correct.

"If you tell me about it now, if you convince me that your people are better able to handle the situation than mine, then I'll step out of your way. But if you won't tell me, I'll blow it wide open."

"I'd be breaking my oath. I'd be putting my neck in the noose."

"No one'll ever know you told me."

"Yeah? Well then, Walt, for Christ's sake, why put me in such an awkward position just to satisfy your curiosity?"

236

Walt looked stung. "It's not as petty as that, damn you. It's not just curiosity."

"Then what is it?"

"One of my men is dead!"

Leaning his head back against the seat, Lem closed his eyes and sighed. Walt had to know *why* he was required to forswear vengeance for the killing of one of his own men. His sense of duty and honor would not allow him to back off without at least that much. His was not exactly an unreasonable position.

"Do I go down there, talk to the reporters?" Walt asked quietly.

Lem opened his eyes, wiped a hand across his damp face. The interior of the car was uncomfortably warm, muggy. He wanted to roll down his window. But now and then men walked past on their way in or out of the house, and he really could not risk anyone overhearing what he was going to tell Walt. "You were right to focus on Banodyne. For a few years they've been doing defense-related research."

"Biological warfare?" Walt asked. "Using recombinant DNA to make nasty new viruses?"

"Maybe that, too," Lem said. "but germ warfare doesn't have anything to do with this case, and I'm only going to tell you about the research that's related to our problems here."

The windows were fogging. Walt started the car. There was no air conditioning, and the fog on the windows continued to spread, but even the vague moist, warm breeze from the vents was welcome.

Lem said, "They were working on several research programs under the heading of the Francis Project. Named for Saint Francis of Assisi."

Blinking in surprise, Walt said, "They'd name a warfare-related project after a saint?"

"It's apt," Lem assured him. "Saint Francis could talk to birds and animals. And at Banodyne, Dr. Davis Weatherby was in charge of a project aimed at making human-animal communication possible."

"Learning the language of porpoises—that sort of thing?"

"No. The idea was to apply the very latest knowledge in genetic engineering to the creation of animals with a much higher order of intelligence, animals capable of nearly human-level thought, animals with whom we might be able to communicate."

Walt stared at him in openmouthed disbelief.

Lem said, "There've been several scientific teams working on very different experiments under the umbrella label of the Francis Project, all of which have been funded for at least five years. For one thing, there were Davis Weatherby's dogs ..."

Dr. Weatherby had been working with the sperm and ova of golden retrievers, which he had chosen because the dogs had been bred with ever greater refinement for more than a hundred years. For one thing, this refinement meant that, in the purest of the breed, all diseases and afflictions of an inheritable nature had been pretty much excised from the animal's genetic code, which insured Weatherby of healthy and bright subjects for his experiments. Then, if the experimental pups were born with abnormalities of any kind, Weatherby could more easily distinguish those mutations of a natural type from those that were an unintended side effect of his own sly tampering with the animal's genetic heritage, and he would be able to learn from his own mistakes.

Over the years, seeking solely to increase the intelligence of the breed without causing a change in its physical appearance, Davis Weatherby had fertilized hundreds of genetically altered retriever ova *in vitro*, then had transferred the fertile eggs to the wombs of bitches who served as surrogate mothers. The bitches carried the test-tube pups to full term, and Weatherby studied these young dogs for indications of increased intelligence.

"There were a hell of a lot of failures," Lem said. "Grotesque physical mutations that had to be destroyed. Stillborn pups. Pups that looked normal but were *less* intelligent than usual. Weatherby was doing cross-species engineering, after all, so you can figure that some pretty horrible possibilities were realized."

Walt stared at the windshiled, now entirely opaqued. Then he frowned at Lem. "Cross-species? What do you mean?"

"Well, you see, he was isolating those genetic determinants of intelligence in species that were brighter than the retriever—"

"Like apes? They'd be brighter than dogs, wouldn't they?"

"Yeah. Apes ... and human beings."

"Jesus," Walt said.

Lem adjusted a dashboard vent to direct the flow of tepid air into his face. "Weatherby was inserting that foreign genetic material into the retriever's genetic code, simultaneously editing out the dog's own genes that limited its intelligence to that of a dog."

Walt rebelled. "That's not possible! This genetic material, as you call it, surely it can't be passed from one species to another."

"It happens in nature all the time," Lem said. "Genetic material is transferred from one species to another, and the carrier is usually a virus. Let's say a virus thrives in rhesus monkeys. While in the monkey, it acquires genetic material from the monkey's cells. These acquired monkey genes become a part of the virus itself. Later, upon infecting a human host, that virus has the capability of leaving the monkey's genetic material in its human host. Consider the AIDS virus, for instance. It's believed AIDS was a disease carried by certain monkeys and by human beings for decades, though neither species was susceptible to it; I mean, we were strictly carriers—we never got sick from what we carried. But then, somehow, something happened in monkeys, a negative genetic change that made them not only carriers but *victims* of the AIDS virus. Monkeys began to die of the disease. Then, when the virus passed to humans, it brought with it this new genetic material specifying susceptibility to AIDS, so before long human beings were also capable of contracting the disease. That's how it works in nature. It's done even more efficiently in the lab.''

As creeping condensation fogged the side windows, Walt said, "So Weatherby really succeeded in breeding a dog with human intelligence?"

"It was a long, slow process, but gradually he made advancements. And a little over a year ago, the miracle pup was born.''

"Thinks like a human being?"

"Not *like* a human being, but maybe *as well as*."

"Yet it looks like an ordinary dog?"

"That's what the Pentagon wanted. Which made Weatherby's job a lot harder, I guess. Apparently, brain size has at least a little bit to do with intelligence, and Weatherby might have made his breakthrough a lot sooner if he'd been able to develop a retriever with a larger brain. But a larger brain would have meant a reconfigured and much larger skull, so the dog would have looked damned unusual.''

All the windows were fogged over now. Neither Walt nor Lem tried to clear the misted glass. Unable to see out of the car, confined to its humid and claustrophobic interior, they seemed to be cut off from the real world, adrift in time and space, a condition that was oddly conducive to the consideration of the wondrous and outrageous acts of creation that genetic engineering made possible.

Walt said, "The Pentagon wanted a dog that looked like a dog but could think like a man? *Why?*"

"Imagine the possibilities for espionage," Lem said. "In times of war, dogs would have no trouble getting deep into enemy territory, scouting installations and troop strength. Intelligent dogs, with whom we could somehow communicate, would then return and tell us what they had seen and what they'd overheard the enemy talking about.''

"*Tell* us? Are you saying dogs could be made to talk, like canine versions of Francis the Mule or Mr. Ed? Shit, Lem, be serious!''

Lem sympathized with his friend's difficulty in absorbing these astounding possibilities. Modern science was advancing so rapidly, with so many revolutionary discoveries to be explored every year, that to laymen there was going to be increasingly less difference between the application of that science and magic. Few nonscientists had any appreciation for how different the world of the next twenty years was going to be from the world of the present, as different as the 1980s were from the 1780s. Change was occurring at an incomprehensible rate, and when you got a glimpse of what might be coming as Walt just had—it was both inspiring and daunting, exhilarating and scary.

Lem said, "In fact, a dog probably could be genetically altered to be able to speak. Might even be easy, I don't know. But to give it the necessary vocal apparatus, the right kind of tongue and lips . . . that'd mean drastically altering its appearance, which is no good for the Pentagon's purpose. So *these* wouldn't speak. Communication would no doubt have to be through an elaborate sign language."

"You're not laughing," Walt said. "This has got to be a fucking joke, so why aren't you laughing?"

"Think about it," Lem said patiently. "In peacetime . . . imagine the president of the United States presenting the Soviet premier with a one-year-old golden retriever as a gift from the American people. Imagine the dog living in the premier's home and office, privy to the most secret talks of the USSR's highest Party officials. Once in a while, every few weeks or months, the dog might manage to slip out at night, to meet with a U.S. agent in Moscow and be debriefed."

"*Debriefed?* This is insane!" Walt said, and he laughed. But his laughter had a sharp, hollow, decidedly nervous quality which, to Lem, indicated that the sheriff's skepticism was slipping away even though he wanted to hold on to it.

"I'm telling you that it's possible, that such a dog was in fact conceived by *in vitro* fertilization of a genetically altered ovum by genetically altered sperm, and carried to term by a surrogate mother. And after a year of confinement at the Banodyne labs, sometime in the early morning hours of Monday, May 17, that dog escaped by a series of incredibly clever actions that cannily circumvented the facility's security system.''

"And the dog's now loose?"

"Yes."

"And that's what been killing—"

"No," Lem said. "The dog is harmless, affectionate, a *wonderful* animal. I was in Weatherby's lab while he was working with the retriever. In a limited way, I communicated with it. Honest to God, Walt, when you see that animal in action, see what Weatherby created, it gives you enormous hope for this sorry species of ours."

Walt stared at him, uncomprehending.

Lem searched for the words to convey what he felt. As he found the language to describe what the dog had meant to him, his chest grew tight with emotion. "Well ... I mean, if we can do these amazing things, if we can bring such a wonder into the world, then there's something of profound value in us no matter what the pessimists and doomsayers believe. If we can do this, we have the power and, potentially, the wisdom of God. We're not only makers of weapons, but makers of *life*. If we could lift members of another species up to our level, create a companion race to share the world ... our beliefs and philosophies would be changed forever. By the very act of altering the retriever, we've altered ourselves. By pulling the dog to a new level of awareness, we are inevitably raising our own awareness as well."

"Jesus, Lem, you sound like a preacher."

"Do I? That's because I've had more time to think about this than you have. In time, you'll understand what I'm talking about. You'll begin to feel it, too, this incredible sense that humankind is on its way to godhood—and that we *deserve* to get there."

Walt Gaines stared at the steamed glass, as if reading something of great interest in the patterns of condensation. Then: "Maybe what you say is right. Maybe we're on the brink of a new world. But for now we've got to live in and deal with the old one. So if it wasn't the dog that

242

killed my deputy—what was it?"

"Something else escaped from Banodyne the same night that the dog got out," Lem said. His euphoria was suddenly tempered by the need to admit that there had been a darker side to the Francis Project. "They called it The Outsider."

5

Nora held up the magazine ad that compared an automobile to a tiger and that showed the car in an iron cage. To Einstein, she said, "All right, let's see what else you can clarify for us. What about this one? What is it that interested you in this photograph—the car?"

Einstein barked once: *No*.

"Was it the tiger?" Travis asked.

One bark.

"The cage?" Nora asked.

Einstein wagged his tail: *Yes*.

"Did you choose this picture because they kept you in a cage?" Nora asked.

Yes.

Travis crawled across the floor until he found the photo of a forlorn man in a prison cell. Returning with it, showing it to the retriever, he said, "And did you choose this one because the cell is like a cage?"

Yes.

"And because the prisoner in the picture reminded you of how you felt when you were in a cage?"

Yes.

"The violin," Nora said. "Did someone at the laboratory play the violin for you?"

Yes.

"Why would they do that, I wonder?" Travis said.

That was one the dog could not answer with a simple yes or no.

"Did you like the violin?" Nora asked.

Yes.

"You like music in general?"

Yes.

"Do you like jazz?"

The dog neither barked nor wagged his tail.

Travis said, "He doesn't know what jazz is. I guess they never let him hear any of that."

"Do you like rock and roll?" Nora asked.

One bark and, simultaneously, a wagging of the tail.

"What's that supposed to mean?" Nora asked.

"Probably means 'yes and no'," Travis said. "He likes some rock and roll but not all of it."

Einstein wagged his tail to confirm Travis's interpretation.

"Classical?" Nora asked.

Yes.

Travis said, "So we've got a dog that's a snob, huh?"

Yes, yes, yes.

Nora laughed in delight, and so did Travis, and Einstein nuzzled and licked them happily.

Travis looked around for another picture, snatched up the one of the man on the exercise treadmill. "They wouldn't want to let you out of the lab, I guess. Yet they'd want to keep you fit. Is this how they exercised you? On a treadmill?"

Yes.

The sense of discovery was exhilarating. Travis would have been no more thrilled, no more excited, no more awe-stricken if he had been communicating with an extraterrestrial intelligence.

6

I'm falling down a rabbit hole, Walt Gaines thought uneasily as he listened to Lem Johnson.

This new high-tech world of space flight, computers in the home, satellite-relayed telephone calls, factory robots, and now biological engineering seemed utterly unrelated to

244

the world in which he was born and grew up. For God's sake, he had been a child during World War II, when there had not even been jet aircraft. He hailed from a simpler world of boatlike Chryslers with tail fins, phones with dials instead of push buttons, clocks with hands instead of digital display boards. Television did not exist when he was born, and the possibility of nuclear Armageddon within his own lifetime was something no one then could have predicted. He felt as though he had stepped through an invisible barrier from his world into another reality that was on a faster track. This new kingdom of high technology could be delightful or frightening—and occasionally both at the same time.

Like now.

The idea of an intelligent dog appealed to the child in him and made him want to smile.

But something else—The Outsider—had escaped from those labs, and it scared the bejesus out of him.

"The dog had no name," Lem Johnson said. "That's not so unusual. Most scientists who work with lab animals never name them. If you've named an animal, you'll inevitably begin to attribute a personality to it, and then your relationship to it will change, and you'll no longer be as objective in your observations as you have to be. So the dog had only a number until it was clear this was the success Weatherby had been working so hard to achieve. Even then, when it was evident that the dog would not have to be destroyed as a failure, no name was given to it. Everyone simply called it 'the dog,' which was enough to differentiate it from all of Weatherby's other pups because they'd been referred to by numbers. Anyway, at the same time, Dr. Yarbeck was working on other, very different research under the Francis Project umbrella, and she, too, finally met with some success."

Yarbeck's objective was to create an animal with dramatically increased intelligence—but one also designed to accompany men into war as police dogs accompanied cops in dangerous urban neighborhoods. Yarbeck sought to engineer a beast that was smart but also deadly, a terror on the battlefield—ferocious, stealthy, cunning, and intelligent enough to be effective in both jungle and urban warfare.

Not quite as intelligent as human beings, of course, not as smart as the dog that Weatherby was developing. It would be sheer madness to create a killing machine as intelligent as the people who would have to use and control it. Everyone had read *Frankenstein* or had seen one of the old Karloff movies, and no one underestimated the dangers inherent in Yarbeck's research.

Choosing to work with monkeys and apes because of their naturally high intelligence and because they already possessed humanlike hands, Yarbeck ultimately selected baboons as the base species for her dark acts of creation. Baboons were among the smartest of primates, good raw material. They were deadly and effective fighters by nature, with impressive claws and fangs, fiercely motivated by the territorial imperative, and eager to attack those whom they perceived as enemies.

"Yarbeck's first task in the *physical* alteration of the baboon was to make it larger, big enough to threaten a grown man," Lem said. "She decided that it would have to stand at least five feet and weigh one hundred to a hundred and ten pounds."

"That's not so big," Walt protested.

"Big enough."

"I could swat down a man that size."

"A man, yes. But not this thing. It's solid muscle, no fat at all, and far quicker than a man. Stop and think of how a fifty-pound pit bull can make mincemeat of a grown man, and you'll realize what a threat Yarbeck's warrior could be at a hundred and ten."

The patrol car's steam-silvered windshield seemed like a movie screen on which Walt saw projected images of brutally murdered men: Wes Dalberg, Teel Porter . . . He closed his eyes but still saw cadavers. "Okay, yeah, I get your point. A hundred and ten pounds would be enough if we're talking about something *designed* to fight and kill."

"So Yarbeck created a breed of baboons that would

grow to greater size. Then she set to work by editing the sperm and ova of her giant primates in other ways, sometimes by editing the baboon's own genetic material, sometimes by introducing genes from other species."

Walt said, "The same sort of cross-species patch-and-stitch that led to the smart dog."

"I wouldn't call it patch-and-stitch ... but yeah, essentially the same techniques. Yarbeck wanted a large, vicious jaw on her warrior, something more like that of a German shepherd, even a jackal, so there would be room for more teeth, and she wanted the teeth to be larger and sharper and perhaps slightly hooked, which meant she had to enlarge the baboon's head and totally alter its facial structure to accommodate all of this. The skull had to be greatly enlarged, anyway, to allow for a bigger brain. Dr. Yarbeck wasn't working under the constraints that required Davis Weatherby to leave his dog's appearance unchanged. In fact, Yarbeck figured that if her creation was hideous, if it was *alien*, it would be an even more effective warrior because it would serve not only to stalk and kill our enemies but terrorize them."

In spite of the warm, muggy air, Walt Gaines felt a coldness in his belly, as if he had swallowed big chunks of ice. "Didn't Yarbeck or anyone else consider the immorality of this, for Christ's sake? Didn't any of them ever read *The Island of Doctor Moreau*? Lem, you have a goddamn moral obligation to let the public know about this, to blow it wide open. And so do I."

"No such thing," Lem said. "The idea that there's good and evil knowledge ... well, that's strictly a religious point of view. Actions can be either moral or immoral, yes, but knowledge can't be labeled that way. To a scientist, to *any* educated man or woman, all knowledge is morally neutral."

"But, shit, *application* of the knowledge, in Yarbeck's case, wasn't morally neutral."

Sitting on one or the other's patio on weekends, drinking Corona, dealing with the weighty problems of the world, they loved to talk about this sort of thing. Backyard philosophers. Beery sages taking smug pleasure in their wisdom. And sometimes the moral dilemmas they discussed on weekends were those that later arose in the course of their police work; however, Walt could not remember any discussion that had had as urgent a bearing on their work as this one.

"Applying knowledge is part of the process of learning more," Lem said. "The scientist has to apply his discoveries to see where each application leads. Moral responsibility is on the shoulders of those who take the technology out of the lab and use it to immoral ends."

"Do you believe that bullshit?"

Lem thought for a moment. "Yeah, I guess I do. I guess, if we held scientists responsible for the bad things that flowed from their work, they'd never go to work in the first place, and there'd be no progress at all. We'd still be living in caves."

Walt pulled a clean handkerchief from his pocket and blotted his face, giving himself a moment to think. It wasn't so much the heat and humidity that had gotten to him. It was the thought of Yarbeck's warrior roaming the Orange County hills that made him break out in a sweat.

He wanted to go public, warn the unwary world that something new and dangerous was loose upon the earth. But that would be playing into the hands of the new Luddites, who would use Yarbeck's warrior to generate public hysteria in an attempt to bring an end to all recombinant-DNA research. Already, such research had created strains of corn and wheat that could grow with less water and in poor soil, relieving world hunger, and years ago they had developed a man-made virus that, as a waste product, produced cheap insulin. If he took word of Yarbeck's monstrosity to the world, he might save a couple of lives in the short run, but he might be playing a role in denying the world the beneficial miracles of recombinant-DNA research, which would *cost* tens of thousands of lives in the long run.

"Shit," Walt said. "It's not a black-and-white issue, is it?"

Lem said, "That's what makes life interesting."

Walt smiled sourly. "Right now, it's a whole hell of a lot more interesting than I care for. Okay. I can see the wisdom of keeping a lid on this. Besides, if we made it public, you'd have a thousand half-assed adventurers out there looking for the thing, and they'd end up victims of it, or they'd gun down one another."

"Exactly."

"But my men could help keep the lid on by joining in the search."

Lem told him about the hundred men from Marine Intelligence units who were still combing the foothills, dressed as civilians, using high-tech tracking gear and, in some cases, bloodhounds. "I've already got more men on line than you could supply. We're already doing as much as can be done. Now will you do the right thing? Will you stay out of it?"

Frowning, Walt said, "For now. But I want to be kept informed."

Lem nodded. "All right."

"And I have more questions. For one thing, why do they call it The Outsider?"

"Well, the dog was the first breakthrough, the first of the lab subjects to display unusual intelligence. This one was next. They were the only two successes: the dog and the other. At first, they added capital letters to the way they pronounced it, The Other, but in time it became The Outsider because that seemed to fit better. It was not an improvement on one of God's creations, as was the dog; it was entirely *outside* of creation, a thing apart. An abomination—though no one actually said as much. And the thing was aware of its status as an outsider, acutely aware."

"Why not just call it the baboon?"

"Because . . . it doesn't really look much of anything like a baboon any more. Not like anything you've ever seen— except in a nightmare."

Walt did not like the expression on his friend's dark face, in his eyes. He decided not to ask for a better description of The Outsider; perhaps that was something he did not need to know.

Instead, he said, "What about the Hudston, Weatherby, and Yarbeck murders? Who was behind all that?"

"We don't know the man who pulled the trigger, but we know the Soviets hired him. They also killed another Banodyne man who was on vacation in Acapulco."

Walt felt as if he were jolting through one of those invisible barriers again, into an even more complicated world. "Soviets? Were we talking about the Soviets? How'd they get into the act?"

"We didn't think they knew about the Francis Project," Lem said. "But they did. Apparently, they even had a mole inside Banodyne who reported out to them on our progress. When the dog and, subsequently, The Outsider escaped, the mole informed the Soviets, and evidently the Soviets decided to take advantage of the chaos and do us even more damage. They killed every project leader—Yarbeck and Weatherby and Haines—plus Hudston, who had once been a project leader but no longer worked at Banodyne. We think they did this for two reasons: first, to bring the Francis Project to a halt; second, to make it harder for us to track down The Outsider."

"How would that make it harder?"

Lem slumped in his seat as if, in talking of the crisis, he was more clearly aware of the burden on his shoulders. "By eliminating Hudston, Haines, and especially Weatherby and Yarbeck, the Soviets cut us off from the people who would have the best idea how The Outsider and the dog think, the people best able to figure out where those animals might go and how they might be recaptured."

"Have you actually pinned it on the Soviets?"

Lem sighed. "Not entirely. I'm focused primarily on recovering the dog and The Outsider, so we have another entire task force trying to track down the Soviet agents behind the murders, arson, and data hijacking. Unfortunately, the Soviets seem to have used freelance hitmen outside of their own network, so we have no idea where to look for the triggermen. That side of the investigation is pretty much stalled."

"And the fire at Banodyne a day or so later?" Walt asked.

"Definitely arson. Another Soviet action. It destroyed all the paper and electronic files on the Francis Project. There were backup computer disks at another location, of course ... but data on them has somehow been erased."

"The Soviets again?"

"We think so. The leaders of the Francis Project and all their files have been wiped out, leaving us in the dark when it comes to trying to figure how either the dog or The Outsider might think, where they might go, how they might be tricked into captivity."

Walt shook his head. "Never thought I'd be on the side of the Russians, but putting a stop to this project seems like a good idea."

"They're far from innocent. From what I hear, they've got a similar project under way at laboratories in the Ukraine. I wouldn't doubt we're working diligently to destroy their files and people the way they've destroyed ours. Anyway, the Soviets would like nothing better than for The Outsider to run wild in some nice peaceable suburb, gutting housewives and chewing the heads off little kids, because if that happens a couple of times ... well, then the whole thing's going to blow up in our face."

Chewing the heads off little kids? Jesus.

Walt shuddered and said, "Is that likely to happen?"

"We don't believe so. The Outsider is aggressive as hell—it was designed to be aggressive, after all—and it has a special hatred for its makers, which is something Yarbeck didn't count on and something she hoped to be able to correct in future generations. The Outsider takes great pleasure in slaughtering us. But it's also smart, and it knows that every killing gives us a new fix on its whereabouts. So it's not going to indulge its hatred too often. It's going to stay away from people most of the time, moving mainly at night. Once in a while, out of curiosity, it might poke into residential areas along the edge of the developed eastern flank of the county—"

"As it did at the Keeshan place."

251

"Yeah. But I bet it didn't go there to kill anyone. Just plain curiosity. It doesn't want to be caught before it accomplishes its main goal."

"Which is?"

"Finding and killing the dog," Lem said.

Walt was surprised. "Why would it care about the dog?"

"We don't really know," Lem said. "But at Banodyne, it harbored a fierce hatred of the dog, worse than what it felt toward people. When Yarbeck worked with it, constructing a sign language with which to communicate complex ideas, The Outsider several times expressed a desire to kill and mutilate the dog, but it would never explain why. It was *obsessed* with the dog."

"So you think now it's tracking the retriever?"

"Yes. Because evidence seems to indicate that the dog was the first to break out of the labs that night in May, and that its escape drove The Outsider mad. The Outsider was kept in a large enclosure inside Yarbeck's lab, and everything belonging to it—bedding, many education devices, toys—was torn and smashed to pieces. Then, apparently realizing that the dog was going to be forever out of its reach if it didn't make good it's own escape, The Outsider put its mind to the problem and, by God, found its own way out."

"But if the dog got a good head start—"

"There's a link between the dog and The Outsider that no one understands. A mental link. Instinctual awareness. We don't know its extent, but we can't rule out the possibility that this link is strong enough for one of them to follow the other over considerable distances. It's apparently a sort of mild sixth sense that was somehow a bonus of the technique of intelligence enhancement used in both Weatherby's and Yarbeck's research. But we're only guessing. We don't really know for sure. There's so fucking much we don't know!"

Both men were silent for a while.

The humid closeness of the car was no longer entirely unpleasant. Given all the dangers loose in the modern world, these steamy confines seemed safe and comfortable, a haven.

Finally, not wanting to ask any more questions, afraid of the answers he might get, Walt nevertheless said, "Banodyne is a high-security building. It's designed to keep unauthorized people from getting in, but it must be hard to get *out* of the place, too. Yet both the dog and The Outsider escaped."

"Yes."

"And obviously no one ever figured they could. Which means they're both smarter than anyone realized."

"Yes."

Walt said, "In the case of the dog . . . well, if it's smarter than anyone figured, so what? The dog is friendly."

Lem, who had been staring at the opaqued windshield, finally met Walt's eyes. "That's right. But if The Outsider is smarter than we thought . . . if it's very nearly as smart as a man, then catching it's going to be even harder."

"Very nearly . . . or *as* smart as a man."

"No. Impossible."

"Or even smarter," Walt said.

"No. That couldn't be."

"Couldn't?"

"No."

"Definitely couldn't?"

Lem sighed, wearily rubbed his eyes, and said nothing. He was not going to start lying to his best friend again.

7

Nora and Travis went through the photographs one by one, learning a little more about Einstein. By barking once or vigorously wagging his tail, the dog answered questions and was able to confirm that he had chosen the advertisement for computers because they reminded him of the computers in the lab where he had been kept. The photo of four young people playing with a striped beach ball appealed to him because one of the scientists in the lab had evidently used balls of various sizes in an intelligence test that Einstein had particularly enjoyed. They were unable to determine the reason for his interest in the parrot, the butterflies, Mickey Mouse, and many other things, but that was only because they could not hit upon the pertinent yes-or-no questions that would have led to explanations.

Even when a hundred questions failed to reveal the meaning of one of the photographs, the three of them remained excited and delighted by the process of discovery. The only time the mood changed for the worse was when they queried Einstein about the magazine picture of the demon from an upcoming horror movie. He became extremely agitated. He tucked his tail between his legs, bared his teeth, growled deep in his throat. Several times, he padded away from the photograph, going behind the sofa or into another room, where he stayed for a minute or two before returning, reluctantly, to face additional questions, and he shivered almost continuously when being quizzed about the demon.

Finally, after trying for at least ten minutes to determine the reason for the dog's dread, Travis pointed to the slab-jawed, wickedly fanged, luminous-eyed movie monster and said, "Maybe you don't understand, Einstein. This isn't a picture of a real, living thing. This is a make-believe demon from a movie. Do you understand what I mean when I say make-believe?"

Einstein wagged his tail: *Yes*.

"Well, this is a make-believe monster."

One bark: *No*.

"Make-believe, phony, not real, just a man in a rubber suit," Nora said.

No.

"Yes," Travis said.

No.

Einstein tried to run off behind the sofa again, but Travis grabbed him by the collar and held him. "Are you claiming to have seen such a thing?"

The dog raised his gaze from the picture, looked into Travis's eyes, shuddered, and whimpered.

The pitiful note of profound fear in Einstein's soft whine

and an indescribably disturbing quality in his dark eyes combined to affect Travis to an extent that surprised him. Holding the collar with one hand, his other hand on Einstein's back, Travis felt the shivers that quaked through the dog—and suddenly he was shivering, too. The dog's stark fear was transmitted to him, and he thought, *By God, he really has seen something like this.*

Sensing the change in Travis, Nora said. "What's wrong?"

Instead of answering her, he repeated the question that Einstein had not yet answered: "Are you claiming to have seen such a thing?"

Yes.

"Something that looks exactly like this demon?"

A bark and a wag: *Yes and no.*

"Something that looks at least a little bit like it?"

Yes.

Letting go of the collar, Travis stroked the dog's back, trying to soothe him, but Einstein continued to shiver. "Is this why you keep a watch at the window some nights?"

Yes.

Clearly puzzled and alarmed by the dog's distress, Nora began to pet him, too. "I thought you were worried that people from the lab would find you."

Einstein barked once.

"You're not afraid people from the lab will find you?"

Yes and no.

Travis said, "But you're more afraid that . . . this other thing will find you."

Yes, yes, yes.

"Is this the same thing that was in the woods that day, the thing that chased us, the thing I shot at?" Travis asked.

Yes, yes, yes.

Travis looked at Nora. She was frowning. "But it's only a movie monster. Nothing in the real world looks even a little bit like it."

Padding across the room, sniffing at the assorted photographs, Einstein paused again at the Blue Cross ad that featured the doctor, mother, and baby in a hospital room.

He brought the magazine to them and dropped it on the floor. He put his nose to the doctor in the picture, then looked at Nora, at Travis, put his nose to the doctor again, and looked up expectantly.

"Before," Nora said, "you told us the doctor represented one of the scientists in that lab."

Yes.

Travis said, "So are you telling me the scientist who worked on you would know what this thing in the woods was?"

Yes.

Einstein went looking through the photographs again, and this time he returned with the ad that showed a car in a cage. He touched his nose to the cage; then, hesitantly, he touched his nose to the picture of the demon.

"Are you saying the thing in the woods belongs in a cage?" Nora asked.

Yes.

"More than that," Travis said, "I think he's telling us that it was in a cage at one time, that he saw it in a cage."

Yes.

"In the same lab where *you* were in a cage?"

Yes, yes, yes.

"Another experimental lab animal?" Nora asked.

Yes.

Travis stared hard at the photograph of the demon, at its thick brow and deeply set yellow eyes, at its deformed snoutlike nose and mouth bristling with teeth. At last he said, "Was it an experiment ... that went wrong?"

Yes and no, Einstein said.

Now at a peak of agitation, the dog crossed the living room to the front window, jumped up and braced his forepaws on the sill, and peered out at the Santa Barbara evening.

Nora and Travis sat on the floor among the opened magazines and books, happy with the progress they had made, beginning to feel the exhaustion that their excitement had masked—and frowning at each other in puzzlement.

She spoke softly. "Do you think Einstein's capable of lying, making up wild stories like children do?"

256

"I don't know. Can dogs lie, or is that just a human skill?" He laughed at the absurdity of his own question. "Can dogs lie? Can a moose be elected to the presidency? Can cows sing?"

Nora laughed, too, and very prettily. "Can ducks tap-dance?"

In a fit of silliness that was a reaction to the difficulty of dealing intellectually and emotionally with the whole idea of a dog as smart as Einstein, Travis said, "I once saw a duck tap-dancing."

"Oh, yeah?"

"Yeah. In Vegas."

Laughing, she said, "What hotel was he performing at?"

"Caesar's Palace. He could sing, too."

"The duck?"

"Yeah. Ask me his name."

"What was his name?"

"Sammy Davis Duck, Jr.," Travis said, and they laughed again. "He was such a big star they didn't even have to put his entire name on the marquee for people to know who was performing there."

"They just put 'Sammy,' huh?"

"No. Just 'Jr'."

Einstein returned from the window and stood watching them, his head cocked, trying to figure out why they were acting so peculiar.

The puzzled expression on the retriever's face struck both Travis and Nora as the most comical thing they had ever seen. They leaned on each other, held each other, and laughed like fools.

With a snort of derision, the retriever went back to the window.

As they gradually regained control of themselves and as their laughter subsided, Travis became aware that he was *holding* Nora, that her head was on his shoulder, that the physical contact between them was greater than any they had allowed themselves before. Her hair smelled clean, fresh. He could feel the body heat pouring off her. Suddenly, he wanted her desperately, and he knew he was going to kiss her when she raised her head from his shoulder. A moment later she looked up, and he did what he knew he'd do—he kissed her—and she kissed him. For a second or two, she did not seem to realize what was happening, what it meant; briefly, it was without significance, sweet and utterly innocent, not a kiss of passion but of friendship and great affection. Then the kiss changed, and her mouth softened. She began to breathe faster, and her hand tightened on his arm, and she tried to pull him closer. A low murmur of need escaped her—and the sound of her own noise brought her to her senses. Abruptly, she stiffened with complete awareness of him as a man, and her beautiful eyes were wide with wonder—and fear—at what had almost happened. Travis instantly drew back because he knew instinctively that the time was not right, not yet perfect. When at last they did make love, it must be exactly right, without hesitation or distraction, because for the rest of their lives they would always remember their first time, and the memory should be all bright and joyous, worth taking out and examining a thousand times as they grew old together. Although it was not quite time to put their future into words and confirm it with vows, Travis had no doubt that he and Nora Devon would be spending their lives with each other, and he realized that, subconsciously, he'd been aware of this inevitability for at least the past few days.

After a moment of awkwardness, as they drew apart and tried to decide whether to comment on the sudden change in their relationship, Nora finally said, "He's still at the window."

Einstein pressed his nose to the glass, staring out at the night.

"Could he be telling the truth?" Nora wondered. "Could there have been something else that escaped from the lab, something *that* bizarre?"

"If they had a dog as smart as him, I guess they might have had other things even more peculiar. And there *was* something in the woods that day."

"But there's no danger of it finding him, surely. Not

after you brought him this far north."

"No danger," Travis agreed. "I don't think Einstein understands how far we came from where I found him. Whatever was in the woods couldn't track him down now. But I'll bet the people from that lab have mounted one hell of a search. It's them I'm worried about. And so is Einstein, which is why he usually plays at being a dumb dog in public and reveals his intelligence only in private to me and now you. He doesn't want to go back."

Nora said, "If they find him ..."

"They won't."

"But if they do, what then?"

"I'll never give him up," Travis said. "Never."

8

By eleven o'clock that night, Deputy Porter's headless corpse and the mutilated body of the construction foreman had been removed from Bordeaux Ridge by the coroner's men. A cover story had been concocted and delivered to the reporters at the police barricades, and the press had seemed to buy it; they had asked their questions, had taken a couple of hundred photographs, and had filled a few thousand feet of videotape with images that would be edited down to a hundred seconds on tomorrow's TV newscast. (In this age of mass murder and terrorism, two victims rated no more than two minutes' airtime: ten seconds for lead-in, a hundred seconds for film, ten seconds for the well-coiffed anchorpersons to look respectfully grim and saddened— then on to a story about a bikini contest, a convention of Edsel owners, or a man who claimed to have seen an alien spacecraft shaped like a Twinkie.) The reporters were gone now, as were the lab men, the uniformed deputies, and all of Lemuel Johnson's agents except Cliff Soames.

Clouds hid the fragment moon. The kliegs were gone, and the only light came from the headlamps of Walt Gaine's car. He had swung his sedan around and aimed his lights at Lem's car, which was parked at the end of the unpaved street, so Lem and Cliff would not have to fumble around in the dark. In the deep gloom beyond the headlamps, half-framed houses loomed like the fossilized skeletons of prehistoric reptiles.

As he walked toward his car, Lem felt as good as he could feel under the circumstances. Walt had agreed to allow federal authorities to assume jurisdiction without a challenge. Although Lem had broken a dozen regulations and had violated his secrecy oath by telling Walt the details of the Francis Project, he was sure Walt could keep his mouth shut. The lid was still on the case, a bit looser than it had been, perhaps, but still in place.

Cliff Soames reached the car first, opened the door, and got in on the passenger's side, and as Lem opened the driver's door he heard Cliff say, "Oh, Jesus, oh God." Cliff was scrambling back out of the car even as Lem looked in from the other side and saw what the uproar was about. A head.

Teel Porter's head, no doubt.

It was on the front seat of the car, propped so it was facing Lem when he opened the door. The mouth was hung open in a silent scream. The eyes were gone.

Reeling back from the car, Lem reached under his coat and pulled his revolver.

Walt Gaines was already out of his car, his own revolver in hand, running toward Lem. "What's wrong?"

Reaching the NSA sedan, Walt looked through the open door and let out a thin, anguished sound when he saw the head.

Cliff came around from the other side of the car, gripping his gun, with the muzzle pointed straight up. "The damn thing was *here* when we arrived, while we were in the house."

"Might still be here," Lem said, anxiously surveying the darkness that crowded them on all sides, beyond the beams from the patrol car's headlights.

Studying the night-swaddled housing development, Walt said, "We'll call in my men, get a search under way."

"No point to it," Lem said. "The thing will take off if it sees your men returning ... if it's not gone already."

They were standing at the edge of Bordeaux Ridge, beyond which lay miles of open land, foothills and mountains, out of which The Outsider had come and into which it could disappear again. Those hills, ridges, and canyons were only vague forms in the meager glow of the partial moon, more sensed than seen.

From somewhere down the unlighted street came a loud clatter, as if a pile of lumber or shingles had been knocked over.

"It *is* here," Walt said.

"Maybe," Lem said. "But we're not going to go looking for it in the dark, not just the three of us. That's what it wants."

They listened.

Nothing more.

"We searched the whole tract when we first got here, before you arrived," Walt said.

Cliff said, "It must've kept one step ahead of you, making a game of dodging your men. Then it saw us arrive, and it recognized Lem."

"Recognized me from the couple of times I visited Banodyne," Lem agreed. "In fact ... The Outsider was probably waiting here just for me. It probably understands my role in all this and knows I'm in charge of the search for it and the dog. So it wanted to leave the deputy's head for me."

"To mock you?" Walt said.

"To mock me."

They were silent, peering uneasily at the blackness within and around the unfinished houses.

The hot June air was motionless.

For a long while, the only sound was the idling engine of the sheriff's car.

"Watching us," Walt said.

Another clatter of overturned construction materials. Nearer this time.

The three men froze, each looking a different direction, guarding against attack.

The subsequent silence lasted almost a minute.

When Lem was about to speak, The Outsider shrieked. The cry was alien, chilling. This time they could identify the direction from which it came: out in the open land, in the night beyond Bordeaux Ridge.

"It's leaving now," Lem said. "It's decided we can't be lured into a search, just the three of us, so it's leaving before we can bring in reinforcements."

It shrieked again, from farther away. The eerie cry was like sharp fingernails raked across Lem's soul.

"In the morning," he said, "we'll move our Marine Intelligence teams into the foothills east of here. We'll nail the damn thing. By God, we will."

Turning to Lem's sedan, evidently contemplating the unpleasant task of dealing with Teel Porter's severed head, Walt said, "Why the eyes? Why does it always tear out the eyes?"

Lem said, "Partly because the creature's just damned aggressive, blood-thirsty. That's in its genes. And partly because it really enjoys spreading terror, I think. But also . . ."

"What?"

"I wish I didn't remember this, but I do, very clearly . . ."

On one of his visits to Banodyne, Lem had witnessed a disturbing conversation (of sorts) between Dr. Yarbeck and The Outsider. Yarbeck and her assistants had taught The Outsider a sign language similar to that developed by the researchers who attempted the first experiments in communication with the higher primates, like gorillas, back in the mid-1970s. The most successful gorilla subject—a female named Koko, which had been the center of countless news stories over the past decade—was reputed to have attained a sign-language vocabulary of approximately four hundred words. When Lem had last seen it, The Outsider boasted a vocabulary considerably larger than Koko's, though still primitive. In Yarbeck's lab, Lem had watched as the man-made monstrosity in the large cage had exchanged complicated series of hand signals with the scientist, while an assistant had whispered a running translation. The Outsider had expressed a fierce hostility toward everyone and everything, frequently interrupting its dialogue with Yarbeck to dash around its cage in uncontrolled rage, banging on the iron bars, screeching furiously. To Lem, the scene was frightening and repellent, but he was also filled with a terrible sadness and pity at the plight of The Outsider: the beast would always be caged, always a freak, alone in the world as no other creature—not even Weatherby's dog—had ever been. The experience had affected him so deeply that he still remembered nearly every exchange of sign language between The Outsider and Yarbeck, and now a pertinent part of that eerie conversation came back to him:

At one point The Outsider had signed: *Tear out your eyes.*

You want to tear out my eyes? Yarbeck signed.

Tear out everyone's eyes.

Why?

So can't see me.

Why don't you want to be seen?

Ugly.

You think you're ugly?

Much ugly.

Where did you get the idea you're ugly?

From people.

What people?

Everyone who see me first time.

Like this man with us today? Yarbeck signed, indicating Lem.

Yes. All think me ugly. Hate me.

No one hates you.

Everyone.

No one's ever told you that you're ugly. How do you know that's what they think?

I know.

How do you know?

I know, I know, I know! It raced around its cage, rattling the bars, shrieking and then it returned to face Yarbeck. *Tear out my own eyes.*

So you won't have to look at yourself?

So won't have to look at people looking at me, the creature had signed, and Lem had pitied it then, deeply, though his pity had in no way diminished his fear of it.

Now, standing in the hot June night, he told Walt Gaines about that exchange in Yarbeck's lab, and the sheriff shivered.

"Jesus," Cliff Soames said. "It hates itself, its otherness, and so it hates its maker even more."

"And now that you've told me this," Walt said, "I'm surprised none of you ever understood why it hates the dog so passionately. This poor damned twisted thing and the dog are essentially the only two children of the Francis Project. The dog is the beloved child, the favored child, and The Outsider has always known that. The dog is the child that the parents want to brag about, while The Outsider is the child they would prefer to keep locked securely in a cellar, and so it resents the dog, *stews* in resentment every minute of every day."

"Of course," Lem said, "you're right. Of course."

"It also gives new meaning to the two smashed mirrors in the upstairs bathrooms in the house where Teel Porter was killed," Walt said. "The thing couldn't bear the sight of itself."

In the distance, very far away, something shrieked, something that was not of God's creation.

SEVEN

1

During the rest of June, Nora did some painting, spent a lot of time with Travis, and tried to teach Einstein to read.

Neither she nor Travis was sure that the dog, although very smart, could be taught such a thing, but it was worth a try. If he understood spoken English, as seemed to be the case, then it followed that he could be taught the printed word as well.

Of course, they could not be absolutely certain that Einstein *did* understand spoken English, even though he responded to it with apt and specific reactions. It was remotely possible that, instead, the dog did not perceive the precise meanings of the words themselves but, by some mild form of telepathy, could read the word-*pictures* in people's minds as they spoke.

"But I don't believe that's the case," Travis said one afternoon as he and Nora sat on his patio, drinking wine coolers and watching Einstein frolic in the spray of a portable lawn sprinkler. "Maybe because I don't want to believe it. The idea that he's both as smart as me *and* telepathic is just too much. If that's the case, then maybe I should be wearing the collar and he should be holding the leash!"

It was a Spanish test that appeared to indicate the

retriever was not, in fact, even slightly telepathic.

In college, Travis had taken three years of Spanish. Later, upon choosing a career in the military and signing on with the elite Delta Force, he'd been encouraged to continue those language studies because his superiors believed the escalating political instability in Central and South America guaranteed that Delta would be required to conduct antiterrorist operations in Spanish-speaking countries with steadily increasing frequency. He had been out of Delta for many years, but contact with the large population of California Hispanics had kept him relatively fluent.

Now, when he gave Einstein orders or asked questions in Spanish, the dog stared at him stupidly, wagging his tail, unresponsive. When Travis persisted in Spanish, the retriever cocked his head and whuffed as if to inquire if this was a joke. Surely, if the dog was reading mental images that arose in the mind of the speaker, he would be able to read them regardless of the language that inspired those images.

"He's no mind reader," Travis said. "There are limits to his genius—thank God!"

Day after day, Nora sat on the floor of Travis's living room or on the patio, explaining the alphabet to Einstein and trying to help him to understand how words were formed from those letters and how those printed words were related to the spoken words that he already understood. Now and then, Travis took charge of the lessons to give Nora a break, but most of the time he sat nearby, reading, because he claimed not to have the patience to be a teacher.

She used a ring-binder notebook to compile her own primer for the dog. On each left-hand page, she taped a picture cut from a magazine, and on each right-hand page she printed, in block letters, the name of the object that was pictured on the left, all simple words: TREE, CAR, HOUSE, MAN, WOMAN, CHAIR ... With Einstein sitting beside her and staring intently at the primer, she would point to the picture first, then to the word, pronouncing it repeatedly.

On the last day of June, Nora spread a score or more of unlabeled pictures on the floor.

"It's test time again," she told Einstein. "Let's see if you can do better than you did on Monday."

Einstein sat very erect, his chest puffed out, his head held high, as if confident of his ability.

Travis was sitting in the armchair, watching. He said, "If you fail, fur face, we're going to trade you in on a poodle that can roll over, play dead, and beg for its supper."

Nora was pleased to see that Einstein ignored Travis. "This is not a time for frivolity," she admonished.

"I stand corrected, professor," Travis said.

Nora held up a flashcard with TREE printed on it. The retriever went unerringly to the photo of a pine tree and indicated it with a touch of his nose. When she held up a card that said CAR, he put a paw on the photo of the car, and when she held up HOUSE, he sniffed at the picture of a colonial mansion. They went through fifty words, and for the first time the dog correctly paired every printed word with the image it represented. Nora was thrilled by his progress, and Einstein could not stop wagging his tail.

Travis said, "Well, Einstein, you're still a hell of a long way from reading Proust."

Rankled by Travis's needling of her star pupil, Nora said, "He's doing fine! Terrific. You can't expect him to be reading at college level overnight. He's learning faster than a child would."

"Is that so?"

"Yes, that's so! *Much* faster than a child would."

"Well then, maybe he deserves a couple of Milk-Bones."

Einstein dashed immediately into the kitchen to get the box of dog biscuits.

2

As the summer wore on, Travis was amazed by the swift progress Nora made in teaching Einstein to read.

By the middle of July, they graduated from her home-made primer to children's picture books by Dr. Seuss, Maurice Sendak, Phil Parks, Susi Bohdal, Sue Dreamer, Mercer Mayer, and many others. Einstein appeared to enjoy all of them immensely, though his favorites were by Parks and especially—for reasons neither Nora nor Travis could discern—the charming Frog and Toad books by Arnold Lobel. They brought armsful of children's books from the city library and purchased additional stacks of them at the bookstore.

At first, Nora read them aloud, carefully moving a finger under each word as she spoke it, and Einstein's eyes followed along as he leaned in toward the book with undivided attention. Later, she did not read the book aloud but held it open for the dog and turned the pages for him when he indicated—by a whimper or some other sign—that he had finished that portion of the text and was ready to proceed to the next page.

Einstein's willingness to sit for hours, focusing on the books, seemed proof that he was actually reading them and not just looking at the cute drawings. Nevertheless, Nora decided to test him on the contents of some of the volumes by posing a number of questions about the story lines.

After Einstein had read *Frog and Toad All Year*, Nora closed the book and said, "All right. Now, answer yes or no to these questions."

They were in the kitchen, where Travis was making a cheese-and-potato casserole for dinner. Nora and Einstein were sitting on chairs at the kitchen table. Travis paused in his cooking to watch the dog take the quiz.

Nora said, "First—when Frog came to see Toad on a winter's day, Toad was in bed and did not want to come outside. Is that right?"

Einstein had to sidle around on his chair to free his tail and wag it. *Yes*.

Nora said, "But finally Frog got Toad outside, and they went ice-skating."

One bark. *No*.

"They went sledding," she said.

268

Yes.

"Very good. Later that same year, at Christmas, Frog gave Toad a gift. Was it a sweater?"

No.

"A new sled?"

No.

"A clock for his mantel?"

Yes, yes, yes.

"Excellent!" Nora said. "Now what shall we read next? How about this one. *Fantastic Mr. Fox.*"

Einstein wagged his tail vigorously.

Travis would have enjoyed taking a more active role in the dog's education, but he could see that working intensely with Einstein was having an enormously beneficial effect on Nora, and he did not want to interfere. Indeed, he sometimes played the curmudgeon, questioning the value of teaching the pooch to read, making wisecracks about the pace of the dog's progress or its taste in reading matter. This mild naysaying was just enough to redouble Nora's determination to stick with the lessons, to spend even more time with the dog, and to prove Travis wrong. Einstein never reacted to those negative remarks, and Travis suspected the dog exhibited a forbearance because he understood the little game of reverse psychology in which Travis was engaged.

Exactly why Nora's teaching chores made her blossom was not clear. Perhaps it was because she had never interacted with anyone—not even with Travis or with her Aunt Violet—as intensely as she had with the dog, and the mere process of extensive communication encouraged her to come farther out of her shell. Or perhaps giving the gift of literacy to the dog was extremely satisfying to her. She was by nature a giving person who took pleasure in sharing with others, yet she had spent all her life as a recluse without a single previous opportunity to express that side of her personality. Now she had a chance to give of herself, and she was generous with her time and energy, and in her own generosity she found joy.

Travis also suspected that, through her relationship with

the retriever, she was expressing a natural talent for mothering. Her great patience was that of a good mother dealing with a child, and she often spoke to Einstein so tenderly and affectionately that she sounded as if she were addressing her own much-loved offspring.

Whatever the reason, Nora became more relaxed and outgoing as she worked with Einstein. Gradually forsaking her shapeless dark dresses for summery white cotton slacks, colorful blouses, jeans and T-shirts, she seemed to grow ten years younger. She had her glorious dark hair redone at the beauty salon and did not brush out all the styling this time. She laughed more often and more engagingly. In conversation, she met Travis's eyes and seldom looked shyly away from him, as she had done previously. She was quicker to touch him, too, and to put an arm around his waist. She liked to be hugged, and they kissed with ease now, although their kissing remained, for the most part, that of uncertain teenagers in the early stages of courting.

On July 14, Nora received news that lifted her spirits even higher. The Santa Barbara District Attorney's Office called to tell her that it was not going to be necessary for her to appear in court to testify against Arthur Streck. In light of his previous criminal record, Streck had changed his mind about pursuing a plea of innocence and waging a defense against charges of attempted rape, assault, and breaking and entering. He had instructed his attorney to plea-bargain with the D.A. As a result, they dropped all charges except assault, and Streck accepted a prison sentence of three years, with a provision that he serve at least two years before being eligible for parole. Nora had dreaded the trial. Suddenly she was free, and in celebration she got slightly tipsy for the first time in her life.

That same day, when Travis brought home a new stack of reading material, Einstein discovered there were Mickey Mouse picture books for children and comic books, and the dog was as jubilant about that discovery as Nora was about the resolution of the charges against Arthur Streck. His fascination with Mickey and Donald Duck and the rest of the Disney gang remained a mystery, but it was undeniable.

Einstein couldn't stop wagging his tail, and he slobbered all over Travis in gratitude.

Everything would have been rosy if, in the middle of the night, Einstein had stopped going through the house from window to window, looking out at the darkness with obvious fear.

3

By Thursday morning, July 15, almost six weeks after the murders at Bordeaux Ridge, two months after the dog and The Outsider had escaped from Banodyne, Lemuel Johnson sat alone in his office on an upper floor of the federal building in Santa Ana, the county seat of Orange County. He stared out the window at the pollutant-rich haze that was trapped under an inversion layer, blanketing the western half of the county and adding to the misery of hundred-degree heat. The bile-yellow day matched his sour mood.

His duties were not limited to the search for the lab escapees, but that case constantly worried him when he was doing other work. He was unable to put the Banodyne affair out of mind even to sleep, and lately he was averaging only four to five hours of rest a night. He could not tolerate failure.

No, in truth, his attitude was much stronger than that: he was *obsessed* with avoiding failure. His father, having started life dirt-poor and having built a successful business, had inculcated in Lem an almost religious belief in the need to achieve, to succeed, and to fulfill all of one's goals. No matter how much success you had, his dad often said, life could pull the rug right out from under you if you weren't diligent. "It's even worse for a black man, Lem. With a black man, success is like a tightrope over the Grand Canyon. He's up there real high, and it's sweet, but when he makes a mistake, when he fails, it's a mile-long drop into an abyss. An *abyss*. Because failure means being poor. And

271

in a lot of people's eyes, even in this enlightened age, a poor miserable failed black man is no man at all, he's just a nigger.'' That was the only time his father ever used the hated word. Lem had grown up with the conviction that any success he achieved was merely a precarious toehold on the cliff of life, that he was always in danger of being blown off that cliff by the winds of adversity, and that he dared not relent in his determination to cling fast and to climb to a wider, safer ledge.

He wasn't sleeping well, and his appetite was no good. When he did eat, the meal was inevitably followed by severe acid indigestion. His bridge game had gone to hell because he could not concentrate on the cards; at their weekly get-togethers with Walt and Audrey Gaines, the Johnsons were taking a beating.

He knew why he was obsessed with closing every case successfully, but that knowledge was of no help in modifying his obsession.

We are what we are, he thought, and maybe the only time we can change what we are is when life throws us such a surprise that it's like hitting a plate-glass window with a baseball bat, shattering the grip of the past.

So he stared out at the blazing July day and brooded, worried.

Back in May, he had surmised that the retriever might have been picked up by someone and given a home. It was, after all, a handsome animal, and if it revealed even a small fraction of its intelligence to anyone, its appeal would be irresistible; it would find sanctuary. Therefore, Lem figured locating the dog would be harder than tracking down The Outsider. A week to locate The Outsider, he had thought, and perhaps a month to lay hands on the retriever.

He had issued bulletins to every animal pound and veterinarian in California, Nevada, and Arizona, urgently requesting assistance in locating the golden retriever. The flyer claimed that the animal had escaped from a medical research lab that was conducting an important cancer experiment. The loss of the dog, the bulletin claimed, would mean the loss of a million dollars of research money and countless hours of researchers' time—and might seriously impede the development of a cure for certain malignancies. The flyer included a photograph of the dog and the information that, on the inside of its left ear, it bore a lab tattoo: the number 33-9. The letter accompanying the flyer requested not only cooperation but confidentiality. The mailing had been repeated every seven days since the breakout at Banodyne, and a score of NSA agents had been doing nothing but phoning animal pounds and vets in the three states to be certain they remembered the flyer and continued to keep a lookout for a retriever with a tattoo.

Meanwhile, the urgent search for The Outsider could, with some confidence, be confined to undeveloped territories because it would be reluctant to show itself. And there was no chance that someone would think *it* was cute enough to take home. Besides, The Outsider had been leaving a trail of death that could be followed.

Subsequent to the murders at Bordeaux Ridge east of Yorba Linda, the creature had fled into the unpopulated Chino Hills. From there it had gone north, crossing into the eastern end of Los Angeles County, where its presence was next pinpointed, on June 9, on the outskirts of semirural Diamond Bar. The Los Angeles County Animal Control Authority had received numerous—and hysterical—reports from Diamond Bar residents regarding wild-animal attacks on domestic pets. Others called the police, believing the slaughter was the work of a deranged man. In two nights, more than a score of Diamond Bar's domestic animals had been torn to pieces, and the condition of the carcasses left no doubt in Lem's mind that the perpetrator was The Outsider.

Then the trail went ice-cold for more than a week, until the morning of June 18, when two young campers at the foot of Johnstone Peak, on the southern flank of the vast Angeles National Forest, reported seeing something they insisted was "from another world." They had locked themselves in their van, but the creature had tried repeatedly to get in at them, going so far as to smash a side window with a rock. Fortunately, the pair kept a .32 pistol in the van,

273

and one of them opened fire on their assailant, driving it off. The press treated the campers as a couple of kooks, and on the evening news the happy-talk anchorpersons got a lot of mileage out of the story.

Lem believed the young couple. On a map, he traced the thinly populated corridor of land by which The Outsider could have gone from Diamond Bar to the area below Johnstone Peak: over the San Jose Hills, through Bonelli Regional Park, between San Dimas and Glendora, then into the wilds. It would have had to cross or go under three freeways that cut through the area, but if it had traveled in the deep of night, when there was little or no traffic, it could have passed unseen. He shifted the hundred men from Marine Intelligence into that portion of the forest, where they continued their search in civilian dress, in groups of three or four.

He hoped the campers had hit The Outsider with at least one shot. But no blood was found at their campsite.

He was beginning to worry that The Outsider might evade capture for a long time. Lying north of the city of Los Angeles, the Angeles National Forest was discouragingly immense.

"Nearly as large as the entire state of Delaware," Cliff Soames said after he had measured the area on the wall map pinned to the bulletin board in Lem's office and had calculated the square miles. Cliff had come from Delaware. He was relatively new to the West and still had a newcomer's amazement at the gigantic scale of everything at this end of the continent. He was also young, with the enthusiasm of youth, and he was almost dangerously optimistic. Cliff's upbringing had been radically different from Lem's, and he did not feel himself to be on a tightrope or at risk of having his life destroyed by just one error, by a single failure. Sometimes Lem envied him.

Lem stared at Cliff's scribbled calculations. "If it takes refuge in the San Gabriel Mountains, feeding on wildlife and content with solitude, venturing out only rarely to vent its rage on the people living along the periphery of the preserve . . . it might never be found."

"But remember," Cliff said, "it hates the dog more than it hates men. It *wants* the dog and has the ability to find it."

"So we think."

"And could it really tolerate a wild existence? I mean, yeah, it's part savage, but it's also smart. Maybe too smart to be content with a hardscrabble life in that rugged country."

"Maybe," Lem said.

"They'll spot it soon, or it'll do something to give us another fix on it," Cliff predicted.

That was June 18.

When they found no trace of The Outsider during the next ten days, the expense of keeping a hundred men in the field grew insupportable. On June 29, Lem finally had to relinquish the Marines that had been put at his disposal and send them back to their bases.

Day by day, Cliff was heartened by the lack of developments and was willing to believe that The Outsider had suffered a mishap, that it was dead, that they would never hear of it again.

Day by day, Lem sank deeper into gloom, certain that he had lost control of the situation and that The Outsider would reappear in a most dramatic fashion, making its existence known to the public. Failure.

The only bright spot was that the beast was now in Los Angeles County, out of Walt Gaines's jurisdiction. If there were additional victims, Walt might not even learn of them and would not have to be persuaded, all over again, to remain out of the case.

By Thursday, July 15, exactly two months after the breakout at Banodyne, almost one month after the campers had been terrorized by a supposed entraterrestrial or smaller cousin of Bigfoot, Lem was convinced he would soon have to consider alternate careers. No one had blamed him for the way things had gone. The heat was on him to deliver, but it was no worse than the heat he had felt on other big investigations. Actually, some of his superiors viewed the lack of developments in the same favorable light as did Cliff Soames. But in his most pessimistic moments,

Lem envisioned himself employed as a uniformed security guard working the night shift in a warehouse, demoted to the status of a make-believe cop with a rinky-dink badge.

Sitting in his office chair, facing the window, staring grimly at the hazy yellow air of the blazing summer day, he said aloud, "Damn it, I've been trained to deal with *human* criminals. How the hell can I be expected to outthink a fugitive from a nightmare?"

A knock sounded at his door, and as he swiveled around in his chair the door opened. Cliff Soames entered in a rush, looking both excited and distraught. "The Outsider," he said. "We've got a new fix on it ... but two people are dead."

Twenty years ago in Vietnam, Lem's NSA chopper pilot had learned everything worth knowing about putting down and taking off in rugged terrain. Now, remaining in constant radio contact with the L.A. County sheriff's deputies who were on the scene already, he had no difficulty locating the site of the murders by visual navigation, making use of natural landmarks. At a few minutes after one o'clock, he put his craft down on a wide section of a barren ridge overlooking Boulder Canyon in the Angeles National Forest, just a hundred yards from the spot where the bodies had been found.

When Lem and Cliff left the chopper and hurried along the crest of the ridge toward the gathered deputies and forest rangers, a hot wind buffeted them. It carried the scent of dry brush and pine. Only tufts of wild grass, parched and brittled by the July sun, had managed to put down roots on this high ground. Low scrub growth—including desert plants like mesquite—marked the upper reaches of the canyon walls that dropped away to the right and left of them, and down on the lower slopes and canyon floors were trees and greener undergrowth.

They were less than four air miles north of the town of Sunland, fourteen air miles north of Hollywood, and twenty miles north of the populous heart of the great city of Los Angeles, yet it seemed they were in a desolation measuring a thousand miles across, disquietingly far from civilization. The sheriff's deputies had parked their four-wheel drive wagons on a crude dirt track three-quarters of a mile away—coming in, Lem's chopper had flown over those vehicles—and they had hiked with ranger guides to the site where the bodies had been found. Now, gathered around the corpses were four deputies, two men from the county crime lab, and three rangers, and they looked as if they, too, felt isolated in a primeval place.

When Lem and Cliff arrived, the sheriff's men had just finished tucking the remains in body bags. The zippers hadn't yet been closed, so Lem saw that one victim was male, the other female, both young and dressed for hiking. Their wounds were grievous; their eyes were gone.

The dead now numbered five innocents, and that toll conjured a specter of guilt that haunted Lem. At times like this, he wished that his father had raised him with no sense of responsibility whatsoever.

Deputy Hal Bockner, tall and tan but with a surprisingly reedy voice, apprised Lem of the identity and condition of the victims: "Based on the ID he was carrying, the male's name was Sidney Tranken, twenty-eight, of Glendale. Body has more than a score of nasty bite marks, even more claw marks, slashes. Throat, as you saw, tore open. Eyes—"

"Yes," Lem said, seeing no need to dwell on these grisly details.

The men from the crime lab pulled the zippers shut on the body bags. It was a cold sound that hung for a moment like a chain of icicles in the hot July air.

Deputy Bockner said, "At first we thought Tranken was probably knifed by some psycho. Once in a while you get a homicidal nut who prowls these forests instead of the streets, preying on hikers. So we figured . . . knifed first, then all this other damage must've been done by animals, scavengers, after the guy was dead. But now . . . we're not so sure."

"I don't see blood on the ground here," Cliff Soames

277

said with a note of puzzlement. "There'd have been a *lot* of it."

"They weren't killed here," Deputy Bockner said, then went on with his summary at his own pace. "Female, twenty-seven, Ruth Kasavaris, also of Glendale. Also vicious bite marks, slashes. Her throat—"

Cutting him off again, Lem said, "When were they killed?"

"Best guess before lab tests is that they died late yesterday. We believe the bodies were carried up here because they'd be found quicker on the ridge top. A popular hiking trail runs along here. But it wasn't other hikers found them. It was a routine fire-patrol plane. Pilot looked down, saw them sprawled here on the bare ridge."

This high ground above Boulder Canyon was more than thirty air miles north-northwest of Johnstone Peak, where the young campers had taken refuge from The Outsider in their van and had later fired at it with a .32 pistol on June 18, twenty-eight days ago. The Outsider would have been reckoning north-northwest by sheer instinct and no doubt would have frequently been required to backtrack out of box canyons; therefore, in this mountainous terrain it had very likely traveled between sixty and ninety miles on the ground to cover those thirty air miles. Still, that was only a pace of three miles a day, at most, and Lem wondered what the creature had been doing during the time it was not traveling or sleeping or chasing down food.

"You'll want to see where these two were killed," Bockner said. "We've found the place. And you'll want to see the den, too."

"Den?"

"The lair," one of the forest rangers said. "The damn lair."

The deputies, rangers, and crime-lab men had been giving Lem and Cliff odd looks ever since they had arrived, but Lem had not been surprised by that. Local authorities always regarded him with suspicion and curiosity because they were not accustomed to having a powerhouse federal agency like the NSA show up and claim jurisdiction; it was a rarity. But now he realized that their curiosity was of a different kind and degree than what he usually encountered, and for the first time he perceived their fear. They had found something —the lair of which they spoke—that gave them reason to believe this case was even stranger than the sudden appearance of the NSA would usually indicate.

In suits, ties, and polished street shoes, neither Lem nor Cliff was properly dressed for a hike down into the canyon, but neither of them hesitated when the rangers led the way. Two deputies, the lab men, and one of the three rangers remained behind with the bodies, which left a party of six for the descent. They followed a shallow channel carved by runoff from rainstorms, then switched to what might have been a deer trail. After descending to the very bottom of the canyon, they turned southeast and proceeded for half a mile. Soon Lem was sweaty and covered with a film of dust, and his socks and pant legs were full of prickling burrs.

"Here's where they were killed," Deputy Bockner said when he led them into a clearing surrounded by scrub pines, cottonwoods, and brush.

The pale, sandy earth and sun-bleached grass were mottled with enormous dark stains. Blood.

"And right back here," one of the rangers said, "is where we found the lair."

It was a shallow cave in the base of the canyon wall, perhaps ten feet deep, twenty feet wide, no more than a dozen steps from the small clearing where the hikers had been murdered. The mouth of the cave was about eight feet wide but low, requiring Lem to stoop a bit as he entered. Once inside, he was able to stand erect, for the ceiling was high. The place had a mildly unpleasant, musty smell. Light found its way through the entrance and through a two-foot-wide water-carved hole in the ceiling, but for the most part the chamber was shadowy and twenty degrees cooler than the canyon outside.

Only Deputy Bockner accompanied Lem and Cliff. Lem sensed that the others held back not out of any concern that the cave would be too crowded, but out of an uneasiness about the place.

Bockner had a flashlight. He switched it on and played the beam over the things he had brought them to see, dispelling some of the shadows and causing others to flit batlike across the room to roost on different perches.

In one corner, dry grass had been piled to a depth of six or eight inches to make a bed on the sandstone floor. Beside the bed was a galvanized bucket full of relatively fresh water carried from the nearest stream, evidently placed there so the sleeper could get a drink upon waking in the middle of the night.

"It was here," Cliff said softly.

"Yes," Lem agreed.

Instinctively he sensed The Outsider had made this bed; somehow, its alien presence was still in the chamber. He stared at the bucket, wondering where the creature had acquired it. Most likely, along the way from Banodyne, it had decided it would eventually find a burrow and hide for a while, and it had realized it would need a few things to make its life in the wild more comfortable. Perhaps breaking into a stable or barn or empty house, it had stolen the bucket and various other things that Bockner now revealed with his flashlight.

A plaid flannel blanket for when the weather turned cooler. A horse blanket, judging by the look of it. What caught Lem's attention was the neatness with which the blanket had been folded and placed on a narrow ledge in the wall beside the entrance.

A flashlight. This was on the same shelf that held the blanket. The Outsider had exceedingly good night vision. That was one of the design requirements with which Dr. Yarbeck had been working: in the dark, a good genetically engineered warrior would be able to see as well as a cat. So why would it want a flashlight? Unless ... maybe even a creature of the night was sometimes afraid of darkness.

That thought jolted Lem, and suddenly he pitied the beast as he had pitied it that day he had watched it communicating by crude sign language with Yarbeck, the day it had said that it wanted to tear its own eyes out so it would never have to look at itself again.

Bockner moved the beam of his own flashlight and focused it on twenty candy wrappers. Apparently, The Outsider had stolen a couple of family packs of candy somewhere along the way. The strange thing was that the wrappers were not crumpled but were smoothed out and laid flat on the floor along the back wall—ten from Reese's peanut butter cups and ten from Clark Bars. Perhaps The Outsider liked the bright colors of the wrappers. Or perhaps it kept them to remind itself of the pleasure that the candy had given it because, once those treats were gone, there was not much other pleasure to be had in the hard life to which it had been driven.

In the farthest corner from the bed, deep in shadows, was a pile of bones. The bones of small animals. Once the candy was eaten, The Outsider had been forced to hunt in order to feed itself. And without the means to light a fire, it had fed savagely on raw meat. Perhaps it kept the bones in the cave because it was afraid that, by disposing of them outside, it would be leaving clues to its whereabouts. By storing them in the darkest, farthest corner of its haven, it seemed to have a civilized sense of neatness and order, but to Lem it also seemed as if The Outsider had hidden the bones in the shadows because it was ashamed of its own savagery.

Most pathetically of all, a peculiar group of items was stored in a niche in the wall above the grassy bed. No, Lem decided, not just stored. The items were carefully arranged, as if for display, the way an aficionado of art glass or ceramics or Mayan pottery might display a valuable collection. There was a round stained-glass bauble of the sort that people hung from their patio covers to sparkle in the sun; it was about four inches in diameter, and it portrayed a blue flower against a pale-yellow background. Beside that bauble was a bright copper pot that had probably once contained a plant on the same—or another —patio. Next to the pot were two things that surely had been taken from inside a house, perhaps from the same place where The Outsider had stolen the candy: first, a fine porcelain study of a pair of red-feathered cardinals sitting

281

on a branch, every detail exquisitely crafted; second, a crystal paperweight. Apparently, even within the alien breast of Yarbeck's monstrosity, there was an appreciation of beauty and a desire to live not as an animal but as a thinking being in an ambience at least lightly touched by civilization.

Lem felt sick at heart as he considered the lonely, tortured, self-hating, inhuman yet self-aware creature that Yarbeck had brought into the world.

Last of all, the niche above the grass bed held a ten-inch-high figure of Mickey Mouse that was also a coin bank.

Lem's pity swelled because he knew why the bank had appealed to The Outsider. At Banodyne, there had been experiments to determine the depth and nature of the dog's and The Outsider's intelligence, to discover how close their perceptions were to those of a human being. One of the experiments had been designed to probe their ability to differentiate between fantasy and reality. On several occasions, the dog and The Outsider had separately been shown a videotape that had been assembled from film clips of all kinds: bits of old John Wayne movies, footage from George Lucas's *Star Wars*, news films, scenes from a wide variety of documentaries—and old Mickey Mouse cartoons. The reactions of the dog and The Outsider were filmed and, later, they were quizzed to see if they understood which segments of the videotape were of real events and which were flights of the imagination. Both creatures had gradually learned to identify fantasy when they saw it; but, strangely, the one fantasy they most wanted to believe in, the fantasy they clung to the longest, was Mickey Mouse. They were enthralled by Mickey's adventures with his cartoon friends. After escaping Banodyne, The Outsider had somehow come across this coin bank and had wanted it badly because the poor damn thing was reminded of the only real pleasure it had ever known while in the lab.

In the beam of Deputy Bockner's flashlight, something on the shelf glinted. It was lying nearly flat beside the coin bank, and they almost overlooked it. Cliff stepped onto the grass bed and plucked the gleaming object out of the wall niche: a three-inch-by-four-inch triangular fragment of mirror.

The Outsider huddled here, Lem thought, trying to take heart from its meager treasures, trying to make as much of a home for itself as was possible. Once in a while it picked up this jagged shard from a mirror and stared at itself, perhaps searching hopefully for an aspect of its countenance that was *not* ugly, perhaps trying to come to terms with what it was. And failing. Surely failing.

"Dear God," Ciff Soames said quietly, for the same thoughts had apparently passed through his mind. "The poor miserable bastard."

The Outsider had possessed one additional item: a copy of *People* magazine. Robert Redford was on the cover. With a claw, sharp stone, or some other instrument, The Outsider had cut out Redford's eyes.

The magazine was rumpled and tattered, as if it had been paged through a hundred times, and now Deputy Bockner handed it to them and suggested they page through it once more. On doing so, Lem saw that the eyes of every person pictured in the issue had been either scratched, cut or crudely torn out.

The thoroughness of this symbolic mutilation—not *one* image in the magazine had been spared—was chilling.

The Outsider was pathetic, yes, and it was to be pitied.

But it was also to be feared.

Five victims—some gutted, some decapitated.

The innocent dead must not be forgotten, not for a moment. Neither an affection for Mickey Mouse nor a love of beauty could excuse such slaughter.

But Jesus . . .

The creature had been given sufficient intelligence to grasp the importance and the benefits of civilization, to long for acceptance and a meaningful existence. Yet a fierce lust for violence, a killing instinct second to none in nature, was also engineered into it because it was meant to be a smart killer on a long invisible leash, a living machine of war. No matter how long it existed in peaceful solitude in its canyon, no matter how many days or weeks it resisted its own violent urges, it could not change what it was. The pressure would build within it until it could no longer contain itself, until the slaughter of small animals would not provide enough psychological relief, and then it would seek larger and more interesting prey. It might damn itself for its savagery, might long to remake itself into a creature that could exist in harmony with the rest of the world, but it was powerless to change what it was. Only hours ago, Lem had pondered how difficult it was for him to become a different man from the one his father had raised, how hard it was for *any* man to change what life had made him, but at least it was possible if one had the determination, willpower, and time. However, for The Outsider change was impossible; murder was in the beast's genes, *locked* in, and it could expect no hope of re-creation or salvation.

"What the hell is this all about?" Deputy Bockner asked, finally unable to repress his curiosity.

"Believe me," Lem said, "you don't want to know."

"What was in this cave?" Bockner asked.

Lem only shook his head. If two more people had to die, it was a stroke of good fortune that they had been murdered in a national forest. This was federal land, which meant much simpler procedures by which the NSA could assume authority in the investigation.

Cliff Soames was still turning the fragment of mirror over and over in his hand, staring at it thoughtfully.

Looking around the eerie chamber one last time, Lem Johnson made a promise to himself and to his dangerous quarry: When I find you, I won't consider trying to take you alive; no net or tranquillizer guns, as the scientists and the military would prefer; instead, I'll shoot you quick and clean, take you down fast.

That was not only the safest plan. It would also be an act of compassion and mercy.

4

By the first of August, Nora had sold all of Aunt Violet's furniture and other possessions. She had phoned a man who dealt in antiques and secondhand furniture, and he had given her one price for everything, and she had accepted it happily. Now—except for dishes, silverware, and the furniture in the bedroom that she had made her own—the rooms were empty from wall to wall. The house seemed cleansed, purified, *exorcized*. All evil spirits had been driven out, and she knew she now had the will to redecorate entirely. But she no longer wanted the place, so she telephoned a real-estate agent and put it on the market.

Her old clothes were gone, too, all of them, and she had an entirely new wardrobe with slacks and skirts and blouses and jeans and dresses like any woman might have. Occasionally, she felt too conspicuous in bright colors, but she always resisted the urge to change into something dark and drab.

She still had not found the courage to put her artistic talent on the market and see if her work was worth anything. Travis nudged her about it now and then, in ways he thought were subtle, but she was not ready to lay her fragile ego on the anvil and give just anyone a chance to swing a hammer at it. Soon, but not yet.

Sometimes, when she looked at herself in a mirror or noticed her reflection in a sun-silvered store window, she realized that, indeed, she was pretty. Not beautiful, perhaps, not gorgeous like some movie star, but moderately pretty. However, she did not seem to be able to hold onto this breakthrough perception of her appearance, at least not for long, because every few days she would be surprised anew by the comeliness of the face looking back at her from the mirror.

On the fifth of August, late in the afternoon, she and Travis were sitting at the table in his kitchen, playing Scrabble, and she was feeling pretty. A few minutes ago, in the bathroom, she'd had another of those revelations when she had looked in the mirror, and in fact she had liked her looks more than ever before. Now, back at the Scrabble board, she felt buoyant, happier than she would have once believed possible—and mischievous. She started using her tiles to spell nonsense words and then vociferously defended them when Travis questioned their legitimacy.

"'Dofnup'?" he said, frowning at the board. "There's no such word as 'dofnup'."

"It's a triangular cap that loggers wear," she said.

"Loggers?"

"Like Paul Bunyan."

"Loggers wear knit caps, what you call toboggan caps, or round leather caps with earflaps."

"I'm not talking about what they wear to work in the woods," she explained patiently. "'Dofnup.' That's the name of the cap they wear to bed."

He laughed and shook his head. "Are you putting me on?"

She kept a straight face. "No. It's true."

"Loggers wear a special cap to bed?"

"Yes. The dofnup."

He was unaccustomed to the very *idea* that Nora would play a joke on him, so he fell for it. "Dofnup? Why do they call it that?"

"Beats me," she said.

Einstein was on the floor, on his belly, reading a novel. Since graduating with startling swiftness from picture books to children's literature like *The Wind in the Willows*, he had been reading eight and ten hours a day, every day. He couldn't get *enough* books. He'd become a prose junkie. Ten days ago, when the dog's obsession with reading had finally outstripped Nora's patience for holding books and turning pages, they had tried to puzzle out an arrangement that would make it possible for Einstein to keep a volume open in front of him and turn the pages himself. At a hospital-supply company, they had found a device designed for patients who had the use of neither arms nor legs. It was a metal stand onto which the boards of the books were clamped; electrically powered mechanical arms, controlled by three push buttons, turned the pages and held them in place. A quadriplegic could operate it with a stylus held in his teeth; Einstein used his nose. The dog seemed immensely pleased by the arrangement. Now, he whimpered softly about something he had just read, pushed one of the buttoms, and turned another page.

Travis spelled "wicked" and picked up a lot of points by using a double-score square, so Nora used her tiles to spell "hurkey," which was worth even more points.

"'Hurkey'?" Travis said doubtfully.

"It's a favorite Yugoslavian meal," she said.

"It is?"

"Yes. The recipe includes both ham and turkey, which is why they call it—" She couldn't finish. She broke into laughter.

He gaped at her in astonishment. "You *are* putting me on. *You* are putting me on! Nora Devon, what's become of you? When I first met you, I said to myself, 'Now, there's the grimmest-damn-most-serious young woman I've ever seen.'"

"And squirrelly."

"Well, not squirrelly."

"Yes, squirrelly," she insisted. "You thought I was squirrelly."

"All right, yeah, I thought you were so squirrelly you probably had the attic of that house packed full of walnuts."

Grinning, she said, "If Violet and I had lived in the south, we'd have been straight out of Faulkner, wouldn't we?"

"Too weird even for Faulkner. But now just look at you! Making up dumb words and dumber jokes, conning me into believing them 'cause I'd never expect Nora Devon, of all people, to do any such thing. You've sure changed in these few months."

"Thanks to you," she said.

"Maybe thanks to Einstein more than me."

"No. You most of all," she said, and abruptly she was stricken by that old shyness that had once all but paralyzed her. She looked away from him, down at her tray of

287

Scrabble tiles, and in a low voice she said, "You most of all. I'd never have met Einstein if I hadn't met you. And you ... cared about me ... worried about me ... saw something in me that I couldn't see. You remade me."

"No," he said. "You give me too much credit. You didn't have to be remade. *This* Nora was always there, inside the old one. Like a flower all cramped up and hidden inside a drab little seed. You just had to be encouraged to ... well, to grow and bloom."

She could not look at him. She felt as if a tremendous stone had been placed on the back of her neck, forcing her to bow her head, and she was blushing. But she found the courage to say, "It's so damn hard to bloom ... to change. Even when you want to change, want it more than anything in the world, it's hard. Desire to change isn't enough. Or desperation. Couldn't be done without ... love." Her voice had dropped to a whisper, and she was unable to lift it. "Love is like the water and the sun that make the seed grow."

He said, "Nora, look at me."

That stone on her neck must have weighed a hundred pounds, a thousand.

"Nora?"

It weighed a *ton*.

"Nora, I love you too."

Somehow with great effort, she lifted her head. She looked at him. His brown eyes, so dark as to be almost black, were warm and kind and beautiful. She loved those eyes. She loved the high bridge and narrow line of his nose. She loved every aspect of his lean and ascetic face.

"I should have told you first," he said, "because it's easier for me to say it than it is for you. I should have said it days ago, weeks ago: Nora, by God, I love you. But I didn't say it because I was afraid. Every time I let myself love someone, I lose them, but this time I think maybe it'll be different. Maybe you'll change things for me the way I helped change them for you, and maybe this time luck's with me."

Her heart raced. She could barely get her breath, but she said, "I love you."

"Will you marry me?"

She was stunned. She did not know what she'd expected to happen, but certainly not *this*. Just hearing him say he loved her, just being able to express the same sentiments to him—that was enough to keep her happy for weeks, months. She expected to have time to walk around their love, as if it were a great and mysterious edifice that, like some newly discovered pyramid, must be studied and pondered from every angle before she dared to undertake an exploration of the interior.

"Will you marry me?" he repeated.

This was too fast, recklessly fast, and just sitting there on a kitchen chair she got as dizzy as if she had been spinning around on a carnival ride, and she was afraid, too, so she tried to tell him to slow down, tried to tell him they had plenty of time to consider the next step before taking it, but to her surprise she heard herself say, "Yes. Oh, yes."

He reached out and took both her hands.

She cried, then, but they were good tears.

Lost in his book, Einstein had nevertheless been aware of what was transpiring. He came to the table, sniffing at both of them, rubbing against their legs, and whining happily.

Travis said, "Next week?"

"Married? But it takes time to get a license and everything."

"Not in Las Vegas. I can call ahead, make arrangements with a wedding chapel in Vegas. We can go next week and be married."

Crying and laughing at the same time, she said, "All right."

"Terrific," Travis said, grinning.

Einstein wagged his tail furiously: *Yes, yes, yes, yes, yes.*

5

On Wednesday, the fourth of August, working on contract for the Tetragna Family of San Francisco, Vince

Nasco hit a little cockroach named Lou Pantangela. The cockroach had turned state's evidence and was scheduled, in September, to testify in court against members of the Tetragna organization.

Johnny The Wire Santini, computer hacker for the mob, had used his high-tech expertise to invade federal computer files and locate Pantangela. The cockroach was living under the protection of two federal marshals in a safe house in, of all places, Redondo Beach, south of L.A. After testifying this autumn, he was scheduled to be given a new identity and a new life in Connecticut, but of course he was not going to live that long.

Because Vince would probably have to waste one or both of the marshals to get at Pantangela, the rubout was going to bring a lot of heat, so the Tetragnas offered him a very high price—$60,000. They had no way of knowing that the need to kill more than one man was a bonus to Vince; it made the job more—not less—attractive.

He ran surveillance on Pantangela for almost a week, using a different vehicle every day to avoid being spotted by the cockroach's bodyguards. They did not often let Pantangela outside, but they were still more confident of their hiding place than they should have been because three or four times a week they allowed him to have a late lunch in public, accompanying him to a little trattoria four blocks from the safe house.

They had changed Pantangela's appearance as much as possible. He had once had thick black hair that he had worn longish, over his collar. Now his hair was cut short and dyed light brown. He'd had a mustache, but they'd made him shave it off. He had been sixty pounds overweight, but after two months in the care of the marshals, he had lost about forty pounds. Nevertheless, Vince recognized him.

On Wednesday, August 4, they took Pantangela to the trattoria at one o'clock, as usual. At ten minutes past one, Vince strolled in to have his own lunch.

The restaurant had only eight tables in the middle and six booths along each side wall. It looked clean but had too much Italian kitsch for Vince's taste: red- and white-checkered tablecloths; garish murals of Roman ruins; empty wine bottles used as candleholders; a thousand bunches of plastic grapes, for God's sake, hanging from lattice fixed to the ceiling and meant to convey the atmosphere of an arbor. Because Californians tend to eat an early dinner, at least by Eastern standards, they also eat an early lunch, and by ten past one, the number of diners had already peaked and was declining. By two o'clock, it was likely that the only customers remaining would be Pantangela, his two bodyguards, and Vince, which was what made it such a good place for the hit.

The trattoria was too small to bother with a hostess at lunch, and a sign told guests to seat themselves. Vince walked back through the room, past the Pantagela party, to an empty booth behind them.

Vince had given a lot of thought to his clothes. He was wearing rope sandals, red cotton shorts, and a white T-shirt on which were blue waves, a yellow sun, and the words ANOTHER CALIFORNIA BODY. His aviator sunglasses were mirrored. He carried an open-topped canvas beach bag that was boldly lettered MY STUFF. If you glanced in the bag when he walked past, you'd see a tightly rolled towel, bottles of tanning lotion, a small radio, and a hairbrush, but you wouldn't see the fully automatic, silencer-equipped Uzi pistol with a forty-round magazine hidden in the bottom. With his deep tan to complement the outfit, he achieved the look he wanted: a very fit but aging surfer; a leisure-sotted, shiftless, and probably harebrained jerk who would be beaching it every day, pretending to be young, and still self-intoxicated when he was sixty.

He only glanced uninterestedly at Pantangela and the marshals, but he was aware of them giving him the once-over, then dismissing him as harmless. Perfect.

The booths had high padded backs, so from where he sat he could not see Pantangela. But he could hear the cockroach and the marshals talking now and then, mostly about baseball and women.

After a week of surveillance, Vince knew that Pantangela never left the trattoria sooner than two-thirty, usually three o'clock, evidently because he insisted on an appetizer, a salad, a main course, and dessert, the whole works. That gave Vince time for a salad and an order of linguini with clam sauce.

His waitress was about twenty, white-blond, pretty, and as deeply tanned as Vince. She had the hip look and sound of a beach girl, and she started coming on to him right away, while taking his order. He figured she was one of those sand nymphs whose brain was as sun-fried as her body. She probably spent every summer evening on the beach, doing dope of every description, spreading her legs for any stud who vaguely interested her—and most of them would interest her—which meant that, no matter how healthy she looked, she was disease-ridden. Just the idea of humping her made him want to puke, but he had to play out the role he'd chosen for himself, so he flirted with her and tried to look as if he could barely keep from drooling at the thought of her naked, writhing body pinned under him.

At five minutes past two, Vince had finished lunch, and the only other customers in the place were Pantangela and the two marshals. One of the waitresses had left for the day, and the other two were in the kitchen. It could not have been better.

The beach bag was on the booth beside him. He reached into it and withdrew the Uzi pistol.

Pantangela and the marshals were talking about the Dodgers' chances of getting in the World Series.

Vince got up, stepped around to their booth, and sprayed them with twenty to thirty rounds from the Uzi. The stubby, high-tech silencer worked beautifully, and the shots sounded like nothing more than a stuttering man having trouble pronouncing a word that began with a sibilant. It went down so fast that the marshals didn't have a chance to reach for their own weapons. They didn't even have time to be surprised.

Ssssnap.
Ssssnap.
Ssssnap.

Pantangela and his guardians were dead in three seconds.

Vince shuddered with intense pleasure, and was briefly overcome by the wealth of life energy that he had just absorbed. He could not speak. Then in a tremulous and raspy voice, he said, "Thank you."

When he turned away from the booth, he saw his waitress standing in the middle of the room, frozen in shock. Her wide blue eyes were fixated on the dead men, but now her gaze shifted slowly to Vince.

Before she could scream, he emptied the rest of the magazine into her, maybe ten shots, and she went down in a rain of blood.

Ssssnap.

"Thank you," he said, then said it again because she had been young and vital and, therefore, of more use to him.

Concerned that someone else would come out of the kitchen—or maybe someone would walk past the restaurant and look in and see the waitress on the floor—Vince stepped quickly to his booth, snatched up the beach bag, and jammed the Uzi pistol under the towel. Putting on his mirrored sunglasses, he got out of there.

He was not worried about fingerprints. He had coated the pads of his fingers with Elmer's glue. It dried nearly transparent and could not be noticed unless he turned his hands palms-up and called people's attention to it. The layer of glue was thick enough to fill the minute lines in the skin, leaving the fingertips smooth.

Outside, he walked to the end of the block, turned the corner, and got into his van, which was parked at the curb. As far as he could tell, no one gave him a second look.

He went to the ocean, looking forward to some time in the sun and an invigorating swim. Going to Redondo Beach, two blocks away, seemed too bold, so he followed the Coast Highway south to Bolsa Chica, just north of where he lived in Huntington Beach.

As he drove, he thought about the dog. He was still paying Johnny The Wire to keep tabs on animal pounds, police agencies, and anyone else who might be dragged into the search for the retriever. He knew about the National

293

Security Agency's bulletin to veterinarians and animal-control authorities in three states, and he also knew that the NSA had so far had no luck.

Maybe the dog had been killed by a car, or by the creature that Hudston had called "The Outsider," or by a coyote pack in the hills. But Vince didn't want to believe it was dead because that would mean an end to his dream of making a huge financial killing with the dog either by ransoming it back to the authorities or selling it to a rich showbiz type who could work up an act with it, or by finding some means of using the animal's secret intelligence to pull a safe and profitable scam on unsuspecting marks.

What he preferred to believe was that someone had found the dog and had taken it home as a pet. If he could just locate the people who had the dog, he could buy it from them—or blow them away and just *take* the mutt.

But where the hell was he supposed to look? How was he supposed to find them? If they were findable, the NSA would surely reach them first.

Most likely, if the dog was not already dead, the best way to get his hands on it was to find The Outsider first and let that beast lead him to the dog, which Hudston had seemed to think it would. But that was not an easy task, either.

Johnny The Wire was also still providing him with information about particularly violent killings of people and animals throughout southern California. Vince knew about the slaughter at the Irvine Park petting zoo, the murder of Wes Dalberg, and the men at Bordeaux Ridge. Johnny had turned up the rash of reports about mutilated pets in the Diamond Bar area, and Vince had actually seen the TV news story about the young couple who had encountered what they thought was an extraterrestrial in the wilds below Johnstone Peak. Three weeks ago, two hikers had been found horribly mauled in the Angeles National Forest, and by hacking his way into the NSA's own computers, Johnny had confirmed that they had taken over jurisdiction in that case, too, which meant it had to be the work of The Outsider.

Since then, nothing.

Vince was not ready to give up. Not by a long shot. He was a patient man. Patience was part of his job. He would wait, watch, keep Johnny The Wire at work, and sooner or later he would get what he was after. He was sure of it. He had decided that the dog, like immortality, was part of his great destiny.

At Bolsa Chica State Beach, he stood for a while with the surf pounding against his thighs, staring out at the great dark masses of surging water. He felt as powerful as the sea. He was filled with scores of lives. He would not have been surprised if electricity had suddenly leaped from his fingertips the way thunderbolts flashed from the hands of the gods in mythology.

Finally, he threw himself forward, into the water, and swam against the powerful incoming waves. He went far out before turning parallel to the shore, swimming first south and then north, keeping at it until, exhausted, he at last allowed the tide to carry him back to shore.

He dozed for a while in the hot afternoon sun. He dreamed of a pregnant woman, her stomach large and round, and in the dream he strangled her to death.

He often dreamed of killing children or, even better, the unborn children of pregnant women because it was something he longed to do in real life. Child murder was, of course, much too dangerous; it was a pleasure he had to deny himself, though a child's life energy would be the richest, the purest, the most worthy of absorption. Too dangerous by far. He couldn't indulge in infanticide until he was certain he had achieved immortality, whereupon he would no longer need to fear the police or anyone else.

Although he often had such dreams, the one he woke from on Bolsa Chica Beach struck him as more meaningful than others of its type. It felt ... different. Prophetic. He sat yawning and blinking in the westering sun, pretending not to notice the bikinied girls who were giving him the eye, and he told himself that this dream was a glimpse of pleasure to come. One day he would actually feel his hands around the throat of a pregnant woman like the one in the dream, and he would know the ultimate thrill, receive the ultimate gift, not only her life energy but the pure, untapped energy of the unborn in her womb.

Feeling like a million bucks, he returned to his van, drove home, showered, and went out to dinner at the nearest Stuart Anderson steak house, where he treated himself to filet mignon.

6

Einstein bolted past Travis, out of the kitchen, across the small dining room, disappearing into the living room. Carrying the leash, Travis went after him. Einstein was hiding behind the sofa.

Travis said, "Listen, it's not going to hurt."

The dog watched him warily.

"We've got to take care of this before we go off to Vegas. The vet will give you a couple of shots, vaccinate you against distemper and rabies. It's for your own good, and it really won't hurt. Really. Then we'll get you a license, which we should've done weeks ago."

One bark. *No*.

"Yes, we will."

No.

Crouching, holding the leash by the clip with which he would attach it to the collar, Travis took a step toward Einstein.

The retriever scrambled away. He ran to the armchair, leaped up, and stood on that observation platform, watching Travis intently.

Coming slowly out from behind the sofa, Travis said, "Now, you listen up, fur face. I'm your master—"

One bark.

Frowning, Travis said, "Oh yes, I *am* your master. You may be one damn smart dog—but you're still the dog, and I'm the man, and I'm telling you that we're going to the vet."

One bark.

Leaning against the dining-room archway, arms folded, smiling, Nora said, "I think he's trying to give you a taste of what children are like, in case we ever decide to have any."

Travis lunged toward the dog.

Einstein flew off his perch and was already out of the room when Travis, unable to halt, fell over the armchair.

Laughing, Nora said, "This is vastly entertaining."

"Where'd he go?" Travis demanded.

She pointed to the hallway that led to the two bedrooms and bath.

He found the retriever in the master bedroom, standing on the bed, facing the doorway. "You can't win," Travis said. "This is for your own good, damn it, and you're going to have those shots whether you like it or not."

Einstein lifted one hind leg and peed on the bed.

Astonished, Travis said, "What in the hell are you doing?"

Einstein stopped peeing, stepped away from the puddle that was soaking into the quilted bedspread, and stared defiantly at Travis.

Travis had heard stories of dogs and cats expressing extreme displeasure by stunts like this. When he had owned the real-estate agency, one of his saleswomen had boarded her miniature collie in a kennel for two weeks while away on vacation. When she returned and bailed out the dog, it punished her by urinating on both her favorite chair and her bed.

But Einstein was not an ordinary dog. Considering his remarkable intellect, the soiling of the bed was even more of an outrage than it would have been if he *had* been ordinary.

Getting angry now, moving toward the dog, Travis said, "This is inexcusable."

Einstein scrambled off the mattress. Realizing the dog would try to slip around him and out of the room, Travis scuttled backward and slammed the door. Cut off from the exit, Einstein swiftly changed directions and dashed to the far end of the bedroom, where he stood in front of the dresser.

"No more fooling around," Travis said sternly, brandishing the leash.

Einstein retreated into a corner.

Closing in at a crouch, spreading his arms to prevent the dog from bolting around either side of him, Travis finally made contact and clipped the leash to the collar. "Ha!"

Huddled defeatedly in the corner, Einstein hung his head and began to shudder.

Travis's sense of triumph was short-lived. He stared in dismay at the dog's bowed and trembling head, at the visible shivers that shook the animal's flanks. Einstein issued low, almost inaudible, pathetic whines of fear.

Stroking the dog, trying to calm and reassure him, Travis said, "This really is for your own good, you know. Distemper, rabies—the sort of stuff you don't want to mess with. And it will be painless, my friend. I swear it will."

The dog would not look at him and refused to take heart from his assurances.

Under Travis's hand, the dog felt as if he were shaking himself to pieces. He stared hard at the retriever, thinking, then said, "In that lab ... did they put a lot of needles in you? Did they hurt you with needles? Is that why you're afraid of getting vaccinations?"

Einstein only whimpered.

Travis pulled the reluctant dog out of the corner, freeing his tail for a question-and-answer session. Dropping the leash, he took Einstein's head in both hands and forced his face up, so they were eye-to-eye.

"Did they hurt you with needles in the lab?"

Yes.

"Is that why you're afraid of the vet?"

Though he did not stop shuddering, the dog barked once: *No.*

"You were hurt by needles, but you're not afraid of them?"

No.

"Then *why* are you like this?"

Einstein just stared at him and made those terrible sounds of distress.

Nora opened the bedroom door a crack and peeked in. "Did you get the leash on him yet, Einstein?" Then she said, "Phew! What happened in here?"

Still holding the dog's head, staring into his eyes, Travis said, "He made a bold statement of displeasure."

"Bold," she agreed, moving to the bed and beginning to strip off the soiled spread, blanket, and sheets.

Trying to puzzle out the reason for the dog's behavior, Travis said, "Einstein, if it's not the needles you're afraid of—is it the vet?"

One bark. *No.*

Frustrated, Travis brooded on his next question while Nora pulled the mattress cover from the bed.

Einstein trembled.

Suddenly, Travis had a flash of understanding that illuminated the dog's contrariness and fear. He cursed his own thickheadedness. "Hell, of course! You're not afraid of the vet—but of who the vet might report you to."

Einstein's shivering subsided a bit, and he wagged his tail briefly. *Yes.*

"If people from that lab are hunting for you—and we know they must be hunting furiously because you have to be the most important experimental animal in history—then they're going to be in touch with every vet in the state, aren't they? Every vet . . . and every dog pound . . . and every dog-licensing agency."

Another burst of vigorous tail wagging, less shivering.

Nora came around the bed and stooped down beside Travis. "But golden retrievers have to be one of the two or three most popular breeds. Vets and animal-licensing bureaucrats deal with them all the time. If our genius dog here hides his light under a bushel and plays dopey mutt—"

"Which he can do quite well."

"—then they'd have no way of knowing he was the fugitive."

Yes, Einstein insisted.

To the dog, Travis said, "What do you mean? Are you saying they would be able to identify you?"

Yes.

"How?" Nora wondered.

Travis said, "A mark of some kind?"

Yes.

"Somewhere under all that fur?" Nora asked.

One bark. *No.*

"Then where?" Travis wondered.

Pulling loose of Travis's hands, Einstein shook his head so hard that his floppy ears made a flapping noise.

"Maybe on the pads of his feet," Nora said.

"No," Travis said even as Einstein barked once. "when I found him, his feet were bleeding from a lot of hard travel, and I had to clean out the wounds with boric acid. I'd have noticed a mark on one of his paws."

Again, Einstein shook his head violently, flapping his ears.

Travis said, "Maybe on the inner lip. They tattoo race-horses on the inner lip to identify them and prevent ringers from being run. Let me peel back your lips and have a look, boy."

Einstein barked once—*No*—and shook his head violently.

At last Travis got the point. He looked in the right ear and found nothing. But in the left ear, he saw something. He urged the dog to go with him to the window, where the light was better, and he discovered that the mark consisted of two numbers, a dash, and a third number tattooed in purple ink on the pink-brown flesh: 33-9.

Looking over Travis's shoulder, Nora said, "They probably had a lot of pups they were experimenting with, from different litters, and they had to be able to identify them."

"Jesus. If I'd taken him to a vet, and if the vet had been told to look for a retriever with a tattoo ..."

"But he has to have shots."

"Maybe he's already had them," Travis said hopefully.

"We don't dare count on that. He was a lab animal in a controlled environment where he might not have needed shots. And maybe the usual inoculations would've interfered with their experiments."

"We can't risk a vet."

"If they do find him," Nora said, "we simply won't give him up."

"They can make us," Travis said worriedly.

"Damned if they can."

"Damned if they can't. More likely than not, the government's financing the research, and *they* can crush us. We can't risk it. More than anything else, Einstein's afraid of going back to the lab."

Yes, yes, yes.

"But," Nora said, "if he contracts rabies or distemper or—"

"We'll get him the shots later," Travis said. "Later. When the situation cools down. When he's not so hot."

The retriever whined happily, nuzzling Travis's neck and face in a sloppy display of gratitude.

Frowning, Nora said, "Einstein is about the number-one miracle of the twentieth century. You really think he's ever going to cool down, that they'll ever stop looking for him?"

"They might not stop for years," Travis admitted, stroking the dog. "But gradually they'll begin to search with less enthusiasm and less hope. And the vets will start forgetting to look in the ears of every retriever that's brought to them. Until then, he'll have to go without the shots, I guess. It's the best thing we can do. It's the only thing we can do."

Ruffling Einstein's coat with one hand, Nora said: "I hope you're right."

"I am."

"I hope so."

"I am."

Travis was badly shaken by how close he had come to risking Einstein's freedom, and for the next few days he brooded about the infamous Cornell Curse. Maybe it was happening all over again. His life had been turned around and made livable because of the love he felt for Nora and for this impossible damn dog. And now maybe fate, which had always dealt with him in a supremely hostile manner, would rip both Nora and the dog away from him.

He knew that fate was only a mythological concept. He did not believe there was actually a pantheon of malevolent gods looking down on him through a celestial keyhole and plotting tragedies for him to endure—yet he could not help looking warily at the sky now and then. Each time he said something even slightly optimistic about the future, he found himself knocking on wood to counter malicious fates. At dinner, when he toppled the salt shaker, he immediately picked up a pinch of the stuff to throw it over his shoulder, then felt foolish and dusted if off his fingers. But his heart began to pound and he was filled with a ridiculous superstitious dread, and he didn't feel right again until he snatched up more salt and tossed it behind him.

Although Nora was surely aware of Travis's eccentric behavior, she had the good grace to say nothing about his jitters. Instead, she countered his mood by quietly loving him every minute of the day, by speaking with great delight about their trip to Vegas, by being in unrelievedly good humor, and by *not* knocking on wood.

She did not know about his nightmares because he did not tell her about them. It was the same bad dream, in fact, two nights in a row.

In the dream, he was wandering in the wooded canyons of the Santa Ana foothills of Orange County, the same woods in which he had first met Einstein. He had gone there with Einstein again, and with Nora, but now he had lost them. Frightened for them, he plunged down steep slopes, scrambled up hills, struggled through clinging brush, calling frantically for Nora, for the dog. Sometimes he heard Nora answering or Einstein barking, and they sounded as if they were in trouble, so he turned in the direction from which their voices came, but each time he heard them they were farther off and in a different place, and no matter how intently he listened or how fast he made his way through the forest, he was losing them, losing them—

—until he woke, breathless, heart racing, a silent scream caught in his throat.

Friday, August 6, was such a blessedly busy day that Travis had little time to worry about hostile fate. First thing in the morning, he telephoned a wedding chapel in Las Vegas and, using his American Express number, made arrangements for a ceremony on Wednesday, August 11, at eleven o'clock. Overcome by a romantic fever, he told the chapel manager that he wanted twenty dozen red roses, twenty dozen white carnations, a good organist (no damn taped music) who could play traditional music, so many candles that the altar would be bright without harsh electric light, a bottle of Dom Perignon with which to conclude events, and a first-rate photographer to record the nuptials. When those details had been agreed upon, he telephoned the Circus Circus Hotel in Las Vegas, which was a family-orientated enterprise that boasted a recreational-vehicle campgrounds behind the hotel itself; he arranged for camp space beginning the night of Sunday, August 8. With another call to an RV campgrounds in Barstow, he also secured reservations for Saturday night, when they would pull off the road halfway to Vegas. Next, he went to a jewelry store, looked at their entire stock, and finally bought an engagement ring with a big, flawless three-carat diamond and a wedding band with twelve quarter-carat stones. With the rings hidden under the seat of the truck, Travis and Einstein went to Nora's house, picked her up, and took her to an appointment with her attorney, Garrison Dilworth.

"Getting married? That's wonderful!" Garrison said, pumping Travis's hand. He kissed Nora on the cheek. He seemed genuinely delighted. "I've asked around about you, Travis."

Surprised, Travis said, "You have?"

"For Nora's sake."

The attorney's statement made Nora blush and protest, but Travis was pleased that Garrison had been concerned about her welfare.

Fixing Travis with a measured stare, the silver-haired

303

attorney said, "I gather you did quite well in real estate before you sold your business."

"I did all right," Travis confirmed modestly, feeling as if he were speaking with Nora's father, trying to make the right impression.

"*Very* well," Garrison said. "And I also hear you've invested the profits rather well."

"I'm not broke," Travis admitted.

Smiling, Garrison said, "I also hear you're a good, reliable man with more than your share of kindness."

It was Travis's turn to blush. He shrugged.

To Nora, Garrison said, "Dear, I'm delighted for you, happier than I can say."

"Thank you." Nora favored Travis with a loving, radiant look that made him want to knock on wood for the first time all day.

Because they intended to take a honeymoon of at least a week or ten days following the wedding, Nora did not want to have to rush back to Santa Barbara in the event her real-estate agent found a taker for Violet Devon's house. She asked Garrison Dilworth to draw up a power of attorney, giving him authority to handle all aspects of such a sale in her name during her absence. This was done in less than half an hour, signed and witnessed. After another round of congratulations and best wishes, they were on their way to buy a travel trailer.

They intended to take Einstein with them not only to the wedding in Vegas but on the honeymoon. Finding good, clean motels that would accept a dog might not always be easy where they were going, so it was prudent to take a motel-on-wheels with them. Furthermore, neither Travis nor Nora could have made love with the retriever in the same room. "It'd be like having another *person* there," Nora said, blushing as bright as a well-polished apple. Staying in motels, they would have to rent two rooms—one for them and one for Einstein—which seemed too awkward.

By four o'clock, they found what they were looking for: a middle-size, silvery, Quonset-shaped Airstream with a kitchenette, a dining nook, a living room, one bedroom, and one bath. When they retired for the night, they could leave Einstein in the front of the trailer and close the bedroom door after themselves. Because Travis's pickup was already equipped with a good trailer hitch, they were able to hook the Airstream to the rear bumper and haul it with them as soon as the sale was concluded.

Einstein, riding in the pickup between Travis and Nora, kept craning his head around to look out the back window at the gleaming, semicylindrical trailer as if amazed at the ingenuity of humankind.

They shopped for trailer curtains, plastic dishes and drinking glasses, food with which to stock the kitchenette cabinets, and a host of other items they needed before they hit the road. By the time they returned to Nora's house and cooked omelettes for a late dinner, they were dragging. For once there was nothing smartass about Einstein's yawns; he was just tired.

That night, at home in his own bed, Travis slept the deep, deep sleep of ancient petrified trees and dinosaur fossils. The dreams of the previous two nights were not repeated.

Saturday morning, they set out on their journey to Vegas and to matrimony. Seeking to travel mostly on wide divided highways on which they would be comfortable with the trailer, they took Route 101 south and then east until it became Route 134, which they followed until it became Interstate 210, with the city of Los Angeles and its suburbs to the south of them and the great Angeles National Forest to the north. Later, on the vast Mojave Desert, Nora was thrilled by the barren yet hauntingly beautiful panoramas of sand, stone, tumbleweed, mesquite, joshua trees, and other cacti. The world, she said, suddenly seemed much bigger than she had ever realized, and Travis took pleasure in her bedazzlement.

Barstow, California, was a sprawling pit stop in that enormous wasteland, and they arrived at the big RV campgrounds by three that afternoon. Frank and Mae Jordan, the middle-aged couple in the next camper space, were from Salt Lake City and were traveling with their pet, a black Labrador named Jack.

To Travis's and Nora's surprise, Einstein had a terrific time playing with Jack. They chased each other around the trailers, took playful nips at each other, tangled and tumbled and sprang up and went chasing again. Frank Jordan tossed a red rubber ball for them, and they sprinted after it, vying to be the champion retriever. The dogs also made a game of trying to get the ball away from each other and then holding on to it as long as possible. Travis was exhausted just watching them.

Einstein was undoubtedly the smartest dog in the world, the smartest dog of all time, a phenomenon, a miracle, as perceptive as any man—but he was also a dog. Sometimes, Travis forgot this fact, but he was charmed every time Einstein did something to remind him.

Later, after sharing charcoal-grilled hamburgers and corn on the cob with the Jordans, and after downing a couple of beers in the clear desert night, they said goodbye to the Salt Lakers, and Einstein seemed to say goodbye to Jack. Inside the Airstream, Travis patted Einstein on the head and told him, "That was very nice of you."

The dog cocked his head, staring at Travis as if to ask what the devil he meant.

Travis said, "You know what I'm talking about, fur face."

"I know, too," Nora said. She hugged the dog. "When you were playing games with Jack, you could have made a fool of him if you'd wanted to, but you let him win his share, didn't you?"

Einstein panted and grinned happily.

After one last nightcap, Nora took the bedroom, and Travis slept on the fold-out sofa bed in the living room. Travis had thought about sleeping with her, and perhaps she had considered allowing him into her bed. After all, the wedding was less than four days away. God knew, Travis wanted her. And although she surely suffered slightly with a virgin's fear, she wanted him, too; he had no doubt of that. Each day, they were touching each other and kissing more often—and more intimately—and the air between them crackled with erotic energy. But why not do things right and proper since they were so close to the day? Why not go to their marriage bed as virgins—she as a virgin to everyone, he to her?

That night, Travis dreamed that Nora and Einstein were lost in the desolate reaches of the Mojave. In the dream, he was for some reason legless, forced to search for them at an agonizingly slow crawl, which was bad because he knew that, wherever they were, they were under attack by ... something ...

Sunday, Monday, and Tuesday in Las Vegas, they prepared for the wedding, watched Einstein playing enthusiastically with other campers' dogs, and took side trips to Charleston Peak and Lake Mead. In the evenings, Nora and Travis left Einstein with his books while they went to stage shows. Travis felt guilty about leaving the retriever alone, but by various means Einstein indicated that he did not want them to stay at the trailer merely because the Strip hotels were so prejudiced and shortsighted as to refuse to allow well-behaved genius dogs into the casinos and showrooms.

Wednesday morning, Travis dressed in a tuxedo, and Nora wore a simple calf-length white dress with spare lace trim at the cuffs and neckline. With Einstein between them, they drove to their wedding in the pickup, leaving the unhitched Airstream at the campgrounds.

The nondenominational, commercial chapel was the funniest place Travis had ever seen, for the design was earnestly romantic, solemn, and tacky all at the same time. Nora thought it was hilarious, too, and upon entering they had trouble suppressing their laughter. The chapel was tucked in among neon-dripping, glitzy, high-rise hotels on Las Vegas Boulevard South. It was only the size of a one-story house, pale-pink stucco with white doors. Engraved in brass above the door was the legend YE SHALL GO TWO BY TWO ... Instead of depicting religious images, the stained-glass windows were aglow with garishly rendered scenes from famous love stories including *Romeo and Juliet, Abelard and Heloise, Aucassin and Nicolette, Gone with the Wind, Casablanca*—and, unbelievably, *I Love Lucy* and *Ozzie & Harriet*.

Curiously, the tackiness did not deflate their buoyant mood. Nothing could diminish this day. Even the outrageous chapel was to be prized, remembered in every gaudy detail to be vividly recalled over the years, and always to be recalled fondly because it was *their* chapel on *their* day and therefore special in its own strange way.

Dogs were not ordinarily admitted. But Travis had generously tipped the entire staff in advance to insure that Einstein would not only be allowed inside but would be made to feel as welcome as anyone.

The minister, the Reverend Dan Dupree— "Please call me Reverend Dan"—was a florid-faced, potbellied fellow, a strenuous smiler and glad-hander who looked like a stereotypical used-car salesman. He was flanked by two paid witnesses—his wife and her sister—who were wearing bright summery dresses for the occasion.

Travis took his place at the front of the chapel.

The woman organist struck up "The Wedding March."

Nora had expressed a deep desire to actually walk down the aisle and meet Travis rather than just beginning the ceremony at the altar railing. Furthermore, she wanted to be "given away," as other brides were. That should have been her father's singular honor, of course, but she had no father. Nor was anyone else at hand who would be a likely candidate for the job, and at first it seemed that she would have to make the walk alone or on the arm of a stranger. But in the pickup, on their way to the ceremony, she had realized that Einstein was available, and she had decided that no one in the world was more suited to accompany her down the aisle than the dog.

Now, as the organist played, Nora entered the back of the

308

nave with the dog at her side. Einstein was acutely aware of the great honor of escorting her, and he walked with all the pride and dignity he could muster, his head held high, his slow steps timed to hers.

No one seemed disturbed—or even surprised—that a dog was giving Nora away. This was, after all, Las Vegas.

"She's one of the loveliest brides I've ever seen," Reverend Dan's wife whispered to Travis, and he sensed that she was sincere, that she did not routinely bestow that compliment.

The photographer's flash blinked repeatedly, but Travis was too involved with the sight of Nora to be bothered by the strobe.

Vases full of roses and carnations filled the small nave with their perfume, and a hundred candles flickered softly, some in clear glass votive cups and others in brass candelabra. By the time Nora arrived at his side, Travis was oblivious to the tacky decor. His love was an architect that entirely remade the reality of the chapel, transforming it into a cathedral as grand as any in the world.

The ceremony was brief and unexpectedly dignified. Travis and Nora exchanged vows, then rings. Tears full of reflected candlelight shimmered in her eyes, and Travis wondered for a moment why her tears should blur *his* vision, then realized that he, too, was on the verge of tears. A burst of dramatic organ music accompanied their first kiss as man and wife, and it was the sweetest kiss he had ever known.

Reverend Dan popped the Dom Perignon and, at Travis's direction, poured a glass for everyone, the organist included. A saucer was found for Einstein. Slurping noisily, the retriever joined in their toast to life, happiness, and love eternal.

Einstein spent the afternoon in the forward end of the trailer, in the living room, reading.

Travis and Nora spent the afternoon at the other end of the trailer, in bed.

After closing the bedroom door, Travis put a second bottle of Dom Perignon in an ice bucket and loaded a compact-disk player with four albums of George Winston's most mellow piano music.

Nora drew down the blind at the only window and switched on a small lamp with a gold cloth shade. The soft amber light lent the room an aura rather like that of a place in a dream.

For a while they lay on the bed, talking, laughing, touching, kissing, then talking less and kissing more.

Gradually, Travis undressed her. He'd never before seen her unclothed, and he found her even more lovely and more exquisitely proportioned than he had imagined. Her slender throat, the delicacy of her shoulders, the fullness of her breasts, the concavity of her belly, the flair of her hips, the round sauciness of her buttocks, the long smooth supple sleekness of her legs—every line and angle and curve excited him but also filled him with great tenderness.

After he undressed himself, he patiently and gently introduced her to the art of love. With a profound desire to please and with full awareness that everything was new to her, he showed Nora—sometimes not without delicious teasing—all the sensations that his tongue, fingers, and manhood could engender in her.

He was prepared to find her hesitant, embarrassed, even fearful, because her first thirty years of life had not prepared her for this degree of intimacy. But she harbored no trace of frigidity and was eager to engage in any act that might pleasure either or both of them. Her soft cries and breathless murmurs of excitement delighted him. Each time that she sighed climactically and surrendered to a shudder of ecstasy, Travis became more aroused, until he was of a size and firmness that he had never attained before, until his need was almost painful.

When at last he let his warm seed flower within her, he buried his face in her throat and called her name and told her that he loved her, told her again and again, and the moment of release seemed so long that he half-thought time had stopped or that he had tapped an inexplicable well that could never be exhausted.

With consummation achieved, they held each other for a long time, silent, not needing to talk. They listened to the music, and in a while they finally spoke of what they felt, both physically and emotionally. They drank some champagne, and in time they made love again. And again.

Although the constant shadow of certain death looms over every day, the pleasures and joys of life can be so fine and deeply affecting that the heart is nearly stilled by astonishment.

From Vegas, they hauled the Airstream north on Route 95, across the immense Nevada barrens. Two days later, on Friday, August 13, they reached Lake Tahoe and connected the trailer to the electric and water lines at an RV campsite on the California side of the border.

Nora was not quite as easily overwhelmed by each new scenic vista and novel experience as she had been. However, Lake Tahoe was so stunningly beautiful that it filled her with childlike wonder again. Twenty-two miles long and twelve miles wide, with the Sierra Nevadas on its western flank and the Carson Range on the east, Tahoe was said to be the clearest body of water in the world, a shimmering jewel in a hundred amazingly iridescent shades of blue and green.

For six days, Nora and Travis and Einstein hiked in the Eldorado, Tahoe, and Toiyabe National Forests, vast primeval tracts of pine, spruce, and fir. They rented a boat and went on the lake, exploring paradisiacal coves and graceful bays. They went sunning and swimming, and Einstein took to the water with the enthusiasm indigenous to his breed.

Sometimes in the morning, sometimes in the late afternoon, more often at night, Nora and Travis made love. She was surprised by her carnal appetite. She could not get enough of him.

"I love your mind and your heart," she told him, "but, God help me, I love your body almost as much! Am I depraved?"

"Good heavens, no. You're just a young healthy woman. In fact, given the life you've led, you're emotionally healthier than you've any right to be. Really, Nora, you stagger me."

"I'd like to straddle you instead."

"Maybe you *are* depraved," he said, and laughed.

Early on the serenely blue morning of Friday the twentieth, they left Tahoe and drove across the state to the Monterey Peninsula. There, where the continental shelf met the sea, the natural beauty was, if possible, even greater than that at Tahoe, and they stayed four days, leaving for home on the afternoon of Wednesday, August 25.

Throughout their trip, the joy of matrimony was so all-consuming that the miracle of Einstein's humanlike intelligence did not occupy their thoughts as much as previously. But Einstein reminded them of his unique nature when they drew near to Santa Barbara late that afternoon. Forty or fifty miles from home, he grew restless. He shifted repeatedly on the seat between Nora and Travis, sat up for a minute, then laid his head on Nora's lap, then sat up again. He began to whimper strangely. By the time they were ten miles from home, he was shivering.

"What's wrong with you, fur face?" she asked.

With his expressive brown eyes, Einstein tried hard to convey a complex and important message, but she could not understand him.

Half an hour before dusk, when they reached the city and departed the freeway for surface streets, Einstein began alternately to whine and growl low in his throat.

"What's wrong with him?" Nora asked.

Frowning, Travis said, "I don't know."

As they pulled into the driveway of Travis's rented house and parked in the shade of the date palm, the retriever began to bark. He had never barked in the truck, not once on their long journey. It was ear-splitting in that confined space, but he would not stop.

312

When they got out of the truck, Einstein bolted past them, positioned himself between them and the house, and continued barking.

Nora moved along the walkway toward the front door, and Einstein darted at her, snarling. He seized one leg of her jeans and tried to pull her off balance. She managed to stay on her feet and, when she retreated to the birdbath, he let go of her.

"What's gotten into him?" she asked Travis.

Staring thoughtfully at the house, Travis said, "He was like this in the woods that first day . . . when he didn't want me to follow the dark trail."

Nora tried to coax the dog closer in order to pet him.

But Einstein would not be coaxed. When Travis tested the dog by approaching the house, Einstein snarled and forced him to retreat.

"Wait here," Travis told Nora. He walked to the Airstream in the driveway and went inside.

Einstein trotted back and forth in front of the house, looking up at the door and windows, growling and whining.

As the sun rolled down the western sky and kissed the surface of the sea, the residential street was quiet, peaceful, ordinary in every respect—yet Nora felt a *wrongness* in the air. A warm wind off the Pacific elicited whispers from the palm and eucalyptus and ficus trees, sounds that might have been pleasant any other day but which now seemed sinister. In the lengthening shadows, in the last orange and purple light of the day, she also perceived an indefinable menace. Except for the dog's behavior, she had no reason to think that danger was near at hand; her uneasiness was not intellectual but instinctual.

When Travis returned from the trailer, he was carrying a large revolver. It had been in a bedroom drawer, unloaded, throughout their honeymoon trip. Now, Travis finished inserting cartridges into the chambers and snapped the cylinder shut.

"Is that necessary?" she asked worriedly.

"Something was in the woods that day," Travis said, "and though I never actually saw it . . . well, it put the hair up on the back of my neck. Yeah, I think the gun might be necessary.''

Her own reaction to the whispering trees and afternoon shadows gave her a hint of what Travis must have felt in the woods, and she had to admit that the gun made her feel at least slightly better.

Einstein had stopped pacing and had taken up his guard position on the walkway again, barring their approach to the house.

To the retriever, Travis said, ''Is someone inside?''

A quick wag of the tail. *Yes.*

''Men from the lab?''

One bark. *No.*

''The other experimental animal you told us about?''

Yes.

''The thing that was in the woods?''

Yes.

''All right, I'm going in there.''

No.

''Yes,'' Travis insisted. ''It's my house, and we're not going to run from this, whatever the hell it is.''

Nora remembered the magazine photograph of the movie monster to which Einstein had reacted so strongly. She did not believe anything even remotely like that creature could actually exist. She believed that Einstein was exaggerating or that they had misunderstood what he had been trying to tell them about the photo. Nevertheless, she suddenly wished they had not only the revolver but a shot gun.

''This is a .357 Magnum,'' Travis told the dog, ''and one shot, even if it hits an arm or a leg, will knock down the biggest, meanest man and keep him down. He'll feel as if he's been hit by a cannonball. I've taken firearms training from the best, and I've done regular target practice over the years to keep my edge. I really know what I'm doing, and I'll be able to handle myself in there. Besides, we can't just call the cops, can we? Because whatever they find in there is going to raise eyebrows, lead to a lot of questions, and sooner or later they'll have you back in that damn lab again.''

Einstein was clearly unhappy with Travis's determination, but the dog padded up the front steps to the stoop and looked back as if to say, *All right, okay, but I'm not letting you go in there alone.*

Nora wanted to go in with them, but Travis was adamant that she remain in the front yard. She reluctantly admitted that—since she lacked both a weapon and the skill to use it—there was nothing she could do to help and that she would most likely only get in the way.

Holding the revolver at his side, Travis joined Einstein on the stoop and inserted his key in the door.

7

Travis disengaged the lock, pocketed the key, and pushed the door inward, covering the room beyond with the .357. Warily, he stepped across the threshold, and Einstein entered at his side.

The house was silent, as it should have been, but the air reeked of a bad smell that did not belong.

Einstein growled softly.

Little of the fast-fading sunlight entered the house through the windows, many of which were partly or entirely covered with drapes. But it was bright enough for Travis to see that the sofa's upholstery was slashed. Shredded foam padding spilled onto the floor. A wooden magazine rack had been hammered to pieces against the wall, gouging holes in the plasterboard. The TV screen had been smashed in with a floor lamp, which still protruded from the set. Books had been taken off the shelves, torn apart, and scattered across the living room.

In spite of the breeze blowing in through the door, the stench seemed to be getting worse.

Travis flicked the wall switch. A corner lamp came on. It did not shed much light, just enough to reveal more details of the rubble.

Looks like somebody went through here with a chainsaw

and then a power mower, he thought.

The house remained silent.

Leaving the door open behind him, he took a couple of steps into the room, and the crumpled pages of the ruined books crunched crisply underfoot. He noticed dark, rusty stains on some of the paper and on the bone-white foam padding, and suddenly he stopped, realizing the stains were blood.

A moment later, he spotted the corpse. It was that of a big man, lying on his side on the floor near the sofa, half-covered by gore-smeared book pages, book boards, and dust jackets.

Einstein's growling grew louder, meaner.

Moving closer to the body, which was just a few feet from the dining-room archway, Travis saw that it was his land-lord, Ted Hockney. Beside him was his Craftsman toolbox. Ted had a key to the house and Travis had no objections to his entering at any time to make repairs. Lately there had been a number of repairs required, including a leaky faucet and broken dishwasher. Evidently, Ted had walked down the block from his own house and entered with the intention of fixing something, Now Ted was broken, too, and beyond repair.

Because of the ripe stink, Travis first thought that the man must have been killed at least a week ago. But on closer inspection, the corpse proved to be neither bloated with the gas of decomposition nor marked by any signs of decay, so it could not have been there for very long. Perhaps only a day, perhaps less. The hideous stench had two other sources: for one thing, the landlord had been disemboweled; furthermore, his killer had apparently defecated and urinated on and around the body.

Ted Hockney's eyes were gone.

Travis felt sick, and not only because he had liked Ted. He would have been sickened by such insane violence regardless of who the dead man had been. A death like this left the victim no dignity whatsoever and somehow diminished the entire human race.

Einstein's low growling gave way to ugly snarling

punctuated with hard, sharp barks.

With a nervous twitch and a sudden hammering of his heart, Travis turned from the corpse and saw that the retriever was facing into the nearby dining room. The shadows were deep in there because the drapes were drawn shut over both windows, and only a thin gray light passed through from the kitchen beyond.

Go, get out, leave! an inner voice told him.

But he did not turn and run because he had never run away from anything in his life. Well, all right, that was not quite true: he had virtually run away from life itself these past few years when he had let despair get the best of him. His descent into isolation had been the ultimate cowardice. However, that was behind him; he was a new man, transformed by Einstein and Nora, and he was not going to run again, damned if he was.

Einstein went rigid. He arched his back, thrust his head down and forward, and barked so furiously that saliva flew from his mouth.

Travis took a step toward the dining-room arch.

The retriever stayed at Travis's side, barking more viciously.

Holding the revolver in front of him, trying to take confidence from the powerful weapon, Travis eased forward another step, treading cautiously in the treacherous rubble. He was only two or three steps from the archway. He squinted into the gloomy dining room.

Einstein's barking resounded through the house until it seemed as if a whole pack of dogs must be loose in the place.

Travis took one more step, then saw something move in the shadowy dining room.

He froze.

Nothing. Nothing moved. Had it been a phantom of the mind?

Beyond the arch, layered shadows hung like gray and black crepe.

He wasn't sure if he had seen movement or merely imagined it.

Back off, get out, now! the inner voice said.

In defiance of it, Travis raised one foot, intending to step into the archway.

The thing in the dining room moved again. This time there was no doubt of its presence, because it rushed out of the deepest darkness at the far side of that chamber, vaulted onto the dining-room table, and came straight at Travis, emitting a blood-freezing shriek. He saw lantern eyes in the gloom, and a nearly man-size figure that—in spite of the poor light—gave an impression of deformity. Then the thing was coming off the table, straight at him.

Einstein charged forward to engage it, but Travis tried to step back and gain an extra second in which to squeeze off a shot. As he pulled the trigger, he slipped on the ruined books that littered the floor, and fell backward. The revolver roared, but Travis knew he had missed, had fired into the ceiling. For an instant, as Einstein scrambled toward the adversary, Travis saw the lantern-eyed thing more clearly, saw it work alligator jaws and crack open an impossibly wide mouth in a lumpish face, revealing wickedly hooked teeth.

"Einstein, no!" he shouted, for he knew the dog would be torn to pieces in any confrontation with this hellish creature, and he fired again, twice wildly, from his position on the floor.

His cry and the shots not only brought Einstein to a halt but gave the enemy second thoughts about going up against an armed man. The thing turned—it was quick, far quicker than a cat—and crossed the unlighted dining room to the kitchen doorway. For a moment, he saw it silhouetted in the murky light from the kitchen doorway, and he had the impression of something that had never been meant to stand erect but was standing erect anyway, something with a misshapen head twice as large as it ought to have been, a hunched back, arms too long and terminating in claws like the tines of a garden rake.

He fired again and came closer the mark. The bullet tore out a chunk of the door frame.

With a shriek, the beast disappeared into the kitchen.

318

What in the name of God was it? Where had it come from? Had it really escaped from the same lab that had produced Einstein? But how had they made this monstrosity? And why? *Why?*

He was a well-read man: in fact, for the last few years, most of his time was devoted to books, so possibilities began to occur to him. Recombinant-DNA research was foremost among them.

Einstein stood in the middle of the dining room, barking, facing the doorway where the thing had vanished.

Lurching to his feet in the living room, Travis called the dog back to his side, and Einstein returned quickly, eagerly.

He shushed the dog, listened intently. He heard Nora frantically calling his name from the yard out front, but he heard nothing in the kitchen.

For Nora's benefit, he shouted, "I'm okay! I'm all right! Stay out there!"

Einstein was shivering.

Travis could hear the loud two-part thudding of his own heart, and he could *almost* hear the sweat trickling down his face and down the small of his back, but he could hear nothing whatsoever to pinpoint that escapee from a nightmare. He did not think it had gone out the back door into the rear yard. For one thing, he figured the creature did not want to be seen by a lot of people and, therefore, only went outside at night, traveled exclusively in the dark, when it could slip even into a fair-sized town like Santa Barbara without being spotted. The day was still light enough to make the thing leery of the outdoors. Furthermore, Travis could sense its presence nearby, the way he might sense that someone was staring at him behind his back, the way he might sense an oncoming thunderstorm on a humid day with a lowering sky. It was out there, all right, waiting in the kitchen, ready and waiting.

Cautiously, Travis returned to the archway and stepped into the half-dark dining room.

Einstein stayed close at his side, neither whining nor growling nor barking. The dog seemed to realize that Travis

319

needed complete silence in order to hear any sound the beast might make.

Travis took two more steps.

Ahead, through the kitchen door, he could see a corner of the table, the sink, part of a counter, half of the dishwasher. The setting sun was at the other end of the house, and the light in the kitchen was dim, gray, so their adversary would not cast a revealing shadow. It might be waiting on either side of the door, or it might have climbed onto the counters from which it could launch itself down at him when he entered the room.

Trying to trick the creature, hoping that it would react without hesitation to the first sign of movement in the doorway, Travis tucked the revolver under his belt, quietly picked up one of the dining-room chairs, eased to within six feet of the kitchen, and pitched the chair through the open door. He snatched the revolver out of his waistband and, as the chair sailed into the kitchen, assumed a shooter's stance. The chair crashed into the Formica-topped table, clattered to the floor, and banged against the dishwasher.

The lantern-eyed enemy did not go for it. Nothing moved. When the chair finished tumbling, the kitchen was again marked by a hushed expectancy.

Einstein was making a curious sound, a quiet shuddery huffing, and after a moment Travis realized the noise was a result of the dog's uncontrollable shivering.

No question about it: the intruder in the kitchen was the very thing that had pursued them through the woods more than three months ago. During the intervening weeks, it had made its way north, probably traveling mostly in the wildlands to the east of the developed part of the state, relentlessly tracking the dog by some means that Travis could not understand and for reasons he could not even guess.

In response to the chair he had thrown, a large white-enameled canister crashed to the floor just beyond the kitchen doorway, and Travis jumped back in surprise, squeezing off a wild shot before he realized he was only being taunted. The lid flew off the container when it hit the floor, and flour spilled across the tile.

By responding to Travis's taunt with one of its own, the intruder had displayed unnerving intelligence. Abruptly Travis realized that, coming from the same research lab as Einstein and being a product of related experiments, the creature might be as smart as the retriever. Which would explain Einstein's fear of it. If Travis had not already accommodated himself to the idea of a dog with humanlike intelligence, he might have been unable to credit this beast with more than mere animal cleverness; however, events of the past few months had primed him to accept—and quickly adapt to—almost anything.

Silence.

Only one round left in the gun.

Deep silence.

He had been so startled by the flour canister that he had not noticed from which side of the doorway it had been flung, and it had fallen in such a fashion that he could not deduce the position of the creature that had hurled it. He still did not know if the intruder was to the left or the right of the doorway.

He was not sure he any longer cared where it was. Even with the .357 in hand, he did not think he would be wise to enter the kitchen. Not if the damn thing was as smart as a man. It would be like doing battle with an intelligent buzz-saw, for Christ's sake.

The light in the east-facing kitchen was dwindling, almost gone. In the dining room, where Travis and Einstein stood, the darkness was deepening. Even behind them, in spite of the open front door and window and the corner lamp, the living room was filling with shadows.

In the kitchen, the intruder hissed loudly, a sound like escaping gas, which was immediately followed by a *click-click-click* that might have been made by its sharply clawed feet or hands tapping against a hard surface.

Travis had caught Einstein's tremors. He felt as if he were a fly on the edge of a spider's wed, about to step into a trap.

He remembered Ted Hockney's bitten, bloodied, eyeless face.

Click-click.

In antiterrorist training, he had been taught how to stalk men, and he had been good at it. But the problem here was that the yellow-eyed intruder was maybe as smart as a man but could not be counted on to *think* like a man, so Travis had no way of knowing what it might do next, how it might respond to any initiative he made. Therefore, he could never outthink it, and by its alien nature the creature had a perpetual and deadly advantage of surprise.

Click.

Travis quietly took a step back from the open kitchen door, then another step, treading with exaggerated care, not wanting the thing to discover that he was retreating because only God knew what it might do if it knew he was slipping out of its reach. Einstein padded silently into the living room, now equally eager to put distance between himself and the intruder.

When he reached Ted Hockney's corpse, Travis glanced away from the dining room, searching for the least littered route to the front door—and he saw Nora standing by the armchair. Frightened by the gunfire, she had gotten a butcher's knife from the kitchenette in the Airstream and had come to see if he needed help.

He was impressed by her courage but horrified to see her there in the glow of the corner lamp. Suddenly it seemed as if his nightmares of losing both Einstein and Nora were on the verge of coming true, the Cornell Curse again, because now they were both inside the house, both vulnerable, both possibly within striking distance of the thing in the kitchen.

She started to speak.

Travis shook his head and raised one hand to his mouth.

Silenced, she bit her lip and glanced from him to the dead man on the floor.

As Travis quietly stepped through the rubble, he was stricken by a feeling that the intruder had gone out the back of the house and was coming around the side, heading for the front door, risking being seen by neighbors in the gloom of twilight, intending to enter behind them, swift and fast. Nora was standing between Travis and the front door so he

322

would not have a clear shot at the creature if it came that way; hell, it would be all over Nora one second after it reached the door. Trying not to panic, trying not to think of Hockney's eyeless face, Travis moved more quickly across the living room, risking the crackle of some debris underfoot, hoping those small noises would not carry to the kitchen if the intruder was still out there. Reaching Nora, he took her by the arm and propelled her toward the front door, out onto the stoop and down the stairs, looking left and right, half-expecting to see the living nightmare rushing at them, but it was nowhere in sight.

The gunshots and Nora's shouting had drawn neighbors as far as their front doors all along the street. A few had even come outside onto porches and lawns. Somebody surely would have called the cops. Because of Einstein's status as a much-wanted fugitive, the police seemed almost as grave a danger as the yellow-eyed thing in the house.

The three of them piled into the pickup. Nora locked her door, and Travis locked his. He started the engine and backed the truck—and the Airstream—out of the driveway, into the street. He was aware of people staring.

The twilight was going to be short-lived, as it always was near the ocean. Already, the sunless sky was blackish in the east, purple overhead, and a steadily darkening blood-red in the west. Travis was grateful for the oncoming cover of nightfall, although he knew the yellow-eyed creature would be sharing it with them.

He drove past the gaping neighbors, none of whom he had ever met during his years of self-imposed solitude, and he turned at the first corner. Nora held Einstein tightly, and Travis drove as fast as he dared. The trailer rocked and swayed behind them when he took the next couple of corners at too great a speed.

"What happened in there?" she asked.

"It killed Hockney earlier today or yesterday—"

"It?"

"—and it was waiting for us to come home."

"*It?*" she repeated.

Einstein mewled.

Travis said, "I'll have to explain later." He wondered if he could explain. No description he gave of the intruder would do it justice; he did not possess the words necessary to convey the degree of its strangeness.

They had gone no more than eight blocks when they heard sirens in the neighborhood that they had just left. Travis drove another four blocks and parked in the empty lot of a high school.

"What now?" Nora asked.

"We abandon the trailer and the truck," he said. "They'll be looking for both."

He put the revolver in her purse, and she insisted on slipping the butcher's knife in there, too, rather than leave it behind.

They got out of the pickup and, in the descending night, walked past the side of the school, across an athletic field, through a gate in a chain-link fence, and onto a residential street lined with mature trees.

With nightfall, the breeze became a blustery wind, warm and parched. It blew a few dry leaves at them and harried dust ghosts along the pavement.

Travis knew they were too conspicuous even without the trailer and truck. The neighbors would be telling police to look for a man, woman, and golden retriever—not the most common trio. They would be wanted for questioning in the death of Ted Hockney, so the search for them would not be perfunctory. They had to get out of sight quickly.

He had no friends with whom they could take refuge. After Paula died, he had withdrawn from his few friends, and he hadn't maintained relationships with any of the real-estate agents who had once worked for him. Nora had no friends, either, thanks to Violet Devon.

The houses they passed, most with warm lights in the windows, seemed to mock them with unattainable sanctuary.

8

Garrison Dilworth lived on the border between Santa Barbara and Montecito, on a lushly landscaped half acre, in a stately Tudor home that did not mesh well with the Californian flora but which perfectly complemented the attorney. When he answered the door, he was wearing black loafers, gray slacks, a navy-blue sports jacket, a white knit shirt, and half-lens tortoiseshell reading glasses over which he peered at them in surprise but, fortunately, not with displeasure. "Well, hello there, newlyweds!"

"Are you alone?" Travis asked as he and Nora and Einstein stepped into a large foyer floored with marble.

"Alone? Yes."

On the way over, Nora had told Travis that the attorney's wife had passed away three years ago and that he was now looked after by a housekeeper named Gladys Murphy.

"Mrs Murphy?" Travis asked.

"She's gone home for the day," the attorney said, closing the door behind them. "You look distraught. What on earth's wrong?"

"We need help," Nora said.

"But," Travis warned, "anyone who helps us may be putting himself in jeopardy with the law."

Garrison raised his eyebrows. "What have you done? Judging by the solemn look of you—I'd say you've kidnapped the president."

"We've done nothing wrong," Nora assured him.

"Yes, we have," Travis disagreed. "And we're still doing it—we're harboring the dog."

Puzzled, Garrison frowned down at the retriever.

Einstein whined, looking suitably miserable and lovable.

"And there's a dead man in my house," Travis said.

Garrison's gaze shifted from the dog to Travis. "Dead man?"

"Travis didn't kill him," Nora said.

Garrison looked at Einstein again.

"Neither did the dog," Travis said. "But I'll be wanted as a material witness, something like that, sure as hell."

"Mmmmm," Garrison said, "why don't we go into my study and get this straightened out?"

He led the way through an enormous and only half-lit living room, along a short hallway, into a den with rich teak paneling and a copper ceiling. The maroon leather armchairs and couch looked expensive and comfortable. The polished teak desk was massive, and a detailed model of a five-masted schooner, all sails rigged, stood on one corner. Nautical items—a ship's wheel, a brass sextant, a carved bullock's horn filled with tallow that held what appeared to be sail-making needles, six types of ship lanterns, a helmsman's bell, and sea charts—were used as decoration. Travis saw photographs of a man and woman on various sailboats, and the man was Garrison.

An open book and half-finished glass of Scotch were on a small table beside one of the armchairs. Evidently, the attorney had been relaxing here when they had rung the doorbell. Now, he offered them a drink, and they both said they would have whatever he was having.

Leaving the couch for Travis and Nora, Einstein took the second armchair. He sat in it, rather than curling up, as if prepared to participate in the discussion to come.

At a corner wet bar, Garrison poured Chivas Regal on the rocks in two glasses. Although Nora was unaccustomed to whiskey, she startled Travis by downing her drink in two long swallows and asking for another. He decided that she had the right idea, so he followed suit and took his empty glass back to the bar while Garrison was refilling Nora's.

"I'd like to tell you everything and have your help," Travis said, "but you really must understand you could be putting yourself on the wrong side of the law."

Recapping the Chivas, Garrison said, "You're talking as a layman now. As an attorney, I assure you the law isn't a line engraved in marble, immovable and unchangeable through the centuries. Rather ... the law is like a string, fixed at both ends but with a great deal of play in it—very loose, the line of the law—so you can stretch it this way or that, rearrange the arc of it so you are nearly always—short of blatant theft or cold-blooded murder—safely on the

326

right side. That's a daunting thing to realize but true. I've no fear that anything you tell me could land my bottom in a prison cell, Travis.''

Half an hour later, Travis and Nora had told him everything about Einstein. For a man only a couple of months shy of his seventy-first birthday, the silver-haired attorney had a quick and open mind. He asked the right questions and did not scoff. When given a ten-minute demonstration of Einstein's uncanny abilities, he did not protest that it was all mere trickery and flummery; he accepted what he saw, and he readjusted his ideas of what was normal and possible in this world. He exhibited greater mental agility and flexibility than most men half his age.

Holding Einstein on his lap in the big leather armchair, gently scratching the dog's ears, Garrison said, ''If you go to the media, hold a press conference, blow the whole thing wide open, then we might be able to sue in court to allow you to keep custody of the dog.''

''Do you really think that would work?'' Nora asked.

''At best,'' Garrison admitted, ''it's a fifty-fifty chance.''

Travis shook his head. 'No. We won't risk it.''

''What have you in mind to do?'' Garrison asked.

''Run,'' Travis said. ''Stay on the move.''

''And what will that accomplish?''

''It'll keep Einstein free.''

The dog woofed in agreement.

''Free—but for how long?'' Garrison asked.

Travis got up and paced, too agitated to sit still any longer. ''They won't stop looking,'' he admitted. ''Not for a few years.''

''Not ever,'' the attorney said.

''All right, it's going to be tough, but it's the only thing we can do. Damned if we'll let them have him. He has a dread of the lab. Besides, he more or less brought me back to life—''

''And he saved me from Streck,'' Nora said.

''He brought us together,'' Travis said.

''Changed our lives.''

"Radically changed us. Now he's as much a part of us as our own child would be," Travis said. He felt a lump of emotion in his throat when he met the dog's grateful gaze. "We fight for him, just as he'd fight for us. We're family. We live together ... or we die together."

Stroking the retriever, Garrison said, "It won't only be the people from the lab looking for you. And not only the police."

"The other thing," Travis said, nodding.

Einstein shivered.

"There, there, easy now," Garrison said reassuringly, patting the dog. To Travis, he said, "What do you think the creature is? I've heard your description of it, but that doesn't help much."

"Whatever it is," Travis said, "God didn't make it. Men made it. Which means it has to be a product of recombinant-DNA research of some kind. God knows why. God knows what they thought they were doing, why they wanted to build something like that. But they did."

"And it seems to have an uncanny ability to track you."

"To track Einstein," Nora said.

"So we'll keep moving," Travis said, "and we'll go a long way."

"That'll require money, but the banks don't open for more than twelve hours," Garrison said. "If you're going to run, something tells me you've got to head out tonight."

"Here's where we could use your help," Travis told him.

Nora opened her purse and withdrew two checkbooks, Travis's and her own. "Garrison, what we'd like to do is write a check on Travis's account and one on mine, payable to you. He's only got three thousand in his checking, but he has a large savings account at the same bank, and they're authorized to transfer funds to prevent overdrawing. My account's the same way. If we give you one of Travis's checks for twenty thousand—backdated so it appears to've been written before all this trouble—and one of mine for twenty, you could deposit them into your account. As soon as they clear, you'd buy eight cashier's checks for five thousand apiece and send them to us."

328

Travis said, "The police will want me for questioning, but they'll know I didn't kill Ted Hockney because no *man* could've torn him apart like that. So they won't put a lock on my accounts."

"If federal agencies are behind the research that produced Einstein and this creature," Garrison said, "then they'll be hot to get their hands on you, and *they* might freeze your accounts."

"Maybe. But probably not right away. You're in the same town, so your bank should clear my check by Monday at the latest."

"What'll you do for funds in the meantime, while you're waiting for me to send you the forty thousand?"

"We've got some cash and traveler's checks left over from the honeymoon," Nora said.

"And my credit cards," Travis added.

"They can track you by credit cards and traveler's checks."

"I know," Travis said. "So I'll use them in a town where we don't intend to stay, and we'll scoot out fast as we can."

"When I've purchased the cashier's checks for forty thousand, where do I send them?"

"We'll be in touch by phone," Travis said, returning to the couch and sitting at Nora's side. "We'll work something out."

"And the rest of your assets—and Nora's?"

"We'll worry about that later," Nora said.

Garrison frowned. "Before you leave here, Travis, you can sign a letter giving me the right to represent you in any legal matters that may arise. If anyone does try to freeze your assets, or Nora's I can beat them off if at all possible—though I'll keep a low profile until they connect me with you."

"Nora's funds are probably safe for a while. She and I haven't told anyone but you about the marriage. The neighbors will tell the police I left in the company of a woman, but they won't know who she is. Have you told anyone about us?"

"Just my secretary, Mrs. Ashcroft. But she's not a gossip."

"All right, then," Travis said. "I don't think the authorities will find out about the marriage license, so they might take quite a while to come up with Nora's name. But when they do, they'll discover you're her attorney. If they monitor my accounts for canceled checks in the hope of learning where I've gone, they'll know about the twenty thousand I paid to you, and they'll come looking for you—"

"That doesn't give me the slightest pause," Garrison said.

"Maybe not," Travis said. "But as soon as they connect me to Nora and both of us to you, they'll be watching you closely. As soon as that happens . . . then the next time we call, you'll have to tell us at once, so we can hang up and break off all contact with you."

"I understand perfectly," the attorney said.

"Garrison," Nora said, "you don't have to involve yourself in this. We're really asking too much of you."

"Listen, my dear, I'm almost seventy-one. I still enjoy my law practice, and I still go sailing . . . but in truth I find life a bit on the dull side these days. This affair is just what I need to get my ancient blood flowing faster. Besides, I do believe you have an obligation to help keep Einstein free, not just for the reasons you mentioned but because . . . mankind has no right to employ its genius in the creation of another intelligent species, then treat it like property. If we've come so far that we can create as God creates, then we have to learn to act with the justice and mercy of God. In this case, justice and mercy require that Einstein remain free."

Einstein raised his head from the attorney's lap, gazed up admiringly, then nuzzled his cold nose under Garrison's chin.

In the three-car garage, Garrison kept a new black Mercedes 560 SEL, an older white Mercedes 500 SEL with pale-blue interior, and a green Jeep that he used primarily

330

to drive down to the marina, where he kept his boat.

"The white one used to belong to Francine, my wife," the attorney said as he led them to the car. "I don't use it much any more, but I keep it in working order, and I drive it often enough to prevent the tires from disintegrating. I should have gotten rid of it when Franny died. It was her car, after all. But ... she loved it so, her flashy white Mercedes, and I can remember the way she looked when she was behind the wheel ... I'd like you to take it."

"A sixty-thousand-dollar getaway car?" Travis said, sliding one hand along the polished hood. "That's going on the run in style."

"No one will be looking for it," Garrison said. "Even if they do eventually connect me with you two, they won't know I've given you one of my cars."

"We can't accept something this expensive," Nora said.

"Call it a loan," the attorney told her. "When you're finished with it, when you've gotten another car, just park this one somewhere—a bus terminal, an airport—and give me a call to tell me where it is. I can send someone to collect it."

Einstein put his forepaws on the driver's door of the Mercedes and peered into the car through the side window. He glanced at Travis and Nora and woofed as if to say he thought they would be foolish if they turned down such an offer.

9

With Travis driving, they left Garrison Dilworth's house at ten-fifteen Wednesday night and took Route 101 north. By twelve-thirty they passed through San Luis Obispo, went by Paso Robles at one o'clock in the morning. They stopped for gasoline at a self-service station at two o'clock, an hour south of Salinas.

Nora felt useless. She was not even able to spell Travis at the wheel because she did not know how to drive. To some extent, that was Violet Devon's fault, not Nora's, just one more result of a lifetime of seclusion and oppression; nonetheless, she felt utterly useless and was displeased with herself. But she was not going to remain helpless the rest of her life. Damn it, no. She was going to learn to drive and to handle firearms. Travis could teach her both skills. Given his background, he could also instruct her in the martial arts, judo or karate. He was a good teacher. He had certainly done a splendid job of teaching her the art of lovemaking. That thought made her smile, and slowly her highly self-critical mood abated.

For the next two and a half hours, as they drove north to Salinas and then on to San Jose. Nora dozed fitfully. When not sleeping, she took comfort in the empty miles they were putting behind them. On both sides of the highway, vast stretches of farmland seemed to roll on to infinity under the frost-pale light of the moon. When the moon set, they drove long stretches in unrelieved darkness before spotting an occasional light at a farm or a cluster of roadside businesses.

The yellow-eyed thing had tracked Einstein from the Santa Ana foothills in Orange County to Santa Barbara—a distance of more than one hundred and twenty-five air miles, Travis had said, and probably close to three hundred miles on foot in the wilds—in three months. Not a fast pace. So if they went three hundred air miles north from Santa Barbara before finding a place to hole up in the San Francisco Bay area, maybe the stalker would not reach them for seven or eight months. Maybe it would never reach them. Over how great a distance could it sniff out Einstein? Surely, there were limits to its uncanny ability to track the dog. Surely.

10

At eleven o'clock Thursday morning, Lemuel Johnson stood in the master bedroom of the small house that Travis

Cornell had rented in Santa Barbara. The dresser mirror had been smashed. The rest of the room had been trashed as well, as if The Outsider had been driven into a jealous rage upon seeing that the dog lived in domestic comfort while it was forced to roam the wildlands and live in comparatively primitive conditions.

In the debris that covered the floor, Lem found four silver-framed photographs that had probably stood on the dresser or nightstands. The first was of Cornell and an attractive blonde. By now Lem had learned enough about Cornell to know that the blonde at his side must be his late wife, Paula. Another photo, a black-and-white shot of a man and woman, was old enough that Lem guessed the people smiling at the camera were Cornell's parents. The third was of a young boy, about eleven or twelve, also black-and-white, also old, which might have been a shot of Travis Cornell himself but which was more likely a picture of the brother who had died young.

The last of the four photos was of ten soldiers grouped on what appeared to be the wooden steps in front of a barracks, grinning at the camera. One of the ten was Travis Cornell. And on a couple of their uniforms, Lem noticed the distinctive patch of Delta Force, the elite antiterrorist corps.

Uneasy about that last photograph, Lem put it on the dresser and headed back toward the living room, where Cliff was continuing to sift through blood-stained rubble. They were looking for something that would mean nothing to the police but might be extremely meaningful to them.

The NSA had been slow to pick up on the Santa Barabara killing, and Lem had not been alerted until almost six o'clock this morning. As a result, the press had already reported the grisly details of Ted Hockney's murder. They were enthusiastically disseminating wild speculations about what might have killed Hockney, focusing primarily on the theory that Cornell kept some kind of exotic and dangerous pet, perhaps a cheetah or panther, and that the animal had attacked the unsuspecting landlord when he had let himself into the house. The TV cameras had lingered lovingly on the shredded and blood-spattered books. It was *National Enquirer* stuff, which did not surprise Lem because he believed the line separating sensational tabloids like the *Enquirer* and the so-called "legitimate" press—especially electronic news media—was often thinner than most journalists cared to admit.

He had already planned and put into operation a disinformation campaign to reinforce the press's wrongheaded hysteria about jungle cats on the loose. NSA-paid informants would come forth, claiming to know Cornell, and would vouch that he did, indeed, keep a panther in the house in addition to a dog. Others who had never met Cornell would, in identifying themselves as his friends, sorrowfully report that they had urged him to have the panther defanged and declawed as it had reached maturity. Police would want to question Cornell—and the unidentified woman—regarding the panther and its current whereabouts.

Lem was confident the press would be nicely deflected from all inquiries that might lead them closer to the truth.

Of course, down in Orange County, Walt Gaines would hear about this murder, would make friendly inquiries with local authorities here, and would swiftly conclude that The Outsider had tracked the dog this far north. Lem was relieved that he had Walt's cooperation.

Entering the living room, where Cliff Soames was at work, Lem said, "Find anything?"

The young agent rose from the debris, dusted his hands together, and said, "Yeah. I put it on the dining-room table."

Lem followed him into the dining room, where a fat ring-binder notebook was the only item on the table. When he opened it and leafed through the contents, he saw photographs that had been cut from glossy magazines and taped to the left-hand pages. Opposite each photo, on the right-hand page, was the name of the pictured object printed in large block letters: TREE, HOUSE, CAR . . .

"What do you make of it?" Cliff asked.

Scowling, saying nothing, Lem continued to leaf through

the book, knowing it was important but at first unable to guess why. Then it hit him: "It's a primer. To teach reading."

"Yeah," Cliff said.

Lem saw that his assistant was smiling. "You think they must know the dog's intelligent, that it must've revealed its abilities to them? And so they ... decided to teach it to read?"

"Looks that way," Cliff said, still smiling. "Good God, do you think it's possible? *Could* it be taught to read?"

"Undoubtedly," Lem said. "In fact, teaching it to read was on Dr. Weatherby's schedule of experiments for this autumn."

Laughing softly, wonderingly, Cliff said, "I'll be damned."

"Before you get too much of a kick out of it," Lem said, "you better consider the situation. This guy knows the dog is amazingly smart. He might've succeeded in teaching it to read. So we have to figure he's worked out a means of com municating with it as well. He know's it's an experimental animal. He must know a lot of people are looking for it."

Cliff said, "He must know about The Outsider, too, because the dog would have found a way of telling him."

"Yes. Yet, knowing all of this, he hasn't chosen to go public. He could've sold the story to the highest bidder. But he didn't. Or if he's a crusading type, he could've called in the press and blasted the Pentagon for funding this kind of research."

"But he didn't" Cliff said, frowning.

"Which means, first and foremost, he's committed to the dog, committed to keeping it for his own and to preventing its recapture."

Nodding, Cliff said, "Which makes sense if what we've heard about him is true. I mean, this guy lost his whole damn family when he was young. Lost his wife after less than a year. Lost all those buddies in Delta Force. So he became a recluse, cut himself off from all his friends. Must've been lonely as hell. Then along comes the dog ..."

"Exactly," Lem said. "And for a man with Delta Force

335

training, staying undercover won't be difficult. And if we *do* find him, he'll know how to fight for the dog. Jesus, will he know how to fight!"

"We haven't confirmed the Delta Force rumor yet," Cliff said hopefully.

"I have," Lem said, and he described the photograph he had seen in the wrecked bedroom.

Cliff sighed. "We're in deep shit now."

"Up to our necks," Lem agreed.

11

They had reached San Francisco at six o'clock Thursday morning and, by six-thirty, had found a suitable motel—a sprawling facility that looked modern and clean. The place did not accept pets, but it was easy to sneak Einstein into the room.

Although a small chance existed that an arrest warrant might have been issued for Travis, he checked into the motel using his ID. He'd no choice because Nora possessed neither credit cars nor a driver's license. These days, desk clerks were willing to accept cash, but not without ID; the chain's computer demanded data on the guests.

He did not, however, give the correct make or license number of his car, for he had parked out of sight of the office for the very purpose of keeping those details from the clerk.

They paid for only one room and kept Einstein with them because they were not going to need privacy for lovemaking. Exhausted, Travis barely managed to kiss Nora before falling into a deep sleep. He dreamed of things with yellow eyes, misshapen heads, and crocodile mouths full of shark's teeth.

He woke five hours later, at twelve-ten Thursday afternoon.

Nora had gotten up before him, showered, and dressed again in the only clothes she had. Her hair was damp and

336

clung alluringly to the nape of her neck. "The water's hot and forceful," she told him.

"So am I," he said, embracing her, kissing her.

"Then you better cool off," she said, pulling away from him. "Little ears are listening."

"Einstein? He has big ears."

In the bathroom, he found Einstein standing on the counter, drinking out of a sinkful of cold water that Nora had drawn for him.

"You know, fur face, for most dogs, the toilet is a perfectly adequate source of drinking water."

Einstein sneezed at him, jumped down from the counter, and padded out of the bathroom.

Travis had no means of shaving, but he decided a day's growth of beard would give him the look he needed for the work he would have to do this evening in the Tenderloin district.

They left the motel and ate at the first McDonald's they could find. After lunch, they drove to a local branch of the Santa Barbara bank where Travis had his checking account. They used his computer-banking card, his Mastercard, and two of his Visa cards to make cash withdrawals totaling fourteen hundred dollars. Next they went to an American Express office, and using one of Travis's checks and his Gold Card, they acquired the maximum allowable five hundred dollars in cash and forty-five hundred in traveler's checks. Combined with the twenty-one hundred in cash and traveler's checks left over from their honeymoon, they had eighty-five hundred in liquid assets.

During the rest of the afternoon and early evening, they went shopping. With credit cards, they bought a complete set of luggage and purchased enough clothes to fill the bags. They got toiletries for both of them and an electric razor for Travis.

Travis also bought a Scrabble game, and Nora said, "You don't really feel in the mood for games, do you?"

"No," he replied cryptically, enjoying her puzzlement. "I'll explain later."

Half an hour before sunset, with their purchases packed

tightly into the spacious trunk of the Mercedes, Travis drove into the heart of San Francisco's Tenderloin, which was the area of the city that lay below O'Farrell Street, wedged between Market Street and Van Ness Avenue. It was a district of sleazy bars featuring topless dancers, go-go joints where the girls wore nothing at all, rap parlors where men paid by the minute to sit with nude young women and talk about sex and where more than talk was usually accomplished.

This degeneracy was a shocking revelation to Nora, who had begun to think of herself as experienced and sophisticated. She was not prepared for the cesspool of the Tenderloin. She gaped at the gaudy neon signs that advertised peep shows, female mud wrestling, female impersonators, gay baths, and massage parlors. The meaning of some of the billboard come-ons at the worst bars baffled her, and she said, "What do they mean when the marquee says 'Get a Wink at the Pink'?"

Looking for a parking place, Travis said, "It means their girls dance entirely nude and that, during the dance, they spread their labia to show themselves more completely."

"No!"

"Yes."

"My God. I don't believe it. I mean, I *do* believe it—but I don't *believe* it. What's it mean—'Extreme Close-Up'?"

"The girls dance right at the customers' tables. The law doesn't allow touching, but the girls dance close, swinging their bare breasts in the customers' faces. You could insert one, maybe two, but not three sheets of paper between their nipples and the men's lips."

In the back seat, Einstein snorted as if with disgust.

"I agree, fella," Travis told him.

They passed a cancerous-looking place with flashing red and yellow bulbs and rippling banks of blue and purple neon, where the sign promised LIVE SEX SHOW.

Appalled, Nora said, "My God, are there other shows where they have sex with the dead?"

Travis laughed so hard he almost back-ended a carload of gawking college boys. "No, no, no. Even the Tenderloin

338

has some limits. They mean 'live' as oppposed to 'on film'. You can see plenty of sex on film, theaters that show only pornography, but that place promises live sex, on stage. I don't know if they deliver on the promise.''

"And I don't care to find out!" Nora said, sounding as if she were Dorothy from Kansas and had just wandered into an unspeakable new neighborhood of Oz. "What're we doing here?"

"This is the place you come to when you're trying to find things they don't sell on Nob Hill—like young boys or really large amounts of dope. Or phony driver's licenses and other counterfeit ID.''

"Oh," she said. "Oh, yes, I see. This area is controlled by the underworld, by people like the Corleones in *The Godfather*.''

"I'm sure the mob owns more of these places than not," he said as he maneuvered the Mercedes into a parking space at the curb. "But don't ever make the mistake of thinking the *real* mob is a bunch of honorable cuties like the Corleones.''

Einstein was agreeable to remaining with the Mercedes.

"Tell you what, fur face. If we're *real* lucky," Travis joked, "we'll get you a new identity, too. We'll make you into a poodle.''

Nora was surprised to discover that, as twilight settled over the city, the breeze off the bay was chilly enough for them to need the nylon, quilt-lined jackets they had bought earlier in the day.

"Even in summer, nights can be cool here," he said. "Soon, the fog rolls in. The stored-up heat of the day pulls it off the water.''

He would have worn his jacket even if the evening air had been mild, for he was carrying his loaded revolver under his belt and needed the jacket to conceal it.

"Is there really a chance you'll need the gun?" she asked as they walked away from the car.

"Not likely. I'm carrying it mainly for ID."

"Huh?"

"You'll see."

She looked back at the car, where Einstein was staring out the rear window, looking forlorn. She felt bad leaving him there. But she was quite certain that even if these establishments would admit dogs such places were not good for Einstein's moral welfare.

Travis seemed interested solely in those bars whose signs were either in both English and Spanish or in Spanish only. Some places were downright shabby and did not conceal the peeling paint and the moldy carpeting, while others used mirrors and glitzy lighting to try to hide their true roach-hole nature. A few were actually clean and expensively decorated. In each, Travis spoke in Spanish with the bartender, sometimes with musicians if there were any and if they were on a break, and a few times he distributed folded twenty-dollar bills. Since she spoke no Spanish, Nora did not know what he was asking about or why he was paying these people.

On the street, searching for another sleazy lounge, he explained that the biggest illegal migration was Mexican, Salvadoran, Nicaraguan—desperate people escaping economic chaos and political repression. Therefore, more Spanish-speaking illegals were in the market for phony papers than were Vietnamese, Chinese, or those in all other language groups put together. "So the quickest way to get a lead on a supplier of phony papers is through the Latino underworld."

"Have you got a lead?"

"Not yet. Just bits and pieces. And probably ninety-nine percent of what I've paid for is nonsense, lies. But don't worry—we'll find what we need. That's why the Tenderloin doesn't go out of business: people who come here *always* find what they need."

The people who came here surprised Nora. In the streets, in the topless bars, all kinds could be found. Asians, Latinos, whites, blacks, and even Indians mingled in an alcholic haze, so it seemed as if racial harmony was a beneficial side effect of the pursuit of sin. Guys swaggered around in leather jackets and jeans, guys who looked like hoods, which she expected. But there were also men in business suits, clean-cut college kids, others dressed like cowboys, and wholesome surfer types who looked as if they had stepped out of an old Annette Funicello movie. Bums sat on the pavement or stood on corners, grizzled old winos in reeking clothes, and even some of the business-suit types had a weird glint in their eyes that made you want to run from them, but it seemed as if most of the people here were those who would pass for ordinary upstanding citizens in any decent neighborhood. Nora was amazed.

Not many women were on the streets or in the company of the men in the bars. No, correct that: there were women to be seen, but they looked more lascivious than the nude dancers, and only a few of them seemed not to be for sale.

At a topless bar called Hot Tips, which had signs in both Spanish and English, the recorded rock music was so loud Nora got a headache. Six beautiful girls with exquisite bodies, wearing only spike heels and sequined bikini panties, were dancing at the tables, wriggling, writhing, swinging their breasts in the sweaty faces of men who were either mesmerized or hooting and clapping. Other topless girls, equally pretty, were waitressing.

While Travis spoke in Spanish with the bartender, Nora noticed some of the customers looking at her appraisingly. They gave her the creeps. She kept one hand on Travis's arm. She couldn't have been torn away from him with a crowbar.

The stink of stale beer and whiskey, body odor, the layered scents of various cheap perfumes, and cigarette smoke made the air as heavy as that in a steambath, though less healthful.

Nora clenched her teeth and thought, I will not be sick and make a fool of myself. I simply will not.

After a couple of minutes of rapid conversation, Travis passed a pair of twenties to the bartender and was directed to the back of the lounge, where a guy as big as Arnold

Schwarzenegger was sitting on a chair beside a doorway that was covered by a densely beaded curtain. He was wearing black leather pants and a white T-shirt. His arms seemed as large as tree trunks. His face looked as if it had been cast in cement, and he had gray eyes almost as transparent as glass. Travis spoke with him in Spanish and passed him two twenties.

The music faded from a thunderous din to a mere roar. A woman, speaking into a microphone, said "All right, boys, if you like what you see, then show it—start stuffin' those pussies."

Nora twitched in shock, but as the music rose again, she saw what was meant by the crude announcement: the customers were expected to slip folded five- and ten-dollar bills into the dancers' panties.

The hulk in black leather pants got off his chair and led them through the beaded curtain, into a room ten feet wide and eighteen or twenty feet long, where six more young women in spike heels and bikini panties were getting ready to take over from the dancers already on the floor. They were checking their makeup in mirrors, applying lipstick, or just chatting with each other. They were all (she saw) as good-looking as the girls out front. Some of them had hard faces, pretty but hard, though others were as fresh-faced as school-teachers. All were the kind of women that men probably had in mind when they talked about girls who were "stacked."

The hulk led Travis—and Travis led Nora, holding her hand—through that dressing room toward the door at the other end. As they went, one of the topless dancers—a striking blonde—put a hand on Nora's shoulder and walked beside her.

"Are you new, honey?"

"Me? No. Oh, no, I don't work here."

The blonde, who was so well-endowed that Nora felt like a boy, said, "You got the equipment, honey."

"Oh, no," was all Nora could say.

"You like my equipment?" the blonde asked.

"Oh, well, you're very pretty," Nora said.

To the blonde, Travis said, "Give it up, sister. The lady doesn't swing that way."

The blonde smiled sweetly. "If she tries it, she might like it."

They went through a door, out of the dressing room and into a narrow, shabby, poorly lit hallway before Nora realized she had been propositioned. By a woman!

She did not know whether to laugh or gag. Probably both.

The hulk took them to an office at the back of the building and left them, saying, "Mr. Van Dyne will be with you in a minute."

The office had gray walls, gray metal chairs, filing cabinets, and a gray metal desk that was battered and scarred. No pictures or calendars hung on the bare walls. No pens or notepads or reports were on the desk. The place looked as if it was seldom used.

Nora and Travis sat on the two metal chairs in front of the desk.

The music from the bar was still audible but no longer deafening. When she caught her breath, Nora said, "Where do they all come from?"

"Who?"

"All those pretty girls with their perfect boobs and tight little bottoms and long legs, and all of them willing to . . . to do *that*. Where do so many of them come from?"

"There's a breeding farm outside of Modesto," Travis said.

She gaped at him.

He laughed and said, "I'm sorry. I keep forgetting how innocent you are, Mrs. Cornell." He kissed her cheek. His stubble scratched a little, but it was nice. In spite of wearing yesterday's clothes and not having shaved, he seemed as clean as a well-scrubbed baby compared to the gauntlet they had run in order to reach this office. He said, "I should answer you straight because you don't know when I'm joking."

She blinked, "Then there *isn't* a breeding farm outside Modesto?"

"No. There's all kinds of girls who do it. Girls who hope

343

to break into showbiz, go to L.A. to be movie stars but can't make it, so they drift into places like this in L.A. or they come north to San Francisco or they go to Vegas. Most are decent enough kids. They see this as temporary. Very good money can be made fast. It's a way to build up a stake before taking another crack at Hollywood. Then there are some, the self-haters, who do it to humiliate themselves. Others are in rebellion from their parents, from their first husbands, from the whole damn world. And some are hookers."

"The hookers meet ... johns here?" she asked.

"Maybe, maybe not. Some probably dance to have an explicable source of income when the IRS knocks on their doors. They report their earnings as dancers, which gives them a better chance of concealing what they make from turning tricks."

"It's sad," she said.

"Yeah. In some cases ... in a *lot* of cases, it's damn sad."

Fascinated, she said, "Will we get false IDs from this Van Dyne?"

"I believe so."

She regarded him solemnly. "You really *do* know your way around, don't you?"

"Does it bother you—that I know places like this?"

She thought a moment. Then: "No. In fact ... if a woman's going to take a husband, I suppose he ought to be a man who knows what to do in any situation. It gives me a lot of confidence."

"In me?"

"In you, yes, and confidence that we're going to get through this all right, that we're going to save Einstein and ourselves."

"Confidence is good. But in Delta Force, one of the first things you learn is that being *overly* confident can get you killed."

The door opened, and the hulk returned with a round-faced man in a gray suit, blue shirt, and black tie.

"Van Dyne," the newcomer said, but he did not offer to

344

shake hands. He went around the desk and sat in a spring-backed chair. He had thinning blond hair and baby-smooth cheeks. He looked like a stockbroker in a television commercial: efficient, smart, as well-meaning as he was well-groomed. "I wanted to talk to you because I want to know who's spreading these falsehoods about me."

Travis said, "We need new ID—driver's licenses, social security cards, the whole works. First-rate, with full backup, not junk."

"That's what I'm talking about," Van Dyne said. He raised his eyebrows quizzically. "Where on earth did you get the idea that I'm in that sort of business? I'm afraid you've been misinformed."

"We need first-rate paper with full backup," Travis repeated.

Van Dyne stared at him, at Nora. "Let me see your wallet. And your purse, miss."

Putting his wallet on the desk, Travis told Nora, "It's okay."

Reluctantly, she put her purse beside the wallet.

"Please stand and let Caesar search you," Van Dyne said.

Travis stood and motioned for Nora to get up as well.

Caesar, the cement-faced hulk, searched Travis with embarrassing thoroughness, found the .357 Magnum, put it on the desk. He was even more thorough with Nora, unbuttoning her blouse and boldly feeling the cups of her bra for a miniature microphone, battery, and recorder. She blushed and would not have permitted these intimacies if Travis had not explained to her what Caesar was looking for. Besides, Caesar remained expressionless throughout, as if he were a machine without the potential for erotic response.

When Caesar was finished with them, they sat down while Van Dyne went through Travis's wallet and then through Nora's purse. She was afraid he was going to take their money without giving them anything in return, but he appeared to be interested in only their ID and the butcher's knife that Nora still carried.

To Travis, Van Dyne said, "Okay. If you were a cop, you wouldn't be allowed to carry a Magnum"— he swung out the cylinder and looked at the ammunition—"loaded with magnums. The ACLU would have your ass." He smiled at Nora. "No policewoman carriers a butcher's knife."

Suddenly she understood what Travis meant when he'd said he was carrying the revolver not for protection but for its value as ID.

Van Dyne and Travis haggled a bit, finally settling on sixty-five hundred as the price for two sets of ID with "full backup."

Their belongings, including the butcher's knife and revolver, were returned to them.

From the gray office, they followed Van Dyne into the narrow hall, where he dismissed Caesar, then to a set of dimly lit concrete stairs leading to a basement beneath Hot Tips, where the rock music was further filtered by the intervening concrete floor.

Nora was not sure what she expected to find in the basement: maybe men who all looked like Edward G. Robinson and wore green eye shades on elastic bands and labored over antique printing presses, producing not just false identification papers but stacks of phony currency. What she found, instead, surprised her.

The steps ended in a stone-walled storage room about forty by thirty feet. Bar supplies were stacked to shoulder height. They walked along a narrow aisle formed by cartons of whiskey, beer, and cocktail napkins, to a steel fire door in the rear wall. Van Dyne pushed a button in the door frame, and a closed-circuit security camera made a purring sound as it panned them.

The door was opened from inside, and they went through into a smaller room with subdued lighting, where two young bearded guys were working at two of seven computers lined up on work tables along one wall. The first guy was wearing soft Rockport shoes, safari pants, a web belt, and a cotton safari shirt. The other wore Reeboks, jeans, and a sweatshirt that featured the Three Stooges. They looked almost like twins, and both resembled young versions of Steven Spielberg. They were so intensely involved with their computer work that they did not look up at Nora and Travis and Van Dyne, but they were having fun, too, talking exuberantly to themselves, to their machines, and to each other in high-tech language that made no sense whatsoever to Nora.

A woman in her early twenties was also at work in the room. She had short blond hair and oddly beautiful eyes the color of pennies. While Van Dyne spoke with the two guys at the computers, the woman took Travis and Nora to the far end of the room, put them in front of a white screen, and photographed them for the phony drivers' licenses.

When the blonde disappeared into a darkroom to develop the film, Travis and Nora rejoined Van Dyne at the computers, where the young men were working happily. Nora watched them accessing the supposedly secure computers of the California Department of Motor Vehicles and the Social Security Administration, as well as those of other federal, state, and local government agencies.

"When I told Mr. Van Dyne that I wanted ID with 'full-backup'," Travis explained, "I meant the driver's licenses must be able to stand up to inspection if we're ever stopped by a highway patrolman who runs a check on them. The licenses we're getting are indistinguishable from the real thing. These guys are inserting our new names into the DMV's files, actually creating computer records of these licenses in the state's data banks."

Van Dyne said, "The addresses are phony, of course. But when you settle down somewhere, under your new names, you just apply to the DMV for a change of address like the law requires, and then you'll be prefectly legit. We're setting these up to expire in about a year, at which time you'll go into a DMV office, take the usual test, and get brand-new licenses because your new names are in their files."

"What're our new names?" Nora wondered.

"You see," Van Dyne said, speaking with the quiet assurance and patience of a stockbroker explaining the market to a new investor, "we have to start with birth certificates. We keep computer files of infant deaths all over the western United States, going back at least fifty years. We've already searched those lists for the years each of you was born, trying to find babies who died with your hair and eye colors—and with your first names, too, just because it's easier for you not to have to change both first and last. We found a little girl, Nora Jean Aimes, born October twelfth of the year you were born and who died one month later, right here in San Francisco. We have a laser printer with virtually an infinite choice of type styles and sizes, with which we've already produced a facsimile of the kind of birth certificate that was in use in San Francisco at that time, and it bears Nora Jean's name, vital statistics. We'll make two Xeroxes of it, and you'll receive both. Next, we tapped into the Social Security files and appropriated a number for Nora Jean Aimes, who never was given one, and we also created a history of Social Security tax payments." He smiled. "You've already paid in enough quarters to qualify for a pension when you retire. Likewise, the IRS now has computer records that show you've worked as a waitress in half a dozen cities and that you've faithfully paid your taxes every year."

Travis said, "With a birth certificate and legitimate Social Security number, they were then able to get a driver's license that would have real ID behind it."

"So I'm Nora Jean Aimes? But if her birth certificate's on record, so is her death certificate. If someone wanted to check—"

Van Dyne shook his head. "In those days, both birth and death certificates were strictly paper documents, no computer files. And because it squanders more money than it spends wisely, the government has never had the funds to transfer records of the precomputer era into electronic data banks. So if someone gets suspicious about you, they can't just search out the death records on computer and learn the truth in two minutes flat. They'd have to go to the courthouse, dig back throught the coroner's files for that year, and find Nora Jean's death certificate. But that won't happen because part of our service involves having Nora

348

Jean's certificate removed from public records and destroyed now that you've bought her identity."

"We're into TRW, the credit-reporting agency," one of the twin Spielberg look-alikes said with obvious delight.

Nora saw data flicking across the green screens, but none of it had any meaning for her.

"They're creating solid credit histories for our new identities," Travis told her. "By the time we do settle down somewhere and put in a change of address with the DMV and TRW, our mailbox will be flooded with offers for credit cards—Visa, Mastercard, probably even American Express and Carte Blanche."

"Nora Jean Aimes," she said numbly, trying to grasp how quickly and thoroughly her new life was being built.

Because they could locate no infant who had died in the year of Travis's birth with his first name, he had to settle for being Samuel Spencer Hyatt, who had been born that January and had perished that March in Portland, Oregon. The death would be expunged from the public record, and Travis's new identity would stand up to fairly intense scrutiny.

Strictly for fun (they said), the bearded young operators created a military record for Travis, crediting him six years in the Marines and awarding him a Purple Heart plus a couple of citations for bravery during a peace-keeping-mission-turned-violent in the Middle East. To their delight, he asked if they could also create a valid real-estate broker's license under his new name, and within twenty-five minutes they cracked into the right data banks and did the job.

"Cake and pie," one of the young men said.

"Cake and pie," the other echoed.

Nora frowned, not understanding.

"Piece of cake," one of them explained.

"Easy as pie," the other said.

"Cake and pie," Nora said, nodding.

The blonde with copper-penny eyes returned, carrying driver's licenses imprinted with Travis's and Nora's pictures. "You're both quite photogenic," she said.

Two hours and twenty minutes after meeting Van Dyne,

they left Hot Tips with two manila envelopes containing a variety of documents supporting their new identities. Out on the street, Nora felt a little dizzy and held onto Travis's arm all the way back to the car.

Fog had rolled through the city while they had been in Hot Tips. The blinking lights and flashing-rippling neon of the Tenderloin were softened yet curiously magnified by the mist, so it seemed as if every cubic centimeter of night air was awash with strange lights, with an aurora borealis brought down to ground level. Those sleazy streets had a certain mystery and cheap allure after dark, in the fog, but not if you'd seen them in daylight first and remembered what you had seen.

In the Mercedes, Einstein was waiting patiently.

"Couldn't arrange to have you turned into a poodle, after all," Nora told him as she buckled her seat belt. "But we sure did ourselves up right. Einstein, say hello to Sam Hyatt and Nora Aimes."

The retriever put his head over the front seat, looked at her, looked at Travis, and snorted once as if to say they could not fool him, that *he* knew who they were.

To Travis, Nora said, "Your antiterrorist training . . . is that where you learned about places like Hot Tips, people like Van Dyne? Is that where terrorists get new ID once they slip into the country?"

"Yeah, some go to people like Van Dyne, though not usually. The Soviets supply papers for most terrorists. Van Dyne services mostly ordinary illegal immigrants, though not the poor ones, and criminal types looking to dodge arrest warrants."

As he started the car, she said, "But if you could find Van Dyne, maybe the people looking for us can find him."

"Maybe. It'll take them a while, but maybe they can."

"Then they'll find out all about our new identities."

"No," Travis said. He turned on the defroster and the windshield wipers to clear the condensation off the outside of the glass. "Van Dyne wouldn't keep records. He doesn't want to be caught with proof of what he does. If the authorities ever tumble to him and go in there with search warrants, they won't find anything in Van Dyne's computers except the accounting and purchasing records for Hot Tips."

As they drove through the city, heading for the Golden Gate Bridge, Nora stared in fascination at the people in the streets and in other cars, not just in the Tenderloin but in every neighborhood through which they passed. She wondered how many of them were living under the names and identities with which they had been born and how many were changelings like her and Travis.

"In less than three hours, we've been totally remade," she said.

"Some world we live in, huh? More than anything else, that's what high technology means—maximum fluidity. The whole world is becoming ever more fluid, malleable. Most financial transactions are now handled with electronic money that flashes from New York to L.A.—or around the world—in seconds. Money crosses borders in a blink; it no longer has to be smuggled out past the guards. Most records are kept in the form of electrical charges that only computers read. So everything's fluid. Identities are fluid. The past is fluid."

Nora said, "Even the genetic structure of a species is fluid these days."

Einstein woofed agreement.

Nora said, "Scary, isn't it?"

"A little," Travis said as they approached the light-bedecked southern entrance to the fog-mantled Golden Gate Bridge, which was all but invisible in the mist. "But maximum fluidity is basically a good thing. Social and financial fluidity guarantee freedom. I believe—and I hope—that we're heading toward an age when the role of governments will inevitably dwindle, when there'll be no way to regulate and control people as thoroughly as was possible in the past. Totalitarian governments won't be able to stay in power."

"How so?"

"Well, how can dictatorship control its citizens in a high-tech society of maximum fluidity? The only way is to refuse to allow high tech to intrude, seal the borders, and live entirely in an earlier age. But that'd be national suicide for any country that tried it. They couldn't compete. In a few decades, they'd be modern aborigines, primitive by the standards of the civilized high-tech world. Right now, for instance, the Soviets try to restrict computers to their defense industry, which can't last. They'll have to computerize their entire economy and teach their people to use computers—and *then* how can they keep the screws tight when their citizens have been given the means to manipulate the system and foil its controls on them?"

At the entrance to the bridge, no northbound toll was collected. They drove onto the span, where the speed limit had been drastically reduced because of the weather.

Looking up at the ghostly skeleton of the bridge, which glistened with condensation and vanished in the fog, Nora said, "You seem to think the world will be paradise in a decade or two."

"Not paradise," he said. "Easier, richer, safer, happier. But not a paradise. After all, there will still be all the problems of the human heart and all the potential sicknesses of the human mind. And the new world's bound to bring us some new dangers as well as blessings."

"Like the thing that killed your landlord," she said.

"Yes."

In the back seat, Einstein growled.

12

That Thursday afternoon, August 26, Vince Nasco drove to Johnny The Wire Santini's place in San Clemente to pick up the past week's report, which was when he learned of the murder of Ted Hockney in Santa Barbara the previous evening. The condition of the corpse, especially the missing eyes, linked it to The Outsider. Johnny had also ascertained that the NSA had quietly assumed jurisdiction in the case, which convinced Vince it was related to the Banodyne fugitives.

That evening, he got a newspaper and, over a dinner of seafood enchiladas and Dos Equis at a Mexican restaurant, he read about Hockney and about the man who had rented the house where the murder occurred—Travis Cornell. The press was reporting that Cornell, a former real-estate broker who had once been a member of Delta Force, kept a panther in the house and that the cat had killed Hockney, but Vince knew that the cat was bullshit, just a cover story. The cops said they wanted to talk to Cornell and to an unidentified woman seen with him, though they had not filed any charges against them.

The story also had one line about Cornell's dog: "Cornell and the woman may be traveling with a golden retriever."

If I can find Cornell, Vince thought, I'll find the dog.

This was the first break he'd had, and it confirmed his feeling that owning the retriever was a part of his great destiny.

To celebrate, he ordered more seafood enchiladas and beer.

13

Travis, Nora, and Einstein stayed Thursday night at a motel in Marin County, north of San Francisco. They got a six-pack of San Miguel at a convenience store and take-out chicken, biscuits, and coleslaw from a fast-food restaurant, and ate a late dinner in the room.

Einstein enjoyed the chicken and showed considerable interest in the beer.

Travis decided to pour half a bottle in the new yellow plastic dish they had gotten the retriever during their shopping spree earlier in the day. "But no more than half a bottle, no matter how much you like it. I want you sober for some questions and answers."

After dinner, the three of them sat on the king-sized bed, and Travis unwrapped the Scrabble game. He put the board upside down on the mattress, with the playing surface concealed, and Nora helped him to sort all the lettered game tiles into twenty-six piles.

Einstein watched with interest and did not seem even slightly woozy from his half-bottle of San Miguel.

"Okay," Travis said, "I need more detailed answers than we've been able to get with yes-and-no questions. It occurred to me that this might work."

"Ingenious," Nora agreed.

To the dog, Travis said, "I ask you a question, and you indicate the letters that are needed to spell out the answer, one letter at a time, word by word. You got it?"

Einstein blinked at Travis, looked at the stacks of lettered tiles, raised his eyes to Travis again, and grinned.

Travis said, "All right. Do you know the name of the laboratory from which you escaped?"

Einstein put his nose to the pile of Bs.

Nora plucked a tile off the stack and put it on the portion of the board that Travis had left clear.

In less than a minute, the dog spelled BANODYNE.

"Banodyne," Travis said thoughtfully. "Never heard of it. Is that the entire name?"

Einstein hesitated, then began to choose more letters until he had spelled out BANODYNE LABORATORIES INC.

On a pad of motel stationery, Travis made a note of the answer, then returned all the tiles to their individual stacks. "Where is Banodyne located?"

IRVINE.

"That makes sense," Travis said. "I found you in the woods of Irvine. All right . . . I found you on Tuesday, May eighteenth. When had you escaped from Banodyne?"

Einstein stared at the tiles, whined, and made no choices.

"In all the reading you've done," Travis said, "you've learned about months, weeks, days, and hours. You have a sense of time now."

Looking at Nora, the dog whined again.

She said, "He has a sense of time now, but he didn't have one when he escaped, so it's hard to remember how long he was on the run."

Einstein immediately began to indicate letters: THATS RIGHT.

"Do you know the names of any researchers at Banodyne?"

DAVIS WEATHERBY.

Travis made a note of the name. "Any others?"

Hesitating frequently to consider possible spellings, Einstein finally produced LAWTON HANES, AL HUDSTUN, and a few more.

After noting all of them on the motel stationery, Travis said, "These will be some of the people looking for you."

YES. AND JOHNSON.

"Johnson?" Nora said. "Is he one of the scientists?"

NO. The retriever thought for a moment, studied the stacks of letters, and finally continued: SECURITY.

"He's head of security at Banodyne?" Travis asked.

NO. BIGGER.

"Probably a federal agent of some kind," Travis told Nora as she returned the letters to their stacks.

To Einstein, Nora said, "Do you know this Johnson's first name?"

Einstein gazed at the letters and mewled, and Travis was about to tell him it was all right if he didn't know Johnson's first name, but then the dog attempted to spell it: LEMOOOL.

"There is no such name," Nora said, taking the letters away.

Einstein tried again: LAMYOULL. Then again: LIMUUL.

"That's not a name, either," Travis said.

A fourth time: LEMB YOU WILL.

Travis realized the dog was struggling to spell the name phonetically. He chose six lettered tiles of his own: LEMUEL.

"Lemuel Johnson," Nora said.

Einstein leaned forward and nuzzled her neck. He was wiggling with pleasure at having gotten the name across to them, and the springs of the motel bed creaked.

Then he stopped nuzzling Nora and spelled DARK LEMUEL.

"Dark?" Travis said. "By 'dark' you mean Johnson is … evil?"

NO. DARK.

Nora restacked the letters and said, "Dangerous?"

Einstein snorted at her, then at Travis, as if to say they were sometimes unbearably thickheaded. NO. DARK.

For a moment they sat in silence, thinking, and at last Travis said, "Black! You mean Lemuel Johnson is a black man."

Einstein chuffed softly, shook his head up and down, swept his tail back and forth on the bedspread. He indicated nineteen letters, his longest answer: THERES HOPE FOR YOU YET.

Nora laughed.

Travis said, "Wiseass."

But he was exhilarated, filled with a joy that he would have been hard-pressed to describe if he had been required to put it into words. They had been communicating with the retriever for many weeks, but the Scrabble tiles provided a far greater dimension to their communication than they had enjoyed previously. More than ever, Einstein seemed to be their own child. But there was also an intoxicating feeling of breaking through the barriers of normal human experience, a feeling of transcendence. Einstein was no ordinary mutt, of course, and his high intelligence was more human than canine, but he *was* a dog—more than anything else, a dog—and his intelligence was still qualitatively different from that of a man, so there was inevitably a strong sense of mystery and great wonder in this interspecies dialogue. Staring at THERES HOPE FOR YOU YET, Travis thought a broader meaning could be read into the message, that it could be directed at all humankind.

For the next half an hour, they continued questioning Einstein, and Travis recorded the dog's answers. In time they discussed the yellow-eyed beast that had killed Ted Hockney.

"What is the damned thing?" Nora asked.

THE OUTSIDER.

Travis said, "'The Outsider'? What do you mean?"

THATS WHAT THEY CALLED IT.

"The people in the lab?" Travis asked. "Why did they call it The Outsider?"

BECAUSE IT DOES NOT BELONG.

Nora said, "I don't understand."

TWO SUCCESSES. ME AND IT. I AM DOG. IT IS NOTHING THAT CAN BE NAMED. OUTSIDER.

Travis said, "It's intelligent, too?"

YES.

"As intelligent as you?"

MAYBE.

"Jesus," Travis said, shaken.

Einstein made an unhappy sound and put his head on Nora's knee, seeking the reassurance that petting could provide him.

Travis said, "Why would they create a thing like that?"

Einstein returned to the stacks of letters: TO KILL FOR THEM.

A chill trickled down Travis's spine and seeped deep into him. "Who did they want it to kill?"

THE ENEMY.

"What enemy?" Nora asked.

IN WAR.

With understanding came revulsion bordering on nausea. Travis sagged back against the headboard. He remembered telling Nora that even a world without want and with universal freedom would fall far short of paradise because of all the problems of the human heart and all the potential sicknesses of the human mind.

To Einstein, he said, "So you're telling us that The Outsider is a prototype of a genetically engineered soldier. Sort of ... a very intelligent, deadly police dog designed for the battlefield."

IT WAS MADE TO KILL. IT WANTS TO KILL.

Reading the words as she laid out the tiles, Nora was appalled. "But this is crazy. How could such a thing ever be controlled? How could it be counted on not to turn against its masters?"

Travis leaned forward from the headboard. To Einstein, he said, "Why is The Outsider looking for you?"

HATES ME.

"Why does it hate you?"

DONT KNOW.

As Nora replaced the letters, Travis said, "Will it continue looking for you?"

YES. FOREVER.

"But how does something like that move unseen?"

AT NIGHT.

"Nevertheless ..."

LIKE RATS MOVE UNSEEN.

Looking puzzled, Nora said. "But how does it track you?"

FEELS ME.

"Feels you? What do you mean?" she asked.

The retriever puzzled over that one for a long time, making several false starts on an answer, and finally said, CANT EXPLAIN.

"Can you feel it, too?" Travis asked.

SOMETIMES.

"Do you feel it now?"

YES. FAR AWAY.

"Very far away," Travis agreed. "Hundreds of miles. Can it really feel you and track you from that far away?"

EVEN FARTHER.

"Is it tracking you now?"

COMING.

The chill in Travis grew icier. "When will it find you?"

DONT KNOW.

The dog looked dejected, and he was shivering again.

"Soon? Will it feel its way to you soon?"

MAYBE NOT SOON.

Travis saw that Nora was pale. He put a hand on her knee and said, "We won't run from it the rest of our lives. Damned if we will. We'll find a place to settle down and wait, a place where we'll be able to prepare a defense and

358

where we'll have the privacy to deal with The Outsider when it arrives.''

Shivering, Einstein indicated more letters with his nose, and Travis laid out the tiles: I SHOULD GO.

"What do you mean?" Travis asked, replacing the tiles. I DANGER YOU.

Nora threw her arms around the retriever and hugged him. "Don't you ever *think* such a thing. You're part of us. You're family, damn you, we're all family, we're all in this together, and we stick it out together because *that's what families do*." She stopped hugging the dog and took his head in both hands, met him nose to nose, peered deep into his eyes. "If I woke up some morning and found you'd left us, it'd break my heart." Tears shimmering in her eyes, a tremor in her voice. "Do you understand me, fur face? It would break my heart if you went off on your own."

The dog pulled away from her and began to choose lettered tiles again: I WOULD DIE.

"You would die if you left us?" Travis asked.

The dog chose more letters, waited for them to study the words, then looked solemnly at each of them to be sure they understood what he meant: I WOULD DIE OF LONELY.

PART TWO

Guardian

EIGHT

1

On the Thursday that Nora drove to Dr. Weingold's office, Travis and Einstein went for a walk across the grassy hills and through the woods behind the house they had bought in the beautiful California coastal region called Big Sur.

On the treeless hills, the autumn sun warmed the stones and cast scattered cloud shadows. The breeze off the Pacific drew a whisper from the dry golden grass. In the sun, the air was mild, neither hot nor cool. Travis was comfortable in jeans and a long-sleeved shirt.

He carried a Mossberg short-barreled pistol-grip pump-action 12-gauge shotgun. He always carried it on his walks. If he ever encountered someone who asked about it, he intended to tell them he was hunting rattlesnakes.

Where the trees grew most vigorously, the bright morning seemed like late afternoon, and the air was cool enough to make Travis glad that his shirt was flannel. Massive pines, a few small groves of giant redwoods, and a variety of foothill hardwoods filtered the sun and left much of the forest floor in perpetual twilight. The undergrowth was dense in places: the vegetation included those low, impenetrable thickets of evergreen oaks sometimes called "chaparral," plus lots of ferns that flourished because of the frequent fog and the constant humidity of the seacoast air.

Einstein repeatedly sniffed out cougar spoor and insisted on showing Travis the tracks of the big cats in the damp forest soil. Fortunately, he fully understood the danger of stalking a mountain lion, and was able to repress his natural urge to prowl after them.

The dog contented himself with merely observing local fauna. Timid deer could often be seen ascending or descending their trails. Raccoons were plentiful and fun to watch, and although some were quite friendly, Einstein knew they could turn nasty if he accidentally frightened them; he chose to keep a respectful distance.

On other walks, the retriever had been dismayed to discover the squirrels, which he could approach safely, were terrified of him. They froze with fear, stared wild-eyed, small hearts pounding visibly.

WHY SQUIRRELS AFRAID? he had asked Travis one evening.

"Instinct," Travis had explained. "You're a dog, and they know instinctively that dogs will attack and kill them."

NOT ME.

"No, not you," Travis agreed, ruffling the dog's coat. "You wouldn't hurt them. But the squirrels don't know you're different, do they? To them, you look like a dog, and you smell like a dog, so you've got to be feared like a dog."

I LIKE SQUIRRELS.

"I know. Unfortunately, they're not smart enough to realize it."

Consequently, Einstein kept his distance from the squirrels and tried hard not to terrify them, often sauntering past with his head turned the other way as if unaware of them.

This special day, their interest in squirrels and deer and birds and raccoons and unusual forest flora was minimal. Even views of the Pacific did not intrigue them. Today, unlike other days, they were walking only to pass the time and to keep their minds off Nora.

Travis repeatedly looked at his watch, and he chose a

circular route that would bring them back to the house at one o'clock, when Nora was expected to return.

It was the twenty-first of October, eight weeks after they had acquired new identities in San Francisco. After considerable thought, they had decided to come south, substantially reducing the distance that The Outsider would have to travel in order to put its hands on Einstein. They would not be able to get on with their new lives until the beast found them, until they killed it; therefore, they wanted to hasten rather than delay that confrontation.

On the other hand, they did not want to risk returning too far south toward Santa Barbara, for The Outsider might cover the distance between them faster than it had traveled from Orange County to Santa Barbara last summer. They could not be certain that it would continue to make only three or four miles a day. If it moved faster this time, it might come upon them before they were ready for it. The Big Sur area, because of its sparse population and because it was a hundred and ninety air miles from Santa Barbara, seemed ideal. If The Outsider got a fix on Einstein and tracked him down as slowly as before, the thing would not arrive for almost five months. If it doubled its speed somehow, swiftly crossing the open farmland and the wild hills between there and here, quickly skirting populated areas, it would still not reach them until the second week of November.

That day was drawing near, but Travis was satisfied that he had made every preparation possible, and he almost welcomed The Outsider's arrival. Thus far, however, Einstein said that he did not feel his adversary was dangerously close. Evidently, they still had plenty of time to test their patience before the showdown.

By twelve-fifty, they reached the end of their circular route through the hills and canyons, returning to the yard behind their new house. It was a two-story structure with bleached-wood walls, a cedar-shingled roof, and massive stone chimneys on both the north and south sides. It boasted front and rear porches on the east and west, and either vantage point offered a view of wooded slopes.

Because no snow ever fell here, the roof was only gently pitched, making it possible to walk all over it, and that was where Travis made one of his first defensive modifications to the house. He looked up now, as he came out of the trees, and saw the herringbone pattern of two-by-fours that he had fixed across the roof. They would make it safer and easier to move quickly across those sloped surfaces. If The Outsider crept up on the house at night, it would not be able to enter by the downstairs windows because, at sundown, those were barricaded with interior locking shutters that Travis had installed himself and that would foil any would-be intruder except, perhaps, a maniacally determined man with an ax. The Outsider would then most likely climb the porch posts onto the front or rear porch roof to have a look at the second-floor windows, which it would find also protected by interior shutters. Meanwhile, warned of the enemy's approach by an infra-red alarm system that he had installed around the house three weeks ago, Travis would go to the roof by way of an attic trap door. Up there, making use of the two-by-four handholds, he would be able to creep to the edge of the main roof, look down on the porch roof or on any portion of the surrounding yard, and open fire on The Outsider from a position where it could not reach him.

Twenty yards behind and east of the house was a small rust-red barn that backed up to the trees. Their property included no tillable land, and the original owner apparently erected the barn to house a couple of horses and some chickens. Travis and Nora used it as a garage because the dirt driveway led two hundred yards in from the highway, past the house, directly to the double doors on the barn.

Travis suspected that, when The Outsider arrived, it would scout the house from the woods and then from the cover of the barn. It might even wait in there, hoping to catch them by surprise when they came out for the Dodge pickup or the Toyota. Therefore, he had rigged the barn with a few surprises.

Their nearest neighbors—whom they had met only once—were over a quarter-mile to the north, out of sight beyond trees and chaparral. The highway, which was closer, was not much traveled at night, when The Outsider was most likely to strike. If the confrontation involved a great deal of gunfire, the shots would echo and reecho through the woods and across the bare hills, so the few people in the area—neighbors or passing motorists—would have trouble determining where the noise originated. He ought to be able to kill the creature and bury it before someone came nosing around.

Now, more worried about Nora than about The Outsider, Travis climbed the back-porch steps, unlocked the two dead bolts on the rear door, and went into the house, with Einstein close behind him. The kitchen was large enough to serve also as the dining room, yet it was cozy: oak walls, a Mexican-tile floor, beige-tile counters, oak cabinets, a hand-textured plaster ceiling, the best appliances. The big plank table with four comfortable padded chairs and a stone fireplace helped make this the center of the house.

There were five other rooms—an enormous living room and a den at the front of the first floor; three bedrooms upstairs—plus one bath down and one up. One of the bedrooms was theirs, and one served as Nora's studio where she had done a little painting since they moved in— and the third was empty, awaiting developments.

Travis switched on the kitchen lights. Although the house seemed isolated, they were only two hundred yards from the highway, and power poles followed the line of their dirt driveway.

"I'm having a beer," Travis said. "You want anything?"

Einstein padded to his empty water dish, which was in the corner beside his food dish, and scooted it across the floor to the sink.

They had not expected to be able to afford such a house so soon after fleeing Santa Barbara—especially not when, during their first call to Garrison Dilworth, the attorney informed them that Travis's bank accounts had, indeed, been frozen. They had been lucky to get the twenty-thousand-dollar check through. Garrison had converted some of both Travis's and Nora's funds into eight cashier's checks as planned, and had sent them to Travis addressed to Mr. Samuel Spence Hyatt (the new persona), care of the Marin County motel where they had stayed for nearly a week. But also, claiming to have sold Nora's house for a handsome six-figure price, he had sent another packet of cashier's checks two days later, to the same motel.

Speaking with him from a pay phone, Nora had said, "But even if you *did* sell it, they can't have paid the money and closed the deal so soon."

"No," Garrison had admitted. "It won't close for a month. But you need the cash now, so I'm advancing it to you."

They had opened two accounts at a bank in Carmel, thirty-odd miles north of where they now lived. They had bought the new pickup, then had taken Garrison's Mercedes north to the San Francisco airport, leaving it there for him. Heading south again, past Carmel and along the coast, they looked for a house in the Big Sur area. When they had found this one, they had been able to pay cash for it. It was wiser to buy than rent, and it was wiser to pay cash rather than finance the house, for fewer questions needed to be answered.

Travis was sure their ID would stand up, but he saw no reason to test the quality of Van Dyne's papers until necessary. Besides, after buying a house, they were more respectable; the purchase added substance to their new identities.

While Travis got a bottle of beer from the refrigerator, twisted off the cap, took a long swallow, then filled Einstein's dish with water, the retriever went to the walk-in pantry. The door was ajar, as always, and the dog opened it all the way. He put one paw on a pedal that Travis had rigged for him just inside the pantry door, and the light came on in there.

In addition to shelves of canned and bottled goods, the huge pantry contained a complex gadget that Travis and Nora had built to facilitate communication with the dog.

The device stood against the rear wall: twenty-eight one-inch-square tubes made of Lucite, lined up side by side in a wooden frame; each tube was eighteen inches tall, open at the top, and fitted with a pedal-release valve at the bottom. In the first twenty-six tubes were stacked lettered tiles from six Scrabble games, so Einstein would have enough letters to be able to form long messages. On the front of each tube was a hand-drawn letter that showed what it contained; A,B,C,D, and so on. The last two tubes held blank game tiles on which Travis had carved commas—or apostrophes—and question marks. (They'd decided they could figure where the periods were supposed to go.) Einstein was able to dispense letters from the tubes by stepping on the pedals, then could use his nose to form the tiles into words on the pantry floor. They had chosen to put the device in there, out of sight, so they would not be required to explain it to neighbors who might drop in unexpectedly.

As Einstein busily pumped pedals and clicked tiles against one another, Travis carried his beer and the dog's water dish out to the front porch, where they would sit and wait for Nora. By the time he came back, Einstein had finished forming a message.

COULD I HAVE SOME HAMBURGER? OR THREE WEENIES?

Travis said, "I'm going to have lunch with Nora when she gets home. Don't you want to wait and eat with us?"

The retriever licked his chops and thought for a moment. Then he studied the letters he had already used, pushed some of them aside, and reused the rest along with a K and a T and an apostrophe that he had to release from the Lucite tubes.

OK. BUT I'M STARVED.

"You'll survive," Travis told him. He gathered up the lettered tiles and sorted them into the open tops of the proper tubes.

He retrieved the pistol-grip shotgun that he'd stood by the back door and carried it out to the front porch, where he put it beside his rocking chair. He heard Einstein turn off the pantry light and follow him.

They sat in anxious silence, Travis in his chair, Einstein on the redwood floor.

Songbirds trilled in the mild October air.

Travis sipped at his beer, and Einstein lapped occasionally at his water, and they stared down at the dirt driveway, into the trees, toward the highway that they could not see.

In the glove compartment of the Toyota, Nora had a .38 pistol loaded with hollow-point cartridges. During the weeks since they had left Marin County, she had learned to drive and, with Travis's help, had become proficient with the .38—also with a fully automatic Uzi pistol and a shotgun. She only had the .38 today, but she'd be safe going and coming from Carmel. Besides, even if The Outsider had crept into the area without Einstein's knowledge, it did not want Nora; it wanted the dog. So she was perfectly safe.

But where was she?

Travis wished he had gone with her. But after thirty years of dependency and fear, solo trips into Carmel were one of the means by which she asserted—and tested—her new strength, independence, and self-confidence. She would not have welcomed his company.

By one-thirty, when Nora was half an hour late, Travis began to get a sick, twisting feeling in his gut.

Einstein began to pace.

Five minutes later, the retriever was the first to hear the car turning into the foot of the driveway at the main road. He dashed down the porch steps, which were at the side of the house, and stood at the edge of the dirt lane.

Travis did not want Nora to see that he had been overly worried because somehow that would seem to indicate a lack of trust in her ability to take care of herself, an ability that she did, indeed, possess and that she prized. He remained in his rocking chair, his bottle of Corona in one hand.

When the blue Toyota appeared, he sighed with relief. As she went by the house, she tooted the horn. Travis waved as if he had not been sitting there under a leaden blanket of fear.

Einstein went to the garage to greet her, and a minute later they both reappeared. She was wearing blue jeans and a yellow- and white-checkered shirt, but Travis thought she looked good enough to waltz onto a dance floor among begowned and bejeweled princesses.

She came to him, leaned down, kissed him. Her lips were warm.

She said, "Miss me terribly?"

"With you gone, there was no sun, no trilling from the birds, no joy." He tried to say it flippantly, but it came out with an underlying note of seriousness.

Einstein rubbed against her and whined to get her attention, then peered up at her and woofed softly, as if to say, *Well?*

"He's right," Travis said. "You're not being fair. Don't keep us in suspense."

"I am," she said.

"You are?"

She grinned. "Knocked up."

"Oh my," he said.

"Preggers. With child. In a family way. A mother-to-be."

He got up and put his arms around her, held her close and kissed her, and said, "Dr. Weingold couldn't be mistaken?" and she said, "No, he's a good doctor," and Travis said, "He must've told you when," and she said, "We can expect the baby the third week of June," and Travis said stupidly, "Next June?" and she laughed and said, "I don't intend to carry this baby for a whole extra year," and finally Einstein insisted on having a chance to nuzzle her and express his delight.

"I brought home a chilled bottle of bubbly to celebrate," she said, thrusting a paper bag into Travis's hands.

In the kitchen, when he took the bottle out of the bag, he saw that it was sparkling apple cider, nonalcoholic. He said, "Isn't this a celebration worth the best champagne?"

Getting glasses from a cupboard, she said, "I'm probably being silly, a world-champion worrier ... but I'm taking no chances, Travis. I never thought I'd have a baby, never dared dream it, and now I've got this hinkey feeling that I was never *meant* to have it and that it's going to be taken away from me if I don't take every precaution, if I don't do everything just right. So I'm not taking another drink until it's born. I'm not going to eat too much red meat, and I'm going to eat more vegetables. I never have smoked, so that's not a worry. I'm going to gain exactly as much weight as Dr. Weingold tells me I should, and I'm going to do my exercises, and I'm going to have the most perfect baby the world has ever seen.''

"Of course you are," he said, filling their wine glasses with sparkling apple cider and pouring some in a dish for Einstein.

"Nothing will go wrong," she said.

"Nothing," he said.

They toasted the baby—and Einstein, who was going to make a terrific godfather, uncle, grandfather, and furry guardian angel.

Nobody mentioned The Outsider.

Later that night, in bed in the dark, after they had made love and were just holding each other, listening to their hearts beating in unison, he dared to say, "Maybe, with what might be coming our way, we shouldn't be having a baby just now."

"Hush," she said.

"But—"

"We didn't plan for this baby," she said. "In fact, we took precautions against it. But it happened anyway. There's something special about the fact that it happened in spite of all our careful precautions. Don't you think? In spite of all I said before, about maybe not being meant to have it ... well, that's just the old Nora talking. The new Nora thinks we *were* meant to have it, that it's a great gift to us—as Einstein was.''

"But considering what may be coming—"

"That doesn't matter," she said. "We'll deal with that.

We'll come out of that all right. We're ready. And then we'll have the baby and really begin our life together. I love you, Travis."

"I love you," he said. "God, I love you."

He realized how much she had changed from the mousy woman he'd met in Santa Barbara last spring. Right now, she was the strong one, the determined one, and *she* was trying to allay *his* fears.

She was doing a good job, too. He felt better. He thought about the baby, and he smiled in the dark, with his face buried in her throat. Though he now had three hostages to fortune—Nora, the unborn baby, and Einstein—he was in finer spirits than he had been in longer than he could remember. Nora had allayed his fears.

2

Vince Nasco sat in an elaborately carved Italian chair with a deep glossy finish that had acquired its remarkable transparency only after a couple of centuries of regular polishing.

To his right was a sofa and two more chairs and a low table of equal elegance, arranged before a backdrop of bookcases filled with leather-bound volumes that had never been read. He knew they had never been read because Mario Tetragna, whose private study this was, had once pointed to them with pride and said, "Expensive books. And as good as the day they were made because they've never been read. Never. Not a one."

In front of him was the immense desk at which Mario Tetragna reviewed earnings reports from his managers, issued memos about new ventures, and ordered people killed. The don was at that desk now, overflowing his leather chair, eyes closed. He looked as if he was dead of clogged arteries and a fat-impacted heart, but he was only considering Vince's request.

Mario "The Screwdriver" Tetragna—respected patriarch

of his immediate blood family, much-feared don of the broader Tetragna Family that controlled drug traffic, gambling, prostitution, loan-sharking, pornography, and other organized criminal activity in San Francisco—was a five-foot-seven-inch, three-hundred-pound tub, with a face as plump and greasy and smooth as an overstuffed sausage casing. It was hard to believe that this rotund specimen could have built an infamous criminal operation. True, Tetragna had been young once, but even then he would have been short, and he had the look of a man who'd been fat all his life. His pudgy, stubby-fingered hands reminded Vince of a baby's hands. But they were the hands that ruled the Family's empire.

When Vince had looked into Mario Tetragna's eyes, he instantly realized that the don's stature and his all too evident decadence were of no importance. The eyes were those of a reptile: flat, cold, hard, watchful. If you weren't careful, if you displeased him, he would hypnotize you with those eyes and take you the way a snake would take a mesmerized mouse; he would choke you down whole and digest you.

Vince admired Tetragna. He knew this was a great man, and he wished he could tell the don that he, too, was a man of destiny. But he had learned never to speak of his immortality, for in the past such talk had earned him ridicule from a man he'd thought would understand.

Now, Don Tetragna opened his reptilian eyes and said, "Let me be certain I understand. You are looking for a man. This is not Family business. It is a private grudge."

"Yes, sir," Vince said.

"You believe this man may have bought counterfeit papers and may be living under a new name. He would know how to obtain such papers, even though he is not a member of any Family, not of the *fratellanza*?"

"Yes, sir. His background is such that ... he would know."

"And you believe he would have obtained these papers in either Los Angeles or here," Don Tetragna said, gesturing toward the window and the city of San Francisco with one soft, pink hand.

Vince said, "On August twenty-fifth he went on the run, starting from Santa Barbara by car because for various reason he couldn't take a plane anywhere. I believe he would've wanted a new identity as quickly as he could get it. At first, I assumed he'd go south and seek out counterfeit ID in Los Angeles because that was closest. But I've spent the better part of two months talking with all the right people in L.A., Orange County, and even San Diego, all the people to whom this man could've gone for high-quality false ID, and I've had a few leads, but none panned out. So if he didn't go south from Santa Barbara, he came north, and the only place in the north where he could get the kind of papers he would want—"

"Is in our fair city," Don Tetragna said, gesturing again toward the window and smiling at the populous slopes below.

Vince supposed that the don was smiling fondly at his beloved San Francisco. But the smile didn't look fond. It looked avaricious.

"And," Don Tetragna said, "you would like for me to give you the names of the people who have my authorization to deal in papers such as this man needed."

"If you can see it in your heart to grant me this favor, I would be most grateful."

"They won't have kept records."

"Yes, sir, but they might remember something."

"They're in the business of *not* remembering."

"But the human mind never forgets, Don Tetragna. No matter how hard it tries, it never really forgets."

"How true. And you swear that the man you seek is not a member of any Family?"

"I swear it."

"This execution must not in any way be traced to my Family."

"I swear it."

Don Tetragna closed his eyes again, but not for as long as he had closed them before. When he opened them, he smiled broadly but, as always, it was a humorless smile. He was the least jolly fat man Vince had ever seen. "When your

375

father married a Swedish girl rather than one of his own people, his family despaired and expected the worst. But your mother was a good wife, unquestioning and obedient. And they produced you—a most handsome son. But you're more than handsome. You're a good soldier, Vincent. You have done fine, clean work for the Families in New York and New Jersey, for those in Chicago, and also for us on this coast. Not very long ago, you did me the great service of crushing the cockroach Pantangela."

"For which you paid me most generously, Don Tetragna."

The Screwdriver waved one hand dismissively. "We're all paid for our labors. But we're not talking money here. Your years of loyalty and good service are worth more than money. Therefore, you are owed at least this one favor."

"Thank you, Don Tetragna."

"You'll be given the names of those who provide such papers in this city, and I'll see that they are all forewarned of your visit. They'll cooperate fully."

"If you say they will," Vince said, rising and bowing with only his head and shoulders, "I know that it is true."

The don motioned him to sit down. "But before you attend to this private affair, I'd like you to take another contract. There's a man in Oakland who is giving me much grief. He thinks I can't touch him because he's politically well connected and well guarded. His name is Ramon Velazquez. This will be a difficult job, Vincent."

Vince carefully concealed his frustration and displeasure. He did not want to take on a troublesome hit right now. He wanted to concentrate on tracking down Travis Cornell and the dog. But he knew Tetragna's contract was more a demand than an offer. To get the names of the people who sold false papers, he must first waste Velazquez.

He said, "I would be honored to squash any insect that has stung you. And there'll be no charge this time."

"Oh, I'd insist on paying you, Vincent."

As ingratiatingly as he knew how, Vince smiled and said, "Please, Don Tetragna, let me do this favor. It would give me great pleasure."

Tetragna appeared to consider the request, though this was what he expected—a free hit in return for helping Vince. He put both hands on his enormous belly and patted himself. "I am such a lucky man. Wherever I turn, people want to do me favors, kindnesses."

"Not lucky, Don Tetragna," Vince said, sick of their mannered conversation. "You reap what you sow, and if you reap kindness it is because of the seeds of greater kindness you've sown so broadly."

Beaming, Tetragna accepted his offer to waste Velazquez for nothing. The nostrils of his porcine nose flared as if he had smelled something good to eat, and he said, "But now tell me ... to satisfy my curiosity, what will you do to this other man when you catch him, this man with whom you have a personal vendetta?"

Blow his brains out and snatch his dog, Vince thought.

But he knew the kind of crap The Screwdriver wanted to hear, the same hard-assed stuff most of these guys wanted to hear from him, their favorite hired killer so he said, "Don Tetragna, I intend to cut off his balls, cut off his ears, cut out his tongue—and only then put an ice pick through his heart and stop his clock."

The fat man's eyes glittered with approval. His nostrils flared.

3

By Thanksgiving, The Outsider had not found the bleached-wood house in Big Sur.

Every night, Travis and Nora locked the shutters over the inside of the windows. They dead-bolted the doors. Retiring to the second floor, they slept with shotguns beside their bed and revolvers on their nightstands.

Sometimes, in the dead hours after midnight, they were awakened by strange noises in the yard or on the porch roof. Einstein padded from window to window, sniffing urgently, but always he indicated that they had nothing to fear. On further investigation, Travis usually found a prowling raccoon or other forest creature.

Travis enjoyed Thanksgiving more than he had thought he would, given the circumstances. He and Nora cooked an elaborate traditional meal for just the three of them: roast turkey with chestnut dressing, a clam casserole, glazed carrots, baked corn, pepper slaw, crescent rolls, and pumpkin pie.

Einstein sampled everything because he had developed a much more sophisticated palate than an ordinary dog. He was still a dog, however, and though the only thing he strongly disliked was the sour pepper slaw, he preferred turkey above all else. That afternoon he spent a lot of time gnawing contentedly on the drumsticks.

Over the weeks, Travis had noticed that, like most dogs, Einstein would go out into the yard occasionally and eat a little grass, though sometimes it seemed to gag him. He did it again on Thanksgiving Day, and when Travis asked him if he liked the taste of grass, Einstein said no. "Then why do you try to eat it sometimes?"

NEED IT.

"Why?"

I DON'T KNOW.

"If you don't know what you need it *for*, then how do you know you need it at all? Instinct?"

YES.

"Just instinct?"

DON'T KNOCK IT.

That evening, the three of them sat in piles of pillows on the living-room floor in front of the big stone fireplace, listening to music. Einstein's golden coat was glossy and thick in the firelight. As Travis sat with one arm around Nora, petting the dog with his free hand, he thought eating grass must be a good idea because Einstein looked healthy and robust. Einstein sneezed a few times and coughed now and then, but those seemed natural reactions to the Thanksgiving overindulgence and to the warm, dry air in front of the fireplace. Travis was not for a moment concerned about the dog's health.

4

On the afternoon of Friday, November 26, the balmy day after Thanksgiving, Garrison Dilworth was aboard his beloved forty-two-foot Hinckley Sou'wester, *Amazing Grace*, in his boat slip in the Santa Barbara harbor. He was polishing brightwork and, diligently bent to his task, almost didn't see the two men in business suits as they approached along the dock. He looked up as they were about to announce themselves, and he knew who they were—not their names, but who they must work for—even before they showed him their credentials.

One was named Johnson.

The other was Soames.

Pretending puzzlement and interest, he invited them aboard.

Stepping off the dock, down onto the deck, the one named Johnson said, "We'd like to ask you a few questions, Mr. Dilworth."

"What about?" Garrison inquired, wiping his hands on a white rag.

Johnson was a black man of ordinary size, even a little gaunt, haggard-looking, yet imposing.

Garrison said, "National Security Agency, you say? Surely, you don't think I'm in the hire of the KGB?"

Johnson smiled thinly. "You've done work for Nora Devon?"

He raised his eyebrows. "Nora? Are you serious? Well, I can assure you that Nora isn't the sort of person to be involved—"

"You are her attorney, then?" Johnson asked.

Garrison glanced at the freckle-faced younger man, Agent Soames, and again raised his eyebrows as if to ask if Johnson was always this chilly. Soames stared expressionlessly, taking his cue from the boss.

Oh my, we're in trouble with these two, Garrison thought.

*   *   *

After his frustrating and unsuccessful questioning of Dilworth, Lem sent Cliff Soames off on a series of errands: begin the procedures to obtain a court order allowing taps to be placed on the attorney's home and office telephones; find the three pay phones nearest his office and the three nearest his house, and arrange for taps to be put on those as well; obtain telephone company records of all long-distance calls made from Dilworth's home and office phones; bring in extra men from the Los Angeles office to staff an around-the-clock surveillance of Dilworth, starting within three hours.

While Cliff was attending to those things, Lem strolled around the boat docks in the harbor, hoping the sounds of the sea and the calming sight of rolling water would help clear his mind and focus his thoughts on his problems. God knew, he needed desperately to *get focused*. Over six months had passed since the dog and The Outsider had escaped from Banodyne, and Lem had lost almost fifteen pounds in the pursuit. He had not slept well in months, had little interest in food, and even his sex life had suffered.

There's such a thing as trying too hard, he told himself. It causes constipation of the mind.

But such admonishments did no good. He was still as blocked as a pipe full of concrete.

For three months, since they found Cornell's Airstream in the school parking lot the day after Hockney's murder, Lem had known that Cornell and the woman had been returning, on that August night, from a trip to Vegas, Tahoe, and Monterey. Nightclub table cards from Vegas, hotel stationery, matchbooks, and gasoline credit-card receipts had been found in the trailer and pickup, pinpointing every stop of their itinerary. He had not known the woman's identity, yet he had assumed she was a girlfriend, nothing more, but of course he should never have assumed any such thing. Only a few days ago, when one of his own agents went to Vegas to marry, Lem had finally realized that Cornell and the woman could have gone to Vegas for that same purpose. Suddenly their trip had looked like a honeymoon. Within hours, he confirmed that

Cornell had, in fact, been married in Clark County, Nevada, on August 11, to Nora Devon of Santa Barbara.

Seeking the woman, he discovered that her house had been sold six weeks ago, after she'd vanished with Cornell. Looking into the sale, he found she had been represented by her attorney, Garrison Dilworth.

By freezing Cornell's assets, Lem thought he had made it harder for the man to continue a fugitive existence, but now he discovered that Dilworth had helped slip twenty thousand out of Cornell's bank and that all of the proceeds from the sale of the woman's house had been transferred to her somehow. Furthermore, through Dilworth, she had closed out her local bank accounts four weeks ago, and that money also was in her hands. She and her husband and the dog might now have sufficient resources to remain in hiding for years.

Standing on the dock, Lem stared at the sun-spangled sea, which slapped rhythmically against the pilings. The motion nauseated him.

He looked up at the soaring, cawing seagulls. Instead of being calmed by their graceful flight, he grew edgy.

Garrison Dilworth was intelligent, clever, a born fighter. Now that the link had been made between him and the Cornells, the attorney promised to take the NSA to court to unfreeze Travis's assets. "You've filed no charges against the man," Dilworth had said. "What toadying judge would grant the power to freeze his accounts? Your manipulation of the legal system to hamper an innocent citizen is unconscionable."

Lem could have filed charges against Travis and Nora Cornell for the violation of all sorts of laws designed to preserve the national security, and by doing so he'd have made it impossible for Dilworth to continue lending assistance to the fugitives. But filing charges meant attracting media attention. Then the harebrained story about Cornell's pet panther—and perhaps the NSA's entire cover-up—would come down like a paper house in a thunderstorm.

His only hope was that Dilworth would try to get in touch

with the Cornells to tell them that his association with them had been at last uncovered and that contact between them would have to be far more circumspect in the future. Then, with luck, Lem would pinpoint the Cornells through their telephone number. He did not have much hope of everything working out that easily. Dilworth was no fool.

Looking around at the Santa Barbara yacht harbor, Lem tried to relax, for he knew he needed to be calm and fresh if he was to outthink the old attorney. The hundreds of pleasure boats at the docks, sails furled or packed away, bobbed gently on the rolling tide, and other boats with unfurled sails glided serenely out toward the open sea, and people in bathing suits were sunning on the decks or having early cocktails, and the gulls darted like stitching needles across the blue and white quilt of the sky, and people were fishing from the stone breakwater, and the scene was achingly picturesque, but it was also an image of leisure, great and calculated leisure, with which Lem Johnson could not identify. To Lem, too much leisure was a dangerous distraction from the cold, hard realities of life, from the competitive world, and any leisure activity that lasted longer than a few hours made him nervous and anxious to get back to work. Here was leisure measured in days, in weeks; here, in these expensive and lovingly crafted boats, was leisure measured in monthlong sailing excursions up and down the coast, so much leisure that it made Lem break into a sweat, made him want to scream.

He had The Outsider to worry about as well. There had been no sign of it since the day Travis Cornell had shot at it in his rented house, back at the end of August. Three months ago. What had the thing been doing in those three months? Where had it been hiding? Was it still after the dog? Was it dead?

Maybe, out in the wilds, it had been bitten by a rattlesnake, or maybe it had fallen off a cliff.

God, Lem thought, let it be dead, please, give me that much of a break. Let it be dead.

But he knew The Outsider was not dead because that would be too easy. Nothing in life was that easy. The damn

382

thing was out there, stalking the dog. It had probably suppressed the urge to kill people it encountered because it knew each murder drew Lem and his men closer to it, and it did not want to be found before it had killed the dog. When the beast had torn the dog and the Cornells to bloody pieces, then it would once again begin to vent its rage on the population at large, and every death would hang heavily on Lem Johnson's conscience.

Meanwhile, the investigation into the murders of the Banodyne scientists was dead in the water. In fact, that second NSA task force had been dismantled. Obviously, the Soviets had hired outsiders for those hits, and there was no way to find out whom they had brought in.

A deeply tanned guy in white shorts and Top-Siders passed Lem and said, "Beautiful day!"

"Like hell," Lem said.

5

The day after Thanksgiving, Travis walked into the kitchen to get a glass of milk and saw Einstein having a sneezing fit, but he did not think much of it. Nora, even quicker than Travis to worry about the retriever's welfare, was also unconcerned. In California, the pollen count peaks in spring and autumn; however, because the climate permits a twelve-month cycle of flowers, no season is pollen-free. Living in the woods, the situation was exacerbated.

That night, Travis was awakened by a sound he could not identify. Instantly alert, every trace of sleep banished, he sat up in the dark and reached for the shotgun on the floor beside the bed. Holding the Mossberg, he listened for the noise, and in a minute or so it came again: in the second-floor hallway.

He eased out of the bed without waking Nora and went cautiously to the doorway. The hall, like most places in the house, was equipped with a low-wattage night-light, and in the pale glow Travis saw that the noise came from the dog. Einstein was standing near the head of the stairs, coughing and shaking his head.

Travis went to him, and the retriever looked up. "You okay?"

A quick wag of the tail: *Yes.*

He stooped and ruffled the dog's coat. "You sure?" *Yes.*

For a minute, the dog pressed against him, enjoying being petted. Then he turned away from Travis, coughed a couple of times, and went downstairs.

Travis followed. In the kitchen, he found Einstein slurping water from the dish.

Having emptied the dish, the retriever went to the pantry, turned on the light, and began to paw lettered tiles out of the Lucite tubes.

THIRSTY.

"Are you sure you feel well?"

FINE. JUST THIRSTY. NIGHTMARE WOKE ME.

Surprised, Travis said, "You dream?"

DON'T YOU?

"Yeah. Too much."

He refilled the retriever's water dish, and Einstein emptied it again, and Travis filled it a second time. By then the dog had had enough. Travis expected him to want to go outside to pee, but the dog went upstairs instead and settled in the hall by the door of the bedroom in which Nora still slept.

In a whisper, Travis said, "Listen, if you want to come in and sleep beside the bed, it's all right."

That was what Einstein wanted. He curled up on the floor on Travis's side of the bed.

In the dark, Travis could reach out and easily touch both the shotgun and Einstein. He took greater reassurance from the presence of the dog than from the gun.

6

Saturday afternoon, just two days after Thanksgiving, Garrison Dilworth got in his Mercedes and drove slowly away from his house. Within two blocks he confirmed that the NSA still had a tail on him. It was a green Ford, probably the same one that had followed him last evening. They stayed well back of him, and they were discreet, but he was not blind.

He still had not called Nora and Travis. Because he was being followed, he suspected his phones were being tapped as well. He could have gone to a pay phone, but he was afraid that the NSA could eavesdrop on the conversation with a directional microphone or some other high-tech gadget. And if they managed to record the push-button tones that he produced by punching in the Cornells' number, they could easily translate those tones into digits and trace the number back to Big Sur. He would have to resort to deception to contact Travis and Nora safely.

He knew he had better act soon, before Travis or Nora phoned him. These days, with the technology available to them, the NSA could trace the call back to its origins as fast as Garrison would be able to warn Travis that the line was tapped.

So at two o'clock Saturday afternoon, chaperoned by the green Ford, he drove to Della Colby's house in Montecito to take her to his boat, the *Amazing Grace*, for a lazy afternoon in the sun. At least that was what he had told her on the phone.

Della was Judge Jack Colby's widow. She and Jack were Garrison's and Francine's best friends for twenty-five years before death broke up the foursome. Jack had died one year after Francine. Della and Garrison remained very close; they frequently went to dinner together, went dancing and walking and sailing. Initially, their relationship had been strictly platonic; they were simply old friends who had the fortune—or misfortune—to outlast everyone they most cared about, and they needed each other because they shared so many good times and memories that would be diminished when there was no longer anyone left with whom to reminisce. A year ago, when they suddenly found themselves in bed together, they had been surprised and overwhelmed with guilt. They felt as if they were cheating on their spouses, though Jack and Francine had died years ago. The guilt passed, of course, and now they were grateful for the companionship and gently burning passion that had unexpectedly brightened their late-autumn years.

When he pulled into Della's driveway, she came out of the house, locked the front door, and hurried to his car. She was dressed in boat shoes, white slacks, a blue- and white-striped sweater, and a blue windbreaker. Although she was sixty-nine, and though her short hair was snow-white, she looked fifteen years younger.

He got out of the Mercedes, gave her a hug and a kiss, and said, "Can we go in your car?"

She blinked. "Are you having trouble with yours?"

"No," he said. "I'd just rather take yours."

"Sure."

She backed her Caddy out of the garage, and he got in on the passenger's side. As she pulled into the street, he said, "I'm afraid my car might be bugged, and I don't want them hearing what I've got to tell you."

Her expression was priceless.

Laughing, he said, "No, I've not gone senile overnight. If you'll keep an eye on the rearview mirror as you drive, you'll see we're being followed. They're very good, very subtle, but they're not invisible."

He gave her time, and after a few blocks Della said, "The green Ford, is it?"

"That's them."

"What've you gotten yourself into, dear?"

"Don't go straight to the harbor. Drive to the farmer's market, and we'll buy some fresh fruit. Then drive to a liquor store, and we'll buy some wine. By then, I'll have told you everything."

"Have you some secret life I've never suspected?" she asked, grinning at him. "Are you a geriatric James Bond?"

* * *

Yesterday, Lem Johnson had reopened a temporary headquarters in a claustrophobic office at the Santa Barbara Courthouse. The room had one narrow window. The walls were dark, and the overhead lighting fixture was so dim it left the corners full of hanging shadows like misplaced scarecrows. The borrowed furniture consisted of rejects from other offices. He had worked out of here in the days following the Hockney killing, but had closed it up after a week, when there was nothing more to be done in the area. Now, with the hope that Dilworth would lead them to the Cornells, Lem reopened the cramped field HQ, plugged in the phones, and waited for developments.

He shared the office with one assisting agent—Jim Vann—who was an almost too-earnest and too-dedicated twenty-five-year-old.

At the moment, Cliff Soames was in charge of the six-man team at the harbor, overseeing not only the NSA agents spotted throughout the area, but also coordinating the coverage of Garrison Dilworth with the Harbor Patrol and the Coast Guard. The shrewd old man apparently realized he was being followed, so Lem expected him to make a break, to try to shake surveillance long enough to place a call to the Cornells in private. The most logical way for Garrison to throw off his tail was to head out to sea, go up or down the coast, put ashore in a launch, and telephone Cornell before his pursuers could relocate him. But he would be surprised to find himself accompanied out of the harbor by the local patrol; then, at sea, he would be followed by a Coast Guard cutter standing by for that purpose.

At three-forty, Cliff called to report that Dilworth and his lady friend were sitting on the deck of the *Amazing Grace*, eating fruit and sipping wine, reminiscing a lot, laughing a little. "From what we can pick up with directional microphones and from what we can see, I'd say they don't have any intention of going anywhere. Except maybe to bed. They sure do seem to be a randy old pair."

"Stay with them," Lem said. "I don't trust him."

Another call came through from the search team that had

secretly entered Dilworth's house minutes after he had left. They had found nothing related to the Cornells or the dog.

Dilworth's office had been carefully searched last night, and nothing had been found there either. Likewise, a study of his phone records did not produce a number for the Cornells; if he had called them in the past, he always did so from a pay phone. An examination of his AT&T credit-card records showed no such calls, so if he *had* used a pay phone, he had not billed it to himself but had reversed the charges to the Cornells, leaving nothing to be traced. Which was not a good sign. Obviously, Dilworth had been exceedingly cautious even before he had known he was being watched.

Saturday, afraid the dog might be coming down with a cold, Travis kept an eye on Einstein. But the retriever sneezed only a couple of times and did not cough at all, and he seemed to be fit.

A freight company delivered ten large cartons containing all of Nora's finished canvases that had been left in Santa Barbara. A couple of weeks ago, using a friend's return address to insure that no link would exist between him and Nora "Aimes," Garrison Dilworth had shipped the paintings to their new house.

Now, unpacking and unwrapping the canvases, creating piles of paper padding in the living room, Nora was transported. Travis knew that, for many years, this work was what she had lived for, and he could see that having the paintings with her again was not only a great joy to her but would probably spur her to return to her new canvases, in the spare room, with greater enthusiasm.

"You want to call Garrison and thank him?" he asked.

"Yes, absolutely!" she said. "But first, let's unpack them all and make sure none of them is damaged."

* * *

388

Posted around the harbor, posing as yacht owners and fishermen, Cliff Soames and the other NSA agents watched Dilworth and Della Colby and eavesdropped on them electronically as the day waned. Twilight descended without any indication that Dilworth intended to put to sea. Soon night fell, yet the attorney and his woman made no move.

Half an hour after dark, Cliff Soames got weary of pretending to fish off the stern of a Cheoy Lee sixty-six-foot sport yacht docked four slips away from Dilworth's. He climbed the steps, went into the pilot's cabin, and pulled the headphones off Hank Gorner, the agent who was monitoring the old couple's conversation through a directional mike. He listened for himself.

"*...the time in Acapulco when Jack hired that fishing boat ... *"

"*...yes, the whole crew looked like pirates!*"

"*...we thought we'd have our throats cut, be dumped at sea ...*"

"*...but then it turned out they were all divinity students ...*"

"*...studying to be missionaries ... and Jack said ... *"

Returning the headphones, Cliff said, "Still reminiscing!"

The other agent nodded. The cabin light was out, and Hank was illuminated only by a small, hooded, built-in work lamp above the chart table, so his features looked elongated and strange. "That's the way it's been all day. At least they have some great stories."

"I'm going to the john," Cliff said wearily. "Be right back."

"Take ten hours if you want. They're not going anywhere."

A few minutes later, when Cliff returned, Hank Gorner pulled off his headphones and said, "They went below decks."

"Something up?"

"Not what we'd hope. They're gonna jump each other's bones."

"Oh."

"Cliff, jeez, I don't want to listen to this."

"Listen," Cliff insisted.

Hank put one earphone to his head. "Jeez, they're undressing each other, and they're as old as my grandparents. This is embarrassing."

Cliff sighed.

"Now they're quiet," Hank said, a frown of distaste creeping over his face. "Any second they're gonna start moaning, Cliff,"

"Listen," Cliff insisted. He snatched a light jacket off the table and went outside again so *he* wouldn't have to listen.

He took up his position in a chair on the stern deck, lifting the fishing pole once more.

The night was cool enough for the jacket, but otherwise it could not have been better. The air was clear and sweet, scented with just a slight tang of the sea. The moonless sky was full of stars. The water slapped lullingly against the dock pilings and against the hulls of the moored boats. Somewhere across the harbor, on another craft, someone was playing love songs from the forties. An engine turned over—*whump-whump-whump*—and there was something romantic about the sound. Cliff thought how nice it would be to own a boat and set out on a long trip through the South Pacific, toward palm-shaded islands—

Suddenly that idling engine roared, and Cliff realized it was the *Amazing Grace*. As he rose from his chair, dropping the fishing pole, he saw Dilworth's boat reversing out of its slip recklessly fast. It was a sailboat, and subconsciously Cliff had not expected it to move with sails furled, but it had auxiliary engines; they knew this, were prepared for this, but still it startled him. He hurried back to the cabin. "Hank, get Harbor Patrol. Dilworth's on the move."

"But they're in the sack."

"Like hell they are!" Cliff ran out to the bow deck and saw that Dilworth had already swung the *Amazing Grace* around and was headed toward the mouth of the harbor.

No lights at the aft end of the boat, the area around the wheel, just one small light forward. Jesus, he was really making a break for it.

By the time they unpacked all one hundred canvases, hung a few, and carried the rest into the unused bedroom, they were starving.

"Garrison's probably having dinner now, too," Nora said. "I don't want to interrupt him. Let's call him after we've eaten."

In the pantry, Einstein released letters from the Lucite tubes and spelled out a message: IT'S DARK. CLOSE THE SHUTTERS FIRST.

Surprised and unsettled by his own uncharacteristic inattention to security, Travis hurried from room to room, closing the interior shutters and slipping the bolt-type latches in place. Fascinated by Nora's paintings and delighted by the pleasure she exhibited in their arrival, he had not even noticed that night had arrived.

Halfway toward the mouth of the harbor, confident that distance and the engine's roar now protected them from electronic eavesdroppers, Garrison said, "Take me close to the outer point of the north breakwater, along the channel's edge."

"Are you sure about this?" Della asked worriedly. "You're not a teenager."

He patted her bottom and said, "I'm better."

"Dreamer."

He kissed her on the cheek and edged forward along the starboard railing, where he got into position for his jump. He was wearing dark blue swim trunks. He should have had a wetsuit because the water would be chilly. But he thought he ought to be able to swim to the breakwater, around the point of it, and haul himself out on the north side, out of

391

sight of the harbor, all in a few minutes, long before the water temperature leached too much body heat from him.

"Company!" Della called from the wheel.

He looked back and saw the Harbor Patrol boat leaving the docks to the south, coming toward them on their port side.

They won't stop us, he thought. They have no legal right.

But he had to go over the side before the Patrol swung in and took up a position astern. From behind, they would see him vault the railing. As long as they were to port, the *Amazing Grace* would conceal his departure, and the boat's phosphorescent wake would cover the first few seconds of his swim around the point of the breakwater, long enough for the Patrol's attention to have moved on with Della.

They were heading out at the highest speed with which Della felt comfortable. The Hinckley Sou'wester jolted through the slightly choppy waters with enough force to make it necessary for Garrison to hold fast to the railing. Still, they seemed to move past the stone wall of the breakwater at a frustratingly slow pace, and the Harbor Patrol drew nearer, but Garrison waited, waited, because he didn't want to go into the harbor a hundred yards short of its end. If he went in too soon, he would not be able to swim all the way out to the point and around it; instead, he would have to swim straight to the breakwater and climb its flank, within full sight of all observers. Now the patrol closed to within a hundred yards—he could see them when he rose from a crouch and looked across the Hinckley's cabin roof—and began to swing around behind them, and Garrison could not wait much longer, could not—

"The point!" Della called from the wheel.

He threw himself over the railing, into the dark water, away from the boat.

The sea was *cold*. It shocked the breath out of him. He sank, could not find the surface, was seized by panic, flailed, thrashed, but then broke through to the air, gasping.

The *Amazing Grace* was surprisingly close. He felt as if he had been thrashing in confusion beneath the surface for a minute or more, but it must have been only a second or two because his boat was not yet far away. The Harbor Patrol was close, too, and he decided that even the churning wake of the *Amazing Grace* did not give him enough cover, so he took a deep breath and went under again, staying down as long as he could. When he came up, both Della and her shadowers were well past the mouth of the harbor, turning south, and he was safe from observation.

The outgoing tide was swiftly carrying him past the point of the northern breakwater, which was a wall of loose boulders and rocks that rose more than twenty feet above the waterline, mottled gray and black ramparts in the night. He not only had to swim around the end of that barrier but had to move toward land against the resistant current. Without further delay, he began to swim, wondering why on earth he had thought this would be a snap.

You're almost seventy-one, he told himself as he stroked past the rocky point, which was illuminated by a navigation-warning light. What ever possessed you to play hero?

But he knew what possessed him: a deep-seated belief that the dog must remain free, that it must not be treated as the government's property. *If we've come so far that we can create as God creates, then we have to learn to act with the justice and mercy of God.* That was what he had told Nora and Travis—and Einstein—on the night Ted Hockney had been killed, and he had meant every word he'd said.

Salt water stung his eyes, blurred his vision. Some had gotten into his mouth, and it burned a small ulcer on his lower lip.

He fought the current, pulled past the point of the breakwater, out of sight of the harbor, then slashed toward the rocks. Reaching them at last, he hung onto the first boulder he touched, gasping, not yet quite able to pull himself out of the water.

In the intervening weeks since Nora and Travis went on the run, Garrison had plenty of time to think about Einstein, and he felt even more strongly that to imprison an intelligent creature, innocent of all crime, was an act of grave injustice, regardless of whether the prisoner was a dog. Garrison had devoted his life to the pursuit of justice that was made possible by the laws of a democracy, and to the maintenance of the freedom that grew from this justice. When a man of ideals decides he is too old to risk everything for what he believes in, then he is no longer a man of ideals. He may no longer be a man at all. That hard truth had driven him, in spite of his age, to make this night swim. Funny—that a long life of idealism should, after seven decades, be put to the ultimate test over the fate of a dog.

But *what* a dog.

And what a wondrous new world we live in, he thought.

Genetic technology might have to be rechristened "genetic art," for every work of art was an act of creation, and no act of creation was finer or more beautiful than the creation of an intelligent mind.

Getting his second wind, he heaved entirely out of the water, onto the sloped north flank of the northern breakwater. That barrier rose between him and the harbor, and he moved inland, along the rocks, while the sea surged at his left side. He'd brought a waterproof penlight, clipped to his trunks, and now he used it to proceed, barefoot, with the greatest caution, afraid of slipping on the wet stones and breaking a leg or an ankle.

He could see the city lights a few hundred yards ahead, and the vague silvery line of the beach.

He was cold but not as cold as he had been in the water. His heart was beating fast but not as fast as before.

He was going to make it.

Lem Johnson drove down from the temporary HQ in the courthouse, and Cliff met him at the empty boat slip where the *Amazing Grace* had been tied up. A wind had risen. Hundreds of craft along the docks were wallowing slightly in their berths; they creaked, and slack sail lines clicked and clinked against their masts. Dock lamps and neighboring boat lanterns cast shimmering patterns of light on the dark, oily-looking water where Dilworth's forty-two-footer had been moored.

"Harbor Patrol?" Lem asked worriedly.

"They followed him out to open sea. Seemed as if he was going to turn north, swung close by the point, but then he went south instead."

"Did Dilworth see them?"

"He had to. As you see—no fog, lots of stars, clear as a bell."

"Good. I want him to be aware. Coast Guard?"

"I've talked to the cutter," Cliff assured him. "They're on the spot, flanking the *Amazing Grace* at a hundred yards, heading south along the coast."

Shivering in the rapidly cooling air, Lem said, "They know he might try putting ashore in a rubber boat or whatever?"

"They know," Cliff said. "He can't do it under their noses."

"Is the Guard sure he sees them?"

"They're lit up like a Christmas tree."

"Good. I want him to know it's hopeless. If we can just keep him from warning the Cornells, then they'll call him sooner or later—and we'll have them. Even if they call him from a pay phone, we'll know their general location."

In addition to taps on Dilworth's home and office phones, the NSA had installed tracing equipment that would lock open a phone line the moment a connection was made, and keep it open even after both parties hung up, until the caller's number and street address were ascertained and verified. Even if Dilworth shouted a warning and hung up the instant he recognized one of the Cornells' voices, it would be too late. The only way he could try to foil the NSA was by not answering his phone at all. But even that would do him no good because, after the sixth ring, every incoming call was being automatically "answered" by the NSA's equipment, which opened the line and began tracing procedures.

"The only thing could screw us now," Lem said, "is if Dilworth gets to a phone we don't have monitored and warns the Cornells not to call him.''

"It's not going to happen," Cliff said. "We're on him tight.''

"I wish you wouldn't say that," Lem worried. As the wind got hold of it, a metal clip on a loose line clanged loudly off a spar, and the sound made Lem jump. "My dad always said the worst happens when you least expect it.''

Cliff shook his head. "With all due respect, sir, the more I hear you quote your father, the more I think he must've been just about the gloomiest man who ever lived.''

Looking around at the wallowing boats and wind-chopped water, feeling as if *he* was moving instead of standing still in a moving world, a little queasy, Lem said, "Yeah ... my dad was a great guy in his way, but he was also ... impossible.''

Hank Gorner shouted, "Hey!" He was running along the dock from the Cheoy Lee where he and Cliff had been stationed all day. "I've just been on with the Guard cutter. They're playing their searchlight over the *Amazing Grace*, intimidating a little, and they tell me they don't see Dilworth. Just the woman.''

Lem said, "But, Christ, he's running the boat!''

"No," Gorner said. "There's no lights in the *Amazing Grace*, but the Guard's searchlight brightens up the whole thing, and they say the woman's at the wheel.''

"It's all right. He's just below deck," Cliff said.

"No," Lem said as his heart started to pound. "He wouldn't be below deck at a time like this. He'd be studying the cutter, deciding whether to keep going or turn back. He's not on the *Amazing Grace*.''

"But he has to be! He didn't get off before she pulled out of the dock.''

Lem stared out across the crystalline-clear harbor, toward the light near the end of the northern breakwater. "You said the damn boat swung out close to the north point, and it looked as if he was going north, but then he suddenly swung south.''

"Shit," Cliff said.

"That's where he dropped off," Lem said. "Out by the

point of the northern breakwater. Without a rubber boat. Swimming, by God.''

"He's too old for that crap," Cliff protested.

"Evidently not. He went around the other side, and he's headed for a phone on one of the northern public beaches. We've got to stop him, and fast.''

Cliff cupped his hands to his mouth and shouted the first names of the four agents who were positioned on other boats along the docks. His voice carried, echoing flatly off the water, in spite of the wind. Men came running, and even as Cliff's shouts faded away across the harbor, Lem was sprinting for his car in the parking lot.

The worst happens when you least expect it.

As Travis was rinsing dinner dishes, Nora said, "Look at this.''

He turned and saw that she was standing by Einstein's food and water dishes. The water was gone, but half his dinner remained.

She said, "When have you known him to leave a single scrap?''

"Never." Frowning, Travis wiped his hands on the kitchen towel. "The last few days ... I've thought maybe he's coming down with a cold or something, but he says he feels fine. And today he hasn't been sneezing or coughing like he was.''

They went into the living room, where the retriever was reading *Black Beauty* with the help of his page-turning machine.

They knelt beside him, and he looked up, and Nora said, "Are you sick, Einstein?''

The retriever barked once, softly: *No.*

"Are you sure?''

A quick wag of the tail: *Yes.*

"You didn't finish your dinner," Travis said.

The dog yawned elaborately.

Nora said, "Are you telling us you're a little tired?''

397

Yes.

"If you were feeling ill," Travis said, "you'd let us know right away, wouldn't you, fur face?"

Yes.

Nora insisted on examining Einstein's eyes, mouth, and ears for obvious signs of infection, but at last she said, "Nothing. He seems okay. I guess even Superdog has a right to be tired once in a while."

The wind had come up fast. It was chilly, and under its lash the waves rose higher than they had been all day.

A mass of gooseflesh, Garrison reach the landward end of the north flank of the harbor's northern breakwater. He was relieved to depart the hard and sometimes jagged stones of that rampart for the sandy beach. He was sure he had scraped and cut both feet; they felt hot, and his left foot stung with each step, forcing him to limp.

At first he stayed close to the surf, away from the tree-lined park that lay behind the beach. Over there, where park lamps lit the walkways and where spotlights dramatically highlighted the palms, he would be more easily seen from the street. He did not think anyone would be looking for him; he was sure his trick had worked. However, if anyone *was* looking for him, he did not want to call attention to himself.

The gusting wind tore foam off the incoming breakers and flung it in Garrison's face, so he felt as if he were continuously running through spiders' webs. The stuff stung his eyes, which had finally stopped tearing from his dunk in the sea, and at last he was forced to move away from the surf line, farther up the beach, where the softer sand met the lawn but where he was still out of the lights.

Young people were on the darkish beach, dressed for the chill of the night: couples on blankets, cuddling; small groups smoking dope, listening to music. Eight or ten teenage boys were gathered around two all-terrain vehicles with balloon tyres, which were not allowed on the beach during the day and most likely weren't allowed at night. They were drinking beer beside a pit they'd dug in the sand to bury their bottles if they saw a cop approaching; they were talking loudly about girls, and indulging in horseplay. No one gave Garrison more than a glance as he hurried by. In California, health-food-and-exercise fanatics were as common as street muggers in New York, and if an old man wanted to take a cold swim and then run on the beach in the dark, he was no more remarkable or noteworthy than a priest in a church.

As he headed north, Garrison scanned the park to his right in search of pay phones. They would probably be in pairs, prominently illuminated, on islands of concrete beside one of the walkways or perhaps near one of the public comfort stations.

He was beginning to despair, certain that he must have passed at least one group of telephones, that his old eyes were failing him, but then he saw what he was looking for. Two pay phones with winglike sound shields. Brightly lighted. They were about a hundred feet in from the beach, midway between the sand and the street that flanked the other side of the park.

Turning his back to the churning sea, he slowed to catch his breath and walked across the grass, under the wind-shaken fronds of a cluster of three stately royal palms. He was still forty feet from the phones when he saw a car, traveling at high speed, suddenly brake and pull to the curb with a squeal of tires, parking in a direct line from the phones. Garrison didn't know who they were, but he decided not to take any chances. He sidled into the cover provided by a huge old double-boled date palm that was, fortunately, not one of those fitted with decorative spotlights. From the notch between the trunks, he had a view of the phones and of the walkway leading out to the curb where the car had parked.

Two men got out of the sedan. One sprinted along the park perimeter, looking inward, searching for something.

The other man rushed straight into the park along the walkway. When he reached the lighted area around the phones, his identity was clear—and shocking.

Lemuel Johnson.

Behind the trunks of the Siamese date palms, Garrison drew his arms and legs closer to his body, sure that the joined bases of the trees provided him with plenty of cover but trying to make himself smaller nevertheless.

Johnson went to the first phone, lifted the handset—and tried to tear it out of the coinbox. It had one of those flexible metal cords, and he yanked on it hard, repeatedly, with little effect. Finally, cursing the instrument's toughness, he ripped the handset loose and threw it across the park. Then he destroyed the second phone.

For a moment, as Johnson turned away from the phones and walked straight toward Garrison, the attorney thought that he had been seen. But Johnson stopped after only a few steps and scanned the seaward end of the park and the beach beyond. His gaze did not appear to rest even momentarily on the date palms behind which Garrison hid.

"You damn crazy old bastard," Johnson said, then hurried back toward his car.

Crouched in shadows behind the palms, Garrison grinned because he knew whom the NSA man was talking about. Suddenly, the attorney did not mind the chill wind sweeping off the night sea behind him.

Damn crazy old bastard or geriatric James Bond—take your pick. Either way, he was still a man to be reckoned with.

In the basement switching room of the telephone company, Agents Rick Olbier and Denny Jones were tending the NSA's electronic tapping and tracing equipment, monitoring Garrison Dilworth's office and home lines. It was dull duty, and they played cards to make the time pass: two-hand pinochle and five-hundred rummy, neither of which was a good game, but the very idea of two-hand poker repelled them.

When a call came through to Dilworth's home number

400

at fourteen minutes past eight o'clock, Olbier and Jones reacted with far more excitement than the situation warranted because they were desperate for action. Olbier dropped his cards on the floor, and Jones threw his on the table, and they reached for the two headsets as if this was World War II and they were expecting to overhear a top-secret conversation between Hitler and Göring.

Their equipment was set to open the line and lock in a tracer pulse if Dilworth did not answer by the sixth ring. Because he knew the attorney was not at home and that the phone would not be answered, Olbier overrode the program and opened the line after the second ring.

On the computer screen, green letters announced: NOW TRACING.

And on the open line, a man said, "Hello?"

"Hello," Jones said into the mike on his headset.

The caller's number and his local Santa Barbara address appeared on the screen. This system worked much like the 911 police emergency computer, providing instant identification of the caller. But now, above the address on the screen, a company's rather than an individual's name appeared: TELEPHONE SOLICITATIONS, INC.

On the line, responding to Denny Jones, the caller said, "Sir, I'm pleased to tell you that you have been selected to receive a free eight-by-ten photograph and ten free pocket prints of any—"

Jones said, "Who is this?"

The computer was now searching data banks of Santa Barbara street addresses to cross-check the ID of the caller.

The voice on the phone said, "Well, I'm calling in behalf of Olin Mills, sir, the photography studio, where the finest quality—"

"Wait a sec," Jones said.

The computer verified the identity of the telephone subscriber who placed the call: Dilworth was getting a sales pitch, nothing more.

"I don't want any!" Jones said sharply, and disconnected.

"Shit," Olbier said.

"Pinochle?" Jones said.

In addition to the six men who had been at the harbor, Lem called in four more from the temporary HQ at the courthouse.

He stationed five along the perimeter of the oceanside park, a few hundred yards apart. Their job was to watch the wide avenue that separated the park from a business district, where there were a lot of motels but also restaurants, yogurt shops, gift shops, and other retail enterprises. All of the businesses had phones, of course, and even some of the motels would have pay phones in their front offices; using any of them, the attorney could alert Travis and Nora Cornell. At this hour on a Saturday evening, some stores were closed, but some of them—and all of the restaurants—were open. Dilworth must not be permitted to cross the street.

The sea wind was stiffening and growing chillier. The men stood with their hands in their jackets, heads tucked down, shivering.

Palm fronds were rattled by sudden gusts. Tree-roosting birds shrilled in alarm, then resettled.

Lem sent another agent to the southwest corner of the park, out by the base of the breakwater that separated the public beach from the harbor on the other side. His job was to prevent Dilworth from returning to the breakwater, climbing it, and sneaking back across the harbor to phones in another part of the city.

A seventh man was dispatched to the northwest corner of the park, down by the water line, to be sure Dilworth did not proceed north onto private beaches and into residential areas where he might persuade someone to allow him to use an unmonitored phone.

Just Lem, Cliff and Hank were left to comb through the park and adjoining beach in search of the attorney. He knew he had too few men for the job, but these ten—plus Olbier and Jones at the telephone company—were the only people he had in town. He could see no point in ordering in more agents from the Los Angeles office; by the time they arrived, Dilworth would either have been found and stopped—or would have succeeded in calling the Cornells.

The roofless all-terrain vehicle was equipped with a roll bar. It had two bucket seats, behind which was a four-foot-long cargo area that could accommodate additional passengers or a considerable amount of gear.

Garrison was flat on his stomach on the floor of the cargo hold, under a blanket. Two teenage boys were in the bucket seats, and two more were in the cargo hold on top of Garrison, sprawled as if they were sitting on nothing more than a pile of blankets. They were trying to keep the worst of their weight off Garrison, but he still felt half-crushed.

The engine sounded like angry wasps: a high, hard buzzing. It deafened Garrison because his right ear was flat against the cargo bed, which transmitted and amplified every vibration.

Fortunately, the soft beach provided a relatively smooth ride.

The vehicle stopped accelerating, slowed, and the engine noise dropped dramatically.

"Shit," one of the boys whispered to Garrison, "there's a guy ahead with a flashlight, flagging us down."

They drew to a halt, and over the whispery idling of the engine, Garrison heard a man say, "Where you boys headed?"

"Up the beach."

"That's private property up there. You have any right up there?"

"It's where we live," Tommy, the driver, responded.

"Is that so?"

"Don't we look like a bunch of spoiled rich kids?" one of them asked, playing wiseass.

"What you been up to?" the man asked suspiciously.

"Beach cruisin', hangin' out. But it got too cold."

"You boys been drinking?"

You dolt, Garrison thought as he listened to the interrogator. These are *teenagers* you're talking to, poor creatures whose hormonal imbalances have thrown them into rebellion against all authority for the next couple of years. I have their sympathy because I'm in flight from the cops, and they'll take my side without even knowing what I've done. If you want their cooperation, you'll never get it by bullying them.

"Drinking? Hell no," another boy said. "Check the cooler in back if you want. Nothing in it but Dr. Pepper."

Garrison, who was pressed up against the ice chest, hoped to God the man would not come around to the back of the vehicle and have a look. If the guy got *that* close he would almost surely see there was something vaguely human about the shape under the blanket on which the boys were sitting.

"Dr. Pepper, huh? What kind of beer was in there before you drank it all?"

"Hey, man," Tommy said. "Why're you hassling us? Are you a cop or what?"

"Yeah, in fact, I am."

"Where's your uniform?" one of the boys asked.

"Undercover. Listen, I'm disposed to let you kids go on, not check your breath for liquor or anything. But I have to know—did you see an old white-haired guy on the beach tonight?"

"Who cares about old guys?" one of the boys asked. "We were looking for *women*."

"You'd have noticed this old character if you'd seen him. He'd most likely have been wearing swim trunks."

"Tonight?" Tommy said. "It's almost December, man. You feel that wind?"

"Maybe he was wearing something else."

"Didn't see him," Tommy said. "No old guy with white hair. Any you guys see him?"

The other three said they had not seen any old fart fitting the description they had been given, and then they were allowed to drive on, north from the public beach, into a residential area of seaside homes and private beaches.

When they had rounded a low hill and were out of sight of the man who had stopped them, they pulled the blanket off Garrison, and he sat up with considerable relief.

Tommy dropped the other three boys off at their houses and took Garrison home with him because his parents were out for the evening. He lived in a house that looked like a ship with multiple decks, slung over a bluff, all glass and angles.

Following Tommy into the foyer, Garrison caught a glimpse of himself in a mirror. He looked nothing like the dignified silver-haired barrister known by everyone in the city's courts. His hair was wet, dirty, and matted. His face was smeared with dirt. Sand, bits of grass, and threads of seaweed were stuck to his bare skin and tangled in his gray chest hair. He grinned happily at himself.

"There's a phone in here," Tommy said from the den.

After preparing dinner, eating, cleaning up, and then worrying about Einstein's loss of appetite, Nora and Travis had forgotten about calling Garrison Dilworth and thanking him for the care with which he had packaged and shipped her paintings. They were sitting in front of the fireplace when she remembered.

In the past, when they had called Garrison, they had done so from public phones in Carmel. That had proved to be an unnecessary precaution. And now, tonight, neither of them was in the mood to get in the car and drive into town.

"We could wait and call him from Carmel tomorrow," Travis said.

"It'll be safe to phone from here," she said. "If they'd made a link between you and Garrison, he'd have called and warned us off."

"He might not know they've made a link," Travis said. "He might not know they're watching him."

"Garrison would know," she said firmly.

Travis nodded. "Yeah, I'm sure he would."

"So it's safe to call him."

She was halfway to the phone when it rang.

The operator said, "I have a collect call for anyone from a Mr. Garrison Dilworth in Santa Barbara. Will you accept the charges?"

A few minutes before ten o'clock, after conducting a thorough but fruitless search of the park and beach, Lem reluctantly admitted that Garrison Dilworth had somehow gotten past him. He sent his men back to the courthouse and harbor.

He and Cliff also drove back to the harbor to the sport yacht from which they had based their surveillance of Dilworth. When they put in a call to the Coast Guard cutter pursuing the *Amazing Grace*, they learned that the attorney's lady had turned around well short of Ventura and was heading north along the coast, back to Santa Barbara.

She entered the harbor at ten thirty-six.

At the empty slip belonging to Garrison, Lem and Cliff huddled in the crisp wind, watching her bring the Hinckley smoothly and gently into its mooring. It was a beautiful boat, beautifully handled.

She had the gall to shout at them, "Don't just stand there! Grab the lines and help tie her up!"

They obliged primarily because they were anxious to speak with her and could not do so until the *Amazing Grace* was secured.

Once their assistance had been rendered, they stepped through the railing gate. Cliff was wearing Top-Siders as part of his boater's disguise, but Lem was in street shoes and not at all sure-footed on the wet deck, especially as the boat was rocking slightly.

Before they could say a word to the woman, a voice behind them said, "Excuse me, gentlemen—"

Lem turned and saw Garrison Dilworth in the glow of a dock lamp, just boarding the boat behind them. He was wearing someone else's clothes. His pants were much too big in the waist, cinched in with a belt. They were too short in the legs, so his bare ankles were revealed. He wore a voluminous shirt.

"—please excuse me, but I've got to get into some warm clothes of my own and have a pot of coffee—"

Lem said, "God *damn* it."

"—to thaw out these old bones."

After a gasp of astonishment, Cliff Soames let out a hard bark of laughter, then glanced at Lem and said, "Sorry."

Lem's stomach cramped and burned with an incipient ulcer. He did not wince with pain, did not double over, did not even put a hand on his gut, gave no indication of discomfort because any such sign from him might increase Dilworth's satisfaction. Lem just glared at the attorney, at the woman, then left without saying a word.

"That damn dog," Cliff said as he fell into step at Lem's side on the dock, "sure inspires one hell of a lot of loyalty."

Later, bedding down in a motel because he was too tired to close the temporary field office tonight and go home to Orange County, Lem Johnson thought about what Cliff had said. Loyalty. One *hell* of a lot of loyalty.

Lem wondered if he had ever felt such a strong bond of loyalty to anyone as the Cornells and Garrison Dilworth apparently felt toward the retriever. He tossed and turned, unable to sleep, and he finally realized there was no use trying to switch off his inner lights until he satisfied himself that he was capable of the degree of loyalty and commitment that he had seen in the Cornells and their attorney.

He sat up in the darkness, leaning against the headboard.

Well, sure, he was damn loyal to his country, which he loved and honored. And he was loyal to the Agency. But to another *person*? All right, Karen. His wife. He was loyal to Karen in every way—in his heart, mind, and gonads. He loved Karen. He had loved her deeply for almost twenty years.

"Yeah," he said aloud in the empty motel room at two o'clock in the morning, "yeah, if you're so loyal to Karen, why aren't you with her now?''

But he wasn't being fair to himself. After all, he had a job to do, an important job.

"That's the trouble," he muttered, "you've always—*always*—got a job to do.''

He slept away from home more than a hundred nights a year, one in three. And when he *was* home, he was distracted half the time, his mind on the latest case. Karen had once wanted children, but Lem had delayed the start of a family, claiming that he could not handle the responsibility of children until he was sure his career was secure.

"Secure?" he said. "Man, you inherited your daddy's money. You started out with more of a cushion than most people.''

If he was as loyal to Karen as those people were to that mutt, then his commitment to her should mean that her desires ought to come before all others. If Karen wanted a family, then family should take precedence over career. Right? At least he should have compromised and started a family when they were in their early thirties. His twenties could have gone to the career, his thirties to child-rearing. Now he was forty-five, almost forty-six, and Karen was forty-three, and the time for starting a family had passed.

Lem was overcome with a great loneliness.

He got out of bed, went into the bathroom in his shorts, switched on the light, and stared hard at himself in the mirror. His eyes were bloodshot and sunken. He had lost so much weight on this case that his face was beginning to look downright skeletal.

Stomach cramps seized him, and he bent over, holding onto the sides of the sink, his face in the basin. He'd been afflicted only for the past month or so, but his condition seemed to be worsening with startling speed. The pain took a long time to pass.

When he confronted his reflection in the mirror again, he said, "You're not even loyal to your own self, you asshole. You're killing yourself, working yourself to death, and you can't stop. Not loyal to Karen, not loyal to yourself. Not really loyal to your country or the Agency, when it comes right down to it. Hell, the only thing you're totally and unswervingly committed to is your old man's crackpot vision of life as a tightrope walk."

Crackpot.

That word seemed to reverberate in the bathroom long after he'd spoken it. He had loved and respected his father, had never said a word against him. Yet today he had admitted to Cliff that his dad had been "impossible." And now—crackpot vision. He still loved his dad and always would. But he was beginning to wonder if a son could love a father and, at the same time, completely reject his father's teachings.

A year ago, a month ago, even a few days ago, he would have said it was impossible to hold fast to that love and still be his own man. But now, by God, it seemed not only possible but essential that he separate his love for his father from his adherence to his father's workaholic code.

What's happening to me? he wondered.

Freedom? Freedom, at last, at forty-five?

Squinting into the mirror, he said, "Almost forty-six."

NINE

1

Sunday, Travis noted that Einstein still had less of an appetite than usual, but by Monday, November 29, the retriever seemed fine. On Monday and Tuesday, Einstein finished every scrap of his meals, and he read new books. He sneezed only once and did not cough at all. He drank more water than in the past, though not an excessive amount. If he seemed to spend more time by the fireplace, if he padded through the house less energetically ... well, winter was swiftly settling upon them, and animals' behavior changed with the seasons.

At a bookstore in Carmel, Nora bought a copy of *The Dog Owner's Home Veterinary Handbook*. She spent a few hours at the kitchen table, reading, researching the possible meanings of Einstein's symptoms. She discovered that listlessness, partial loss of appetite, sneezing, coughing, and unusual thirst could signify a hundred ailments—or mean nothing at all. "About the only thing it couldn't be is a cold," she said. "Dogs don't get colds like we do." But by the time she got the book, Einstein's symptons had diminished to such an extent that she decided he was probably perfectly healthy.

In the pantry off the kitchen, Einstein used the Scrabble tiles to tell them: FIT AS A FIDDLE.

Stooping beside the dog, stroking him, Travis said, "I guess you ought to know better than anyone."

WHY SAY FIT AS A FIDDLE?

Replacing the tiles in their Lucite tubes, Travis said, "Well, because it means—healthy."

BUT WHY DOES IT MEAN HEALTHY?

Travis thought about the metaphor—fit as a fiddle—and realized he was not sure why it meant what it did. He asked Nora, and she came to the pantry door, but she had no explanation for the phrase, either.

Pawing out more letters, pushing them around with his nose, the retriever asked: WHY SAY SOUND AS A DOLLAR?

"Sound as a dollar—meaning healthy or reliable," Travis said.

Stooping beside them, speaking to the dog, Nora said, "That one's easier. The United States dollar was once the soundest, most stable currency in the world. Still is, I suppose. For decades, there was no terrible inflation in the dollar like in some other currencies, no reason to lose faith in it, so folks said, 'I'm as sound as a dollar.' Of course, the dollar isn't what it once was, and the phrase isn't as fitting as it used to be, but we still use it."

WHY STILL USE IT?

"Because ... we've always used it," Nora said, shrugging.

WHY SAY HEALTHY AS A HORSE? HORSES NEVER SICK?

Gathering up the tiles and sorting them back into their tubes, Travis said, "No, in fact, horses are fairly delicate animals in spite of their size. They get sick pretty easily."

Einstein looked expectantly from Travis to Nora.

Nora said, "We probably say we're healthy as a horse because horses *look* strong and seem like they shouldn't ever get sick, even though they get sick all the time."

"Face it," Travis told the dog, "we humans say things all the time that don't make sense."

Pumping the letter-dispensing pedals with his paw, the retriever told them: YOU ARE A STRANGE PEOPLE.

Travis looked at Nora, and they both laughed.

Beneath YOU ARE A STRANGE PEOPLE, the retriever spelled: BUT I LIKE YOU ANYWAY.

Einstein's inquisitiveness and sense of humor seemed, more than anything else, to indicate that, if he had been mildly ill, he was now recovered.

That was Tuesday.

On Wednesday, December 1, while Nora painted in her second-floor studio, Travis devoted the day to inspecting his security system and to routine weapons maintenance.

In every room, a firearm was carefully concealed under furniture or behind a drape or in a closet, but always within easy reach. They owned two Mossberg pistol-grip shotguns, four Smith & Wesson Model 19 Combat Magnums loaded with .357s, two .38 pistols that they carried with them in the pickup and Toyota, an Uzi carbine, two Uzi pistols. They could have obtained their entire arsenal legally, from a local gun shop, once they purchased a house and established residence in the county, but Travis had not been willing to wait that long. He had wanted to have the weapons on the first night they settled into their new home; therefore, through Van Dyne in San Francisco, he and Nora had located an illegal arms salesman and had acquired what they needed. Of course, they could not have bought conversion kits for the Uzis from a licensed gun dealer. But they were able to purchase three such kits in San Francisco, and now the Uzi carbine and pistols were fully automatic.

Travis moved from room to room, checking that the weapons were properly positioned, that they were free of dust, that they did not need to be oiled, and that their magazines were fully loaded. He knew that everything would be in order, but he just felt more comfortable if he conducted this inspection once a week. Though he had been out of uniform for many years, the old military training and methodology were still a part of him, and under pressure they surfaced more quickly than he had expected.

Taking a Mossberg with them, he and Einstein also walked around the house, stopping at each of the small infrared sensors that were, as much as possible, placed inconspicuously against backdrops of rocks or plants, snug against the trunks of a few trees, at the corners of the house, and beside an old rotting pine stump at the edge of the driveway. He had bought the components on the open market, from an electronics dealer in San Francisco. It was dated stuff, not at all state-of-the-art security technology, but he chose it because he was familiar with it from his days in Delta Force, and it was good enough for his purposes. Lines from the sensors ran underground, to an alarm box in one of the kitchen cupboards. When the system was switched on at night nothing larger than a raccoon could come within thirty feet of the house—or enter the barn at the back of the property—without tripping the alarm. No bells would ring, and no sirens would blare because that would alert The Outsider and might run it off. They didn't want to chase it away; they wanted to *kill* it. Therefore, when the system was tripped, it turned on clock radios in every room of the house, all of which were set at a low volume so as not to frighten off an intruder but high enough to warn Travis and Nora.

Today, all the sensors were in place, as usual. All he had to do was wipe off the light film of dust that had coated the lenses.

"The palace moat is in good repair, m'lord," Travis said.

Einstein woofed approval.

In the rust-red barn, Travis and Einstein examined the equipment that, they hoped, would provide a nasty surprise for The Outsider.

In the northwest corner of the shadowy interior, to the left of the big rolling door, a pressurized steel tank was clamped in a wall rack. In the diagonally opposite southeast corner at the back of the building, beyond the pickup and car, an identical vessel was bolted to an identical rack. They resembled large propane tanks of the sort people used at summer cabins for gas cooking, but they did not hold propane. They were filled with nitrous oxide, which was sometimes inaccurately called "laughing gas." The first whiff *did* exhilarate you and make you want to laugh, but the second whiff knocked you out before the laugh could escape your lips. Dentists and surgeons frequently used nitrous oxide as an anesthetic. Travis had purchased it from a medical-supply house in San Francisco.

After switching on the barn lights, Travis checked the gauges on both tanks. Full pressure.

In addition to the large rolling door at the front of the barn, there was a smaller, man-size door at the rear. These were the only two entrances. Travis had boarded over a pair of windows in the loft. At night, when the alarm system was engaged, the smaller rear door was left unlocked in the hope that The Outsider, intending to scout the house from the cover of the barn, would let itself into the trap. When it opened the door and crept into the barn, it would trigger a mechanism that would slam and lock the door behind it. The front door, already locked from outside, would prevent an exit in that direction.

Simultaneous with the springing of the trap, the large tanks of nitrous oxide would release their entire contents in less than one minute because Travis had fitted them with high-pressure emergency-release valves tied in with the alarm system. He had caulked all of the draft-admitting cracks in the barn and had insulated the place as thoroughly as possible in order to insure that the nitrous oxide would be contained within the structure until one of the doors was unlocked from outside and opened to vent the gas.

The Outsider could not take refuge in the pickup or the Toyota, for they would be locked. No corner in the barn would be free of the gas. Within less than a minute, the creature would collapse. Travis had considered using poisonous gas of some kind, which he probably could have obtained on the underground market, but he had decided against going to that extreme because, if something went wrong, the danger to him and Nora and Einstein would be too great.

Once gas had been released and The Outsider had succumbed, Travis could simply open one of the doors, vent the barn, enter with the Uzi carbine, and kill the beast where it lay unconscious. At worst, even if the time taken airing out the building gave The Outsider a chance to regain consciousness, it would still be groggy and disoriented and easily dispatched.

When they had ascertained that everything in the barn was as it should be, Travis and Einstein returned to the yard behind the house. The December day was cool but windless. The forest surrounding the property was preternaturally still. The trees stood motionless under a low sky of slate-colored clouds.

Travis said, "Is The Outsider still coming?"

With a quick wag of the tail, Einstein said, *Yes*.

"Is it close?"

Einstein sniffed the clean, winter-crisp air. He padded across the yard to the perimeter of the northern woods and sniffed again, cocked his head, peered intently into the trees. He repeated this ritual at the southern end of the property.

Travis had the feeling that Einstein was not actually employing his eyes, ears, and nose in search of The Outsider. He had some way of monitoring The Outsider that was far different from the means by which he would track a cougar or squirrel. Travis perceived that the dog was employing an inexplicable sixth sense—call it psychic or at least quasi-psychic. The retriever's use of its ordinary senses was probably either the trigger by which it engaged that psychic ability—or mere habit.

At last, Einstein returned to him and whined curiously.

"Is it close?" Travis asked.

Einstein sniffed the air and surveyed the gloom of the encircling forest, as if he could not decide on an answer.

"Einstein? Is something wrong?"

Finally, the retriever barked once: *No*.

"Is The Outsider getting close?"

A hesitation. Then: *No*.

"Are you sure?"

Yes.

"Really sure?"

Yes.

At the house, as Travis opened the door, Einstein turned

away from him, padded across the back porch, and stood at the top of the wooden steps, taking one final look around at the yard and at the peaceful, shadowed, soundless forest. Then, with a faint shiver, he followed Travis inside.

Throughout the inspection of the defenses during the afternoon, Einstein had been more affectionate than usual, rubbing against Travis's legs a great deal, nuzzling, seeking by one means or another to be petted or patted or scratched. That evening, as they watched television, then played a three-way game of Scrabble on the living-room floor, the dog continued to seek attention. He kept putting his head in Nora's lap, then in Travis's. He seemed as if he would be content to be stroked and have his ears gently scratched until next summer.

From the day of their first encounter in the Santa Ana foothills, Einstein had gone through spells of purely doggy behavior, when it was hard to believe that he was, in his own way, as intelligent as a man. Tonight, he was in one of those moods again. In spite of his cleverness at Scrabble— in which his score was second only to Nora's, and in which he took devilish pleasure forming words that made sly references to her as yet unnoticeable pregnancy—he was nonetheless, this night, more of a dog than not.

Nora and Travis chose to finish the evening with a little light reading—detective stories—but Einstein did not want them to bother inserting a book in his page-turning machine. Instead, he lay on the floor in front of Nora's armchair and went instantly to sleep.

"He still seems a little draggy," she said to Travis.

"He ate all his dinner, though. And we did have a long day."

The dog's breathing, as it slept, was normal, and Travis was not worried. Actually, he was feeling better about their future than he had for some time. The inspection of their defenses had given him renewed confidence in their preparations, and he believed they would be able to handle The Outsider when it arrived. And thanks to Garrison Dilworth's courage and dedication to their cause, the government had been stymied, perhaps for good, in its efforts to track them down. Nora was painting again with great enthusiasm, and Travis had decided to use his real-estate license, under the name of Samuel Hyatt, to go back to work once The Outsider had been destroyed. And if Einstein was still a little draggy ... well, he was certainly more energetic than he had been for a while and was sure to be himself by tomorrow or the day after, at the latest.

That night, Travis slept without dreaming.

In the morning, he was up before Nora. By the time he showered and dressed, she was up, too. On her way into the shower, she kissed him, nibbled on his lip, and mumbled sleepy vows of love. Her eyes were puffy, and her hair was mussed, and her breath was sour, but he would have rushed her straight back into bed if she had not said, "Try me this afternoon, Romeo. Right now, the only lust in my heart is for a couple of eggs, bacon, toast, and coffee."

He went downstairs and, starting in the living room, opened the interior shutters to let in the morning light. The sky looked as low and gray as it had been yesterday, and he would not be surprised if rain fell before twilight.

In the kitchen, he noticed that the pantry door was open, the light on. He looked in to see if Einstein was there, but the only sign of the dog was the message that he had spelled out sometime during the night.

FIDDLE BROKE. NO DOCTOR. PLEASE. DON'T WANT TO GO BACK TO LAB. AFRAID. AFRAID.

Oh shit. Oh Jesus.

Travis stepped out of the pantry and shouted, "*Einstein!*"

No bark. No sound of padding feet.

The shutters still covered the kitchen windows, and most of the room was not illuminated by the glow from the pantry. Travis snapped on the lights.

Einstein was not there.

He ran into the den. The dog was not there, either.

Heart pounding almost painfully, Travis climbed the stairs two at a time, looked in the third bedroom that would one day be a nursery and then in the room that Nora used as a studio, but Einstein was not in either place, and he was

418

not in the master bedroom, not even under the bed where Travis was desperate enough to check, and for a moment he could not figure out where in the hell the dog had gone, and he stood listening to Nora singing in the shower—she was oblivious of what was happening—and he started into the bathroom to tell her that something was wrong, horribly wrong, which was when he thought of the downstairs bath, so he ran out of the bedroom and along the hall and descended the stairs so fast he almost lost his balance, almost fell, and in the first-floor bath, between the kitchen and the den, he found what he most feared to find.

The bathroom stank. The dog, ever considerate, had vomited in the toilet but had not possessed the strength—or perhaps the clarity of mind—to flush. Einstein was lying on the bathroom floor, on his side. Travis knelt next to him. Einstein was still but not dead, not dead, because he was breathing; he inhaled and exhaled with a rasping noise. He tried to lift his head when Travis spoke to him, but he did not have the strength to move.

His eyes. Jesus, his eyes.

Ever so gently, Travis lifted the retriever's head and saw that those wonderfully expressive brown eyes were slightly milky. A watery yellow discharge oozed from the eyes; it had crusted in the golden fur. A similar sticky discharge bubbled in Einstein's nostrils.

Putting a hand on the retriever's neck, Travis felt a laboring and irregular heartbeat.

"No," Travis said. "Oh, no, no. It's not going to be like this, boy. I'm not going to let it happen like this."

He lowered the retriever's head to the floor, got up, turned toward the door—Einstein whimpered almost inaudibly, as if to say that he did not want to be left alone.

"I'll be right back, right back," Travis promised. "Just hold on, boy. I'll be right back."

He ran to the stairs and climbed faster than before. Now, his heart was beating with such tremendous force that he felt as if it would tear loose of him. He was breathing too fast, hyperventilating.

In the master bathroom, Nora was just stepping out of

the shower, naked and dripping.

Travis's words ran together in panic: "Get dressed quick we've got to get to the vet now for God's sake hurry."

Shocked, she said, "What's happened?"

"Einstein! Hurry! I think he's dying."

He grabbed a blanket off the bed, left Nora to dress, and hurried downstairs to the bathroom. The retriever's ragged breathing seemed to have gotten worse in just the minute that Travis had been away. He folded the blanket twice, to a fourth of its size, then eased the dog onto it.

Einstein made a pained sound, as if the movement hurt him.

Travis said, "Easy, easy. You'll be all right."

At the door, Nora appeared, still buttoning her blouse, which was damp because she had not taken time to towel off before dressing. Her wet hair hung straight.

In a voice choked with emotion, she said, "Oh, fur face, no, no."

She wanted to stoop and touch the retriever, but there was no time to delay. Travis said, "Bring the pickup alongside the house."

While Nora sprinted to the barn, Travis folded the blanket around Einstein as best he could, so only the retriever's head, tail, and hind legs protruded. Trying unsuccessfully not to elicit another whimper of pain, Travis lifted the dog in his arms and carried him out of the bathroom, across the kitchen, out of the house, pulling the door shut behind him but leaving it unlocked, not giving a damn about security right now.

The air was cold. Yesterday's calm was gone. Evergreens swayed, shivered, and there was something ominous in the way their bristling, needled branches pawed at the air. Other leafless trees raised black, bony arms toward the somber sky.

In the barn, Nora started the pickup. The engine roared.

Travis cautiously descended the porch steps and went out to the driveway, walking as if he were carrying an armload of fragile antique china. The blustery wind stood Travis's hair straight up, flapped the loose ends of the blanket, and ruffled the fur on Einstein's exposed head, as if it were a wind with a malevolent consciousness, as if it wanted to tear the dog away from him.

Nora swung the pickup around, heading out, and stopped where Travis waited. She would drive.

It was true what they said: sometimes, in certain special moments of crisis, in times of great emotional tribulation, women are better able to bite the bullet and do what must be done than men often are. Sitting in the truck's passenger seat, cradling the blanket-wrapped dog in his arms, Travis was in no condition to drive. He was shaking badly, and he realized that he had been crying from the time he had found Einstein on the bathroom floor. He had seen difficult military service, and he had never panicked or been paralyzed with fear while on dangerous Delta Force operations, but this was different, this was Einstein, *this was his child*. If he had been required to drive, he'd probably have run straight into a tree, or off the road into a ditch. There were tears in Nora's eyes, too, but she didn't surrender to them. She bit her lip and drove as if she had been trained for stunt work in the movies. At the end of the dirt lane, they turned right, heading north on the twisty Pacific Coast Highway toward Carmel, where there was sure to be at least one veterinarian.

During the drive, Travis talked to Einstein, trying to soothe and encourage him. "Everything's going to be all right, just fine, it's not as bad as it seems, you'll be as good as new."

Einstein whimpered and struggled weakly in Travis's arms for a moment, and Travis knew what the dog was thinking. He was afraid that the vet would see the tattoo in his ear, would know what it meant, and would send him back to Banodyne.

"Don't you worry about that, fur face. Nobody's going to take you away from us. By God, they aren't. They'll have to walk through me first, and they aren't going to be able to do that, no way."

"No way," Nora agreed grimly.

But in the blanket, cradled against Travis's chest, Einstein trembled violently.

Travis remembered the letter tiles on the pantry floor: FIDDLE BROKE ... AFRAID ... AFRAID.

"Don't be afraid," he pleaded with the dog. "Don't be afraid. There's no reason to be afraid."

In spite of Travis's heartfelt assurances, Einstein shivered and was afraid—and Travis was afraid, too.

2

Stopping at an Arco service station on the outskirts of Carmel, Nora found the vet's address in a phone book and called him to be sure he was in. Dr. James Keene's office was on Dolores Avenue at the southern end of town. They pulled up in front of the place at a few minutes before nine.

Nora had been expecting a typically sterile-looking veterinary clinic and was surprised to find that Dr. Keene's offices were in his home, a quaint two-story Country English house of stone and plaster and exposed timbers with a roof that curved over the eaves.

As they hurried up the stone walk with Einstein, Dr. Keene opened the door before they reached it, as if he had been on the lookout for them. A sign indicated that the entrance to the surgery was around the side of the house, but the vet took them in at the front door. He was a tall, sorrowful-faced man with sallow skin and sad brown eyes, but his smile was warm, and his manner was gracious.

Closing the door, Dr. Keene said, "Bring him this way, please."

He led them swiftly along a hallway with an oak parquet floor protected by a long, narrow oriental carpet. On the left, through an archway, lay a pleasantly furnished living room that actually looked *lived*-in, with footstools in front of the chairs, reading lamps, laden bookshelves, and crocheted afghans folded neatly and conveniently over the backs of some chairs for when the evenings were chilly. A dog stood just inside the archway, a black labrador. It watched them solemnly, as if it understood the gravity of

Einstein's condition, and it did not follow them.

At the rear of the large house, on the left side of the hall, the vet took them through a door into a clean white surgery. Lined along the walls were white-enameled and stainless-steel cabinets with glass fronts, which were filled with bottles of drugs, serums, tablets, capsules, and the many powdered ingredients needed to compound more exotic medicines.

Travis gently lowered Einstein onto an examination table and folded the blanket back from him.

Nora realized that she and Travis looked every bit as distraught as they would have if they'd been bringing a dying child to a doctor. Travis's eyes were red, and though he was not actively crying at the moment, he continually blew his nose. The moment she had parked the pickup in front of the house and had pulled on the hand brake, Nora had ceased to be able to repress her own tears. Now she stood on the other side of the examination table from Dr. Keene, with one arm around Travis, and she wept quietly.

The vet was apparently used to strong emotional reactions from pet owners, for he never once glanced curiously at Nora or Travis, never once indicated by any means that he found their anxiety and grief to be excessive.

Dr. Keene listened to the retriever's heart and lungs with a stethoscope, palpated his abdomen, examined his oozing eyes with an ophthalmoscope. Through those and several other procedures, Einstein remained limp, as if paralyzed. The only indications that the dog still clung to life were his faint whimpers and ragged breathing.

It's not as serious as it seems, Nora told herself as she blotted her eyes with a Kleenex.

Looking up from the dog, Dr. Keene said, "What's his name?"

"Einstein," Travis said.

"How long have you owned him?"

"Only a few months."

"Has he had his shots?"

"No," Travis said. "Damn it, no."

"Why not?"

"It's ... complicated," Travis said. "But there're reasons that shots couldn't be gotten for him."

"No reason's good enough," Keene said disapprovingly. "He's got no license, no shots. It's very irresponsible not to see that your dog is properly licensed and vaccinated."

"I know," Travis said miserably. "I know."

"What's wrong with Einstein?" Nora said.

And she thought-hoped-prayed: It's not as serious as it seems.

Lightly stroking the retriever, Keene said, "He's got distemper."

Einstein had been moved to a corner of the surgery, where he lay on a thick, dog-size foam mattress that was protected by a zippered plastic coverlet. To prevent him from moving around—if at any time he had the strength to move—he was tethered on a short leash to a ringbolt in the wall.

Dr. Keene had given the retriver an injection. "Antibiotics," he explained. "No antibiotics are effective against distemper, but they're indicated to avoid secondary bacteriological infections."

He had also inserted a needle in one of the dog's leg veins and had hooked him to an IV drip to counteract dehydration.

When the vet tried to put a muzzle on Einstein, both Nora and Travis objected strenuously.

"It's not because I'm afraid he'll bite," Dr. Keene explained. "It's for his own protection, to prevent him from chewing at the needle. If he has the strength, he'll do what dogs always do to a wound—lick and bite at the source of the irritation."

"Not this dog," Travis said. "This dog's different." He pushed past Keene and removed the device that bound Einstein's jaws together.

The vet started to protest, then thought better of it. "All right. For now. He's too weak anyway."

424

Still trying to deny the awful truth, Nora said, "But how could it be so serious? He showed only the mildest symptoms, and even those went away over a couple of days."

"Half the dogs who get distemper never show any symptoms at all," the vet said as he returned a bottle of antibiotics to one of the glass-fronted cabinets and tossed a disposable syringe in a wastecan. "Others have only a mild illness, symptoms come and go from one day to the next. Some, like Einstein, get very ill. It can be a gradually worsening illness, or it can change suddenly from mild symptoms to ... this. But there is a bright side here."

Travis was crouched beside Einstein, where the dog could see him without lifting his head or rolling his eyes, and could therefore feel attended, watched over, loved. When he heard Keene mention a bright side, Travis looked up eagerly. "What bright side? What do you mean?"

"The dog's condition, before it contracts distemper, frequently determines the course of the disease. The illness is most acute in animals that are ill-kept and poorly nourished. It's clear to me that Einstein was given good care."

Travis said, "We tried to feed him well, to make sure he got plenty of exercise."

"He was bathed and groomed almost *too* often," Nora added.

Smiling, nodding approval, Dr. Keene said, "Then we have an edge. We have real hope."

Nora looked at Travis, and he could meet her eyes only briefly before he had to look away, down at Einstein. It was left to her to ask the dreaded question: "Doctor, he's going to be all right, isn't he? He won't—he won't die, will he?"

Apparently, James Keene was aware that his naturally glum face and drooping eyes presented, merely in repose, an expression that did little to inspire confidence. He cultivated a warm smile, a soft yet confident tone of voice, and an almost grandfatherly manner that, although perhaps calculated, seemed genuine and helped balance the perpetual gloom God had seen fit to visit upon his countenance.

He came to Nora, put his hands on her shoulders. "My dear, you love this dog like a baby, don't you?"

She bit her lip and nodded.

"Then have faith. Have faith in God, who watches over sparrows, so they say, and have a little faith in me too. Believe it or not, I'm pretty good at what I do, and I deserve your faith."

"I believe you are good," she told him.

Still squatting beside Einstein, Travis said thickly, "But the chances. What're the chances? Tell us straight?"

Letting go of Nora, turning to Travis, Keene said, "Well, the discharge from his eyes and nose isn't as thick as it can get. Not nearly. No pus blisters on the abdomen. You say he's vomited, but you've seen no diarrhea?"

"No. Just vomiting," Travis said.

"His fever's high but not dangerously so. Has he been slobbering excessively?"

"No," Nora said.

"Fits of head-shaking and chewing on air, sort of as if he had a bad taste in his mouth?"

"No," Travis and Nora said simultaneously.

"Have you seen him run in circles or fall down without reason? Have you seen him lie on his side and kick violently, as if he were running? Aimless wandering around a room, bumping into walls, jerking and twitching—anything like that?"

"No, no," Travis said.

And Nora said, "My God, could he *get* like that?"

"If he goes into second-stage distemper, yes," Keene said. "Then there's brain involvement. Epileptic-like seizures. Encephalitis."

Travis came to his feet in a sudden lurch. He staggered toward Keene, then stopped, swaying. His face was pale. His eyes filled with a terrible fear. "Brain involvement? If he recovered, would there be ... brain damage?"

An oily nausea rippled in Nora. She thought of Einstein with brain damage—as intelligent as a man, intelligent enough to remember that he had once been special, and to know that something had been lost, and to know that he

426

was now living in a dullness, a grayness, that his life was somehow less than what it had once been. Sick and dizzy with fear, she had to lean against the examination table.

Keene said, "Most dogs in second-stage distemper don't survive. But if he made it, there would, of course, be some brain damage. Nothing that would require he be put to sleep. He might have lifelong chorea, for instance, which is involuntary jerking or twitching, rather like palsy, and often limited to the head. But he could be relatively happy with that, lead a pain-free existence, and he could still be a fine pet."

Travis almost shouted at the vet: "To hell with whether he'd make a fine pet or not. I'm not concerned about *physical* effects of the brain damage. What about his *mind*?"

"Well, he'd recognize his masters," the doctor said. "He'd know you and remain affectionate toward you. No problem there. He might sleep a lot. He might have periods of listlessness. But he'd almost certainly remain housebroken. He wouldn't forget that training—"

Shaking, Travis said, "I don't give a damn if he pisses all over the house as long as he can still *think*!"

"Think?" Dr. Keene said, clearly perplexed. "Well ... what do you mean exactly? He is a dog, after all."

The vet had accepted their anxious, grief-racked behavior as within the parameters of normal pet-owner reactions in a case like this. But now, at last, he began to look at them strangely.

Partly to change the subject and dampen the vet's suspicion, partly because she simply had to know the answer, Nora said, "All right, but is Einstein *in* second-stage distemper?"

Keene said, "From what I've seen so far, he's still in the first stage. And now that treatment has begun, if we don't see any of the more violent symptoms during the next twenty-four hours, I think we have a good chance of keeping him in first stage and rolling it back."

"And there's no brain involvement in first stage?"

Travis asked with an urgency that again caused Keene to furrow his brow.

"No. Not in first stage."

"And if he stays in first stage," Nora said, "he won't die?"

In his softest voice and most comforting manner, James Keene said, "Well, now, the chances are very high that he'd survive just first-stage distemper—and without any after effects. I want you to realize that his chances of recovery *are* quite high. But at the same time, I don't want to give you false hope. That'd be cruel. Even if the disease proceeds no further than first stage ... Einstein could die. The percentages are on the side of life, but death is possible."

Nora was crying again. She thought she had gotten a grip on herself. She thought she was ready to be strong. But now she was crying. She went to Einstein, sat on the floor beside him, and put one hand on his shoulder, just to let him know that she was there.

Keene was becoming slightly impatient with—and thoroughly baffled by—their tumultuous emotional response to the bad news. A new note of sternness entered his voice as he said, "Listen, all we can do is give him top-flight care and hope for the best. He'll have to remain here, of course, because distemper treatment is complex and ought to be administered under veterinary supervision. I'll have to keep him on the intravenous fluids, antibiotics ... and there'll be regular anticonvulsants and sedatives if he begins to have seizures."

Under Nora's hand, Einstein shivered as if he had heard and understood the grim possibilities.

"All right, okay, yes," Travis said, "obviously, he's got to stay here in your office. We'll stay with him."

"There's no need—" Keene began.

"Right, yes, no need," Travis said quickly, "but we want to stay, we'll be okay, we can sleep here on the floor tonight."

"Oh, I'm afraid that's not possible," Keene said.

"Yes, it is, oh yes, entirely possible," Travis said,

babbling now in his eagerness to convince the vet. "Don't worry about us, Doctor. We'll manage just fine. Einstein needs us here, so we'll stay, the important thing is that we stay, and of course we'll pay you extra for the inconvenience."

"But I'm not running a hotel!"

"We must stay," Nora said firmly.

Keene said, "Now, really, I am a reasonable man, but—"

With both hands, Travis seized the vet's right hand and held it tightly, startling Keene. "Listen, Dr. Keene, please, let me try to explain. I know this is an unusual request. I know we must sound like a couple of lunatics to you, but we've got our reasons, and they're good ones. This is no ordinary dog, Dr. Keene. He saved my life—"

"And he saved mine, too," Nora said. "In a separate incident."

"And he brought us together," Travis said. "Without Einstein, we would never have met, never married, and we'd both be dead."

Astonished, Keene looked from one to the other. "You mean he saved your lives—literally? And in two separate incidents?"

"Literally," Nora said.

"And then brought you together?"

"Yes," Travis said. "Changed our lives in more ways than we can count or ever explain."

Held fast in Travis's hands, the vet looked at Nora, lowered his kind eyes to the wheezing retriever, shook his head, and said, "I'm a sucker for heroic dog stories. I'll want to hear this one, for sure."

"We'll tell you all about it," Nora promised. But, she thought, it'll be a carefully edited version.

"When I was five years old," James Keene said, "I was saved from drowning by a black labrador."

Nora remembered the beautiful black lab in the living room and wondered if it was actually a descendant of the animal that had saved Keene—or just a reminder of the great debt he owed to dogs.

"All right," Keene said, "you may stay."

"Thank you." Travis's voice cracked. "Thank you."

Freeing his hand from Travis, Keene said, "But it'll be at least forty-eight hours before we can be at all confident that Einstein will survive. It'll be a long haul."

"Forty-eight hours is nothing," Travis said. "Two nights of sleeping on the floor. We can handle that."

Keene said, "I have a hunch that, for you two, forty-eight hours is going to be an eternity, under the circumstances." He looked at his wristwatch and said, "Now, my assistant will arrive in about ten minutes, and shortly after that we'll open the office for morning hours. I can't have you underfoot in here while I'm seeing other patients. And you wouldn't want to wait in the patient lounge with a bunch of other anxious owners and sick animals; that would only depress you. You can wait in the living room, and when the office is closed late this afternoon, you can return here to be with Einstein."

"Can we peek in on him during the day?" Travis asked.

Smiling, Keene said, "All right. But just a peek."

Under Nora's hand, Einstein finally stopped shivering. Some of the tension went out of him, and he relaxed, as if he had heard they would be allowed to remain close by, and was immensely comforted.

The morning passed at an agonizingly slow pace. Dr. Keene's living room had a television set, books, and magazines, but neither Nora nor Travis could get interested in TV or reading.

Every half hour or so, they slipped down the hall, one at a time, and peeked in at Einstein. He never seemed worse, but he never seemed any better, either.

Keene came in once and said, "By the way, feel free to use the bathroom. and there's cold drinks in the refrigerator. Make coffee if you want." He smiled down at the black lab at his side. "And this fella is Pooka. He'll love you to death if you give him a chance."

Pooka was, indeed, one of the friendliest dogs Nora had ever seen. Without encouragement, he would roll over, play dead, sit up on his haunches, and then come snuffling around, tail wagging, to be rewarded with some petting and scratching.

All morning, Travis ignored the dog's pleas for affection, as if petting Pooka would in some way be a betrayal of Einstein and would insure Einstein's death of distemper.

However, Nora took comfort from the dog and gave it the attention it desired. She told herself that treating Pooka well would please the gods and that the gods would then look favorably upon Einstein. Her desperation produced in her a superstition just as fierce as—if different from—that which gripped her husband.

Travis paced. He sat on the edge of a chair, head bowed, his face in his hands. For long periods, he stood at one of the windows, staring out, not seeing the street that lay out there but some dark vision of his own. He blamed himself for what had happened, and the truth of the situation (which Nora recalled for him) did nothing to lessen his irrational sense of guilt.

Facing a window, hugging himself as if he were cold, Travis said quietly, "Do you think Keene saw the tattoo?"

"I don't know. Maybe not."

"Do you think there's been a description of Einstein circulated to vets? Will Keene know what the tattoo means?"

"Maybe not," she said. "Maybe we're too paranoid about this."

But after hearing from Garrison and learning of the lengths to which the government had gone to prevent him from getting a warning to them, they knew that an enormous and urgent search for the dog must be still under way. So there was no such thing as being "too paranoid."

From noon until two, Dr. Keene closed the office for lunch. He invited Nora and Travis to eat with him in the

431

big kitchen. He was a bachelor who knew how to take care of himself, and he had a freezer stocked with frozen entrées that he had prepared and packaged himself. He defrosted individually wrapped slabs of homemade lasagna and, with their help, made three salads. The food was good, but neither Nora nor Travis was able to eat much of it.

The more Nora knew of James Keene, the more she liked him. He was lighthearted in spite of his morose appearance, and his sense of humor ran toward self-deprecation. His love of animals was a light within that gave him a special glow. Dogs were his greatest love, and when he spoke of them his enthusiasm transformed his homely features and made of him a handsomer and quite appealing man.

The doctor told them of the black lab, King, that had saved him from drowning when he was a child, and he encouraged them to tell him how Einstein saved their lives. Travis recounted a colorful story about going hiking and almost walking into an injured and angry bear. He described how Einstein warned him off and then, when the half-mad bear gave chase, how Einstein challenged and repeatedly foiled the beast. Nora was able to tell a story closer to the truth: harassment by a sexual psychopath whose attack had been interrupted by Einstein and who had been held by the retriever until the police arrived.

Keene was impressed. "He really is a hero!"

Nora sensed that the stories about Einstein had so completely won the vet over that, if he *did* spot the tattoo and knew what it meant, he might conceivably put it out of his mind and might let them go in peace once Einstein was recovered. *If* Einstein recovered.

But as they were gathering up the dishes, Keene said, "Sam, I've been wondering why your wife calls you 'Travis'."

They were prepared for this. Since assuming new identities, they had decided that it was easier and safer for Nora to continue calling him Travis, rather than trying to use Sam all the time and then, at some crucial moment, slipping up. They could claim that Travis was a nickname she'd given him, that the origin was a private joke; with

432

winks at each other and foolish grins, they could imply there was something sexual about it, something much too embarrassing to explain further. That was how they handled Keene's question, but they were in no mood to wink and grin foolishly with any conviction, so Nora was not sure they carried it off. In fact she thought their nervous and inept performance might increase Keene's suspicions if he had any.

Just before afternoon office hours were to begin, Keene received a call from his assistant, who'd had a headache when she had gone to lunch, and who now reported that the headache had been complicated by an upset stomach. The vet was left to handle his patients alone, so Travis quickly volunteered his and Nora's services.

"We've got no veterinary training, of course. But we can handle any manual labor involved."

"Sure," Nora agreed, "and between us we've got one pretty good brain. We could do just about anything else you showed us how to do."

They spent the afternoon restraining recalcitrant cats and dogs and parrots and all sorts of other animals while Jim Keene treated them. There were bandages to be laid out, medicines to be retrieved from the cabinets, instruments to be washed and sterilized, fees to be collected and receipts written. Some pets, afflicted with vomiting and diarrhea, left messes to be cleaned up, but Travis and Nora tended to those unpleasantnesses as uncomplainingly and unhesitatingly as they performed other tasks.

They had two motives, the first of which was that, by assisting Keene, they had a chance to be in the surgery with Einstein throughout the afternoon. Between chores, they stole a few moments to pet the retriever, speak a few encouraging words to him, and reassure themselves that he was getting no worse. The downside of being around Einstein continuously was that they could see, to their dismay, that he did not seem to be getting any *better*, either.

433

Their other purpose was to further ingratiate themselves with the vet, to give him a reason to be beholden to them, so he would not reconsider his decision to allow them to stay the night.

The patient load was far greater than usual, Keene said, and they were not able to close the office until after six o'clock. Weariness—and the labor they shared—generated a warm feeling of camaraderie. As they made and ate dinner together, Jim Keene entertained them with a treasure of amusing animal stories culled from his experiences, and they were almost as comfortable and friendly as they would have been if they had known the vet for months instead of less than one day.

Keene prepared the guest bedroom for them, and provided a few blankets with which to make a crude bed on the floor of the surgery. Travis and Nora would sleep in the real bed in shifts, each spending half the night on the floor with Einstein.

Travis had the first shift, from ten o'clock until three in the morning. Only one light was left on in the far corner of the surgery, and Travis alternately sat and stretched out on the piled blankets in the shadows where Einstein lay.

Sometimes, Einstein slept, and the sound of his breathing was more normal, less frightening. But sometimes he was awake, and his respiration was horribly labored, and he whimpered in pain and—Travis somehow knew—in fear. When Einstein was awake, Travis talked to him, reminiscing about experiences they had shared, the many good moments and happy times over the past six months, and the retriever seemed to be at least slightly soothed by Travis's voice.

Unable to move at all, the dog was of necessity incontinent. A couple of times he peed on the plastic-covered mattress. With no distaste whatsoever, with the same tenderness and compassion a father might show in caring for a gravely ill child, Travis cleaned up. In a curious way, Travis was even pleased by the mess because, every time Einstein peed, it was proof that he still lived, still functioned, in some ways, as normally as ever.

434

Rainsqualls came and went during the night. The sound of rain on the roof was mournful, like funeral drums.

Twice during the first shift, Jim Keene appeared in pajamas and a robe. The first time, he examined Einstein carefully and changed his IV bottle. Later, he administered an injection after the examination. On both occasions, he assured Travis that right now they did not have to see signs of improvement to be encouraged; right now, it was good enough that there were no indications of deterioration in the dog's condition.

Frequently during the night, Travis wandered to the other end of the surgery and read the words of a simply framed scroll that hung above the scrub sink:

TRIBUTE TO A DOG

The one absolutely unselfish friend that man can have in this selfish world, the one that never deserts him, the one that never proves ungrateful or treacherous, is his dog. A man's dog stands by him in prosperity and in poverty, in health and in sickness. He will sleep on the cold ground, where the wintry winds blow and the snow drives fiercely, if only he may be near his master's side. He will kiss the hand that has no food to offer; he will lick the wounds and sores that come in encounter with the roughness of the world. He guards the sleep of his pauper master as if he were a prince. When all other friends desert, he remains. When riches take wing and reputation falls to pieces, he is as constant in his love as the sun in its journey through the heavens.
—Senator George Vest, 1870

Each time he read the tribute, Travis was filled anew with wonder at Einstein's existence. What fantasy of children was more common than that their dogs were fully as perceptive and wise and clever as any adult? What gift from God would more delight a young mind than to have the family dog prove able to communicate on a human level and to share triumphs and tragedies with full understanding of their meaning and importance? What miracle could bring more joy, more respect for the mysteries of nature,

435

more sheer exuberance over the unanticipated wonders of life? Somehow, in the very idea of a dog's personality *and* human intelligence combined in a single creature, one had a hope of a species at once as gifted as humankind but more noble and worthy. And what fantasy of adults was more common than that, one day, another intelligent species would be found to share the vast, cold universe and, by sharing it, would at last provide some relief from our race's unspeakable loneliness and sense of quiet desperation?

And what other loss could be more devastating than the loss of Einstein, this first hopeful evidence that humankind carried within it the seeds not merely of greatness but of godhood?

These thoughts, which Travis could not suppress, shook him and drew from him a thick sob of grief. Damning himself for being an emotional basket case, he went into the downstairs hall, where Einstein would not be aware of—and perhaps be frightened by—his tears.

Nora relieved him at three in the morning. She had to insist that he go upstairs, for he was reluctant to leave Keene's surgery.

Exhausted but protesting that he would not sleep, Travis tumbled into bed and slept.

He dreamed of being pursued by a yellow-eyed thing with wicked talons and foreshortened alligator jaws. He was trying to protect Einstein and Nora, pushing them in front of him, encouraging them to run, run, run. But somehow the monster got around Travis and tore Einstein to pieces, then savaged Nora—it was the Cornell Curse, which could not be avoided by a simple change of name to Samuel Hyatt—and at last Travis stopped running and fell to his knees and lowered his head because, having failed Nora and the dog, he wanted to die, and he heard the thing approaching—*click-click-click*—and he was afraid but he also welcomed the death that it promised—

Nora woke him shortly before five in the morning.

"Einstein," she said urgently. "He's having convulsions."

When Nora led Travis into the white-walled surgery, Jim Keene was crouched over Einstein, ministering to him. They could do nothing but stay out of the vet's way, give him room to work.

She and Travis held each other.

After a few minutes, the vet stood up. He looked worried, and he did not make his usual effort to smile or try to lift their hopes. "I've given him additional anticonvulsants. I think ... he'll be all right now."

"Has he gone into second stage?" Travis asked.

"Maybe not," Keene said.

"Could he be having convulsions and still be in first stage?"

"It's possible," Keene said.

"But not likely."

"Not likely," Keene said. "But ... not impossible."

Second-stage distemper, Nora thought miserably.

She held Travis tighter than ever.

Second stage. Brain involvement. Encephalitis. Chorea. Brain damage. *Brain damage*.

Travis would not return to bed. He remained in the surgery with Nora and Einstein the rest of that night.

They turned on another light, brightening the room somewhat but not enough to bother Einstein, and they watched him closely for signs that the distemper had progressed to the second stage: the jerking and twitching and chewing movements of which Jim Keene had spoken.

Travis was unable to extract any hope from the fact that no such symptoms were exhibited. Even if Einstein was in the first stage of the disease and remained there, he appeared to be dying.

*   *   *

The next day, Friday, December 3, Jim Keene's assistant was still too sick to come to work, so Nora and Travis helped out again.

By lunchtime, Einstein's fever had not fallen. His eyes and nose continued to ooze a clear though yellowish fluid. His breathing was slightly less labored, but in her despair Nora wondered if the dog's respiration only sounded easier because he was not making as great an effort to breathe and was, in fact, beginning to give up.

She could not eat even a bite of lunch. She washed and ironed both Travis's clothes and her own, while they sat around in two of Jim Keene's spare bathrobes, which were too big for them.

That afternoon, the office was busy again. Nora and Travis were kept in constant motion, and Nora was glad to be overworked.

At four-forty, a time that she would never forget for as long as she lived, just after they finished helping Jim deal with a difficult Irish setter, Einstein yipped twice from his bed in the corner. Nora and Travis turned, both gasping, both expecting the worst, for this was the first sound other than whimpers that Einstein had made since his arrival at the surgery. But the retriever had lifted his head—the first time he'd had the strength to lift it—and was blinking at them; he looked around curiously, as if to ask where on earth he was.

Jim knelt beside the dog and, while Travis and Nora crouched expectantly behind him, he thoroughly examined Einstein. "Look at his eyes. They're slightly milky but not at all like they were, and they've stopped actively leaking." With a damp cloth, he cleaned the crusted fur beneath Einstein's eyes and wiped off his nose; the nostrils no longer bubbled with fresh excretions. With a rectal thermometer he took Einstein's temperature and, reading it, said, "Falling. Down two full degrees."

"Thank God," Travis said.

And Nora discovered that her eyes were filling with tears again.

Jim said, "He's not out of the woods yet. His heartbeat

is more regular, less accelerated, though still not good. Nora, get one of those dishes over there and fill it with some water."

Nora returned from the sink a moment later and put the dish down on the floor, at the vet's side.

Jim pushed it close to Einstein. "What do you think, fella?"

Einstein raised his head off the mattress again and stared at the dish. His lolling tongue looked dry and was coated with a gummy substance. He whined and licked his chops.

"Maybe," Travis said, "if we help him—"

"No," Jim Keene said. "Let him consider it. He'll know if he feels up to it. We don't want to force water that's going to make him vomit again. He'll know by instinct if the time is right."

With some groaning and wheezing, Einstein shifted on the foam mattress, rolling off his side, half onto his belly. He put his nose to the dish, sniffed the water, put his tongue to it tentatively, liked the first taste, had another, and drank a third of it before sighing and lying down again.

Stroking the retriever, Jim Keene said, "I'd be very surprised if he doesn't recover, fully recover, in time."

In time.

That phrase bothered Travis.

How much time would Einstein require for a full recovery? When The Outsider finally arrived, they would all be better off if Einstein was healthy and if all of his senses were functioning sharply. The infrared alarms notwithstanding, Einstein was their primary early-warning system.

After the last patient left at five-thirty, Jim Keene slipped out for half an hour on a mysterious errand, and when he returned he had a bottle of champagne. "I'm not much of a drinking man, but certain occasions demand a nip or two."

Nora had pledged to drink nothing during her pregnancy,

but even the most solemn pledge could be stretched under these circumstances.

They got glasses and drank in the surgery, toasting Einstein, who watched them for a few minutes but, exhausted, soon fell asleep.

"But a natural sleep," Jim noted. "Not induced with sedatives."

Travis said, "How long will he need to recover?"

"To shake off distemper— a few more days, a week. I'd like to keep him here two more days, anyway. You could go home now, if you want, but you're also welcome to stay. You've been quite a help."

"We'll stay," Nora said at once.

"But after the distemper is beaten," Travis said, "he's going to be weak, isn't he?"

"At first, very weak," Jim said. "But gradually he'll get most if not all of his old strength back. I'm sure now that he never went into second-stage distemper, in spite of the convulsions. So perhaps by the first of the year he'll be his old self, and there should be no lasting infirmities, no palsied shaking or anything like that."

The first of the year.

Travis hoped that would be soon enough.

Again, Nora and Travis split the night into two shifts. Travis took the first watch, and she relieved him in the surgery at three o'clock in the morning.

Fog had seethed into Carmel. It roiled at the windows, softly insistent.

Einstein was sleeping when Nora arrived, and she said, "Has he been awake much?"

"Yeah," Travis said. "Now and then."

"Have you ... talked to him?"

"Yeah."

"Well?"

Travis's face was lined, haggard, and his expression was

440

grave. "I've asked him questions that can be answered with a yes or no."

"And?"

"He doesn't answer them. He just blinks at me, or yawns, or he goes back to sleep."

"He's very tired yet," she said, desperately hoping that was the explanation for the retriever's uncommunicative behavior. "He doesn't have the strength even for questions and answers."

Pale and obviously depressed, Travis said, "Maybe. I don't know ... but I think ... he seems ... confused."

"He hasn't shaken the disease yet," she said. "He's still in the grip of it, beating the damn stuff, but still in its grip. He's bound to be a little muddleheaded for a while yet."

"Confused," Travis repeated.

"It'll pass."

"Yeah," he said. "Yeah, it'll pass."

But he sounded as if he believed that Einstein would never be the same again.

Nora knew what Travis must be thinking: it was the Cornell Curse again, which he professed not to believe in but which he still feared in his heart of hearts. Everyone he loved was doomed to suffer and die young. Everyone he cared about was torn from him.

That was all nonsense, of course, and Nora did not believe in it for a moment. But she knew how hard it was to shake off the past, to face only toward the future, and she sympathized with his inability to be optimistic just now. She also knew there was nothing she could do for him to haul him out of that pit of private anguish—nothing except kiss him, hold him for a moment, then send him off to bed to get some sleep.

When Travis was gone, Nora sat on the floor beside Einstein and said, "There're some things I have to tell you, fur face. I guess you're asleep and can't hear me, and maybe even if you were awake you wouldn't understand what I'm saying. Maybe you'll never again understand, which is why I want to say these things now, while there's at least still *hope* that your mind's intact."

441

She paused and took a deep breath and looked around at the still surgery, where the dim lights gleamed in the stainless-steel fixtures and in the glass of the enameled cabinets. It was a lonely place at three-thirty in the morning.

Einstein's breath came and went with a soft hiss, an occasional rattle. He didn't stir. Not even his tail moved.

"I thought of you as my guardian, Einstein. That's what I called you once, when you saved me from Arthur Streck. My guardian. You not only rescued me from that awful man—you also saved me from loneliness and terrible despair. And you saved Travis from the darkness within him, brought us together, and in a hundred other ways you were as perfect as any guardian angel might hope to be. In that good, pure heart of yours, you never asked for or wanted anything in return for all you did. Some Milk-Bones once in a while, a bit of chocolate now and then. But you'd have done it all even if you'd been fed nothing but Dog Chow. You did it because you love, and being loved in return was reward enough. And by just being what you are, fur face, you taught me a great lesson, a lesson I can't easily put into words ..."

For a while, silent and unable to speak, she sat in the shadows beside her friend, her child, her teacher, her guardian.

"But damn it," she said at last, "I've *got* to find words because maybe this is the last time I can even pretend you're able to understand them. It's like this ... you taught me that I'm *your* guardian, too, that I'm Travis's guardian, and that he is my guardian and yours. We have a responsibility to stand watch over one another, we are watchers, all of us, watchers guarding against the darkness. You've taught me that we're all needed, even those who sometimes think we're worthless, plain, and dull. If we love and allow ourselves to be loved ... well, a person who loves is the most precious thing in the world, worth all the fortunes that ever were. That's what you've taught me, fur face, and because of you I'll never be the same."

442

The rest of the long night, Einstein lay motionless, lost in a deep sleep.

Saturday, Jim Keene kept hours only in the morning. At noon he locked the office entrance at the side of his big, cozy house.

During the morning, Einstein had exhibited encouraging signs of recovery. He drank more water and spent some time on his belly instead of lying limply on his side. Head raised, he looked around with interest at the activity in the vet's surgery. He even slurped up a raw-egg-and-gravy mixture that Jim put in front of him, downing half the contents of the dish, and he did not regurgitate what he had eaten. He was now entirely off intravenous fluids.

But he still dozed a lot. And his responses to Travis and Nora were only those of an ordinary dog.

After lunch, as they were sitting with Jim at the kitchen table, having a final cup of coffee, the vet sighed and said, "Well, I don't see how this can be put off any longer." From an inner pocket of his old, well-worn corduroy jacket, he withdrew a folded sheet of paper and put it on the table in front of Travis.

For a moment, Nora thought it was the bill for his services. But when Travis unfolded the paper, she saw that it was a wanted flyer put out by the people looking for Einstein.

Travis's shoulders sagged.

Feeling as if her heart had begun to sink down through her body, Nora moved closer to Travis so they could read the bulletin together. It was dated last week. In addition to a description of Einstein that included the three-number tattoo in his ear, the flyer stated the dog would most likely be found in the possession of a man named Travis Cornell and his wife, Nora, who might be living under different names. Descriptions—and photographs—of Nora and Travis were at the bottom of the sheet.

"How long have you known?" Travis asked.

443

Jim Keene said, "Within an hour after I first saw him, Thursday morning. I've been getting weekly updates of that bulletin for six months—and I've had three follow-up calls from the Federal Cancer Institute to make sure I'll remember to examine any golden retriever for a lab tattoo and report it at once."

"And have you reported him?" Nora asked.

"Not yet. Didn't see any point arguing about it until we saw whether he was going to pull through."

Travis said, "Will you report him now?"

His hound-dog face settling into an expression that was even more glum than usual, Jim Keene said, "According to the Cancer Institute, this dog was at the very center of extremely important experiments that might lead to a cancer cure. Says there that millions of dollars of research money will have been spent for nothing if the dog isn't found and returned to the lab to complete their studies."

"It's all lies," Travis said.

"Let me make one thing very clear to you," Jim said, leaning forward in his chair and folding his large hands around his coffee cup. "I'm an animal lover to the bone. I've dedicated my life to animals. And I love dogs more than anything else. But I'm afraid I don't have a lot of sympathy for people who believe that we should stop all animal experimentation, people who think medical advancements that help save human lives are not worth harming one guinea pig, one cat, one dog. People who raid labs and steal animals, ruining years of important research ... they make me want to spit. It's good and right to love life, to dearly love it in all its most humble forms. But these people don't love life—they *revere* it, which is a pagan and ignorant and perhaps even savage attitude."

"This isn't like that," Nora said. "Einstein was never used in cancer research. That's just a cover story. The Cancer Institute isn't hunting for Einstein. It's the National Security Agency that wants him." She looked at Travis and said, "Well, what do we do now?"

Travis smiled grimly, and said, "Well, I sure can't kill Jim here to stop him—"

444

The vet looked startled.

"So I guess we've got to persuade him," Travis finished.

"The truth?" Nora asked.

Travis stared at Jim Keene for a long time, and at last said, "Yeah. The truth. It's the only thing that might convince him to throw that damn wanted poster in the trash."

Taking a deep breath, Nora said, "Jim, Einstein is as smart as you or me or Travis."

"Smarter, I sometimes think," Travis said.

The vet stared at them, uncomprehending.

"Let's make another pot of coffee," Nora said. "This is going to be a long long afternoon."

Hours later, at ten minutes past five, Saturday afternoon, Nora and Travis and Jim Keene crowded in front of the mattress on which Einstein lay.

The dog had just taken a few more ounces of water. He looked at them with interest, too.

Travis tried to decide if those large brown eyes still had the strange depth, uncanny alertness, and undoglike awareness that he had seen in them so many times before. Damn. He was not sure—and his uncertainty scared him.

Jim examined Einstein, noting aloud that his eyes were clearer, almost normal, and that his temperature was still falling. "Heart's sounding a little better, too."

Worn out by the ten-minute examination, Einstein flopped onto his side and issued a long weary sigh. In a moment, he dozed again.

The vet said, "He sure doesn't seem much like a genius dog."

"He's still sick," Nora said. "All he needs is a little more time to recover, and he'll be able to show you that everything we've said is true."

"When do you think he'll be on his feet?" Travis asked.

Jim thought about that, then said, "Maybe tomorrow. He'll be very shaky at first, but maybe tomorrow. We'll just have to see."

"When he's on his feet," Travis said, "when he's got his sense of balance back and is interested in moving around, that ought to indicate he's clearer in his head, too. So when he's up and about—that's when we'll give him a test to prove to you how smart he is."

"Fair enough," Jim said.

"And if he proves it," Nora said, "you'll not turn him in?"

"Turn him in to people who'd create this Outsider you've told me about? Turn him in to the liars who cooked up that baloney wanted flyer? Nora, what sort of man do you take me for?"

Nora said, "A good man."

Twenty-four hours later, on Sunday evening, in Jim Keene's surgery, Einstein was tottering around as if he were a little old four-legged man.

Nora scooted along the floor on her knees beside him, telling him what a fine and brave fellow he was, quietly encouraging him to keep going. Every step he took thrilled her as if he were her own baby learning to walk. But what thrilled her more was the look he gave her a few times: it was a look that seemed to express chagrin at his infirmity, but there was also a sense of humor in it, as if he were saying, *Hey, Nora, am I a spectacle—or what? Isn't this just plain ridiculous?*

Saturday night he had eaten a little solid food, and all day Sunday he had nibbled at easily digestible vittles that the vet provided. He was drinking well, and the most encouraging sign of improvement was his insistence on going outside to make his toilet. He could not stay on his feet for long periods of time, and once in a while he wobbled and plopped backwards on his butt; however, he did not bump into walls or walk in circles.

Yesterday, Nora had gone shopping and had returned with three Scrabble games. Now, Travis had separated the lettered tiles into twenty-six piles at one end of the surgery, where there was a lot of open floor space.

"We're ready," Jim Keene said. He was sitting on the floor with Travis, his legs drawn up under him Indian-style.

Pooka was lying at his master's side, watching with baffled eyes.

Nora led Einstein back across the room to the Scrabble tiles. Taking his head in her hands, looking straight into his eyes, she said, "Okay, fur face. Let's prove to Dr. Jim that you're not just some pathetic lab animal involved in cancer tests. Let's show him what you *really* are and prove to him what those nasty people really want you for."

She tried to believe that she saw the old awareness in the retriever's dark gaze.

With evident nervousness and fear, Travis said, "Who asks the first question?"

"I will," Nora said unhesitatingly. To Einstein, she said, "How's the fiddle?"

They had told Jim Keene about the message that Travis had found the morning Einstein had been so very ill—FIDDLE BROKE—so the vet understood what Nora was asking.

Einstein blinked at her, then looked at the letters, blinked at her again, sniffed the letters, and she was getting a sick feeling in her stomach when, suddenly, he began to choose tiles and push them around with his nose.

FIDDLE JUST OUT OF TUNE.

Travis shuddered as if the dread he had contained was a powerful electric charge that had leapt out of him in an instant. He said, "Thank God, thank you God," and he laughed with delight.

"Holy shit," Jim Keene said.

Pooka raised his head very high and pricked his ears, aware that something important was happening but not sure what it was.

Her heart swelling with relief and excitement and love, Nora returned the letters to their separate piles and said, "Einstein, who is your master? Tell us his name."

The retriever looked at her, at Travis, then made a considered reply.

NO MASTER. FRIENDS.

Travis laughed. "By God, I'll settle for that! No one can be his master, but anyone should be damned proud to be his friend."

Funny—this proof of Einstein's undamaged intellect made Travis laugh with delight, the first laughter of which he had been capable in days, but it made Nora weep with relief.

Jim Keene looked on in wide-eyed wonder, grinning stupidly. He said, "I feel like a child who's sneaked downstairs on Christmas Eve and actually seen the real Santa Claus putting gifts under the tree."

"My turn," Travis said, sliding forward and putting a hand on Einstein's head, patting him. "Jim just mentioned Christmas, and it's not far away. Twenty days from now. So tell me, Einstein, what would you most like to have Santa bring you?"

Twice Einstein started to line up the lettered tiles, but both times he had second thoughts and disarranged them. He tottered and thumped down on his butt, looked around sheepishly, saw that they were all expectant, got up again, and this time produced a three-word request for Santa.

MICKEY MOUSE VIDEOS.

They didn't get to bed until two in the morning because Jim Keene was intoxicated, not drunk from beer or wine or whiskey but from sheer joy over Einstein's intelligence. "Like a man's, yes, but still the dog, still the dog, wonderfully like, yet wonderfully different from, a man's thinking, based on what little I've seen." But Jim did not press for more than a dozen examples of the dog's wit, and he was the first to say that they must not tire their patient. Still, he was electrified, so excited he could barely contain himself. Travis would not have been too surprised if the vet had suddenly just exploded.

In the kitchen, Jim pleaded with them to retell stories about Einstein: the *Modern Bride* business in Solvang; the way he had taken it upon himself to add cold water to the first hot bath that Travis had given him; and many more. Jim actually retold some of the same stories himself, almost as if Travis and Nora had never heard them, but they were happy to indulge him.

With a flourish, he snatched the wanted flyer off the table, struck a kitchen match, and burned the sheet in the sink. He washed the ashes down the drain. "To hell with the small minds who'd keep a creature like that locked up to be poked and prodded and studied. They might've had the genius to make Einstein, but they don't understand the meaning of what they themselves have done. They don't understand the greatness of it, because if they did they wouldn't want to cage him."

At last, when Jim Keene reluctantly agreed that they were all in need of sleep, Travis carried Einstein (already sleeping) up to the guest room. They made a blanket-cushioned place for him on the floor next to the bed.

In the dark, under the covers, with Einstein's soft snoring to comfort them, Travis and Nora held each other.

She said, "Everything's going to be all right now."

"There's still some trouble coming," he said. He felt as if Einstein's recovery had weakened the curse of untimely death that had followed him all of his life. But he was not ready to hope that the curse had been banished altogether. The Outsider was still out there somewhere ... coming.

TEN

1

On Tuesday afternoon, December 7, when they took Einstein home, Jim Keene was reluctant to let them go. He followed them out to the pickup and stood at the driver's window, restating the treatment that must be continued for the next couple of weeks, reminding them that he wanted to see Einstein once a week for the rest of the month, and urging them to visit him not only for the dog's medical care but for drinks, dinner, conversation.

Travis knew the vet was trying to say he wanted to remain a part of Einstein's life, wanted to participate in the magic of it. "Jim, believe me, we'll be back. And before Christmas, you'll have to come out to our place, spend the day with us."

"I'd like that."

"So would we," Travis said sincerely.

On the drive home, Nora held Einstein in her lap, wrapped in a blanket once more. He still did not have his old appetite, and he was weak. His immune system had taken severe punishment, so he would be more than usually susceptible to illness for a while. He was to be kept in the house as much as possible and pampered until he had regained his previous vigor—probably after the first of the year, according to Jim Keene.

The bruised and swollen sky bulged with saturated dark clouds. The Pacific Ocean was so hard and gray that it did not appear to be water but looked more like billions of shards and slabs of slate being continuously agitated by some geological upheaval in the earth below.

The bleak weather could not dampen their high spirits. Nora was beaming, and Travis found himself whistling. Einstein studied the scenery with great interest, clearly treasuring even the somber beauty of this nearly colorless winter day. Perhaps he had never expected to see the world outside Jim Keene's office again, in which case even a sea of jumbled stone and a contusive sky were precious sights.

When they reached home, Travis left Nora in the pickup with the retriever and entered the house alone, by the back door, carrying the .38 pistol they kept in the truck. In the kitchen, where the lights had been on ever since their hasty departure last week, he immediately took an Uzi automatic pistol from its hiding place in a cabinet, and put the lighter gun aside. He proceeded cautiously from room to room, looking behind every large item of furniture and in every closet.

He saw no signs of burglary, and he expected none. This rural area was relatively crime-free. You could leave your door unlocked for days at a time without risking thieves who would take everything down to the wallpaper.

The Outsider, not a burglar, worried him.

The house was deserted.

Travis checked the barn, too, before driving the pickup inside, but it was also safe.

In the house, Nora put Einstein down and pulled the blanket off him. He tottered around the kitchen, sniffing at things. In the living room he looked at the cold fireplace and inspected his page-turning machine.

He returned to the kitchen pantry, clicked on the light with his foot pedal, and pawed letters out of the Lucite tubes.

HOME.

Stooping beside the dog, Travis said, "It's sure good to be here, isn't it?"

452

Einstein nuzzled Travis's throat and licked his neck. The golden coat was fluffy and smelled clean because Jim Keene had given the dog a bath, in his surgery, under carefully controlled conditions. But as fluffy and fresh as he was, Einstein still did not look himself; he seemed tired, and he was thinner, too, having lost a few pounds in less than a week.

Pawing out more letters, Einstein spelled the same word again, as if to emphasize his pleasure: HOME.

Standing at the pantry door, Nora said, "Home is where the heart is, and there's plenty of heart in this one. Hey, let's have an early dinner and eat it in the living room while we run the videotape of *Mickey's Christmas Carol*. Would you like that?"

Einstein wagged his tail vigorously.

Travis said, "Do you think you could handle your favorite food—a few weenies for dinner?"

Einstein licked his chops. He dispensed more letters, with which he expressed his enthusiastic approval of Travis's suggestion.

HOME IS WHERE THE WEENIES ARE.

When Travis woke in the middle of the night, Einstein was at the bedroom window, on his hind feet with his forepaws braced on the sill. He was barely visible in the second-hand glow of the night-light in the adjoining bathroom. The interior shutter was bolted over the window, so the dog had no view of the front yard. But perhaps, for getting a fix on The Outsider, sight was the sense on which he least depended.

"Something out there, boy?" Travis asked quietly, not wanting to wake Nora unnecessarily.

Einstein dropped from the window, padded to Travis's side of the bed, and put his head up on the mattress.

Petting the dog, Travis whispered, "Is it coming?"

Replying with only a cryptic mewl, Einstein settled down on the floor beside the bed and went to sleep again.

In a few minutes, Travis slept, too.

He woke again near dawn to find Nora sitting on the edge of the bed, petting Einstein. "Go back to sleep," she told Travis.

"What's wrong?"

"Nothing," she whispered drowsily. "I woke up and saw him at the window, but it's nothing. Go to sleep."

He did manage to fall asleep a third time, but he dreamed that The Outsider had been smart enough to learn how to use tools during its six-month-long pursuit of Einstein and now, yellow eyes gleaming, it was smashing its way through the bedroom shutters with an ax.

2

They gave Einstein his medicines on schedule, and he swallowed his pills obediently. They explained to him that he needed to eat well in order to regain his strength. He tried, but his appetite was returning only slowly. He would need a few weeks to regain the pounds he had lost and to recover his old vitality. But day by day his improvement was perceptible.

By Friday, December 10, Einstein seemed strong enough to risk a short walk outside. He still wobbled a little now and then, but he no longer tottered with every step. He'd had all of his shots at the veterinary clinic; there was no chance of picking up rabies on top of the distemper he'd just beaten.

The weather was milder than it had been in recent weeks, with temperatures in the low sixties and no wind. The scattered clouds were white, and the sun, when not hidden, laid a warm life-giving caress on the skin.

Einstein accompanied Travis on an inspection tour of the infrared sensors around the house and the nitrous-oxide tanks in the barn. They moved a bit more slowly than the last time they had walked this line together, but Einstein seemed to enjoy being back on duty.

Nora was in her studio, working diligently on a new painting: a portrait of Einstein. He was not aware that he was the subject of her latest canvas. The picture was to be one of his Christmas gifts and would, once opened on the holiday, be hung above the fireplace in the living room.

When Travis and Einstein came out of the barn, into the yard, Travis said, "Is it getting closer?"

Upon being asked that question, Einstein went through his usual routine, though with less exertion, less sniffing of the air, and less study of the shadowy forest around them. Returning to Travis, the dog whined anxiously.

"Is it out there?" Travis asked.

Einstein gave no answer. He merely surveyed the woods again—puzzled.

"Is it still coming?" Travis asked.

The dog did not reply.

"Is it nearer than it was?"

Einstein padded in a circle, sniffed the ground, sniffed the air, cocked his head one way and then the other. Finally he returned to the house and stood at the door, looking at Travis, waiting patiently.

Inside, Einstein went directly to the pantry.

MUZZY.

Travis stared at the word on the floor, "Muzzy?"

Einstein dispensed more letters and nosed them into place.

MUFFLED. FUZZY.

"Are you talking about your ability to sense The Outsider?"

A quick tail wag! *Yes*.

"You can't sense it any more?"

One bark: *No*.

"Do you think ... it's dead?"

DON'T KNOW.

"Or maybe this sixth sense of yours doesn't work when you're sick—or debilitated like you are now."

MAYBE.

Gathering up the lettered tiles and sorting them into the tubes, Travis thought for a minute. Bad thoughts.

Unnerving thoughts. They had an alarm system around the property, yes, but to some extent they were depending on Einstein for an early warning. Travis should have felt comfortable with the precautions he had taken and with his own abilities, as a former Delta Force man, to exterminate The Outsider. But he was tormented by the feeling that he had overlooked a hole in their defenses and that, come the crisis, he would need Einstein's full powers and strength to help him deal with the unexpected.

"You're going to have to get well as fast as you can," he told the retriever. "You're going to have to try to eat even when you have no real appetite. You're going to have to sleep as much as you can, give your body a chance to knit up, and don't spend half the night at the windows, worrying."

CHICKEN SOUP.

Laughing, Travis said, "Might as well try that, too."

A BOILERMAKER KILLS GERMS DEAD.

"Where'd you get that idea?"

BOOK. WHAT'S BOILERMAKER?

Travis said, "A shot of whiskey dropped into a glass of beer."

Einstein considered that for a moment.

KILL GERMS BUT BECOME ALCOHOLIC.

Travis laughed and ruffled Einstein's coat. "You're a regular comedian, fur face."

MAYBE I SHOULD PLAY VEGAS.

"I bet you could."

HEADLINER.

"You certainly would be."

ME AND PIA ZADORA.

He hugged the dog, and they sat in the pantry laughing, each in his own way.

In spite of the joking, Travis knew that Einstein was deeply troubled by the loss of his ability to sense The Outsider. The jokes were a defensive mechanism, a way to hold off fear.

That afternoon, exhausted from their short walk around the house, Einstein slept while Nora painted feverishly in her studio. Travis sat by a front window, staring out at the woods, repeatedly going over the defenses in his mind, looking for a hole.

On Sunday, December 12, Jim Keene came out to their place in the afternoon and stayed for dinner. He examined Einstein and was pleased with the dog's improvement.

"Seems slow to us," Nora said fretfully.

"I told you, it'll take time," Jim said.

He made a couple of changes in Einstein's medication and left new bottles of pills.

Einstein had fun demonstrating his page-turning machine and his letter-dispensing device in the pantry. He graciously accepted praise for his ability to hold a pencil in his teeth and use it to operate the television and the videotape recorder without bothering Nora and Travis for help.

Nora was at first surprised that the veterinarian looked less sad-eyed and sorrowful than she remembered. But she decided his face was the same; the only thing that had changed was her perception of him. Now that she knew him better, now that he was a friend of the first rank, she saw not only the glum features nature had given him but the kindness and humor beneath his somber surface.

Over dinner, Jim said, "I've been doing a little research into tattooing—to see if maybe I can remove the numbers in his ear."

Einstein had been lying on the floor nearby, listening to their conversation. He got to his feet, wobbled a moment, then hurried to the kitchen table and jumped into one of the empty chairs. He sat very erect and stared at Jim expectantly.

"Well," the vet said, putting down a forkful of curried chicken that he'd lifted halfway to his mouth, "most but not all tattoos can be eradicated. If I know what sort of ink was used and by what method it was embedded under the skin, I might be able to erase it."

"That would be terrific," Nora said. "Then even if they found us and tried to take Einstein back, they couldn't prove he's the dog they lost."

"There'd still be traces of the tattoo that would show up under close inspection," Travis said. "Under a magnifying glass."

Einstein looked from Travis to Jim Keene as if to say, *Yeah, what about that?*

"Most labs just tag research animals," Jim said. "Of those that tattoo, there're a couple of different standard inks used. I might be able to remove it and leave no trace except a natural-looking mottling of the flesh. Microscopic examination wouldn't reveal traces of the ink, not a hint of the numbers. It's a small tattoo, after all, which makes the job easier. I'm still researching techniques, but in a few weeks we might try it—if Einstein doesn't mind some discomfort."

The retriever left the table and padded into the pantry. They could hear the pumping of the letter-dispensing pedals.

Nora went to see what message Einstein was composing.

DON'T WANT TO BE BRANDED. AM NOT A COW.

His desire to be free of the tattoo went deeper than Nora had thought. He wanted the mark removed in order to escape identification by the people at the lab. But evidently he also hated carrying those three numbers in his ear because they marked him as mere property, a condition that was an affront to his dignity and a violation of his rights as an intelligent creature.

FREEDOM.

"Yes," Nora said respectfully, putting a hand on his head, "I do understand. You are a ... a *person*, and a person with" —this was the first time she had thought of this aspect of the situation—"a soul."

Was it blasphemous to think Einstein had a soul? No. She did not think blasphemy entered into it. Man had made the dog; however, if there was a God, He obviously approved of Einstein—not least of all because Einstein's ability to differentiate right from wrong, his ability to love,

458

his courage, and his selflessness made him closer to the image of God than were many human beings who walked the earth.

"Freedom," she said. "If you've got a soul—and I know you do—then you were born with free will and the right to self-determination. The number in your ear is an insult, and we'll get rid of it."

After dinner, Einstein clearly wanted to monitor—and participate—in the conversation, but he ran out of energy and slept by the fire.

Over a short brandy and coffee, Jim Keene listened as Travis outlined their defenses against The Outsider. Encouraged to find holes in their preparations, the vet could think of nothing except the vulnerability of their power supply. "If the thing was smart enough to bring down the line that runs in from the main highway, it could plunge you into darkness in the middle of the night and render your alarm useless. And without power those tricky mechanisms in the barn wouldn't slam the door behind the beast or release the nitrous oxide."

Nora and Travis took him downstairs, into the half-basement under the rear of the house, to show him the emergency generator. It was powered by a forty-gallon tank of gasoline buried in the yard, and it would restore electricity to the house and barn and alarm system after only a ten-second delay following the loss of the main supply.

"As far as I can see," Jim said, "you've thought of everything."

"I think we have, too," Nora said.

But Travis scowled. "I wonder."

On Wednesday, December 22, they drove into Carmel. Leaving Einstein with Jim Keene, they spent the day buying Christmas gifts, decorations for the house, ornaments for a tree, and the tree itself.

With the threat of The Outsider moving inexorably closer

to them, it seemed almost frivolous to make plans for the holiday. But Travis said, "Life is short. You never know how much time you've got left, so you can't let Christmas slide by without celebrating, no matter what. Besides, my Christmases haven't been so terrific these last few years. I intend to make up for that."

"Aunt Violet didn't believe in making an event of Christmas. She didn't believe in exchanging gifts or putting up a tree."

"She didn't believe in *life*," Travis said. "And that's just one more reason to do this Christmas up right. It'll be your first good one, as well as Einstein's first."

Starting next year, Nora thought, there'll be a baby in the house with which to share Christmas, and won't *that* be a hoot!

Aside from suffering a little mild morning sickness and having put on a couple of pounds, she'd not yet shown any signs of pregnancy. Her belly was still flat, and Dr. Weingold said that, considering her body type, she had a chance of being one of those women whose abdomen underwent only moderate distension. She hoped she was lucky in that regard because, after the birth, getting back into shape would be a lot easier. Of course, the baby was not due for six months yet, which gave her plenty of time to get as big as a walrus.

Returning from Carmel in the pickup—the back of which was filled with packages and a perfectly formed Christmas tree— Einstein slept half on Nora's lap. He was worn out from his busy day with Jim and Pooka. They got home less than an hour before dark. Einstein led the way toward the house—

—but suddenly stopped and looked around curiously. He sniffed the chilly air, then moved across the yard, nose to the ground, as if tracking a scent.

Heading toward the back door with her arms full of packages, Nora did not at first see anything unusual in the dog's behavior, but she noticed that Travis had halted and was staring hard at Einstein. She said, "What is it?"

"Wait a second."

Einstein crossed the yard to the edge of the woods on the south side. He stood rigid, head thrust forward, then shook himself and moved on along the perimeter of the forest. He stopped repeatedly, standing motionless each time, and in a couple of minutes he came all the way around to the north.

When the retriever returned to them, Travis said, "Something?"

Einstein wagged his tail briefly and barked once: *Yes and no*.

Inside, in the pantry, the retriever laid out a message.

FELT SOMETHING.

"What?" Travis asked.

DON'T KNOW.

"The Outsider?"

MAYBE.

"Close?"

DON'T KNOW.

"Are you getting your sixth sense back?" Nora asked.

DON'T KNOW. JUST FELT.

"Felt what?" Travis asked.

The dog composed an answer only after considerable deliberation.

BIG DARKNESS.

"You felt a big darkness?"

Yes.

"What's that mean?" Nora asked uneasily.

CAN'T EXPLAIN BETTER. JUST FELT IT.

Nora looked at Travis and saw a concern in his eyes that probably mirrored the expression in her own.

A big darkness was out there somewhere, and it was coming.

3

Christmas was joyous and fine.

In the morning, sitting around the light-bedecked tree,

461

drinking milk and eating homemade cookies, they opened presents. As a joke, the first gift that Nora gave Travis was a box of underwear. He gave her a bright orange and yellow muumuu obviously sized for a three-hundred-pound woman: "For March, when you'll be too big for anything else. Of course, by May you'll have outgrown it." They exchanged serious gifts, also—jewelry and sweaters and books.

But Nora, like Travis, felt the day belonged to Einstein more than to anyone else. She gave him the portrait on which she had been working all month, and the retriever seemed stunned and flattered and delighted that she had seen fit to immortalize him in paint. He got three new Mickey Mouse videotapes, a pair of fancy metal food and water bowls with his name engraved on them to replace the plastic dishes he had been using, his own small battery-powered clock that he could take with him to any room in the house (he was showing an increasing interest in time), and several other presents, but he was repeatedly drawn to the portrait, which they propped against the wall for his inspection. Later, when they hung it above the living-room fireplace, Einstein stood on the hearth and peered up at the picture, pleased and proud.

Like any kid, Einstein perversely took almost as much pleasure in playing with empty boxes, crumpled wrapping paper, and ribbons as he did with the gifts themselves. And one of his favorite things was a joke gift: a red Santa cap with a white pom-pom on the tip, which was held on his head by an elastic strap. Nora put it on him just for fun. When he saw himself in a mirror, he was so taken with his appearance that he objected when, a few minutes later, she tried to take the cap off him. He kept it on most of the day.

Jim Keene and Pooka arrived in the early afternoon, and Einstein herded them straight into the living room to look at his portrait above the mantel. For an hour, watched over by Jim and Travis, the two dogs played together in the back yard. That activity, having been preceded by the excitement of the morning's gift-giving, left Einstein in need of a nap, so they returned to the house, where Jim and Travis helped Nora prepare Christmas dinner.

After his nap, Einstein tried to interest Pooka in Mickey Mouse cartoons, but Nora saw that he met with only limited success. Pooka's attention span didn't even last long enough for Donald or Goofy or Pluto to get Mickey into trouble. In respect of his companion's lower IQ, and apparently not bored with such company, Einstein turned the television off and engaged in strictly doggy activities: some light wrestling in the den and a lot of lying around, nose to nose, silently communing with each other about canine concerns.

By early evening, the house was filled with the aromas of turkey, baked corn, yams, and other goodies. Christmas music played. And in spite of the interior shutters that had been bolted over the windows when the early-winter night had fallen, in spite of the guns near at hand, in spite of the demonic presence of The Outsider that always lurked in the back of her mind, Nora had never been happier.

During dinner, they talked about the baby, and Jim asked if they had given any thought to names. Einstein, eating in the corner with Pooka, was instantly intrigued by the idea of participating in the naming of their firstborn. He dashed immediately to the pantry to spell out his suggestion.

Nora left the table to see what name the dog thought suitable.

MICKEY.

"Absolutely not!" she said. "We're not naming the baby after a cartoon mouse."

DONALD.

"Nor a duck."

PLUTO.

"Pluto? Get serious, fur face."

GOOFY.

Nora firmly restrained him from pushing the letter-dispensing pedals any more, gathered up the used tiles and put them away, turned off the pantry light, and went back to the table. "You may think it's hilarious," she told Travis

463

and Jim, who were choking with laughter, "but *he's* serious!"

After dinner, sitting around the tree in the living room, they talked about many things, including Jim's intention of getting another dog. "Pooka needs to have another of his kind," the vet said. "He's almost a year and a half old now, and I'm of the belief that human companionship isn't enough for them after they're well past the puppy stage. They get lonely like we do. And since I'm going to get him a companion, I might as well get a female purebred lab and maybe wind up with some nice puppies to sell later. So he's going to have not only a friend but a mate."

Nora had not noticed that Einstein was any more interested in that part of the conversation than in any other. However, after Jim and Pooka had gone home, Travis found a message in the pantry and called Nora over to have a look at it.

MATE. A COMPANION, PARTNER, ONE OF A PAIR.

The retriever had been waiting for them to notice the carefully arranged tiles. Now he appeared behind them and regarded them quizzically.

Nora said, "Do you think you'd like a mate?"

Einstein slipped between them, into the pantry, disarranged the tiles, and made a reply.

IT'S WORTH THINKING ABOUT.

"But, listen, fur face," Travis said, "you're one of a kind. There's no other dog like you, with your IQ."

The retriever considered that point but was not dissuaded.

LIFE IS MORE THAN INTELLECT.

"True enough," Travis said. "But I think this needs a lot of consideration."

LIFE IS FEELINGS.

"All right," Nora said. "We'll think about it."

LIFE IS MATE. SHARING.

"We promise to think about it and then discuss it with you some more," Travis said. "Now it's getting late."

Einstein quickly made one more message.

BABY MICKEY?

"Absolutely not!" Nora said.

That night, in bed, after she and Travis made love, Nora said, "I'll bet he *is* lonely."

"Jim Keene?"

"Well, yes, I bet he's lonely, too. He's such a nice man, and he'd make someone a great husband. But women are just as choosy about looks as men are, don't you think? They don't go for husbands with hound-dog faces. They marry the good-looking ones who half the time treat them like dirt. But I didn't mean Jim. I meant Einstein. He must get lonely now and then."

"We're with him all the time."

"No, we're really not. I paint, and you do things in which poor Einstein doesn't get included. And if you do go back to real estate eventually, there'll be a lot of time when Einstein's without anyone."

"He has his books. He loves books."

"Maybe books aren't enough," she said.

They were silent for so long that she thought Travis had fallen asleep. Then he said, "If Einstein mated and produced puppies, what would they be like?"

"You mean—would they be as smart as he is?"

"I wonder ... Seems to me there's three possibilities. First, his intelligence isn't inheritable, so his puppies would just be ordinary puppies. Second, it *is* inheritable, but the genes of his mate would dilute the intelligence, so the puppies would be smart but not as smart as their father; and each succeeding generation would get dimmer, duller, until eventually his great-great-great grandpups would just be ordinary dogs."

"What's the third possibility?"

"Intelligence, being a survival trait, might be genetically dominant, very dominant."

"In which case his puppies would be as smart as he is."

"And their puppies after them, on and on, until in time

465

you'd have a colony of intelligent golden retrievers, thousands of them all over the world.''

They were silent again.

Finally she said, "Wow."

Travis said, "He's right."

"What?"

"It *is* something worth thinking about."

4

Vince Nasco had never anticipated, back in November, that he would need a full month to get a whack at Ramon Velazquez, the guy in Oakland who was a thorn in the side of Don Mario Tetragna. Until he wasted Velazquez, Vince would not be given the names of people in San Francisco who dealt in false ID and who might help him track down Travis Cornell, the woman, and the dog. So he had an urgent need to reduce Velazquez to a hunk of putrifying meat.

But Velazquez was a goddamn shadow. The man did not make a step without two bodyguards at his side, which should have made him more rather than less conspicuous. However, he conducted his gambling and drug enterprises—infringing on the Tetragna franchise in Oakland— with all the stealth of Howard Hughes. He slipped and slithered on his errands, using a *fleet* of different cars, never taking the same route two days in a row, never meeting in the same place, using the street as an office, never staying anywhere long enough to be made, marked, and wiped out. He was a hopeless paranoid who believed everyone was out to get him. Vince couldn't keep the man in sight long enough to match him with the photograph that the Tetragnas had supplied. Ramon Velazquez was *smoke*.

Vince didn't get him until Christmas Day, and it was a hell of a mess when it went down. Ramon was at home with a lot of relatives. Vince came at the Velazquez property from the house behind it, over the high brick wall between one big lot and the other. Coming down on the other side, he saw Velazquez and some people at a barbecue on the patio near the pool, where they were roasting an enormous turkey—did people barbecue turkeys anywhere but in California?—and they all spotted him immediately though he was half an acre away. He saw the bodyguards reaching for weapons in their shoulder holsters, so he had no choice but to fire indiscriminately with his Uzi, spraying the entire patio area, taking out Velazquez, both bodyguards, a middle-aged woman who must have been somebody's wife, and an old dame who had to be somebody's grandmother.

Ssssnap.

Ssssnap.

Ssssnap.

Ssssnap.

Ssssnap.

Everyone else, inside and outside of the house, was screaming and diving for cover. Vince had to climb the wall back into the yard of the house next door—where nobody was home, thank God—and as he was hauling his ass over the top, a bunch of Latino types at the Velazquez place opened fire on him. He barely got away with his hide intact.

The day after Christmas, when he showed up at a San Francisco restaurant owned by Don Tetragna, to meet with Frank Dicenziano, a trusted Family *capo* who answered only to the don himself, Vince was worried. The *fratellanza* had a code about assassinations. Hell, they had a code about everything—probably even bowel movements—and they took their codes seriously, but the code of assassination was maybe taken a little more seriously than others. The first rule of that code was: You don't hit a man in the company of his family unless he's gone to ground and you just can't reach him any other way. Vince felt fairly safe on that score. But another rule was that you never shot a man's wife or kids or his grandmother in order to get at him. Any hit man who did such a thing would probably wind up dead himself, wasted by the very people who had hired him. Vince hoped to convince Frank Dicenziano that Velazquez was a special case—no other target had ever eluded Vince for a month—and that what had happened in Oakland on Christmas Day was regrettable but unavoidable.

Just in case Dicenziano—and by extension, the don—was too furious to listen to reason, Vince went prepared with more than a gun. He knew that, if they wanted him dead, they would crowd him and take the gun away from him before he could use it, as soon as he walked into the restaurant and before he knew the score. So he wired himself with plastic explosives and was prepared to detonate them, wiping out the entire restaurant, if they tried to fit him for a coffin.

Vince was not sure if he would survive the explosion. He had absorbed the life energies of so many people recently that he thought he must be getting close to the immortality he had been seeking—or was already there—but he could not know how strong he was until he put himself to the test. If his choice was standing at the heart of an explosion ... or letting a couple of wiseguys pump a hundred rounds into him and encase him in concrete for a dunk in the bay ... he decided the former was more appealing and, perhaps, offered him a marginally better chance of survival.

To his surprise, Dicenziano—who resembled a squirrel with meatballs in his cheeks—was delighted with how the Velazquez contract had been fulfilled. He said the don had the highest praise for Vince. No one searched Vince when he entered the restaurant. At a corner booth, as the first men in the room, he and Frank were served a special lunch of dishes not on the menu. They drank three-hundred-dollar Cabernet Sauvignon, a gift from Mario Tetragna.

When Vince cautiously raised the issue of the dead wife and grandmother, Dicenziano said, "Listen, my friend, we knew this was going to be a hard hit, a demanding job, and that rules might have to be broken. Besides, these people were not *our* kind of people. They were just a bunch of wetback spics. They don't belong in this business. If they try to force their way into it, they can't expect us to play by the rules."

Relieved, Vince went to the men's room halfway through

lunch and disconnected the detonator. He didn't want to set the Plastique off accidentally now that the crisis was past.

At the end of lunch, Frank gave Vince the list. Nine names. "These people—who are not all Family people, by the way—pay the don for the right to operate their ID businesses in his territory. Back in November, in anticipation of your success with Velazquez, I spoke to these nine, and they'll remember that the don wants them to cooperate with you in any way they can."

Vince set out the same afternoon, looking for someone who would remember Travis Cornell.

Initially, he was frustrated. Two of the first four people on the list could not be reached. They had closed up shop and gone away for the holidays. To Vince, it seemed wrong that the criminal underworld would take off for Christmas and New Year's as if they were schoolteachers.

But the fifth man, Anson Van Dyne, was at work in the basement beneath his topless club, Hot Tips, and at five-thirty, December 26, Vince found what he was after. Van Dyne looked at a photograph of Travis Cornell, which Vince had obtained from the back-issue files of the Santa Barbara newspaper. "Yeah, I remember him. He's not one you forget. Not a foreigner looking to become an instant American like half my customers. And not the usual sad-assed loser who needs to change his name and hide his face. He's not a big guy, and he doesn't come on tough or anything, but you get the feeling he could mop up the floor with anyone who crossed him. Very self-contained. Very watchful. I couldn't forget him."

"What you couldn't forget," said one of the two bearded boy wonders at the computers, "is that gorgeous quiff he was with."

"For her, even a dead man could get it up," the other one said.

The first said, "Yeah, even a dead man. Cake and pie."

Vince was both offended and confused by their contributions to the conversation, so he ignored them. To Van Dyne, he said, "Is there any chance you'd remember the new names you gave them?"

"Sure. We got it on file," Van Dyne said.

Vince could not believe what he had heard. "I thought people in your line of work didn't keep records? Safer for you and essential for your clients."

Van Dyne shrugged. "Fuck the clients. Maybe one day the feds or the locals hit us, put us out of business. Maybe I find myself needing a steady flow of cash for lawyers' fees. What better than to have a list of a couple of thousand bozos living under phony names, bozos who'd be willing to be squeezed a little rather than have to start all over again with new lives."

"Blackmail," Vince said.

"An ugly word," Van Dyne said. "But apt, I'm afraid. Anyway, all we care about is that *we* are safe, that there aren't any records here to incriminate *us*. We don't keep the data in this dump. Soon as we provide someone with a new ID, we transmit the record of it over a safe phone line from the computer here to a computer we keep elsewhere. The way *that* computer is programmed, the data can't be pulled out of it from here; it's a one-way road; so if we are busted, the police hackers can't reach our records from these machines. Hell, they won't even know the records exist."

This new high-tech criminal world made Vince woozy. Even the don, a man of infinite criminal cleverness, had thought these people kept no records and had not realized how computers had made it safe to do so. Vince thought about what Van Dyne had told him, getting it all sorted out in his mind. He said, "So you can take me to this other computer and look up Cornell's new ID?"

"For a friend of Don Tetragna's," Van Dyne said, "I'll do just about anything but slit my own throat. Come with me."

Van Dyne drove Vince to a busy Chinese restaurant in Chinatown. The place must have seated a hundred and fifty, and every table was occupied, mostly by Anglos rather than Asians. Although the joint was enormous and was decorated with paper lanterns, dragon murals, imitation rosewood screens, and strings of brass wind chimes in the shapes of Chinese ideograms, it reminded Vince of the kitschy Italian trattoria in which he had murdered the cockroach Pantangela and the two federal marshals last August. All ethnic art and decor—from Chinese to Italian to Polish to Irish—were, when boiled down to their essence, perfectly alike.

The owner was a Chinese man in his thirties, who was introduced to Vince simply as Yuan. With bottles of Tsingtao provided by Yuan, Van Dyne and Vince went into the owner's basement office, where two computers stood on two desks, one out in the main work area and the other shoved into a corner. The one in the corner was switched on, though nobody was working at it.

"This is my computer," Van Dyne said. "No one here ever works with it. They never even *touch* it, except to open the phone line to put the modem in operation every morning and to close it at night. My computers at Hot Tips are linked to this one."

"You trust Yuan?"

"I got him the loan that started this business. He owes me his good fortune. And it's pretty much a clean loan, nothing that can be linked to me in any way, or to Don Tetragna, so Yuan remains an upstanding citizen who's of no interest to the cops. All he does for me in return is let me keep the computer here."

Sitting in front of the terminal, Van Dyne began to use the keyboard. In two minutes he had Travis Cornell's new name: Samuel Spencer Hyatt.

"And here," Van Dyne said as new data flickered up. "This is the woman who was with him. Her real name was Nora Louise Devon of Santa Barbara. Now, she's Nora Jean Aimes."

"Okay," Vince said. "Now wipe them off your records."

"What do you mean?"

"Erase them. Take them out of the computer. They're not yours any more. They're mine. Nobody else's. Just *mine*."

* * *

471

A short while later, they were back at Hot Tips, which was a decadent place that revolted Vince.

In the basement, Van Dyne gave the name of Hyatt and Aimes to the bearded boy wonders who seemed to live down there around the clock, like a couple of trolls.

First, the trolls broke into the Department of Motor Vehicle computers. They wanted to see whether, in the three months since acquiring new identities, Hyatt and Aimes had settled down somewhere and filed a change of address with the state.

"Bingo," one of them said.

An address appeared on the screen, and the bearded operator ordered a printout.

Anson Van Dyne tore the paper off the printer and handed it to Vince.

Travis Cornell and Nora Devon—now Hyatt and Aimes—were living at a rural address on Pacific Coast Highway south of the town of Carmel.

5

On Wednesday, December 29, Nora drove into Carmel alone for an appointment with Dr. Weingold.

The sky was overcast, so dark that the white seagulls, swooping against the backdrop of clouds, were by contrast almost as bright as incandescent lights. The weather had been much the same since the day after Christmas, but the promised rain never came.

Today, however, it came in torrents just as she pulled the pickup into one of the spaces in the small parking lot behind Dr. Weingold's office. She was wearing a nylon jacket with a hood, just in case, and she pulled the hood over her head before dashing from the truck into the one-story brick building.

Dr. Weingold gave her the usual thorough examination and pronounced her fit as a fiddle, which would have amused Einstein.

"I've never seen a woman at the three-month mark in better shape," the doctor said.

"I want this to be a very healthy baby, a perfect baby."

"And so it shall be."

The doctor believed that her name was Aimes and her husband's name Hyatt, but he never once indicated disapproval of her marital status. The situation embarrassed Nora, but she supposed that the modern world, into which she had fluttered from the cocoon of the Devon house, was liberal-minded about these things.

Dr. Weingold suggested, as he had done before, that she consider a test to determine the baby's sex, and as before she declined. She wanted to be surprised. Besides, if they found out they were going to have a girl, Einstein would start campaigning for the name "Minnie."

After huddling with the doctor's receptionist to schedule the next appointment, Nora pulled the hood over her head again and went out into the driving rain. It was coming down hard, drizzling off a section of roof that had no gutters, sluicing across the sidewalk, forming deep puddles on the macadam of the parking lot. She sloshed through a miniature river on her way to the pickup, and in seconds her running shoes were saturated.

As she reached the truck, she saw a man getting out of a red Honda parked beside her. She didn't notice much about him—just that he was a big guy in a small car, and that he was not dressed for the rain. He was wearing jeans and a blue pullover, and Nora thought: The poor man is going to get soaked to the skin.

She opened the driver's door and started to get into the truck. The next thing she knew, the man in the blue sweater was coming in after her, shoving her across the seat and clambering behind the wheel. He said, "If you yell, bitch, I'll blow your guts out," and she realized that he was jamming a revolver into her side.

She almost yelled anyway, involuntarily, almost tried to keep on going across the front seat and out the door on the passenger's side. But something in his voice, brutal and dark, made her hesitate. He sounded as if he would shoot her in the back rather than let her escape.

He slammed the driver's door, and now they were alone in the truck, beyond help, virtually concealed from the world by the rain that streamed down the windows and made the glass opaque. It didn't matter: the doctor's parking lot was deserted, and it could not be seen from the street, so even out of the truck she would have had no one to whom to turn.

He was a *very* big man, and muscular, but it was not his size that was most frightening. His broad face was placid, virtually expressionless; that serenity, completely unsuited to these circumstances, scared Nora. His eyes were worse. Green eyes—and cold.

"Who are you?" she demanded, trying to conceal her fear, sure that visible terror would excite him. He seemed to be balanced on a thin line. "What do you want with me?"

"I want the dog."

She had thought: robber. She had thought: rapist. She had thought: psychopathic thrill killer. But she had not for a moment thought that he might be a government agent. Yet who else would be looking for Einstein? No one else even knew the dog existed.

"What're you talking about?" she said.

He pushed the muzzle of the revolver deeper into her side, until it hurt.

She thought of the baby growing within her. "All right, okay, obviously you know about the dog, so there's no point playing games."

"No point." He spoke so quietly that she could hardly hear him above the roar of the rain that drummed on the roof of the cab and snapped against the windshield.

He reached over and pulled down the hood of her jacket, opened the zipper, and slid his hand down her breasts, over her belly. For a moment she was terrified that he was, after all, intent on rape.

Instead, he said, "This Weingold is a gynecologist-obstetrician. So what's your problem? You have some damn social disease or are you pregnant?" He almost spit

474

out the words "social disease," as if merely pronouncing those syllables made him sick with disgust.

"You're no government agent." She spoke entirely from instinct.

"I asked you a question, bitch," he said in a voice barely louder than a whisper. He leaned close, digging the gun into her side again. The air in the truck was humid. The all-enveloping sound of rain combined with the stuffiness to create a claustrophobic atmosphere that was nearly intolerable. He said, "Which is it? You got herpes, syphilis, clap, some other crotch rot? Or are you pregnant?"

Thinking that pregnancy might gain her a dispensation from the violence of which he seemed so capable, she said, "I'm going to have a baby. I'm three months pregnant."

Something happened in his eyes. *A shifting*. Like movement in a subtle kaleidoscopic pattern that was composed of bits of glass all the same shade of green.

Nora knew that admitting pregnancy was the worst thing she could have done, but she did not know *why*.

She thought about the .38 pistol in the glove compartment. She could not possibly open the glove box, grab the gun, and shoot him before he pulled the trigger of the revolver. Still, she'd have to remain constantly on the lookout for an opportunity, for a laxness on his part, that would give her a chance to go for her own weapon.

Suddenly he was climbing on top of her, and again she thought he was going to rape her in broad daylight, in the veiling curtains of rain but still daylight. Then she realized he was just changing places with her, urging her behind the wheel while he moved into the passenger's seat, keeping the muzzle of the revolver on her the whole time.

"Drive," he said.

"Where?"

"Back to your place."

"But—"

"Keep your mouth shut and drive."

Now she was at the opposite side of the cab from the glove box. To get to it, she would have to reach in front of him. He would never be *that* lax.

Determined to keep a rein on her galloping fear, she now found that she had to rein in despair as well.

She started the truck, drove out of the parking lot, and turned right in the street.

The windshield wipers thumped nearly as loud as her heart. She wasn't sure how much of the oppressive sound was made by the impacting rain and how much of it was the roar of her own blood in her ears.

Block by block, Nora searched for a cop—although she had no idea what she should do if she saw one. She never had to figure it out because no cops were anywhere to be seen.

Until they were out of Carmel and on the Pacific Coast Highway, the blustering wind not only drove rain against the windshield but also flung bristling bits of cypress and pine needles from the huge old trees that sheltered the town's streets. South along the coast, as they headed into steadily less populated areas, no trees overhung the road, but the wind off the ocean hit the pickup full force. Nora frequently felt it pulling at the wheel. And the rain, slashing straight at them from the sea, seemed to pummel the truck hard enough to leave dents in the sheet metal.

After at least five minutes of silence, which seemed like an hour, she could no longer obey his order to keep her mouth shut. "How did you find us?"

"Been watching your place for more than a day," he said in that cool, quiet voice that matched his placid face. "When you left this morning, I followed you, hoping you'd give me an opening."

"No, I mean, how did you know where we lived?"

He smiled. "Van Dyne."

"That double-crossing creep."

"Special circumstances," he assured her. "The Big Man in San Francisco owed me a favor, so he put pressure on Van Dyne."

"Big Man?"

"Tetragna."

"Who's he?"

"You don't know anything, do you?" he said. "Except

476

how to make babies, huh? You know about that, huh?"

The hard taunting note in his voice was not merely sexually suggestive: it was darker, stranger, and more terrifying than that. She was so frightened of the fierce tension that she sensed in him each time he approached the subject of sex that she did not dare reply to him.

She turned on the headlights as they encountered thin fog. She kept her attention on the rain-washed highway, squinting through the smeary windshield.

He said, "You're very pretty. If I was going to stick it into anyone, I'd stick it into you."

Nora bit her lip.

"But even as pretty as you are," he said, "you're like all the others, I'll bet. If I stuck it into you, then it'd rot and fall off because you're diseased like all the others—aren't you? Yeah. You are. Sex is death. I'm one of the few who seem to know it, even though proof is everywhere. Sex is death. But you're very pretty ... "

As she listened to him, her throat got tight. She was having difficulty drawing a deep breath.

Suddenly his taciturnity was gone. He talked fast, still soft-voiced and unnervingly calm, considering the crazy things he was saying, but very fast: "I'm going to be bigger than Tetragna, more important. I've got scores of lives in me. I've absorbed energies from more than you'd believe, experienced The Moment, felt The Snap. It's my Gift. When Tetragna's dead and gone, I'll be here. When everyone now alive is dead, I'll be here because I'm immortal."

She didn't know what to say. He had come out of nowhere, somehow knowing about Einstein, and he was a lunatic, and there seemed to be nothing she could do. She was as angry about the unfairness of it as she was afraid. They had made careful preparations for The Outsider, and they had taken elaborate steps to elude the government— but how were they supposed to have prepared for this? It wasn't *fair*.

Silent again, he stared at her intently for a minute or more, another eternity. She could feel his icy green gaze on her as surely as she would have felt a cold, fondling hand.

"You don't know what I'm talking about, do you?" he said.

"No."

Perhaps because he found her pretty, he chose to explain. "I've only ever told one person before, and he made fun of me. His name was Danny Slowicz, and we both worked for the Carramazza Family in New York, biggest of the five Mafia Families. Little muscle work, once in a while killing people who needed killed."

Nora felt sick because he was not merely crazy and not merely a killer but a crazy *professional* killer.

Unaware of her reaction, switching his gaze from the rain-swept road to her face, he continued, "See, we were having dinner in this restaurant, Danny and me, washing down clams with Valpolicella, and I explained to him that I was destined to lead a long life because of my ability to acquire the vital energies of people I wasted. I told him, 'See, Danny, people are like batteries, walking batteries, filled with this mysterious energy we call life. When I off someone, his energy becomes *my* energy, and I get stronger. I'm a bull, Danny,' I says. 'Look at me—am I a bull or what? And I got to be a bull 'cause I have this Gift of being able to take the energy from a guy.' And you know what Danny says?"

"What?" she asked numbly.

"Well, Danny was a serious eater, so he kept his attention on his plate, face in his food, until he scarfs a few more clams. Then he looks up, his lips and chin dripping clam sauce, and he says, 'Yeah, Vince, so where'd you learn this trick, huh? Where'd you learn how to absorb these life energies?' I said, 'Well, it's my Gift,' and he said, 'You mean like from God?' So I had to think about that, and I said, 'Who knows where from? It's my Gift like Mantle's hitting was a gift, like Sinatra's voice was a gift.' And Danny says, 'Tell me this—suppose you waste a guy who's an electrician. After you absorb his energy, would you all of a sudden know how to rewire a house?' I didn't realize he was putting me on. I thought it was a serious question, so I explained how I absorb life energy, not personality, not all the stuff the guy knows, just his energy. And then Danny says, 'So if you blew away a carnival geek, you wouldn't all of a sudden get the urge to bite the heads off chickens.' Right then I knew Danny thought I was either drunk or nuts, so I ate clams and didn't say any more about my Gift, and that's the last time I told anyone until I'm here telling you.''

He had called himself Vince, so now she knew his name. She did not see what good it would do her to know it.

He had told his story without any indication that he was aware of the insane black humor in it. He was a deadly serious man. Unless Travis could deal with him, this guy was not going to let them live.

"So," Vince said, "I couldn't risk Danny going around telling anyone what I'd told him, because he'd color it up, make it sound funny, and people would think I was nuts. The big bosses don't hire crazy hit men; they want cool, logical, balanced guys who can do the work clean. Which is what I am, cool and balanced, but Danny would have had them thinking the other way. So that night I slit his throat, took him to this deserted factory I knew, cut him into pieces, put him in a vat, and poured a lot of sulfuric acid over him. He was a favorite nephew of the don's, so I couldn't take a chance of anyone finding a body that might be traced back to me. Now, I got Danny's energy in me, along with a lot of others.''

The gun was in the glove box.

Some small hope could be taken from the knowledge that the gun was in the glove box.

While Nora was visiting Dr. Weingold, Travis whipped up and baked a double batch of chocolate cookies with peanut-butter chips. Living alone, he had learned to cook, but he had never taken pleasure in it. During the past few months, however, Nora had improved his culinary skills to such an extent that he enjoyed cooking, especially baking.

Einstein, who usually hung around dutifully throughout

a baking session, in the anticipation of receiving a sweet morsel, deserted him before he had finished mixing the batter. The dog was agitated and moved around the house from window to window, staring out at the rain.

After a while, Travis got edgy about the dog's behavior and asked if something was wrong.

In the pantry, Einstein made his reply.

I FEEL A LITTLE STRANGE.

"Sick?" Travis asked, worried about a relapse. The retriever was recovering well, but still recovering. His immune system was not in condition for a major new challenge.

NOT SICK.

"Then what? You sense … The Outsider?"

NO . NOT LIKE BEFORE.

"But you sense something?"

BAD DAY.

"Maybe it's the rain."

MAYBE.

Relieved but still edgy, Travis returned to his baking.

The highway was silver with rain.

The daytime fog grew slightly thicker as they drove south along the coast, forcing Nora to slow to forty miles an hour, thirty in some places.

Using the fog as an excuse, could she slow the truck enough to risk throwing open her door and leaping out? No. Probably not. She would have to let their speed drop below five miles an hour in order not to hurt herself or her unborn child, and the fog simply was not dense enough to justify reducing speed that far. Besides, Vince kept the revolver pointed at her while he talked, and he would shoot her in the back as she turned to make her exit.

The pickup's headlamps and those of the few oncoming cars were refracted by the mist. Halos of light and scintillant rainbows bounced off the shifting curtains of fog, briefly seen, then gone.

She considered running the truck off the road, over the edge in one of the few places where she knew the embankment to be gentle and the drop endurable. But she was afraid she would misjudge where she was and, by mistake, drive off the brink into a two-hundred-foot emptiness, crashing with terrible force into the rocky coastline below. Even if she went over at the right point, a calculated and survivable crash might might her unconscious or induce a miscarriage, and if possible she wanted to get out of this with her life and the life of the child within her.

Once Vince started talking to her, he could not stop. For years he had husbanded his great secrets, had hidden his dreams of power and immortality from the world, but his desire to speak of his supposed greatness evidently had never diminished after the fiasco with Danny Slowicz. It was as if he had stored up all the words he had wanted to say to people, had put them on reels and reels of mental recording tape, and now he was playing them back at high speed, spewing out all this craziness that made Nora sick with dread.

He told her how he had learned of Einstein—the killing of the research scientists in charge of various programs under the Francis Project at Banodyne. He knew of The Outsider, too, but was not afraid of it. He was, he said, on the brink of immortality, and gaining ownership of the dog was one of the final tasks he had to complete in order to achieve his Destiny. He and the dog were destined to be together because each of them was unique in this world, one of a kind. Once Vince had achieved his Destiny, he said, nothing could stop him, not even The Outsider.

Half the time, Nora didn't understand what he was saying. She supposed that if she *did* understand it, she would be as insane as he clearly was.

But though she did not always grasp his meaning, she knew what he intended to do to her and to Travis once he had the retriever. At first, she was afraid of speaking about her fate, as if putting it into words would somehow make it irrevocable. At last, however, when they were no more than five miles from the dirt lane that turned off the

481

highway and led up to the bleached-wood house, she said, "You won't let us go when you've got the dog, will you?"

He stared at her, caressing her with his gaze. "What do you think, Nora?"

"I think you'll kill us."

"Of course."

She was surprised that his confirmation of her fears did not fill her with greater terror. His smug response only infuriated her, dampening her fear while increasing her determination to spoil his neat plans.

She knew, then, that she was a radically changed woman from the Nora of last May, who would have been reduced to uncontrollable shudders by this man's bold self-assurance.

"I could run this truck right off the road, take my chances with an accident," she said.

"The moment you pulled on the wheel," he said, 'I'd have to shoot you and then try to regain control."

"Maybe you couldn't. Maybe you'd die, too."

"Me? Die? Maybe. But not in anything as minor as a traffic accident. No, no. I've got too many lives in me to go that easily. And I don't believe you'll try it anyway. In your heart of hearts, you believe that man of yours will pull a sharp one, save you and the dog and himself. You're wrong, of course, but you can't stop believing in him. He won't do anything because he'll be afraid of hurting you. I'll go in there with a gun in your belly, and that will paralyze him long enough for me to blow his head off. That's why I've only got the revolver. It's all I need. His caring for you, his fear of hurting you, will get him killed."

Nora decided it was very important that she not let her fury show. She must try to look frightened, weak, utterly unsure of herself. If he underestimated her, he might slip up and give her some small advantage.

Taking her eyes off the rainy highway for only a second, she glanced at him and saw that he was staring at her not with amusement or psychopathic rage, as she would have expected, and not with his usual bovine placidity either, but with something that looked very much like affection and maybe gratitude.

"I've dreamed for years of killing a pregnant woman," he said, as if that was a goal no less worthwhile and commendable than wanting to build a business empire or feed the hungry or nurse the sick. "I have never been in a situation where the risk of killing a pregnant woman was low enough to justify it. But in that isolated house of yours, once I've dealt with Cornell, the conditions will be ideal."

"Please, no," she said shakily, playing the weakling, though she didn't have to fake the nervous quiver in her voice.

Still speaking calmly but with a trace more emotion than before, he said, "There'll be your life energy, still young and rich, but in the instant you die, I'll also receive the energy of the child. And that'll be perfectly pure, unused, a life that's unsoiled by the many contaminants of this sick and degenerate world. You're my first pregnant woman, Nora, and I'll always remember you."

Tears shimmered at the corners of her eyes, which was not just good acting, either. Although she *did* believe Travis would find some way to handle this man, she was afraid that, in the turmoil, she or Einstein would die. And she did not know how Travis would be able to cope with his failure to save all of them.

"Don't despair, Nora," Vince said. "You and your baby will not entirely cease to exist. You'll both become a part of me, and in me you'll live forever."

Travis took the first tray of cookies out of the oven and put them on a rack to cool.

Einstein came sniffing around, and Travis said, "They're too hot yet."

The dog returned to the living room to look out the front window at the rain.

*   *   *

Just before Nora turned off the Coast Highway, Vince slid down on the seat, below the window level, out of sight. He kept the gun on her. "I'll blow that baby right out of your belly if you make the slightest wrong move."

She believed him.

Turning onto the dirt lane, which was muddy and slippery, Nora drove up the hill toward the house. The overhanging trees shielded the road from the worst of the rain but collected the water on their branches and sent it to the ground in fatter droplets or rivulets.

She saw Einstein at a front window, and she tried to come up with some signal that would mean "trouble," that the dog would instantly understand. She couldn't think of anything.

Looking up at her, Vince said, "Don't go all the way to the barn. Stop right beside the house."

His plan was obvious. The corner of the house where the pantry and cellar stairs were located had no windows. Travis and Einstein would not be able to see the man getting out of the truck with her. Vince could hustle her around the corner, onto the back porch, and inside before Travis realized something was wrong.

Maybe Einstein's canine sense would detect danger. Maybe. But ... Einstein had been so ill.

Einstein padded into the kitchen, excited.

Travis said, "Was that Nora's truck?"

Yes.

The retriever went to the back door and did a dance of impatience—then stood still, cocked his head.

Nora's stroke of luck came when she least expected it.

When she parked alongside the house, engaged the hand brake, and switched off the engine, Vince grabbed her and dragged her across the seat, out of his side of the truck because that was the side against the back end of the house and most difficult to see from windows at the front corner of the structure. Climbing from the pickup, pulling her by one hand, he was looking around to be sure Travis was not nearby; distracted, he couldn't keep his revolver on Nora as closely as before. As she slid across the seat, past the glove box, she popped open the door and snatched up the .38 pistol. Vince must have heard or sensed something because he swung toward her, but he was too late. She jammed the .38 into his belly and, before he could raise his gun and blow her head off, she squeezed the trigger three times.

With a look of shock, he slammed back against the house, which was only three feet behind him.

She was amazed by her own cold-bloodedness. Crazily, she thought that no one was so dangerous as a mother protecting her children, even if one child was unborn and the other was a *dog*. She fired once more, point-blank, at his chest.

Vince went down hard, face-first on the wet ground.

She turned from him and ran. At the corner of the house she almost collided with Travis, who vaulted over the porch railing and landed in a crouch in front of her, holding the Uzi carbine.

"I killed him," she said, hearing hysteria in her voice, fighting to control it. "I shot him four times, I killed him, my *God*."

Travis rose from a crouch, bewildered. Nora threw her arms around him and put her head against his chest. As chilling rain beat upon them, she reveled in the living warmth of him.

"Who—" Travis begun.

Behind Nora, Vince issued a shrill breathless cry and, rolling onto his back, fired at them. The bullet struck Travis high in the shoulder and knocked him backward. If it had been two inches to the right, it would have hit Nora in the head.

She was almost pulled off her feet when Travis fell because she was holding him. But she let go fast enough and went to the left, in front of the truck, out of the line of fire. She got only a quick look at Vince, who was holding his revolver in one hand and clutching his stomach with the other, trying to get off the ground.

In that glimpse before she cowered down in front of the pickup, she had not seen any blood on the man.

What was happening here? He could not possibly have survived three rounds in the stomach and one in the chest. Not unless he actually *was* immortal.

Even as Nora scrambled for the cover of the truck, Travis had been getting off his back, sitting up in the mud. Blood was visible on *him*, spreading across his chest from his shoulder, soaking his shirt. He still had the Uzi in his right hand, which functioned in spite of the wound in that shoulder. As Vince pulled off a wild second shot, Travis opened fire with the Uzi. His position was no better than Vince's; the spray of bullets snapped into the house and ricocheted along the side of the truck, indiscriminate fire.

He stopped shooting. "Shit." He struggled to his feet.

Nora said, "Did you get him?"

"He made it around the front of the house," Travis said, and headed that way.

Vince figured he was approaching immortality, almost there, if he had not already arrived. He was in need of—at most—only a few more lives, and his only concern was that he would be snuffed out when he was *that* close to his Destiny. As a result, he took precautions. Like the latest and most expensive model Kevlar bulletproof vest. He was wearing one under his sweater, which was what had stopped the four shots the bitch had tried to pump into him. The slugs had flattened against the vest, drawing no blood whatsoever. But, Jesus, they had hurt. The impact had knocked him against the wall of the house and had driven the breath out of him. He felt as if he had lain on a giant anvil while someone repeatedly pounded a blacksmith's hammer into his gut.

Hunched over his pain, hobbling toward the front of the house, trying to get out of the way of the damn Uzi, he was sure he was going to be shot in the back. But somehow he made it to the corner, climbed the porch steps, and got out of Cornell's line of fire.

Vince took some satisfaction in having wounded Cornell, though he knew it wasn't mortal. And having lost the element of surprise, he was in for a protracted battle. Hell, the woman looked to be almost as formidable as Cornell himself—a crazy Amazon.

He could have sworn there was something of the timid mouse in the woman, that it was her nature to submit. Obviously, he misjudged her—and that spooked him. Vince Nasco was not accustomed to making such mistakes; mistakes were for lesser men, not for the child of Destiny.

Scuttling across the front porch, certain that Cornell was coming fast behind him, Vince decided to go into the house instead of heading for the woods. They would expect him to run for the trees, take cover, and reconsider his strategy. Instead, he'd go straight into the house and find a position from which he could see both the front and rear doors. Maybe he'd take them by surprise yet.

He was passing a large window, heading for the front door, when something exploded through the glass.

Vince cried out in surprise and fired his revolver, but the shot went into the porch ceiling, and the dog—Jesus, that's what it was, the dog—hit him hard. The gun flew out of his hand. He was knocked backward. The dog clung to him, claws snagged in his clothes, teeth sunk in his shoulder. The porch railing disintegrated. They tumbled out into the front yard, into the rain.

Screaming, Vince hammered at the dog with his big fists until it squealed and let go of him. Then it went for his throat, and he just knocked it off in time to prevent it tearing open his windpipe.

His gut still throbbed, but he hitched and stumbled back to the porch, looking for his revolver—and found Cornell instead. Bleeding from his shoulder, Cornell was on the porch, looking down at Vince.

Vince felt a great wild surge of confidence. He knew that he had been right all along, knew that he was invincible, immortal, because he could look straight into the muzzle of the Uzi without fear, without the *slightest* fear, so he grinned up at Cornell. "Look at me, *look*! I'm your worst nightmare."

Cornell said, "Not even close," and opened fire.

In the kitchen Travis sat in a chair, with Einstein at his side, while Nora dressed his wound. As she worked, she told him what she knew about the man who had forced his way into the truck.

"He was a damn wild card," Travis said. "No way we could ever have known he was out there."

"I hope he's the *only wild* card."

Wincing as Nora poured alcohol and iodine into the bullet hole, wincing again as she bound the wound with gauze by passing it under his armpit, he said, "Don't worry about making a great job of it. The bleeding's not that bad. No artery's been hit."

The bullet had gone through, leaving a hideous exit wound, and he was in considerable pain, but for a while yet he would be able to function. He would have to seek medical attention later, maybe from Jim Keene to avoid the questions that any other doctor would surely insist on having answered. For now, he was only concerned that the wound be bound tight enough to allow him to dispose of the dead man.

Einstein was battered, too. Fortunately, he had not been cut when he smashed through the front window. He did not seem to have any broken bones, but he had taken several hard blows. Not in the best of shape to begin with, he looked bad—muddy and rain-soaked and in pain. He would need to see Jim Keene, too.

Outside, rain was falling harder than ever, pounding on the roof, gurgling noisily through gutters and downspouts. It was slanting across the front porch and through the shattered window, but they did not have time to worry about water damage.

"Thank God for the rain," Travis said. "No one in the area will have heard the gunfire in this downpour."

Nora said, "Where will we dump the body?"

"I'm thinking." And it was hard to think clearly because the pain in his shoulder throbbed up and into his head.

She said, "We could bury him here, in the woods—"

"No. We'd always know he was there. We'd always worry about the body being dug up by wild animals, found by hikers. Better ... there're places along the Coast Highway where we could pull over, wait until there's no traffic, drag him out of the bed of the truck, and toss him over the side. If we pick a place where the sea comes in right to the base of the slope, it'll carry him out, move him away, before anyone notices him down there."

As Nora finished the bandage, Einstein abruptly got up, whined. He sniffed the air. He went to the back door, stood staring at it for a moment, then disappeared into the living room.

"I'm afraid he's hurt worse than he seems to be," Nora said, applying a final strip of adhesive tape.

"Maybe," Travis said. "But maybe not. He's just been acting peculiar all day, ever since you left this morning. He told me it smelled like a bad day."

"He was right," she said.

Einstein returned from the living room at a run and went straight to the pantry, switching on the lights and pumping the pedals that released lettered tiles.

"Maybe he has an idea about disposing of the body," Nora said.

As Nora gathered up the leftover iodine, alcohol, gauze, and tape, Travis painfully pulled on his shirt and went to the pantry to see what Einstein had to say.

THE OUTSIDER IS HERE.

Travis slammed a new magazine into the butt of the Uzi

489

carbine, put an extra in one pocket, and gave Nora one of the Uzi pistols that was kept in the pantry.

Judging by Einstein's sense of urgency, they had no time to go through the house, closing and bolting shutters.

The clever scheme to gas The Outsider in the barn had been built upon the certainty that it would approach at night and reconnoiter. Now that it had come in daylight and had reconnoitered while they were distracted by Vince, that plan was useless.

They stood in the kitchen, listening, but nothing could be heard above the relentless roar of the rain.

Einstein was not able to give them a more precise fix on their adversary's location. His sixth sense was still not working up to par. They were just lucky that he had sensed the beast at all. His morning-long anxiety had evidently not been related to any presentiment about the man who had come home with Nora but had been, even without his knowledge, caused by the approach of The Outsider.

"Upstairs," Travis said. "Let's go."

Down here, the creature could enter by doors or windows, but on the second floor they would at least have only windows to worry about. And maybe they could get shutters closed over some of those.

Nora climbed the stairs with Einstein. Travis brought up the rear, moving backward, keeping the Uzi aimed down at the first floor. The ascent made him dizzy. He was acutely aware that the pain and weakness in his injured shoulder was slowly spreading outward through his entire body like an ink stain through a blotter.

On the second floor, at the head of the stairs, he said, "If we hear it come in, we can back off, wait until it starts to climb toward us, then step forward and catch it by surprise, blow it away."

She nodded.

They had to be silent now, give it a chance to creep into the downstairs, give it time to decide they were on the second floor, let it gain confidence, let it approach the stairs with a sense of security.

A strobe-flash of lightning—the first of the storm—

pulsed at the window at the end of the hall, and thunder cracked. The sky seemed to have been shattered by the blast, and all the rain stored in the heavens collapsed upon the earth in one tremendous fall.

At the end of the hallway, one of Nora's canvases flew out of her studio and crashed against the wall.

Nora cried out in surprise, and for an instant all three of them stared stupidly at the painting lying on the hall floor, half thinking that its poltergeist-like flight had been related to the great crash of thunder and the lightning.

A second painting sailed out of her studio, hit the wall, and Travis saw the canvas was shredded.

The Outsider was already in the house.

They were at one end of the short hall. The master bedroom and future nursery were on the left, the bathroom and then Nora's studio on the right. The thing was just two doors away, in Nora's studio, demolishing her paintings.

Another canvas flew into the hallway.

Rain-soaked, muddied, battered, still somewhat weak from his battle with distemper, Einstein nevertheless barked viciously, trying to warn off The Outsider.

Holding the Uzi, Travis moved one step down the hall.

Nora grabbed his arm. "Let's not. Let's get out."

"No. We've got to face it."

"On *our* terms," she said.

"These are the best terms we're going to get."

Two more paintings flew out of the studio and clattered down on top of the growing pile of wrecked canvases.

Einstein was no longer barking but growling deep in his throat.

Together, they moved along the hall, toward the open door of Nora's studio.

Travis's experience and training told him they ought to split up, spread out, instead of grouping into a single target. But this was not Delta Force. And their enemy was not a mere terrorist. If they spread out, they would lose some of the courage they needed to face the thing. Their very closeness gave them strength.

They were halfway to the studio door when The Outsider

shrieked. It was an icy sound that stabbed right through Travis and quick-froze his bone marrow. He and Nora halted, but Einstein took two more steps before stopping.

The dog was shuddering violently.

Travis realized he, too, was shaking. The tremors aggravated the pain in his shoulder.

Breaking fear's hold, he rushed to the open door, treading on ruined canvases, spraying bullets into the studio. The weapon's recoil, though minimal, was like a chisel chipping into his wound.

He hit nothing, heard nothing scream, saw no sign of the enemy.

The floor in there was littered with a dozen mangled paintings and glass from the broken window by which the thing had entered after climbing onto the front porch roof.

Waiting, Travis stood with his legs spread wide. The gun in both hands. Blinking sweat out of his eyes. Trying to ignore the seething pain in his right shoulder. Waiting.

The Outsider must be to the left of the door—or behind it on the right, crouched, ready to spring. If he gave it time, maybe it would grow tired of waiting and would rush him, and he could cut it down in the doorway.

No, it's as smart as Einstein, he told himself. Would Einstein be so dumb as to rush me through a narrow doorway? No. No, it'll do something more intelligent, unexpected.

The sky exploded with thunder so powerful it vibrated the windows and shook the house. Chain lightning sizzled through the sky.

Come on you bastard, show yourself.

He glanced at Nora and Einstein, who stood a few steps away from him, with the master bedroom on one side of them and the bathroom on the other side, the stairs behind them.

He looked again through the doorway, at the window glass among the debris on the floor. Suddenly he was certain that The Outsider was no longer in the studio, that it had gone out through the window, onto the roof of the front porch, and that it was coming at them from another part of the house, through another door, perhaps out of one of the bedrooms, or from the bathroom—or maybe it would explode at them, shrieking, from the top of the steps.

He motioned Nora forward, to his side. "Cover me."

Before she could object, he went through the doorway, into the studio, moving in a crouch. He nearly fell in the rubble, but stayed on his feet and spun around, ready to open fire if the thing was looming over him.

It was gone.

The closet door was open. Nothing in there.

He went to the broken window and cautiously looked out onto the roof of the rain-washed porch. Nothing.

Wind keened over the dangerously sharp shards of glass still bristling from the window frame.

He started back toward the upstairs hall. He could see Nora out there, looking at him, scared, but gamely clutching her Uzi. Behind her, the door to the future nursery opened, and it was *there*, yellow eyes aglow. Its monstrous jaws cracked wide, full of teeth far sharper than the wicked glass shards in the window frame.

She was aware of it, started to turn, but it struck at her before she had a chance to fire. It tore the Uzi out of her hands.

It had no chance to gut her with its razor-edged six-inch claws because, even as the beast was tearing the pistol out of her hands, Einstein charged it, snarling. With catlike quickness, The Outsider shifted its attention from Nora to the dog. It whipped around on him, lashed out as if its long arms were constructed with more than one elbow joint. It snatched Einstein up in both horrendous hands.

Crossing the studio to the hall door, Travis had no clear shot at The Outsider because Nora was between him and that hateful thing. As Travis reached the doorway, he cried out for her to fall down, to give him a line of fire, and she did, immediately, but too late. The Outsider scooped Einstein into the nursery and slammed the door, as if it were an evil nightmare-spawned jack-in-the-box that had popped out and popped back in with its prey, all in the blink of an eye.

Einstein squealed, and Nora rushed the nursery door.

"No!" Travis shouted, pulling her aside.

He aimed the automatic carbine at the closed door and emptied the rest of the magazine into it, punching at least thirty holes in the wood, crying out through clenched teeth as pain flared through his shoulder. There was some risk of hitting Einstein, but the retriever would be in worse danger if Travis did *not* open fire. When the gun stopped spitting bullets, he ripped out the empty magazine, took the full magazine from his pocket and slammed that into the gun. Then he kicked open the ruined door and went into the nursery.

The window stood open, curtains blowing in the wind.

The Outsider was gone.

Einstein was on the floor, against one wall, motionless, covered with blood.

Nora made a wrenching sound of grief when she saw the retriever.

At the window, Travis spotted splashes of blood leading across the porch roof. Rain was swiftly washing the gore away.

Movement caught his eye, and he looked toward the barn, where The Outsider disappeared through the big door.

Crouching over the dog, Nora said, "Oh my God, Travis, my God, after all he's come through and now he has to die like this."

"I'm going after the son-of-a-bitching bastard," Travis said ferociously. "It's in the barn."

She moved toward the door, too, and he said, "No! Call Jim Keene and then stay with Einstein, stay with Einstein."

"But you're the one who needs me. You can't go after it alone."

"*Einstein* needs you."

"Einstein is dead," she said through tears.

"Don't say that!" he screamed at her. He was aware that he was irrational, as if he believed Einstein would not really be dead until they *said* he was dead, but he could not control himself. "Don't say he's dead. Stay here with him, damn it. I've already hurt that fucking fugitive from a nightmare, hurt it bad I think, it's bleeding, and I can finish it off myself. Call Jim Keene, stay with Einstein.''

He was also afraid that, in all of this activity, she was going to induce a miscarriage, if she had not already done so. Then they would have lost not only Einstein but the baby.

He left the room at a run.

You're in no condition to go into that barn, he told himself. You've got to cool down first. Telling Nora to call a vet for a dead dog, telling her to stay with it when, in fact, you could have used her at your side ... No good. Letting rage and a thirst for vengeance get the best of you. No good.

But he could not stop. All of his life he had lost people he loved, and except in Delta Force he'd never had anyone to strike back at because you can't take vengeance on fate. Even in Delta, the enemy was so faceless—the lumpish mass of maniacs and fanatics who were ''international terrorism''—that vengeance provided little satisfaction. But here was an enemy of unparalleled evil, an enemy worthy of the name, and he would make it pay for what it had done to Einstein.

He raced down the hallway, descended the stairs two and three at a time, was hit by a wave of dizziness and nausea, and nearly fell. He grabbed at the banister to steady himself. He leaned on the wrong arm, and hot pain flared in his wounded shoulder. Letting go of the railing, he lost his balance and tumbled down the last flight, hitting the bottom hard.

He was in worse shape than he had thought.

Clutching the Uzi, he got to his feet and staggered to the back door, onto the porch, down the steps, into the yard. The cold rain cleared his fuzzy head, and he stood for a moment on the lawn, letting the storm wash some of the dizziness out of him.

An image of Einstein's broken, bloody body flashed through his mind. He thought of the amusing messages that would never be formed on the pantry floor, and he thought of Christmases to come without Einstein padding around in his Santa cap, and he thought of love that would never be given or received, and he thought of all the genius puppies who would never be born, and the weight of all that loss nearly crushed him into the ground.

He used his grief to sharpen his rage, honed his fury until it had a razored edge.

Then he went to the barn.

The place swarmed with shadows. He stood at the open door, letting the rain beat on his head and back, peering into the barn, squinting at the layered gloom, hoping to spot the yellow eyes.

Nothing.

He went through the door, bold with rage, and sidled to the light switches on the north wall. Even when the lights came on, he could not see The Outsider.

Fighting off dizziness, clenching his teeth in pain, he moved past the empty space where the truck belonged, past the back of the Toyota, slowly along the side of the car.

The loft.

He would be moving out from under the loft in a couple of steps. If the thing was up there, it could leap down on him—

That speculation proved a dead end, for The Outsider was at the back of the barn, beyond the front end of the Toyota, crouched on the concrete floor, whimpering and hugging itself with both long, powerful arms. The floor around it was smeared with its blood.

He stood beside the car for almost a minute, fifteen feet from the creature, studying it with disgust, fear, horror, and a weird fascination. He believed he could see the body structure of an ape, maybe a baboon—something in the simian family, anyway. But it was neither mostly one species nor merely a patchwork of the recognizable parts of many animals. It was, instead, a thing unto itself. With its oversized and lumpish face, immense yellow eyes, steam-shovel jaw, and long curved teeth, with its hunched back and matted coat and too-long arms, it attained a frightful individuality.

It was staring at him, waiting.

He took two steps forward, bringing up the gun.

Lifting its head, working its jaws, it issued a raspy, crackled, slurred, but still intelligible word that he could hear even above the sounds of the storm: *"Hurt."*

Travis was more horrified than amazed. The creature had not been designed to be capable of speech, yet it had the intelligence to learn language and to desire communication. Evidently, during the months it pursued Einstein, that desire had grown great enough to allow it to conquer, to some extent, its physical limitations. It had practiced speech, finding ways to wring a few tortured words from its fibrous voice box and malformed mouth. Travis was horrified not at the sight of a demon speaking but at the thought of how desperately the thing must have wanted to communicate with someone, anyone. He did not want to pity it, did not dare pity it, because he wanted to feel *good* about blowing it off the face of the earth.

"Come far. Now done," it said with tremendous effort, as if each word had to be torn from its throat.

Its eyes were too alien ever to inspire empathy, and every limb was unmistakably an instrument of murder.

Unwrapping one long arm from around its body, it picked up something that had been on the floor beside it but that Travis had not noticed until now: one of the Mickey Mouse tapes Einstein had gotten for Christmas. The famous mouse was pictured on the cassette holder, wearing the same outfit he always wore, smiling that familiar smile, waving.

"Mickey," The Outsider said, and as wretched and strange and barely intelligible as its voice was, it somehow conveyed a sense of terrible loss and loneliness. *"Mickey."*

Then it dropped the cassette and clutched itself and rocked back and forth in agony.

Travis took another step forward.

The Outsider's hideous face was so repulsive that there was almost something exquisite about it. In its unique ugliness, it was darkly, strangely seductive.

This time, when the thunder crashed, the barn lights flickered and nearly went out.

Raising its head again, speaking in that same scratchy voice but with cold, insane glee, it said, *"Kill dog, kill dog, kill dog,"* and it made a sound that might have been laughter.

He almost shot it to pieces. But before he could pull the trigger, The Outsider's laughter gave way to what seemed to be sobbing. Travis watched, mesmerized.

Fixing Travis with its lantern eyes, it again said, *"Kill dog, kill dog, kill dog,"* but this time it seemed racked with grief, as if it grasped the magnitude of the crime that it had been genetically compelled to commit.

It looked at the cartoon of Mickey Mouse on the cassette holder.

Finally, pleadingly, it said, *"Kill me."*

Travis did not know if he was acting more out of rage or out of pity when he squeezed the trigger and emptied the Uzi magazine into The Outsider. What man had begun, man now ended.

He dropped the carbine and walked outside. He could not find the strength to return to the house. He sat down on the lawn, huddled in the rain, and wept.

He was still weeping when Jim Keene drove up the muddy lane from the Coast Highway.

ELEVEN

1

On Thursday afternoon, January 13, Lem Johnson left
Cliff Soames and three other men at the foot of the dirt
lane, where it met the Pacific Coast Highway. Their
instructions were to allow no one past them but to remain
on station until—and if—Lem called for them.

Cliff Soames seemed to think this was a strange way to
handle things, but he did not voice his objections.

Lem explained that, since Travis Cornell was an ex-Delta
Force man with considerable combat skills, he ought to be
handled with care. "If we go storming in there, he'll know
who we are as soon as he sees us coming, and he might react
violently. If I go in alone, I'll be able to get him to talk to
me, and maybe I can persuade him to just give it up."

That was a flimsy explanation for his unorthodox
procedure, and it did not wipe the frown off Cliff's face.

Lem didn't care about Cliff's frown. He went in alone,
driving one of the sedans, and parked in front of the
bleached-wood house.

Birds were singing in the trees. Winter had temporarily
relaxed its hold on the northern California coast, and the
day was warm.

Lem climbed the steps and knocked on the front door.
Travis Cornell answered the knock and stared at him

through the screen door before saying, "Mr. Johnson, I suppose."

"How did you ... oh yes, of course, Garrison Dilworth would have told you about me that night he got his call through."

To Lem's surprise, Cornell opened the screen door. "You might as well come in."

Cornell was wearing a sleeveless T-shirt, apparently because of a sizable bandage encasing most of his right shoulder. He led Lem through the front room and into the kitchen, where his wife sat at the table, peeling apples for a pie.

"Mr. Johnson," she said.

Lem smiled and said, "I'm widely known, I see."

Cornell sat at the table and lifted a cup of coffee. He offered no coffee to Lem.

Standing awkwardly for a moment, Lem eventually sat with them. He said, "Well, it was inevitable, you know. We had to catch up with you sooner or later."

She peeled apples and said nothing. Her husband stared into his coffee.

What's wrong with them? Lem wondered.

This was not remotely like any scenario he had imagined. He was prepared for panic, anger, despondency, and many other things, but not for this strange apathy. They did not seem to care that he had at last tracked them down.

He said, "Aren't you interested in how we located you?"

The woman shook her head.

Cornell said, "If you really want to tell us, go ahead and have your fun."

Frowning, puzzled, Lem said, "Well, it was simple. We knew that Mr. Dilworth had to've called you from some house or business within a few blocks of that park north of the harbor. So we tied our own computers into the telephone company's records—with their permission, of course—and put men to work on examining all the long-distance calls charged to all the numbers within three blocks of that park, on that one night. Nothing led us to you. But then we realized that, when charges are reversed, the call

500

isn't billed to the number from which the call is placed; it appears on the records of the person who accepts the reversed charges—which was you. *But* it also appears in a special phone-company file so they'll be able to document the call if the person who accepted the charges later refuses to pay. We went through that special file which is very small, and quickly found a call placed from a house along the coast, just north of the beach park, to your number here. When we went around to talk to the people there—the Essenby family—we focused on their son, a teenager named Tommy, and although it took some time, we ascertained that it had, indeed, been Dilworth who used their phone. The first part was terribly time-consuming, weeks and weeks, but after that ... child's play.''

"Do you want a medal or what?" Cornell asked.

The woman picked up another apple, quartered it, and began to strip off the peel.

They were not making this easy for him—but then his intentions were much different from what they would be expecting. They could not be criticized for being cool toward him when they did not yet know that he had come as a friend.

He said, "Listen, I've left my men at the end of the lane. Told them you might panic, do something stupid, if you saw us coming up in a group. But why I really came alone was ... to make you an offer."

They both met his eyes at last, with interest.

He said, "I'm getting out of this goddamn job by spring. Why I'm getting out ... you don't have to know or care. Just say that I've gone through a sea change. Learned to deal with failure, and now it doesn't scare me any more." He sighed and shrugged. "Anyway, the dog doesn't belong in a cage. I don't give a good goddamn what they say, what they want—I know what's right. I know what it's like being in a cage. I've been in one most of my life, until recently. The dog shouldn't have to go back to that. What I'm going to suggest is that you get him out here now, Mr. Cornell, take him off through the woods, let him somewhere that he'll be safe, then come back and face the music. Say that the dog ran off a couple of months ago, in some other place, and you think he must be dead by now, or in the hands of people who're taking good care of him. There'll still be the problem of The Outsider, which you must know about, but you and I can work up a way to deal with that when it comes. I'll put men on a surveillance of you, but after a few weeks I'll pull them, say it's a lost cause—"

Cornell stood up and stepped to Lem's chair. With his left hand he grabbed hold of Lem's shirt and hauled him to his feet. "You're sixteen days too late, you son of a bitch."

"What do you mean?"

"The dog is dead. The Outsider killed him, and I killed The Outsider."

The woman laid down her paring knife and a piece of apple. She put her face in her hands and sat forward in her chair, shoulders hunched, making soft, sad sounds.

"Ah, Jesus," Lem said.

Cornell let go of him. Embarrassed, depressed, Lem straightened his tie, smoothed the wrinkles out of his shirt. He looked down at his pants—brushed them off.

"Ah, Jesus," he repeated.

Cornell was willing to lead them to the place in the forest where he had buried The Outsider.

Lem's men dug it up. The monstrosity was wrapped in plastic, but they didn't have to unwrap it to know that it was Yarbeck's creation.

The weather had been cool since the thing had been killed, but it was getting rank.

Cornell would not tell them where the dog was buried. "He never had much of a chance to live in peace," Cornell said sullenly, "but, by God, he's going to rest in peace now. No one's going to put him on an autopsy table and hack him up. No way."

"In a case where the national security is at stake, you can be forced—"

"Let them," Cornell said. "If they haul me up before a judge and try to make me tell them where I buried Einstein, I'll spill the whole story to the press. But if they leave Einstein alone, if they leave me and mine alone, I'll keep my mouth shut. I don't intend to go back to Santa Barbara, to pick up as Travis Cornell. I'm Hyatt now, and that's what I'm going to stay. My old life's gone forever. There's no reason to go back. And if the government's smart, it'll let me be Hyatt and stay out of my way."

Lem stared at him a long time. Then: "Yeah, if they're smart, I think they'll do just that."

Later that same day, as Jim Keene was cooking dinner, his phone rang. It was Garrison Dilworth, whom he had never met but had gotten to know during the past week by acting as liaison between the attorney and Travis and Nora. Garrison was calling from a pay phone in Santa Barbara.

"They show up yet?" the attorney asked.

"Early this afternoon," Jim said. "That Tommy Essenby must be a good kid."

"Not bad, really. But he didn't come to see me and warn me out of the goodness of his heart. He's in rebellion against authority. When they pressured him into admitting that I made the call from his house that night, he resented them. As inevitably as billy goats ram their heads into board fences, Tommy came straight to me."

"They took away The Outsider."

"What about the dog?"

"Travis said he wouldn't show them where the grave was. Made them believe that he'd kick a lot of ass and pull down the whole temple on everyone's heads if they pushed him."

"How's Nora?" Dilworth asked.

"She won't lose the baby."

"Thank God. That must be a great comfort."

Eight months later, on the big Labor Day weekend in September, the Johnson and Gaines families got together for a barbecue at the sheriff's house. They played bridge most of the afternoon. Lem and Karen won more often than they lost, which was unusual these days, because Lem no longer approached the game with the fanatical need to win that had once been his style.

He had left the NSA in June. Since then, he had been living on the income from the money he had long ago inherited from his father. By next spring, he expected to settle on a new line of work, a small business of some kind, in which he would be his own boss, able to set his own hours.

Late in the afternoon, while their wives made salads in the kitchen, Lem and Walt stood out on the patio, tending to the steaks on the barbecue.

"So you're still known at the Agency as the man who screwed up the Banodyne crisis?"

"That's how I'll be known until time immemorial."

"Still get a pension though," Walt said.

"Well, I did put in twenty-three years."

"Doesn't seem right, though, that a man could screw up the biggest case of the century and still walk away, at forty-six, with a full pension."

"Three-quarter pension."

Walt breathed deeply of the fragrant smoke rising off the charring steaks. "Still. What is our country coming to? In less liberal times, screwups like you would have been flogged and put in the stocks, at least." He took another deep whiff of the steaks and said, "Tell me again about that moment in their kitchen."

Lem had told it a hundred times, but Walt never got tired of hearing it again. "Well, the place was neat as a pin. Everything gleamed. And both Cornell and his wife are neat about themselves, too. They're well-groomed, well-scrubbed people. So they tell me the dog's been dead two weeks, dead and buried. Cornell throws this angry fit, hauls me out of my chair by my shirt, and glares at me like maybe he's going to rip my head off. When he lets go of me, I straighten my tie, smooth my shirt ... and I look down at my pants, sort of out of habit, and I notice these golden hairs. Dog hairs. *Retriever* hairs, sure as hell. Now could it have been that these neat people, especially trying to fill their empty days and take their minds off their tragedy, didn't find the time to clean the house in more than two weeks?''

"Hairs were just all *over* your pants?" Walt said.

"A hundred hairs."

"Like the dog had just been sitting there minutes before you came in."

"Like, if I'd been two minutes sooner, I'd have set right down on the dog himself."

Walt turned the steaks on the barbecue. "You're a pretty observant man, Lem, which ought to've taken you far in the line of work you were in. I just don't understand how, with all your talents, you managed to screw up the Banodyne case so thoroughly."

They both laughed, as they always did.

"Just luck, I guess," Lem said, which was what he always said, and he laughed again.

3

When James Garrison Hyatt celebrated his third birthday on June 28, his mother was pregnant with his first sibling, who eventually became his sister.

They threw a party at the bleached-wood house on the forested slopes above the Pacific. Because the Hyatts would soon be moving to a new and larger house a bit farther up the coast, they made it a party to remember, not merely a birthday bash but a goodbye to the house that had first sheltered them as a family.

Jim Keene drove in from Carmel with Pooka and Sadie, his two black labs, and his young golden retriever,

Leonardo, who was usually called Leo. A few close friends came in from the real-estate office where Sam—"Travis" to everyone—worked in Carmel Highlands, and from the gallery in Carmel where Nora's paintings were exhibited and sold. These friends brought their retrievers, too, all of them second-litter offspring of Einstein and his mate, Minnie.

Only Garrison Dilworth was missing. He had died in his sleep the previous year.

They had a fine day, a grand time, not merely because they were friends and happy to be with one another, but because they shared a secret wonder and joy that would forever bind them into one enormous extended family.

All members of the first litter, which Travis and Nora could not have borne adopting out, and which lived at the bleached-wood house, were also present: Mickey, Donald, Daisy, Huey, Dewey, Louie.

The dogs had an even better time than the people, frolicking on the lawn, playing hide-and-seek in the woods, and watching videotapes on the TV in the living room.

The canine patriarch participated in some of the games, but he spent much of his time with Travis and Nora and, as usual, stayed close to Minnie. He limped—as he would for the rest of his life—because his right hind leg had been cruelly mangled by The Outsider and would not have been usable at all if his vet had not been so dedicated to the restoration of the limb's function.

Travis often wondered whether The Outsider had thrown Einstein against the nursery wall with great force and then had assumed he was dead. Or at the moment when it held the retriever's life in its hands, perhaps the thing had reached down within itself and found some drop of mercy that its makers had not designed into it but which had somehow been there anyway. Perhaps it remembered the one pleasure it and the dog had shared in the lab—the cartoons. And in remembering the sharing, perhaps it saw itself, for the first time, as having a dim potential to be like other living things. Seeing itself as like others, perhaps it then could not kill Einstein as easily as it had expected.

After all, with a flick of those talons, it could have gutted him.

But though he had acquired the limp, Einstein had lost the tattoo in his ear, thanks to Jim Keene. No one could ever prove that he was the dog from Banodyne—and he could still play "dumb dog" very well when he wished.

At times during young Jimmy's third birthday extravaganza, Minnie regarded her mate and offspring with charmed befuddlement, perplexed by their attitudes and antics. Although she could never fully understand them, no mother of dogs ever received half the love that she was given by those she'd brought into the world. She watched over them, and they watched over her, guardians of each other.

At the dark end of that good day, when the guests were gone, when Jimmy was asleep in his room, when Minnie and her first litter were settling down for the night, Einstein and Travis and Nora gathered at the pantry off the kitchen.

The Scrabble-tile dispenser was gone. In its place, an IBM computer stood on the floor. Einstein took a stylus in his mouth and tapped the keyboard. The message appeared on the screen:

THEY GROW UP FAST.

"Yes, they do," Nora said. "Yours faster than ours."

ONE DAY THEY WILL BE EVERYWHERE.

"One day, given time and lots of litters," Travis said, "they'll be all over the world."

SO FAR FROM ME. IT'S A SADNESS.

"Yes, it is," Nora said. "But all young birds fly from the nest sooner or later."

AND WHEN I'M GONE?

"What do you mean?" Travis asked, stooping and ruffling the dog's thick coat.

WILL THEY REMEMBER ME?

"Oh yes, fur face," Nora said, kneeling and hugging him. "As long as there are dogs and as long as there are people fit to walk with them, they will all remember you."

INFORMED CONSENT

A MEDICAL CHILLER BY

HAROLD L. KLAWANS

Dr Paul Richardson is top
neurologist at one of Chicago's largest
medical centres. His speciality —
complex experimental brain surgery —
is highly controversial,
and when one of his patients brings a big
malpractice suit, Paul's entire
reputation is at stake, unless he can
track down the mysteriously
missing medical consent form.

His only witness is Jackie Baumer, a
dedicated nurse whose insatiable sexual
appetite is the talk of the hospital...
and then Nurse Baumer is butchered in
an insane act of sexual sadism.
The deadly hunt is on. And as tension
mounts, shocking revelations
of perverted sex and unthinkable medical
evil turn the giant hospital
into a deadly chamber of horrors...

Fiction/Medical Thriller   0 7472 3081 1

More compulsive fiction from Headline:

CHET WILLIAMSON
Beware the whirlwind horror of the

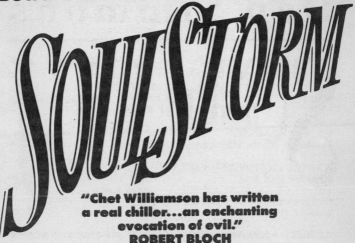

SOULSTORM

"Chet Williamson has written a real chiller...an enchanting evocation of evil."
ROBERT BLOCH

Three men are each tempted with a million dollars to spend just one month in a huge and isolated mansion called The Pines.

There they confront murder, madness and the ultimate evil – so that billionaire host David Neville will find the key to life beyond the grave.

For The Pines is the dwelling of all the psychotic, vengeful and violent dead souls from the beginning of time.

The soulstorm is waiting...

Williamson has *"located hell on a lonely mountaintop in northern Pennsylvania – and he manages to convince us it's true."*
T.E.D KLEIN,
author of *The Ceremonies*

Fiction/Horror   0 7472 3072 2

A selection of bestsellers from Headline

FICTION

GASLIGHT IN PAGE STREET	Harry Bowling	£4.99 □
LOVE SONG	Katherine Stone	£4.99 □
WULF	Steve Harris	£4.99 □
COLD FIRE	Dean R Koontz	£4.99 □
ROSE'S GIRLS	Merle Jones	£4.99 □
LIVES OF VALUE	Sharleen Cooper Cohen	£4.99 □
THE STEEL ALBATROSS	Scott Carpenter	£4.99 □
THE OLD FOX DECEIV'D	Martha Grimes	£4.50 □

NON-FICTION

THE SUNDAY TIMES SLIM PLAN	Prue Leith	£5.99 □
MICHAEL JACKSON The Magic and the Madness	J Randy Taraborrelli	£5.99 □

SCIENCE FICTION AND FANTASY

SORCERY IN SHAD	Brian Lumley	£4.50 □
THE EDGE OF VENGEANCE	Jenny Jones	£5.99 □
ENCHANTMENTS END Wells of Ythan 4	Marc Alexander	£4.99 □

All Headline books are available at your local bookshop or newsagent, or can be ordered direct from the publisher. Just tick the titles you want and fill in the form below. Prices and availability subject to change without notice.

Headline Book Publishing PLC, Cash Sales Department, PO Box 11, Falmouth, Cornwall, TR10 9EN, England.

Please enclose a cheque or postal order to the value of the cover price and allow the following for postage and packing:
UK & BFPO: £1.00 for the first book, 50p for the second book and 30p for each additional book ordered up to a maximum charge of £3.00.
OVERSEAS & EIRE: £2.00 for the first book, £1.00 for the second book and 50p for each additional book.

Name ....

Address ....

....

....